SING ROSES FOR ME

BEN MARNEY

SING ROSES FOR ME

A NOVEL

Written by
Ben Marney

Copyright © 2017 by Ben Marney
Published by: Ben Marney Books
ISBN: 9781521428757
www.benmarneybooks.com

Lyrics to "What Am I Doing Wrong" written by Ben Marney
What Am I Doing Wrong published by: Marney Media Group-BMI

This book is a work of fiction. All characters in this book are fictional coming from the author's imagination. Any similarities to anyone living or dead is purely coincidental.

DEDICATION

For my brother Ron
You were right, there are no rivers too wide to cross.
I miss you

Dedicated to my wife Dana
Thank you for all the lonely hours you spent while I wrote this book. I know
it was difficult for you. Even though we were in the same room, I know I
really wasn't there. I'll try to be better and not completely disappear into my
strange little writing world on the next one.
I love you

EPIGRAPH

The years have healed my wounds and the bleeding has stopped, but the scars on my life will never go away.

— MAX ALLEN

MAX ALLEN

CHAPTER ONE

My name is Max Allen. Yes, "The" Max Allen–the guy in the news, the guy you think you know all about, but you are wrong, you don't know it all–not the whole story...

This began, September 1, 1983. It was the worst day of my life, a memory so haunting, so horrible it's hard to believe it really happened, but it did. Even now, 20 plus years later, the pain comes rushing back and still makes me cry every time I think about it.

It was an unusual day for Houston, especially for that time of year–a glorious morning, cool, around 70 degrees with very little humidity and not a cloud in the sky. I'd actually stopped in Memorial Park on my drive to work that morning to finish my coffee, eat my doughnut and admire the splendor of the day. As I sat there listening to music, watching the ducks swim in the pond, I had a feeling of euphoria running through me.

The planets had aligned, my life for the first time in a long time had some form of direction, but most importantly, I was finally, after thirty years, bonding with my older brother. For the first time in our adult lives, Dean was treating me with respect. We were actually working together, had become friends, and had somehow overcome our silly childhood sibling rivalries.

Dean had become a very successful real estate developer and had built several high-rise office buildings around the Houston area, as well as several apartment buildings and condo complexes. He was rolling in cash and finally had convinced me to give up my life long dreams of being a country music star and go to work for him. He would tell me, "Give me ten years little brother and we'll buy Nashville." Although I'd had some good luck and minor success in the music business, I certainly wasn't a star. I was 32 years old and had finally come to the crossroads–I had to choose between possibly never making it in show business, facing a future barely scratching out a living doing what I loved, or give it all up, go in with my brother and make some serious cash. Reluctantly, I cut my hair, put down my guitar and moved from Nashville, Tennessee back home to Houston, Texas.

When I finished my coffee in the park, I cranked up my truck and headed to North Point Central–my office and our newest office tower under development. The traffic was horrible, as usual, backed up for miles, so it was almost 9:30 a.m. before I walked into my office. Taped to my phone was a message–*Call Dean. He wants you to fly to Louisiana with him this morning.* I tried to call him but he was on the phone, so I left a message with Peggy, his personal assistant, for him to call me back.

Things had picked up around the office and I'd honestly forgotten about Dean until the phone rang on my desk. It was almost 1 p.m.

"How fast can you get to Andrough Airport?" Dean asked.

"I don't know. The traffic was hell this morning, maybe an hour or so I guess. Why?"

"I've got to go to Lafayette to take this dumb ass coon ass cash money to close the deal on a new quarter horse. Hey! What do you think about that? A dumb ass coon ass! Sounds like a country song to me. Write that down little brother it might be a hit."

"You know... it's a damn good thing you've got a shit load of money, because if you're considering a career change to show business you're gonna need it, other wise you'd starve your ass off."

"Little brother you always were jealous of my singing voice. Seri-

ously, can you make it to Andrough by two? I've got to take off by
then to make it back in time."

"Are we flying in the new one, the Merlin?" I asked.

"Nah, the damn nose gear is still out on the Merlin, my pilot's
coming to get me in a Beach Baron. I hate those damn planes, but he
says this is a good one. He flies it all the time. It's got six seats, so why
don't you leave now and head that way? If you make it, we'll take a cab
downtown and get some crawfish ettoufee' or some gumbo while
we're there."

"I'll do my best to get there by 2, but it's going to be close."

"Ah, one more thing little brother."

"What's that?"

"I know your heart ain't in this construction business, but stick
with me on this for a while. As soon as we've got your pockets lined
with a little gold, we just might ship your ass back to Nashville and
see what you can do. Hell, we might even start our own record
company one of these days. I figure you got a hit or two in you."

I was so taken aback I didn't know how to respond. That was the
first time he'd ever said anything positive about my music. He'd
always been my worst critic, but now out of nowhere he was talking
like this? "Be careful what you're suggesting, big brother, I just may
hold you to it one day."

"I think it's something we need to talk about. " Dean said. "Look,
get your ass to the airport and we'll talk about it on the plane. See you
there. Hurry up."

I rushed out of the office and started working my way to southwest Houston through the bumper-to-bumper traffic. I looked at my
watch, it was 1:45 and I wasn't even close, so I took the next exit and
tried to call his car phone. There was no answer. Back on the freeway,
it was obvious that I'd never make it in time, so I gave up, took the
next exit and began driving down the side streets to Dean's office
complex near Gessner and Westheimer. His office suite took up an
entire floor of a beautiful, three-story, mostly glass building he'd built
a few years earlier. I had a small office there, so I figured I'd finish out

the day there rather than fighting the traffic back to North Point Central.

At 2:15, I heard a special announcement over my truck radio. A local businessman and his pilot had been killed in a crash at Andrough Airport. The reporter said the crash happened as they were taking off at 2:05 P.M. Both were killed instantly. A wave of fear came over my entire body as I wondered if it could be Dean. I began pondering all the horrible consequences of his death. How could I tell Mom and Dad? What would happen to his company? His kids? How could I go on without him—without his wisdom and guidance? His love? If this was true and it was his plane, suddenly I'd be working for Camille, his wife. Oh, God! What a horrible thought.

Camille was Dean's second wife, not the mother of his children. Their relationship was a real life cliché, the same old story—married boss, hot secretary... you know the rest. Camille was an absolute knock out. She had a beautiful face, a tiny waist, huge tits, but definitely was *not* a dumb, blonde. She was smart, real smart, but a conniving kind of smart that was obvious to everyone who knew her, but Dean.

For whatever reason, she didn't think much of me, so I did my best to just stay out of her way. I assumed that she'd heard one too many dumb little kid stories about me from Dean, because she always treated me with aloofness—not rude, just a total lack of respect for my intelligence and complete disregard for anything I had to say.

She was one of those obstacles you try to side step in life. She had few redeeming qualities, but she was Dean's fairy princess. He loved her and because he loved her so much, he was completely blind to her faults, so I just kept my mouth shut and tried to avoid her.

If this horrible scenario was true and Dean was dead, there was no way I could work for her. She didn't have the intelligence or experience to run the company, but I was sure her arrogance and giant ego would convince her that she could. Oh God! What in the world would I do next? This couldn't be happening. The thought was so horrible and preposterous I quickly put it out of my mind. After all, Andro008 was a very busy airport with private planes taking off every few minutes; it could have been anyone. No way could it have been Dean's plane. No possible way!

It had taken me another thirty minutes to reach the office, so the thought of the plane crash was far from my mind. I was in a great mood, winked and said "Hey there," to the receptionist as I walked past her desk. She didn't respond to me—nothing. She just sat there staring forward. It was a bit strange, but I didn't think much of it and walked on by her down the hall to my office.

When I sat down behind my desk, I overheard Peggy, my brother's personal assistant, talking to Camille. "I don't think Max knows," she said. "Someone's got to tell him."

The moment Camille and Peggy walked into my office, I knew. They didn't have to say a word. My brother was dead.

THE FUNERAL

CHAPTER TWO

Houston motorcycle cop told me that it was the longest line of cars he'd ever led. The parade stretched for almost two miles and created a major traffic problem on the Katy Freeway backing traffic up all the way to the 610 loop as we crept along working our way to the gravesite. Soon the nightmare I'd been living the last three days would be over. Dean would be in the ground and the rest of us would have to figure out how to go on with our lives without him. We all knew that wasn't going to be easy, but we had no choice.

I'd been quiet, not saying much to anyone since it had happened. The last person I'd talked to was my father and I'm not sure those were actual words. My dad and I have always been very close and as long as I can remember, we've had a slight telepathic communication between us. I never really had to go into deep detail about anything with my father. He just always seemed to know what I needed or wanted. When I knocked on his door only hours after Dean's plane crash, my father took one look at me and instantly knew.

At the gravesite, I sat on one of the small green chairs reserved for the family and listened to the preacher pray for my brother's soul. It seemed like an eternity, but it actually only took a few minutes. When it was finally over and everyone moved out from under the small canopy cover, I just stood there with my hand on his casket. To this day, I can still see it clearly. It was made out of beautiful dark mahogany wood and was so highly polished I could see my reflection.

As I stood there with my hand on that cold wood, the memory of the last time I'd seen him alive flashed through my mind. It was only a few days earlier at a party at his ranch. Dean loved throwing big Texas size parties and this was one of his best. One of Dean's side businesses was racing and breeding quarter horses. The purpose of this party was to celebrate the success of one of his horses that had just been named the *Aged Champion Stallion*. It was a big deal and lots of people, dressed up in all of their finest boots and hats, showed up. Dean had asked me to put my old band back together for the entertainment, so I did and we were a big hit with his friends. It was one of those magical musical nights for me; things had gone especially well. During my breaks, everyone was coming up slapping Dean on the back talking about what a great singer his little brother was. Although he never said it, I know he was proud of me that night.

When the party was over and most of the guests had left, he came up to me as I was packing up my guitar. "Would you do one more song for me little brother?" he asked.

"Sure." I said, "What would you like to hear?"

"Sing Roses for me again," he said, smiling. "I love that song."

He was talking about a song called *Run For The Roses*, by Dan Fogleberg. I'd already sung it three times during the night, always at his request. "Hang on a second, I'll round up the band."

"You don't need the band. Sing it for me here at the table. Just you and your guitar."

I pulled up a chair and sang it for him one last time. Every time I'd come to the chorus, he'd lean back in his chair and join in, singing at the top of his lungs. I didn't realize it at the time, but that was a monumental three minutes in my life – a performance forever imprinted in my brain.

When the gravesite service was over, I went back to Dean's house. Within an hour, the place was packed with some of Dean's closest friends and everyone had a story to tell about him. Some were about his generosity, some were about his intelligence, but all were from the heart. After listening to one story after another, I soon realized that I didn't really know Dean at all. He had so many dimensions, so many layers. I only knew what he chose to expose to me. The more I learned about him, the more I felt a little cheated. I'd missed out on so much of his life, knowing who he really was.

The biggest surprise of the day came when four of his closest friends came to me and said, "Come with us, there's something we have to do." I had no idea what they were up to, but I could tell it was important, so I went with them without hesitation.

They took me upstairs to Dean's library and sat me down in his favorite chair. Bob Hugley opened the bar and poured five tall scotches, neat. Randy Woodham opened the doors to the stereo and began searching through the albums. To my surprise, he pulled out one of mine and put it on the record player. Before I could protest, my voice was blaring out of the speakers. It was almost as if they'd rehearsed what to do next. Bob handed me a scotch and sat in the chair next to me. Randy, Howard and Sidney sat on the couch. For the next hour, no one said a word; we just sipped our scotch and listened to my music, all three albums.

I was very confused at all of this, but didn't question it, because for whatever reason his friends were enjoying it. Each one of them lost in deep thought, no doubt memories of Dean. It was all very bizarre and surreal.

When it was over and my music had finally been turned off, I asked them, "What was that all about?"

The four of them looked at me with shocked expressions. "You're kidding right?" Howard Stone said.

"No, I'm not kidding. Why did you guys want to listen to my music?"

"Because that's what Dean loved to do," Bob said. "That's what we always did up here: drank scotch and listened to your albums."

"My albums? You listened to my music?" I asked.

"Of course, your albums. Max, he loved your music," Randy said.

I had to sit down. My legs felt like rubber and my head was spinning. I tried not to cry, but I couldn't hold it in. "I didn't know," I said, wiping my eyes. "He never told me."

Sid sat down next to me and put his arm around me. "He knew every word of every song. He thought you were brilliant. It was all he ever talked about."

"Yeah, he drove us all nuts with it." Randy added. "I can't tell you how many times he made us sit here with him and listen to your damn albums. To be honest, I'm a little sick of hearing you sing." He broke into a loud belly laugh. Soon everyone was laughing, even me.

That experience was a true revelation in my life. It made me realize something I'd hidden away from myself for over thirty years; I'd been living my life not for me, but for Dean. Everything I'd ever done I did hoping that it would garner his acceptance and somehow meet his standard of excellence. Until that day, I thought I'd always missed the mark somehow. I was sure that everything I'd ever accomplished was not quite good enough; just slightly sub-standard. That day I found out that I *had* done something Dean approved of... my music. He loved my music.

I guess if Dean had not died, I would have never known what he thought and would have continued living my life not believing in my talents and myself. Why he couldn't tell me, I'll never understand. I guess he had his reasons; however, from that day forward, I changed. From then on, I lived my life for *me* and no one else. It had taken my brother's death and 32 years, but I'd finally grown up.

As I expected, working for Dean's widow, Camille was a futile effort. Without Dean's ingenuity there *was* no company, only the shell remained. It was time to move on, so I packed my bags, said goodbye to my parents and headed back to Nashville.

EDWARD CECIL, SR.

CHAPTER THREE

E
dward Cecil, Sr. had everything a man could want: a gorgeous wife, two beautiful children and a good job. He started working at the box factory when he was only 15 years old. Each day after school, he would walk to the factory to do his daily chores of sweeping the floors and cleaning the bathrooms. Legally, he was too young to work there, but old man Jackson took a liking to him and hired him anyway, paying him in cash each week until his 16th birthday. Finally of age, he became a full-fledged employee of the Jackson Box Factory. Two years later, when he graduated from high school, he was old enough to go on the line. Five years later, he was promoted to line foreman.

Over the next ten years, he labored vigorously and learned everything he could about the manufacture of corrugated cardboard boxes. He proved himself a dedicated employee and because of this, was promoted three more times until at age 35 he became the youngest general manager in the factory's history. He'd reached the top as far as he was concerned and he was proud of himself.

Along the way, he'd married Judy and had two beautiful children. Every time he looked at his wife, he said a small prayer giving thanks for his good fortune. She was extraordinarily beautiful, exotic with her dark skin, long black hair and deep blue eyes. She could have married anyone, but she had picked him.

Their meeting as cliché as it sounds, was truly love at first sight. They met at a church picnic by accident when she spilled her drink on him. She'd just moved to town; he had never seen her before that day, but when she looked into his eyes, he was lost and he knew instantly he'd finally found the one he'd been searching for. They were married six months later; he was twenty-seven and she was twenty-five. On his twenty-ninth birthday, Judy delivered their first child. They named her Carla after his father, Carl; five years later Edward Cecil, Jr. was born.

IT WAS A STRANGE PHONE CALL. Edward could hear the stress in old man Jackson's voice, but didn't ask what was wrong on the phone. Jackson told him to drop everything and come to his office, ASAP. On his way, he racked his brain but couldn't think of anything he'd done wrong. He had no idea why he was being called in so suddenly. It must be something big, he thought, as he walked up the long stairs to the main office.

When he opened the office door, Brenda, Jackson's secretary was crying and looked up at him with sad eyes. "Go on in Ed, he's expecting you," she said softly.

Jackson was sitting behind his desk. His eyes were swollen and bright red. "Have a seat Ed."

"What's wrong?" Edward's heart was pounding fast in his chest. He could sense that something was terribly wrong.

"Ed, I... I... just don't know how to tell you this. It's the hardest thing I've ever had to do."

"Just say it, sir. Tell me please."

"It's Judy. She's been in a horrible accident."

"Oh my God! Is she alright?" Edward yelled.

"Ed, son, " Jackson stared at the floor and fumbled for words,

"They did everything they could for her. I'm so sorry to have to tell you this, but she's gone."

Edward did not react.

"Ed, did you hear me?"

As if in a trance he slowly stood up, looked at Jackson and whispered, "Where is she?"

"She's at the hospital, but..." Edward didn't let him finish. He rushed out of the room and ran to his truck.

At the hospital, they stopped him at the emergency room doors. "No, Ed. You don't want to see her like this." The doctor told him. "Please listen to me. It was a head on collision. She's pretty messed up. Trust me on this Ed. You don't want to see her this way."

"I want to be with her!" He yelled. "I have to see her. Is she dead... really dead?"

The doctor put his arm around him. "I did my best Ed. I'm so sorry, but yes, she's gone."

Edward looked into the doctor's eyes. "She's gone?" His knees went limp and his body began to shake uncontrollably.

The doctor could feel him begin to slump under his arm. "Ed, I called John at the funeral home. He's on his way to pick her up. You know he'll do a good job on her; he loved her too. We all loved her. Please let us do this for you first. You can see her in a few hours. Let him make her pretty for you."

Edward collapsed to the floor, holding his head in his hands... weeping from the depths of his soul.

He buried Judy on Saturday morning. On Sunday, he gathered up his eleven-year old daughter, his six-year old son and headed for Padre Island. For the next two weeks, they swam in the Gulf of Mexico, made sand castles on the beach and searched for seashells, all the while trying his best to explain to his young children why they wouldn't ever see their mother again.

At the funeral, Carla seemed to understand what was going on, but little Edward just couldn't grasp it. "Is Mommy asleep? When will she wake up?"

"Yes Eddy, she is asleep in a way," he struggled. "It is sort of like sleeping, but she can't wake up from this sleep."

"Go kiss her, Daddy. That will make her wake up. Like in *Sleeping Beauty*." He said it loud enough for everyone in the chapel to hear. It was the saddest thing anyone had ever heard. Edward's heart sank. Oh, how he wished it was true.

Everyday at the beach, little Eddy would ask a million questions and Edward would do his best to try to make him understand, but only seemed to confuse him further with each one of his answers. On the drive home, Carla who had been very quiet, having not talked much since the funeral, finally spoke.

"Eddy, do you remember what happened to your goldfish?" she asked him.

"Yeah," he said, sadly. "They died. I fed them too much."

"Do you remember what we did with them?"

"Sure, we buried them in the back yard under the big tree."

"Have you ever seen them again?"

"No way. I can't," he said, with a puzzled look on his face.

"Why not?"

"Cause they're dead."

"That's right. Do you still love them?"

"Yeah, sure."

"Do you think they still love you?"

He thought for a moment. "Yeah, I guess they do."

"Well, that's the same thing that happened to Mommy. She died, but it's important to remember that even though she's not here anymore, she still loves you and it's ok for you to still love her."

Eddy smiled and said. "Ohhhhh." He finally understood.

Edward Sr. was stunned. He couldn't believe what he'd just heard come out of his little girl's mouth. For over two weeks, he'd stumbled and fumbled for the right words but they never came. Now, in less than three minutes, his eleven-year old daughter had explained it simply and with compassion to her six-year old brother. Inside he felt a strange wave of relief come over him and he knew that things were going to be all right with his children.

On the long drive home, he listened carefully to everything else his daughter had to say, which wasn't much. She listened more than she talked, but when she did say something, it was always well thought out and very astute. The more he listened, the more obvious it became that she had an intellect far beyond her years. No doubt, she was a gifted child. He wondered how he had not noticed her brilliance before.

EDWARD HAD to force himself to return to his job after his beach trip with his children, however, once he got there he realized that "work" was exactly what he needed. When he was busy, the time flew by and kept his mind occupied. For the next year, he worked long hours neglecting everything and everyone in his life, except his job and his children.

Each night he would rush home from work, so he could lie on the floor and help Carla and Eddie with their homework. After homework, they would have dinner. After dinner, they'd play games together or just talk to each other about their day. He loved this time with his children. It was the only time he ever smiled, the only time he was truly happy.

Spending these nights together made him realize how distinctly unique each child was. Carla was the quiet one, but quick to anger and very vocal when she was mad. Eddie was the loud one, always talking about something, asking a million questions, but sweet, never losing his temper and always forgiving, even when Carla was mean to him. Eddie was always in a positive, happy mood; Carla was usually brooding and dark, but always thinking. She was very intelligent, never really needing his help with her homework. Eddie was always confused with his schoolwork and always needed his help. The only thing they seemed to have in common was their looks. They both had his blonde hair and their mother's blue eyes.

Each day Carla's intellect became more obvious to him. Frequently, she shocked him with answers to questions that most little girls her age wouldn't even understand. To be certain, he contacted her school principal and arranged for her to be tested. He found out that his suspicions were correct; her test results were so high it astounded everyone at her school. Soon she was bumped up a grade, then another and another until she was the youngest child attending Tyler high school. At 12 years old, she finished her junior year at the top of her class. When she turned 13, she was tested again: she had an IQ of 163, technically a genius. One month later, she became the youngest freshman ever to be accepted at Rice University, the Texas equivalent to Harvard or Yale.

To be fair, Edward had little Eddie tested as well, but was not surprised with the results: Eddie was normal. In fact, he was slightly below average for a child his age. In his mind, he rationalized that little Eddie had taken after him and Carla after her mother, because he certainly was no genius and had always struggled in school.

It was hard for him to let his 13-year old daughter leave his house to go away to college. She was so young and innocent, but she was also a certified genius and had outgrown Tyler, Texas. Although he hated it, he knew he had to let her go; she couldn't grow any further there. Everyone told him he was doing the right thing, so reluctantly he packed her bags, drove the two hundred miles to Houston and moved Carla into her new home for the next four years.

Because Carla was so young, she wasn't allowed to live in a dormitory like the other freshman students. The dean felt she might have trouble fitting in and wouldn't feel comfortable there, so he made special arrangements for her to live with a local family. The man and the woman were both graduates of Rice, big supporters of the college and pillars of the community. The wife was on the university faculty, a professor of history. The husband was a well respected, Texas state court judge. They were childless and very excited to take Carla in, especially since she was such a gifted child. Conveniently, their house was located only a few blocks from the campus, allowing Carla to walk to her classes.

It was a perfect solution, but something just didn't seem right to Edward. He couldn't put his finger on it, but deep inside he had a bad feeling about leaving his daughter with these people. They seemed nice enough, but perhaps just a bit too nice. His intuition told him to call the whole thing off, but Carla was a gifted child and deserved to go to college and unfortunately, this appeared to be the only way. It was going to be hard enough for him to cover her tuition each year, and paying for additional housing on top of that was just simply out of the question. He had no other choice.

It was a very nice house located in the prestigious University area and the room they'd fixed up for Carla was beautiful, all pink and frilly with antique white furniture and an unusually large four posted canopy bed. Maybe he was just jealous, he thought to himself. He could never afford to live in a house like this or fix up a room this nicely for Carla. He convinced himself that all his ill feelings were just that—jealousy. It was the hardest thing he'd ever had to do, but somehow he forced himself to kiss his beloved Carla goodbye and leave her crying in the doorway holding hands with the honorable Judge Bradford Doss.

THOMAS

CHAPTER FOUR

estosterone pumped through his body. It was all part of the experience and he savored the tingling sensation.

Holding what was left of the butt between his stubby fingers, Thomas touched a new one to the cherry and fired up the sixth cigarette of this chain. Thomas was the name he always used when he played, and although Thomas was his real name, it was his middle name–a name few people knew. He was confident that no one would ever connect that name back to him.

Settling back into the passenger seat of the stolen Ford van he watched the children play in the open field across the street. He studied them carefully watching the little girls playing hopscotch, their dresses flying up exposing white lace panties and multicolored knee socks. He could feel his heart pounding in his chest. He focused on the little boys kicking a white soccer ball, running and laughing. His heart raced faster.

Which one would it be, he wondered. Perhaps the little girl with the long blonde hair flying behind her as she ran; maybe the dark skinned little boy, it didn't matter. He really didn't care. They were all so... delicious.

He glanced at his watch; it was time to move. Soon the bell would ring and recess would be over and he didn't want to cause any unwanted suspicion. Sliding over to the driver's seat, he turned the ignition key. He'd be back at exactly 2:30 p.m., then he'd make his choice. It was going to be so easy, he thought to himself, just so easy. He pulled away from the curb and drove slowly past the children at play. No one gave him a second look.

"See you later kids," he said out loud, as he drove away.

AT 2:25 P.M., Thomas pulled to the curb two blocks south of the elementary school. In front of the building, there was a long line of cars and minivans driven by soccer moms and divorced dads. They were all waiting for the bell to ring and the onslaught of screaming kids to come rushing out of the front doors. There was also a line of yellow school buses waiting to pick up and deliver the rest of the little ones around the city, hopefully safely home. He smiled as he heard the bell ring. It was playtime. His plan was to wait for the buses to load then let all of the cars and minivans move through the circle drive. That's when he'd make his move. This was going to be so easy.

He was confident there would be a few stray children in front of the school left alone; it never failed. There were always four or five left standing in front of the school waiting for their moms or dads, late for one reason or another. Eventually, the tardy parents would fly into the circle drive and load up their waiting children—finally on their way home, safe and sound… but not today.

He waited for three minutes after the last car pulled out before he started the van and rolled into the circular drive. As expected, there they were—three little girls and two little boys standing on the front steps, holding their lunch boxes and books, waiting patiently for their moms or dads to arrive. Slowly, he pulled to a stop in front of the unsuspecting children and rolled down his window.

"Excuse me children, I'm looking for Bobby. Is he still here?" he asked with a big smile on his face.

The kids looked confused, shaking their heads no. "I may not have the right name. What's your name?" he asked, still smiling broadly.

"Edward," a beautiful blonde haired boy said back to him.

"Yeah, that's the name! Edward. Does your mommy call you Eddy?"

"I don't have a mommy. She died."

"I meant your dad. Does he call you Eddy?"

The little boy looked down at his shoes and shyly said, "Sometimes."

"Eddy, your daddy's been in a terrible accident and told me to come and get you today. He's in the hospital. Jump in and I'll take you to him. Hurry now!" He said, firmly.

Obediently, Edward climbed into the passenger seat. Thomas reached over, slammed the door behind him and sped away. "Why don't you come stand over here so I can hold on to you as I drive, I wouldn't want you to get hurt falling out of your seat."

Edward slid down out of the seat and stood next to him as he drove. He wrapped an arm around the boy's waist and reached into his pocket with his other hand, steering the van with his knees. In one swift motion, Thomas covered Edward's face with an ether soaked rag. The tiny boy struggled, but was no match for his firm grip. After a moment, Edward calmed down and slumped to the floor between the seats, out cold. "So easy." He said, laughing, "so fucking easy."

Fifteen minutes later, glancing in his rear view mirror, he watched the police car suddenly whip around and begin following him. He stiffened in his seat and could feel beads of perspiration forming on his forehead. It couldn't be the kid; there wasn't enough time for that. It had to be the stolen van.

"Damn! The owner must have reported it already!" That surprised him. He assumed he'd have a few hours before the owner even missed it. "Fuck!" he shouted, when the blue lights flashed in his rear view mirror. He gunned the van and flew off the next exit accelerating to 80 miles per hour. The police siren blasted close behind him as he sped down the feeder road. A few miles past the exit, he slid sideways turning down a gravel road leading to a thick wooded area. The cop

was directly behind him, inches from his bumper. He had to do something quick before other police units arrived on the scene. He floored
the accelerator, zooming away from the cop car, flying over a small
hill in the road. He was going so fast that the van went airborne,
landing hard spewing a huge cloud of gravel and dirt behind him.
Checking his rear view mirror, he saw no sign of the cop car. The cop
had been forced to slow down because of the dust cloud, allowing him
to gain a few seconds lead. Ahead, he could see a steep incline. As he
topped the hill, he slammed on the brakes coming to a dead stop in
the middle of the gravel road. In a panic, he pulled his seat belt over
his shoulder, snapped it closed and braced himself.

The police officer didn't see the stopped van until it was too late–
crashing into it at full speed. The impact slammed Thomas back into
his seat, snapping his head against the headrest, but his shoulder belt
held him firmly in place and his inflated airbag stopped his forward
momentum. In slow motion, he watched the back of the van rip open
like a tin can and fly away in pieces. He watched Edward's small body
fly up into the air and crash headfirst into the windshield. The glass
exploded, opening a jagged hole that ripped the flesh from Edward's
face and neck, splattering blood everywhere as he flew out the
windshield.

Thomas lost consciousness, but only for a few seconds. When he
came to, he was in a daze–disoriented and light-headed. When he
tried to move, a severe pain shot down his shoulder from his neck all
the way to his legs. It felt like a bolt of electricity shocking his body. It
was all he could do to move, but the pain helped raise his level of
consciousness and brought him back to the reality of his situation.

He forced his door open and rolled out of the van onto the ground.
Slowly he pulled himself up and walked to the back of the van to
check on the police car. Peering through the window, he could see the
cop's bloody face looking back at him. His body was twisted in a
strange pretzel shape, wedged between the seat and the floorboard.
His eyes were wide open, but he wasn't seeing anything. His head
must have hit the steering wheel hard, because he had a large open

gash across his forehead and Thomas could see small bits of gray brain matter on the steering wheel. No doubt, the cop was dead.

His neck was throbbing and he was having trouble walking, but somehow he worked himself to the front of the van where he found Edward's body. There was nothing left of his face; his body was mangled and covered in blood. He leaned over and felt for a pulse, but nine-year old Edward Cecil, Jr. was dead.

"Now isn't that a shame." he said, as he stood up. "I was planning on having a lot of fun with you, boy."

The pain in his neck was getting worse, more intense by the moment. Taking small steps, he slowly made his way across the dirt road, away from the wrecked van and police car.

"Another time, another place, another boy." he said, looking back one last time. Then, the Honorable Judge Bradford "Thomas" Doss turned and limped away, disappearing deep into the woods... without a trace.

THE SONG

CHAPTER FIVE

I t had only been three months since I had buried my brother, so the pain from his loss was still throbbing deep inside my heart when I finally took the exit off the freeway that dropped me in downtown Music City. Although, I dreaded my future there and didn't look forward to the difficulties that lay ahead, I knew I had to try one more time because this time, I wasn't there to impress my brother. I'd already done that. This time I was there for me, and as I drove the surface streets toward my new apartment, somehow the bright lights of Music Row seemed a bit dimmer and less intimidating.

NASHVILLE, TENNESSEE IS CALLED "MUSIC CITY" because a lot of music comes out of that city; however, it's the worst place on earth to find a gig. Oh, there's tons of work if you happen to be a monster musician and somehow worm your way into the inner circle of producers that control the town. If you can do that, life is sweet; you can make tons of money playing sessions in one of the 100 or more recording studios located there, however, if you're not a monster musician or considered one of the good old boys, you either starve, hit the road playing the Holiday Inn circuit, or move back to where you came from.

I'm a guitar player. I've played guitar all my life and I'm pretty good at it, but in Nashville, *good* just doesn't cut it; you have to be great. The term "monster musician" refers to a very elite group of players who are so skillful on their instruments, they perform on an entirely different level; they are almost inhuman music machines. They are quick, extremely creative and almost never make mistakes. For someone like me, it's a very humiliating and humbling experience to watch these guys in action.

I'm also a singer. Except the few years I worked with my brother, I'd made my living playing my guitar and singing. Most people tell me that I'm a good singer, but again, to make it in Nashville as a session singer (background singer) you have to be great, a vocal "monster" to coin a new term. The background vocalists in Nashville can hear a song one time and instantly know what harmony parts fit perfectly. They are so fast and accurate there was just no way I could compete.

It didn't take me long to realize that making a living in the recording studios in Nashville was out of the question; I simply wasn't good enough. The next logical step was to look for a gig in one of the clubs or beer joints there, but as you can imagine, there were about a million other singers and musicians doing the same thing, so finding a gig in Nashville was a dead end street. I kept reminding myself that Randy Travis was cooking at a steak house to make ends meet before he was discovered, but it didn't help. I'm a rotten waiter and a lousy cook.

I was running out of money and I was just about to give up and move back to Texas, when quite by accident, I met the country music legend, Waylon Jones.

I was sitting alone in a Denny's restaurant when he walked up to me and said, "Son, you look depressed, mind if I sit down?"

When I looked up and realized it was Waylon, I was so shocked I couldn't talk.

He sat down and yelled at the waitress. "Darlene, honey, would you bring me another cup and give my friend here a refill." Then he turned and looked me in the eye. "You a picker, son?"

I was still in a state of shock, so I just shook my head yes. "Are you Waylon Jones?" I asked, in a voice I'd never heard come out of my mouth before.

He smiled with a wide grin. "In the flesh, but don't hold that against me. I'm here to help you, son."

I didn't know what to say, so I just sat there mumbling to myself like a star struck idiot. The waitress brought us our coffee and after he poured about half the sugar container into it, Waylon took a long sip and leaned back into the booth.

"Let me guess. Back home, you're some kind of hot shit, packing all the local beer joints. Every time you play all the girls scream and all the rest of the drunks yell and tell you how great you are. Am I right?"

I finally got my normal voice back. "Yeah, that's happened before," I said.

"So you packed up everything you owned and headed to Nashville to become a big star."

It sounded so naïve and stupid when he said it, I was embarrassed to admit it was true, so I didn't respond.

"How long you been here, son?" He asked.

"Six months."

"You mean to tell me that you're all depressed, crying in your coffee and you've only been here six months!" He started laughing. "What'd you think, cowboy, that you'd just waltz in here and take over the town?"

"No. I just thought that maybe I could find some work here and see what could happen, but…"

"Son, there's lots of work here." He interrupted. "Just not in the music business."

"Yeah, I've figured that out. I guess I was just fooling myself coming here."

Waylon took a long sip of his coffee then leaned over the table and looked me directly in the eyes. "How are you doing that?" "Doing what?" I asked.

"How are you talking with your head stuck so far up your ass?" He laughed hard and leaned further back into the booth.

I smiled at him. "I guess I am a little depressed, but there's so much talent here... I just don't think I'm good enough to..."

"What's your name, son?"

"Uh... It's Max, Max Allen."

He reached over the table and shook my hand. "Nice to meet you, Max. OK, Max, I want you to listen to me carefully. I don't normally do this sort of thing, but I've been sitting over there watching you talking to yourself. At first, I thought you were some kind of wacko, but after watching a while I figured out that you were a picker who's just discovered how tough things are here in Nashville. This city is iniquitous. Do you know what that word means: iniquitous?"

"Honestly, no. I haven't got a clue. Big words were my brother's forte, not mine."

He smiled at me. "It's sort of a hobby of mine, looking up big words and trying to use them in conversation and I've got to tell you it ain't easy to do around here with all of these blockheads. Look it up, son. 'Iniquitous' is the perfect description of this town."

WHEN I WAS A KID, I had three interests: girls, guitars and sports. Expanding my mind and making good grades was not one of my main priorities. I did all right, I made A's and B's, but I must admit I wasn't the best student. My brother, Dean was my polar opposite. He was completely tone deaf and rhythmically challenged. His talent was his intellect and his interests leaned more toward being a member of the National Honor Society or the president of the math club. One of his life goals was to graduate Valedictorian of our high school, which he accomplished.

Dean's tragic death was still fresh in my mind and it didn't take much for me to drift away, lost in one of his memories. Suddenly, I was sitting at the dining room table, me doing my dreaded homework and Dean reading the Webster's Dictionary. He used to spend hours searching that dictionary for new words. When he'd find one, he would write it on the front of a 3x5 index card and the definition on the back. Then, when his friends would come over, he'd pull out the cards and they would play the word game. The object of this game was to give the new word's definition and then use it correctly in a proper sentence. Dean and his nerd friends actually thought this was fun.

I COULDN'T HELP but laugh thinking about Waylon's new word, Iniquitous. Of all the people in the world to play my brothers geeky word game, Waylon Jones would be the last one I'd ever expect.

"Iniquitous," I said. "Ok, the next time I'm around a dictionary I'll look it up."

"You do that, look it up." Waylon smiled at me then leaned forward. "Max, this town will suck you dry and kill your spirit if you let it. The trick is, not to let it."

"How the hell do you do that?" I said, "I can't even get in the front door around here."

Waylon smiled at me. "Are you worth a shit?"

"What?"

"Are you worth a shit? Can you sing? Do you have any real talent? Do you think you're good at what you do?"

"Well, yeah... I guess." I stammered.

"You guess! What the hell does that mean? You're either worth a shit or you're not worth a shit. It's just that simple. If you don't know, then how the hell do you expect to convince anyone up here?" He said firmly.

I had to think about that one for a moment. I know this may sound strange, but that was the first time I'd ever been asked that before. I started singing when I was 12 years old, formed my first band when I was 13 and had been making a living as a singer for almost 20 years, but no one had ever asked me if I thought I was any good. I'd always been told that I was good, but no one had ever asked me what I thought. I knew I could sing, but did I think I was a good singer or "worth a shit" as he put it? I'd never really thought about it. Singing was just something I could do and something that made me easy money. I'd never analyzed it before, I just did it.

So there I was, staring a country legend in the eyes, trying to decide if I was "worth a shit" or not.

"Well, uh… Yeah, I think I sing pretty well," I began. "I know I sing good enough to make a living at it, because I've been doing that for 20 years, but I'm not sure that I have the talent to become a big star like you."

"Max, I'm not sure why I came over here today, because I don't really have any answers for you. All I know is that if you believe in yourself and you actually have talent, you can make it in this business one way or the other. The only ones who fail in this business are the ones who quit. Never stop trying and never give up, but I think it's important for you to understand that whether you become a big star or not has very little to do with talent. Don't get me wrong, you have to have talent to make it, but talent isn't necessarily the determining factor for success around here. It has everything to do with two things: politics and luck… stupid luck. You can be the most talented guy in Nashville, but if you're not in the right place at the right time it ain't going to happen and that's something that's out of your hands. It's fate, plain and simple and if the gods aren't smiling down on you, you're just screwed, but you can't let it get you down."

Waylon stood up and put on his hat. "I'm only going to say one more thing to you, son. If you can make a living as a singer, big star or not, you're one lucky son-of-a-bitch. If you don't believe that, then go spend a day watching some poor bastard digging a ditch somewhere. The music business may suck, but it beats the hell out of working for a living. Don't forget, 'iniquitous.' Look it up." With that, he tipped his hat and walked out the front door.

I looked it up. Iniquitous: *immoral, especially in a way that results in great injustice or unfairness.*

I gained two things from my impromptu meeting with Waylon Jones that day. He convinced me not to give up on the music business.

He was right, it beat digging ditches. He also made me rethink my goals and realize that perhaps it was time to stop obsessing about becoming a star.

A few weeks earlier, I'd met a good talent agent who had offered to book me a year in advance in some of the best clubs in the country making damn good money, so I took the gigs. It would take me out of Nashville and away from the recording industry, but at least I could pay my bills singing for a living.

I'D BEEN on the road for almost two years, traveling from one coast to the other. My dreams of becoming a big star had finally waned and I'd accepted my fate, when out-of-the-blue, life blind-sided me again.

After my set one night in a small club in Jacksonville, Arkansas, a couple asked if they could buy me a drink. I didn't normally drink with the customers, but I'd noticed how much they seemed to appreciate my music, so I agreed and sat down with them. They were both a bit on the portly side, but they made a cute couple and were extremely friendly. The wife was sort of quiet, but the husband was a real card, cracking one joke after another. He was hilarious and I enjoyed my time with them.

As I was leaving, the husband stood up to shake my hand, "It was great getting to know you. I just know that you're going to be a big star someday."

"I wouldn't hold your breath," I responded.

"It's going to happen, we both know it. Just promise us something."

"What's that?" I asked.

"When you get depressed, you'll just ask yourself, 'What am I doing wrong?' and then try to figure out how to do it right." His belly shook as he laughed. "It really just that simple. You're gonna be a big star someday, just be patient. Promise me when that happens you won't let living high on the hog make a pig out of you. Promise us you won't change and become some arrogant asshole."

"I promise," I said laughing as I walked away.

As I was walking back to the stage to get my equipment, I heard the guy–very loudly–tell the table next to him, "Hope ya'll have a great night, we're heading on home now. Yep, I'm taking this little lady home and when I get there, I'm dropping a Viagra pill into a glass and then I'm gonna pour myself a stiff one!" I guess the entire bar was listening to him, because the place erupted in laughter.

All the way back to my hotel room, I had this strange feeling churning in my gut. I didn't know what it was, but it wouldn't go away. That night I tried to get some sleep, but my mind was whirling like a top. Finally, I got out of bed and grabbed my guitar– my guitar has always been my tranquilizer. In the dark, I started strumming and without thinking about it, these words came out of my mouth,

"Don't get me wrong I'm not the type to complain, but I still think someone should explain.

Why every time I get my feet on the ground, something always comes up and knocks me down.

What am I doing wrong, whoa oh, what am I doing wrong?'

Won't somebody cut me some slack and get old Murphy off my back.

What am I doing wrong, whoa oh, what am I doing wrong?"

I started smiling. It was a good line a lot of people could relate to. I sang it again. I knew I had something.

For the next three hours, I wrote words and music to go with that line. When I finished the song, I broke out my tape recorder and cut it a few times until I had a good recording of it. It was now four in the morning and I was hungry as hell, so I threw on some clothes and headed to the I-Hop. The place was empty except for two drunk rednecks in the smoking section and the waitresses. After I devoured my pancakes, I hit the play button on my tape player and held it up to my ear. The volume was louder than I realized and soon I had two waitresses standing around my table.

"What song is that?" one asked.

"That sounds like my life," the other one said. "Play it again and turn it up this time." So I did.

Before I knew it, I had five waitresses, two cooks and the drunks from the smoking section dancing between the I-Hop tables, all singing along with my new song. I was a huge hit at the local pancake house and best of all... my breakfast was free.

I woke up my band members at 8 A.M. They were not happy that I wanted to rehearse a new song that early in morning, but they all showed up anyway. With everyone gathered around, I played them my new song. When I started, they were all half-asleep, barely listening, but when I finished, they were all laughing and singing along.

"Man, you've got to cut that," my drummer said. Everyone in the band chimed in with agreement.

"Max, that's a hit song," my bass player said. "A fucking, huge hit song."

I knew I had something with this new song, but I'd been down that slimy Nashville road so many times before, I wouldn't allow myself to get too excited. "Let's just learn it and play it to our audience for a while and see what they think," I told them.

That night we played it for the first time and the crowd went wild. We had to play it four times before we finished. Everyone kept requesting it over and over. They loved it. By the end of the night, I knew I had a potential smash hit on my hands.

There was a small recording studio in Jacksonville, Arkansas. It wasn't as state of the art as the Nashville studios I was used to, but it had adequate equipment to cut a quality demo. I planned on shopping the tape around Music Row on my next break, but as things turned out, that wasn't necessary.

Jacksonville is a very small town and, as in most small towns, everyone knows everyone else's business. The engineer (who was also the owner of the studio we recorded in) was so fired up about my song, without asking me he called the local country radio station and played it for them. I almost drove off the road the next day when I realized the song I was singing along with was my song. *What Am I Doing Wrong* had hit the airwaves and the second it was over the phone lines at the radio station lit up. They told me that within fifteen minutes the station received over 500 requests to play it again. It was the most requested song they'd ever played on their station.

The next day the station manager called to ask if it would be OK for him to send a copy of my song to their sister station in Little Rock. Of course, I agreed and within a week *What Am I doing Wrong* was the most requested song on that station as well. Suddenly I became a hot property and the switchboard of the Jacksonville Holiday Inn got busy. I got calls from every big shot in Nashville–all wanting to talk to me. I stopped answering the phone after the first day and let the front desk at the hotel take the messages. Every hour or so, I would walk to the lobby of the hotel to pick them up. It was amazing to read them. I had urgent messages from people I'd been trying to see for years. The same people who were always busy in a meeting or out of the office when I'd drop by with my new tape. Now, when I returned their calls, instead of being blown off with some lame excuse by the secretary, I'd instantly be put through. I have to admit it was exciting, but at the same time it was infuriating. When the phony bastards answered their phones, it was as if I was one of their long lost friends calling. The most exasperating call of all was the one I got from Jimmy Proud.

I WAS, or at least used to be, a friend of Jimmy Proud. We'd started together, in a way. When we met, he was a struggling record producer – an up and comer. There was an instant friendship and musical connection between us, so we teamed up and he produced my first serious album project. Together, we walked the streets of Nashville knocking on doors, shopping the project. It was full of my best songs, cut by the best studio musicians in Nashville, but the timing wasn't right and we failed at getting a label to pick it up. We collaborated on two more projects with, unfortunately, the same results. The last time I'd seen Jimmy was in my house in Nashville. He actually cried that night, blaming his lack of talent as a producer for our failure. At that time, I honestly thought Jimmy believed in my talent as a singer/songwriter and recording artist; he appeared to be very sincere.

A year after I moved to Houston to work with my brother, Jimmy produced Travis White's first album for RCA. It was a smash hit, selling three million copies in three months and suddenly Jimmy Proud was THE producer in Nashville, a real hot shot.

During his rise, I'd sent him a few letters from Houston offering him congratulations, but never received anything back. When I'd call him, he was always in a meeting or out of his office. I hadn't talked to him in over a year and I'd only been back in Nashville three weeks, when I accidentally ran into him in a restaurant. He hugged my neck and slapped me on the back. We talked for a few minutes. I told him about the loss of my brother and why I was back in Nashville. He seemed genuinely happy to see me; however, when I brought up the subject of our old projects, he suddenly changed his expression and demeanor.

"I'm sorry, Max, there's nothing I can do. I'd love to help you, but that would be considered unsolicited material and you know Mammoth doesn't listen to unsolicited material, even from an old friend. Sorry old buddy, but my hands are tied, but hey, good luck anyway." He said that looking me in the eye with a smile on his face. He shook my hand and walked out of the restaurant. I felt like I'd been kicked in the stomach. I was numb. I could not believe what had just happened.

Inside every performer, there is a dream that someday, someone will discover you. You dream that this mystical person will recognize your talent and instantly sign you up. Against all odds, you keep trying, because deep inside you know that someday, somehow that special contact will find you and your life will change. That's what keeps you singing in all those beer joints and hotel bars night after night. It's what keeps your confidence and faith in your talent.

Jimmy *was* my mystical person of power. With a snap of his fingers, he could have changed my life. He'd heard my best songs, he'd seen me perform on stage and yet, he didn't sign me up. I went home that day in a state of shock with my hopes and dreams shattered.

Lack of confidence festered inside my head for months after that and I wasn't sure I would ever get over the damage Jimmy Proud did to me that day. Now, two years later, there I was sitting in a hotel room in Jacksonville, Arkansas holding an urgent message from him. Suddenly, my confidence was back. The tide had changed and the revenge tasted sweet.

AMNESIA

CHAPTER SIX

When Bradford Doss opened the door and walked into his house he hid his pain. He did not limp or let his internal agony show. His mysterious injuries would have been hard to explain to his wife, but he knew that even if he slipped and limped a bit, more than likely she wouldn't notice. In fact, she barely acknowledged his existence when he walked in the front door and carefully made his way to his bedroom–his private bedroom. He hadn't shared a bed with his wife for years and he knew that once he was safely inside that room, he could tend to his wounds without fear of discovery. His wife *never* entered his private domain.

He couldn't remember the last time he'd had sex with his wife or even touched her for that matter. Personal contact stopped shortly after she discovered her infertility. The day the doctor told her that she could never have children she began to back away from him. It was a subtle transition. When they had sex, it became increasingly obvious that it repulsed her, so he just stopped and a few months later moved into the bedroom next to his study. He never explained why he moved out and she never asked. They both knew. After his move, her mood improved and she seemed visibly relieved. In reality, it wasn't that big of a change to either one of them; sex had never been a significant part of their relationship. He was attracted to her intelligence. She was a brilliant person, a great cook and a dedicated wife in every other area. It was a marriage of convenience–she wanted social status, he wanted occasional companionship and someone to look after his house. It was a congenial union. The fact that his marriage was sexless wasn't a problem; he had other sexual outlets that were much more erotic and satisfying, however, this time his search for erotic sex had gone terribly awry. For the first time he'd come very close to getting caught. He'd been discovered and chased by a policeman, he'd been in a serious car crash, and two people had died in the process. It was a close call, but somehow he'd managed to escape.

Safe in his bedroom, he couldn't help but smile thinking about how lucky he'd been. He did regret causing the accident and the deaths of the policeman and the young boy — especially the young boy. What was his name? Oh yeah, Eddie something. He didn't get his last name, things had happened so fast. Honestly, the death of the cop didn't bother him, but he *was* sorry the boy had died. He was beautiful and would have been fun to play with, however, he had no choice in the matter. He had to do what he had to do and sometimes bad things just happen. It wasn't his fault.

When he removed his shirt and looked into the bathroom mirror, the only visible injury was the long blue and red bruise that crossed his chest diagonally, the imprint of the shoulder strap that secured him in his seat during the crash. Although the strap had probably saved his life, it had also broken several of his ribs in the process. It was difficult to breathe and when he coughed, the pain almost caused him to black out. He needed medical attention, but that was impossible. He realized that he could have sustained serious internal injuries, but he couldn't go to a doctor. It would be obvious to a doctor that he'd been in a car accident and they are required by law to report mysterious injuries to the police. All he could do was hope he didn't bleed to death from internal injuries and hide his pain until he healed.

It was ironic that he'd gotten hurt and almost caught this time, because it was going to be his last–his final abduction of a stranger. The last time simply because he had no reason to do it any longer.

After all, he had a beautiful young 13-year-old girl living in his house. And now, finally, he knew how to get to her.

Unfortunately, to get his hands on the drugs that would make it all possible–safely and untraceable back to him–would take a few weeks. But the anticipation, his vivid fantasies, had driven him to uncontrollable heights. He didn't want anyone to die, he was only trying to get some sexual relief. It was not his fault. It was those damn cameras that drove him to this–watching her lying there... naked.

THE CAMERAS WERE ONLY a few inches long and easily camouflaged. There were four of them: two in the bedroom and two in the bathroom. The Judge was impressed at the quality of the video he was receiving from such small devices. The images were only black and white, but very detailed and intensely erotic. Like the tiny cameras, the viewing room was also small: only large enough for a chair and a desk where the four television monitors were placed. From there, he could watch Carla's every move. Cameras one and two showed two clear views of the bedroom. He could watch her in bed when she slept or when she was dressing. He could actually zoom both cameras in and out to get a better look.

In the bathroom, cameras three and four allowed him to see every inch of her, but his favorite view was camera four, the overhead shot of the bathtub. Watching her soap her young, firm breasts and legs was all it took to bring him to an explosive orgasm.

Overall, he was pleased with the setup, but now that she was there and he realized how beautiful she was he wished he'd installed twice as many cameras.

Everything had happened so fast. Only two weeks had passed from the time he'd received the call from the dean asking if he and his wife would be interested in looking after a brilliant 13 year old girl while she attended college. Of course, he instantly said yes without even consulting his wife. Honestly, he didn't care what his wife thought; it was a dream come true.

When Carla first arrived, she only took showers, but the steam fogged the camera and blocked his view. To solve this, he surprised her with a fancy wrapped package containing a large bottle of perfumed bubble bath. She was very excited to receive his gift. He told her that taking a bath each night, rather than a shower was much more relaxing and would help her to sleep better. She was easily swayed and soon watching Carla bathe became his nightly ritual.

He realized what he was doing was extremely risky. He'd never done anything like this, this close to home, this close to his wife, but the intense jeopardy only seemed to heighten the erotic excitement of it all.

Each evening after dinner, he would insist that Carla hurry up to her room to bathe and get ready for bed. Then as usual, not to cause any suspicion, he would kiss his wife goodnight and retire to his home office to review case documents and prepare for his next busy day in court: nothing out of the normal, nothing unusual. Then later, usually well after midnight after checking to see that his wife was sound asleep, he would go to his secret viewing room in the attic, rewind videotapes and masturbate repeatedly to Carla's young erotic images.

However, with each passing day, his desires for the young girl grew more intense. Soon his nightly voyeuristic viewing became more of a sexual frustration than a sexual satisfaction. Her young supple body was all he could think about, keeping him in a constant state of arousal. It was having a negative effect on his work, making it difficult for him to concentrate on his cases. He couldn't wait much longer—something had to be done. He had to have her soon.

He was losing control… and then… a simple court hearing showed him the way.

∽

THE CASE, according to the nervous young Houston assistant district attorney standing before the honorable Judge Bradford Doss, was simple. "Your Honor, the girl was raped, plain and simple," he said, in his slow Texas drawl.

"It was not consensual sex as the defense will argue. It was rape. We are aware, Your Honor, that the defense has witnesses that will testify that the girl was all over the defendant and appeared to be more than willing. We have no argument to the fact, but Your Honor, the girl was acting under the influence of a combination of drugs. One called 'Ecstasy' and the other called 'Scopolamine' commonly known as the 'amnesia drug.' When Scopolamine is combined with Morphine, these drugs put you into something know as 'twilight sleep'; you are awake, but can't remember what happened to you when the drugs wear off. It's a very effective drug commonly used by doctors when they need a patient awake during a medical procedure and yet, want them to forget the pain and discomfort after the procedure is completed. When these three drugs are used in tandem, a virtual sex slave with no memory is created and that's exactly what happened to this girl. It's a horrible thing to do to another human being, but as horrific as it may sound, that's exactly what this man did. He secretly drugged this girl and when she was under their influence, he raped her. She had no self-control and worse, no recollection of the event afterward. The drugs... unfortunately... worked well, Your Honor."

The case had Doss' full attention. After listening to the defense's opening, he ordered a two-day continuance to research the effects of the drugs. He wanted to know everything about Ecstasy and Scopolamine, but not necessarily for this case. Slamming down his gavel, he walked out of the courtroom his mind whirling with thoughts of a firm, 13 year old naked body squirming on the bed, out of control, begging him for more and best of all, not remembering a single thing the next day.

COINCIDENCE

CHAPTER SEVEN

he two Vicoden and four Tylenol PM tablets had knocked him out so deep he didn't hear the doorbell ring at 4:00 A.M. but he quickly sat up in bed when his bedroom door creaked open. Groggy, he opened his eyes to see his wife and two uniformed Houston police officers standing in his doorway. Instantly, adrenalin rushed through his body, jarring him awake.

"What's going on?" he asked, as calmly as he could.

"Bradford, something horrible has happened," his wife said, her voice quivering. "Get dressed, these police officers need to talk to you."

His mind raced with horrific scenarios. How could they have found him so quickly? What evidence did he leave behind?

"Give me a second," he said to his wife. "I'll be right there."

Keep your head, Bradford. He fortified himself. Think before you speak.

As a Texas State Court Judge, hearing case after case, year after year, it doesn't take long to understand why most criminals get caught–they all make the same stupid mistakes. As he dressed, he racked his brain retracing the episode moment by moment. He had shaved his body, had worn gloves the entire time, he'd worn a hat that covered his hair and the overalls covered his whole body: there was no way he could have left prints or DNA behind. But what if he had, they'd be no way to connect him... not this quickly. They couldn't have DNA test results or a print match this fast, not overnight. Perhaps someone recognized him. That was a possibility, but unlikely. He'd stolen the van out of a deserted parking lot and was sure no one had seen him. He'd driven two hours north to a town he'd never been to before... it was a random abduction, he'd never seen the boy before... there *was* no connection.

He reminded himself of another common mistake made by most criminals: panic. When they are cornered, they usually run or confess. He would not panic. He would not run. He would not confess. There *was* no connection. He was clean; they had nothing on him.

Before he left his bedroom, he gathered up the gloves, hat and overalls from the bathroom floor and stuffed them into the dirty clothes hamper in the back of his closet. He would burn them later.

The last thing he did was to place the tiny shoe he'd taken off the dead boy's foot in the floor safe next to his bed. The shoe was his only souvenir and the only real connection to the event. Deep down he knew that keeping a souvenir was a huge risk, but he couldn't help himself; he always took something. Sometimes he would take the souvenirs out of the safe and rub them on his erection. It helped bring back the moments in vivid detail and always brought him to an intense orgasm.

As he walked out of his bedroom, his legal mind took over and assured him they didn't have a search warrant or they would have already served it. All he had to do was answer a few questions, explain his whereabouts for the last few hours and not panic. The cops would be intimidated just talking to him. After all, he was the honorable Judge Bradford Doss. They had nothing on him.

DOSS TALKED to the two cops for over an hour, shook their hands and watched them drive away. Back in his house, it took him fifteen more minutes to convince his wife that the best thing to do was wait until morning to tell Carla the bad news about her little brother. Finally, back in the safety of his bedroom, he sat on the edge of his bed and considered his predicament. His mind boggled with the impossibility of it all.

What were the odds? He'd done everything possible not to have a connection to this abduction; he'd driven two hours to a strange town, picked a child he'd never seen before and... damn! The kid was Carla's brother. The strange town he'd driven to... Tyler, Texas. It was Carla's hometown. It was the mother of all coincidences and a dangerous situation he could not ignore. He couldn't let something as stupid and unlucky as this lead to his demise. He had no choice, he had to embed himself into this investigation and misdirect any attention that might come his way.

EDWARD CECIL SR. showed no emotion during little Eddie's funeral. He didn't cry, moan or sniffle. He just sat there motionless in silence staring forward. He didn't hear the loving eulogy given by the pastor, nor the soft compassionate words of comfort from his friends as they filed by Eddie's casket. He heard nothing and felt nothing. His mind was blank and his body was numb.

Carla, holding on to her father tightly, guided him from the church to the limousine, from the limousine to the gravesite and finally back to the limousine for the slow ride home. Not once during this time did Edward speak or show any signs of comprehension. His once brilliant green eyes now appeared colorless and sunk deep into their sockets.

It had only been two months since Carla had seen her Dad, but when she opened the door and saw him there in his bed, she had to fight back her tears and hide her shock. The young, happy, vibrant man was gone. In his place was a broken pathetic shell of the father she once knew.

It had taken her two hours to get him up and dressed. She wasn't sure dressing him for the funeral was the right thing, but it was all she could think to do. She too, was devastated about Eddie's death and wanted nothing more than to be held by her father and cry her hurt away in his arms, but that wasn't going to happen. Something was terribly wrong with her father and she had to be there for him now. The roles had been reversed; she had to be the strong one. She tried to talk to him, but he didn't respond. She didn't know what else to do, so she took charge of the situation, forced him into his clothes and walked him out the door to the waiting limousine. She was hoping that once the funeral was over, her dad would get better. Perhaps then they could talk and figure out what to do next.

Unfortunately, things didn't change after the funeral. Edward remained completely non-responsive and soon it became obvious that something had to be done. Edward Cecil Sr. was adrift existing somewhere deep in his mind, a dark place far from the pain of his tragic life. Carla was overwhelmed and desperate for help, but couldn't bring herself to call the judge. She couldn't explain why, but deep inside she had a feeling of admonition when it came to the judge; however, when he appeared at her doorstep, she burst into tears and cried for twenty minutes as he held her in his arms.

Everyone in Tyler, Texas was overwhelmed at the seemingly limitless generosity of the honorable Judge Bradford Doss. When it became obvious that Edward Sr. was incapacitated, Judge Doss magnanimously took over. He paid for all of the costs connected to little Eddie's funeral and quickly arranged for Edward Sr. to be placed in a psychiatric ward at a hospital in Houston, of course at his expense. He was the talk of the town. Carla was very lucky to be in his care. He was truly a great man in the eyes of the people in Tyler; even old man Jackson praised him.

Over the next six months, Edward showed no signs of recovery. In fact, he'd digressed; falling further into a complete vegetable state kept alive by a feeding tube. So when the judge filed the guardianship papers, it made perfect sense to everyone. Although Carla was a freshman in college and had the IQ of a genius, she was only 13 years old and needed someone to look after her interests.

Edward's tragic demise had saddened everyone in town. In less than two years, he'd lost it all. "It was more than anyone could take," the locals would say. "Who wouldn't have gone crazy?" What had happened to Edward was terrible, they all agreed. The only positive thing they could point to was the honorable Judge Bradford Doss. At least, thank God, young Carla was in good hands.

EVERY FRIDAY at 2:30 p.m., after her last class, Carla walked twenty blocks from Rice University to the Houston Medical Center. She would sit on the edge of her father's hospital bed, take his hand in hers and tell him everything she'd learned in college that week. She talked to him for hours, but Edward never responded. He would just lay there motionless, staring out the window.

"I'm not sure yet, Dad, but I'm leaning toward a career in the financial world. I may even change my major next semester and go for a degree in economics. After I graduate, I might become a stockbroker or maybe an investment banker. Everyone tells me that I'd make a fortune as a stockbroker and I must admit that it all sounds sort of glamorous and exciting. Oh, I know it would be hard work, but fun at the same time. I know this may sound strange to you, but I have a knack for picking stocks. Don't laugh, I'm really good at it. I've come up with my own formula and it works real well. Oh, don't worry, Dad, I'm not really buying stocks, it's just pretend. In one of my economic classes, we did a mock stock purchase. Each student got to pick fifty thousand dollars worth of stocks on any companies they wanted. We wrote down the prices at that time and followed their progress. After four months, we had to give a report on their successes or failures. Listen to this, Dad; out of 1,200 students, my stock picks were the best. I did better than anyone else in the entire economic department, even the seniors. Dad, I started with fifty thousand dollars and grew it to over a million dollars in sixteen weeks. My professors were amazed and are begging me to show them how I did it. What do you think? Should I tell them?"

Carla looked at her father as if she was expecting him to answer, but he just continued his trance like gaze out the window. "I think I'll tell them it was just simple fat luck and keep the formula to myself. If I work real hard and save my money, I may have fifty thousand real dollars to invest someday, then I could make us rich. What do you think Dad? Wouldn't you like to be rich? We could move into a big fancy house and I could take care of you. I could work out of the house buying and selling stocks and we could be so happy there. Come on Dad! Talk to me. What do you think? Come on! Come out of this! Wake up, please. I need you. Please talk to me!"

Carla fell across his bed and cried, her small body shaking violently with each convulsion. This had become a ritual, a long talk with her dad and then a good cry. She realized that it probably wasn't a healthy thing to look forward to each week, but it always made her feel better. She felt safe in his hospital room. She didn't know why exactly, but it was the only place she truly felt content. The only place she could let her emotions out. The only place she could talk out her problems and she had a lot of them.

She told her father about the strange things that had been happening to her, things she couldn't explain. She went into detail telling him about the black outs and about the entire days that were somehow erased from her memory. She talked about the mornings when she would wake up confused and disorientated, but she didn't mention the physical pain that always accompanied the time loss–the horrible aching in her bottom. Even in his condition, there were things she just couldn't tell her father. Anyway, the physical pain always went away after a few days. That wasn't the most troubling of her problems; the loss of memory and time was what petrified her. Was she losing her mind or worse, could she have a brain tumor or some horrible disease?

"What should I do, Dad? I'm so scared. Tell me what should I do?"

Carla believed deep down he was listening, hearing every word she was saying. Every night she prayed that one day he'd wake up and come back to her.

ON FRIDAYS, Judge Doss always adjourned his court for the weekend by 3 p.m. Supposedly, he used this extra time to catch up on paper work and organize his caseload, but in reality, the moment he slammed down his gavel, his mind shifted from the law to much more pleasurable things. Leaving early allowed him to miss the heavy Houston traffic and usually got him home by 3:30. With Carla visiting her father in his hospital room and his wife working late in her office at the university, he had the house to himself for hours, plenty of time to get things set and ready.

He knew Carla would be thirsty after her long walk home from the hospital, and he always had a nice ice-cold glass of lemonade waiting for her when she arrived.

When she walked in, she immediately began drinking the drug-laced lemonade. It was difficult to contain his anticipation. Be patient, he told himself, it wouldn't be long. Soon she'd be out and he'd be playing with her young, firm body again.

IT HAD TAKEN four times to get the combination of drugs to work correctly. The first time was a disaster. He'd given her way too much for her small body. She never regained consciousness and just lay there motionless. Although he loved nibbling and kissing every inch of her body, it would have been nice for her to respond to him just a little. Unfortunately, afterward the bed was covered in blood. He had broken her hymen and she bled for almost two hours. After he was sure the bleeding had stopped, he bathed her, changed the sheets and placed her back in bed dressed in her favorite yellow nightgown. It was almost noon the next day, when Carla finally stumbled down the stairs. She was confused and disoriented for almost two days.

He reduced the dosage for the second session with similar results. He reduced it again on the third time, but it was still too much. Frustratingly, she remained unconscious during the sex, however, she didn't seem as affected the next day. Finally, on the fourth try, she had opened her eyes and tried to push him away, fighting him off with her tiny fists. He was ecstatic; he wanted her conscious, this was what he had been waiting for.

The vivid memory of Carla's young firm body squirming beneath him was irrepressible. Three times in the past week, he had abruptly recessed his court rushing back to his chambers to masturbate.

Every day the growing intoxicating passion inside him became increasingly more difficult to control. The temptation to abandon his plan of only on Friday nights was a constant battle. Several times each day he would have to remind himself that Friday was the only safe time, the only night he could be absolutely sure he'd be alone with the girl. His wife taught an 8 P. M. class and always worked in her office afterward until 11:30 p.m. In five years, she'd never been home before midnight on Friday. It was the only night to do it. He had to stick with the plan, so with each passing minute he suppressed his desires and counted the days.

THIS VISIT with her dad had been exceptionally difficult. She had seen no signs of improvement from her last visit. In many ways, he seemed worse, slipping deeper and further away from her. Standing next to his bed, she leaned over and kissed his cheek. "Guess I better go, Dad. I'm real tired. It's going to get dark soon and I have a long walk home."

Walking down the hall, suddenly she felt weak and dizzy. Her head began to spin, her vision narrowed, tunneling smaller and smaller and soon she was walking blindly with rubbery legs, frantically clinging to the stainless steel railings bolted to the corridor wall.

"Are you alright, Honey?" she heard a voice say behind her.

"I... I... don't know what's wrong with me..." she said as she slid down the wall to the floor. Her ears began to ring, everything turned white and then to black.

When she woke up, she was laying on a hospital bed encircled with a light blue curtain. It took her a few minutes to realize that she was in the emergency room of her father's hospital. Looking under her sheet, she saw that she was naked, covered only by a small blue cotton gown that tied in the back; she had no idea how she'd gotten there. She lay there listening for sounds on the other side of the curtain, but didn't hear any.

"Is anyone there?" she yelled. "Hello! Is anyone there?"

The curtain slid back and a tall man dressed in green hospital scrubs walked up to her bed. "Hello, I'm Dr. White. Glad to see you're back among the living. How do you feel?" he said.

"A little confused, how did I get here? What happened to me?"

"You fainted upstairs in the corridor."

"I fainted? I've never done that before."

"There's nothing to be concerned about. People faint for a number of reasons and most are not serious. I've taken some blood and as soon as the test results come back, we'll know for sure. Just try to relax," he said reassuringly. "I hope you don't mind, but we took the liberty of looking in your purse for identification. You are Carla Cecil?" he asked.

"Yes."

"You're a student at Rice University?"

"Yes, that's right."

"It says here on your student ID that you're only thirteen years old. Is that a mistake?"

"No, that's correct. I'm thirteen, almost fourteen."

"Wow! Thirteen and going to Rice University! You must be a very smart thirteen year old," Dr. White said smiling.

Blushing, Carla smiled and said, "I'm not that smart. Just smart enough to go to college a little early."

"A little early?" Doctor White mocked.

"Going to college this early wasn't my idea. It was sort of forced on me. I guess I should be thankful, but honestly, I hate it." Carla wiped away a small tear that had formed in the corner of her eye.

"It must be very tough for someone so young. Are you having trouble keeping up with the lectures?"

"No, I don't mean that. It's not the classes. I love going to the lectures... it's just... everything else. That's what I hate."

A nurse pulled back the curtain. "Doctor White, I think you need to look at this," she said abruptly, handing him a folder. The doctor scanned the papers slowly reading and re-reading the pages. "Carla, I'll be back in a few minutes. Just try to rest."

Carla sensed a change. His soft understanding eyes had suddenly become strained and he was doing his best not to make eye contact with her. It confused her. Whatever was in that folder concerned her and it couldn't have been good, she thought.

For the next thirty minutes, she laid on her hospital bed waiting for someone to tell her something. Finally, the curtain slid open. "Miss Cecil, we need to do a more comprehensive physical exam on you. Just a few more tests, nothing painful. I promise."

Ten minutes later, Carla was wheeled into an examination room, helped out of the wheel chair and onto a table. "Please put your feet into the stirrups." The nurse said.

"Put my feet where?" Carla asked. "What kind of examination is this?"

"It's a pelvic examination. Please put your feet into these," she said pointing to the metal foot rests on each side of the table. "The doctor will be in shortly."

Carla knew what a pelvic examination was, she'd read about them and knew what they were for, but it had never been done to her. No one had ever touched her down there before.

Carla jumped off the bed. "I just fainted. There is no reason for a pelvic exam. I want to go home now. Where are my clothes? I want my clothes," she demanded.

"I'm sorry but we can't let you leave just now," a voice said behind her.

Carla looked around and saw Dr. White standing there. "Dr. White! I want to go home. Please let me go home. I just fainted. I don't want an exam. Please don't let them give me that exam."

"I'm sorry Carla, but it's out of my hands. We have to check you for several things and we can't let you leave the hospital right now. In fact, I'm afraid we're going to have to contact the police."

"The police? Why? What have I done? I just fainted." She began to cry, wiping her eyes with her hands.

"I can't tell you everything, but I will tell you that you've done nothing wrong, but we did find something unusual in your blood and these additional tests are, well, let's just say required. That's all I can tell you at this time. Please, Carla, just cooperate and everything will be over very soon."

Carla had never been so frightened and humiliated in her life, but she didn't resist and let Dr. White do what he needed to do. The pelvic exam was mortifying, but it only hurt slightly and was over in a few seconds.

Fifty-five minutes later, the curtain opened and Dr. White walked in and sat on the edge of her bed. "Carla, the last thing I want to do is to make you more upset than you already are, but I have to talk to you about something. I'm sorry, but I have no choice."

Confused and scared, Carla pulled her legs up to her chest and rocked back and forth. There was tension and hesitancy in the doctor's eyes. "What did you find in my blood? Am I dying? Oh, God! What is it? Please tell me." Tears began rolling down her cheeks.

"Oh, no, nothing like that. You're fine," Dr. White said, wiping her cheeks with his handkerchief. In fact, you're a very healthy girl. I'm so sorry, I didn't mean to mislead you."

"Then... what's wrong with me? You said something about the police? What is it? Please tell me."

Dr. White stood up and looked into her eyes. "Carla, do you have a boyfriend? Someone you're intimate with?"

"A boyfriend? Intimate? Are you talking about sex? Are you asking if I'm sexually intimate with someone?" Carla was stunned at the question. "Dr. White, I'm only thirteen. I'm a virgin. I've never even been on a date. Why would you ask me something like that?"

He'd known the answer before he asked the question. The perplexed look in her eyes convinced him that as far as she knew, she was a virgin. His suspicions were confirmed and it sickened and angered him inside. This sweet, innocent 13-year old girl had been drugged and savagely raped several times. He was in an awkward position. She may have the IQ of a grown woman, but she was still just a little girl, with little girl emotions. She deserved to know what had happened to her, but it wasn't his place to tell her. News like this should come from someone who knew her well; someone she loved and trusted, someone who could help her get through this.

"Carla, I understand your father is upstairs in the psychiatric ward. What about your mother? Where is she?"

"She's dead. She was killed in an automobile accident two years ago."

"Any siblings, brothers or sisters?"

Carla dropped her head. "I had a younger brother, but he was kidnapped and killed six months ago. That's what drove my father over the edge. That's why he's upstairs."

"What about grandparents, an aunt, or an uncle?"

"No. I have none." Carla looked up, her face wet with tears. "Why are you asking me all of this? What is going on?"

Dr. White sat back down on the edge of her bed. "I wish I could tell you, but..." his heart ached for this little girl. What kind of monster could be doing this to her? She was so helpless, so innocent and all alone in the world. "Trust me, no one's going to hurt you anymore. Everything's going to be alright."

Carla stopped crying and reclined back on the bed. "What do you mean, no one's going to hurt me anymore?"

Dr. White stood. "I'm sorry, Carla, I don't mean to be so cryptic, but soon you'll understand everything."

The curtain slid open and a nurse walked in and handed the doctor a note. After reading the note, Dr. White grinned. "Why didn't you tell me that your guardian was Judge Doss?"

"I don't know. I... Ah... You didn't ask me. What difference does that make?"

"It means that I have someone to talk to. It means that we have someone I can release you to. I can't tell you how happy I am to know that Judge Doss is looking after you. You are a lucky girl, he's a great man. I'm going to go call him now. Just try to relax, I'll be back soon."

On the phone, Dr. White gave a lengthy explanation of Carla's situation to Judge Doss, but was taken aback by his immediate negative response. "Judge Doss, I would like your permission to get her upstairs to a rape specialist as soon as possible. She needs to know what's happened to..."

"I appreciate your concern, Dr. White," Doss growled into his ear, "but that will not be necessary. Listen to me very carefully, doctor. You do *not* have my permission to take Carla anywhere. Do you understand?"

"Yes of course, but Judge Doss, She is only 13 years old and she's been drugged and raped. If this is not handled correctly there could be enormous negative psychological repercussions and..."

"I don't mean to be rude, doctor, but what exactly is your medical specialty?" Doss interrupted.

"Ah... well, I'm board certified in emergency medicine. I'm an E. R. trauma doctor."

"As I expected. You are not trained or hold any degrees in psychology. Am I correct?"

"Well no, that's why I suggested a rape specialist, they are trained psychol..."

"I'm sorry doctor, but it's obvious to me that you do not have the expertise to make this call. So, I will reiterate. Do NOT under any circumstances tell Carla what has happened to her or take her to see anyone else. I am on my way to the hospital to collect her and I will take it from there. I will see that she sees a psychologist if I deem that to be necessary. Do you understand my instructions, doctor?"

"Yes, I understand, Judge Doss. I don't agree with you, but I understand."

"Whether you agree is of no consequence. Just make sure you do what I say. I'm not trying to be difficult, but I think I know what is best for her. I am Carla's legal guardian and I warn you doctor, if you go against my wishes, I will have your license within the week."

Dr. White was shocked and angered by the obvious threat, but there was nothing he could do about it. His hands were tied. "OK, if that's what you think is best, but as you know, Carla's a very intelligent young girl, she knows that something serious has transpired and is going to want answers soon. I'll do my best to dodge her questions. I won't tell her anything specific, but it's not going to be easy."

"One last question, doctor. Does anyone else know about this, other than the nurses and people working in the lab? I am specifically talking about the authorities. I know you are required by law to report potential crimes to the police. Have you done this?"

"Yes I have. In fact, that's how I learned that Carla was in your charge. I talked to officer John Colby at the fifth precinct. He immediately recognized Carla's name and told me that you were her guardian. I'm sure there's nothing to worry about there, he informed me that he wouldn't file any official papers until he heard from you."

"Very good, Doctor. Yes, Officer Colby's been in my courtroom many times. Dr. White, I realize you may not completely understand my position here, unfortunately I am a high profile political figure in this state and I can't afford for something like this to get out; the press would have a field day blowing it out of proportion. I hope you understand the necessity of keeping this confidential."

Dr. White *didn't* understand and hung up the phone with an uneasy feeling in his gut. He thought that he'd experienced every possible human reaction to this kind of news. Usually, bad news spawned instant shock, then tears followed by a total loss of emotions, however this was the first time it had produced selfishness and apparent indifference.

Dr. White slid back the curtain encircling Carla's bed startling her awake. "Sorry, I didn't realize you were sleeping," he said. "How are you doing?"

"That's OK, I must have dozed off. I'm doing OK, I guess. You tell me." She said rubbing her eyes.

"You're going to be just fine. In fact, I just got off the phone with Judge Doss and he's on his way. I'll have the nurse bring you your clothes so you can get dressed. He'll be here soon to take you home."

"Dr. White, don't you think I have a right to know what's

happened to me?"

"Yes, Carla I do and I'm sure Judge Doss will tell you everything and get you to the right people to help you get through this."

"There you go again...'People to help me get through this?' What people? Through what?"

Dr. White pulled a card out of his pocket and handed it to her. "Here are my numbers. My office number is printed on the front and I've written my home phone on the back. After you've talked to the judge and if you still want to talk, give me a call. But just in case you'd rather talk to a woman about this, I've also given you Dr. Jane Griswald's number. She's a good friend and a specialist in this area. She'd be a good person for you to talk to. I know this must be very confusing and I'm sorry, but it's all I can say right now. Just remember I'm here for you if you need me." Dr. White patted her on the head and walked to the foot of her bed. He unhooked her chart and wrote in it. After re-attaching the chart, he smiled and walked out, closing the curtain behind him.

Carla had no idea what the doctor had been talking about. Dr. Griswald was a specialist in this area? What area?

The nurse brought in her clothes and left her alone to dress. As she dressed, she noticed the chart hanging on the end of her bed. Quietly, she lifted the chart off its hook and read it carefully line by line. It took her a while to find what she was looking for and when she did, she had to read it several times to comprehend it. Her blood tested positive for Ecstasy, Morphine and Scopolamine.

She read it again. What it said was impossible. She didn't take drugs, not even aspirin. How could these drugs be in her blood? She checked and saw where the lab had run the blood tests twice. There was no question about it, it *was* her blood. She read the report again and memorized the spelling of Ecstasy, Morphine and Scopolamine. Turning the page, she scanned the doctor's personal comments. What she read was unfathomable.

The patient's hymen has been ruptured. Further examination shows slight tears in the walls of the vagina and anus; obvious signs of regular vaginal and anal penetration, conclusive evidence of frequent aggressive sexual activity. The patient has tested negative for HIV, Hepatitis A, B, C and all other known sexually transmitted diseases. Due to this evidence and my strong suspicions of drug-induced date rape, the police have been contacted. Also, due to the patient's age, psychological counseling has been strongly advised to her guardian.

NEITHER CARLA nor Judge Doss spoke a word on the short drive home. Once inside, Carla ran up the stairs to her room, threw herself on her bed and burst into tears.

A few minutes later, her door opened and Doss walked in carrying a tray of food. "I thought you might be hungry," he said, setting the tray on her bed. "Come on now, there's no need to cry, it was all just a big mistake. I'll take care of everything, don't you worry about a thing. Try to eat something. It will make you feel better. I'll be in my study if you need me for anything. Goodnight."

"Am I in trouble?" She asked, wiping away her tears from her cheeks.

"In trouble? With whom?"

"The police. They had to report to the police. The doctor told me..."

"No one reported anything. It was just a big mistake made by the lab, just a simple mistake. You're not in trouble. Now stop worrying. I told you I'd take care of everything and I have."

"But the doctor said I had stuff in my blood and that I may need to see a specialist."

Doss suddenly stiffened and spun around to look at Carla, his eyes were gray and hard, his brow furrowed and wrinkled. "What did he tell you? What do you know about this? Tell me exactly what that doctor told you."

Carla was startled by the Judge's sudden change in demeanor. He seemed enraged. His body language hardened and his voice was husky and anxious. She had planned on telling him everything. Even about reading her hospital chart and about the date rape, but the Judge's sudden and strange reaction gave her an intuitive caution. She was confused and needed time to think, so she played dumb. "Honest, Judge Doss, I don't know anything. Only that they found something bad in my blood. The doctor wouldn't tell me what it was, but it must have been serious if he had to report it to the police. I swear I've never taken any drugs. I swear." For effect, she faked a small cry, whimpering, falling back onto her bed. Through the cracks of her fingers covering her face, she watched his reaction carefully.

Observing Carla crying her heart out, covering her face with her tiny hands so he couldn't see her tears, convinced Doss that she didn't know anything more. Carla watched him relax his body and let out a sigh of relief. Then she saw him smile with a disturbing, sinister gaze in his eyes and slowly walk out of the room. A chill raced through her body.

Doss was relieved that Carla didn't know more, however, the doctor knew everything. Something would have to be done about him, as well as the police officer. He regretted it, but once again, he had to resolve a serious problem that was not his fault, none of his doing. Killing was something he'd become skilled at, but did not enjoy. He had no choice in the matter, the doctor and the cop knew too much and simply had to die.

As he walked down the stairs to his study, Doss couldn't help but smile. He was a lucky man. Anyone could have answered the phone at the police station when the doctor had called. Some other police officer that didn't know Carla was in his charge could have answered that phone and simply filed the report, but that didn't happen. Once again, he had escaped catastrophe by inches. It was a sign from God that Carla was his fate and more proof that what he was doing was not wrong. Carla was his destiny and they were meant to be together.

After arranging to meet privately with Officer John Colby on the following night, Doss climbed the stairs to his private video room and watched impatiently as Carla slowly ate her food and finally drank the coke he'd left for her on the tray. His body tingled; he could barely wait for the drugs to work. Soon she'd be naked and again, he'd feel her warm skin next to his.

THE FALL

CHAPTER EIGHT

By the end of the week, I had received three urgent messages from Jimmy Proud at Mammoth Records. Although I savored the instant reverse of power, it was time to cash in, so reluctantly, I made the call. His voice was so cheerful it turned my stomach. Listening to him relive all the good times we'd shared together in the past was painful and it was all I could do not to hang up in his ear. The more I listened, the more I realized what kind of snake in the grass this guy really was. For almost twenty minutes, he embellished about the good old days remembering one story after another then finally, he changed the subject and came to the point.

"Max, when will you be back in Nashville?" he asked.

"In a couple of weeks. Why?" I asked.

"I guess there's no other way to say this, so I'll just spit it out. Max, you're a hot property and I want you on the Mammoth label. I know you must be getting calls from everybody in the business by now. All I'm asking is to let an old buddy have the first shot at cutting a deal with you. What do you say?"

I could actually feel my temperature rising and the blood thumping in my head. I wanted to tell him *hell no* or to go fuck himself, but I didn't. Cutting a deal with a major record label was my dream and I wasn't about to let my temper or hatred for Jimmy Proud screw me out of my big chance. I had to be smart and play it out slowly and carefully, so I bit my lip and agreed to call him the second I got back to Nashville.

The next morning my phone rang at 6:00 a.m. Still asleep, I grabbed the receiver and growled, "This better be important."

"The word for today is 'fortuity.'" A low voice on the other end boomed.

"Waylon, is that you?"

"In the flesh, son. I had one heck of a time finding you. What the hell are you doing in Jacksonville, Arkansas?"

"Just trying to make a living... singing my ass off."

"I guess you know that you're the talk of the town up here."

"Yeah, I guess I am. I've been getting about a million calls a day from those guys."

"Alas, the point of this call. I'm going to ask you this one more time. What the hell are you doing in Jacksonville, Arkansas? Why in God's name aren't you here cashing in on all this fortuity you've fallen into?"

"Waylon, give me a break. It's early and I don't have a dictionary. What the hell does 'fortuity' mean?"

"What a blockhead. How did you ever get out of high school? The definition of 'fortuity' is simply, something that happens by chance or accident. In a word, this is your lucky break, son. So I'll ask one last time, what are you doing in Jacksonville?"

"I'm in the middle of a gig, I'm contracted to play here for two more weeks. I'll be there as soon as I finish."

"Max, don't be obtuse. Go talk to your boss, cut a deal with him and get your ass back to Nashville, now. Trust me. Don't wait two weeks. In two weeks, they may not remember your name. Don't fuck this up, son, you've got to strike while the iron is hot and that time is now."

He was right. Everything had happened fast and could go away just as fast. "Thanks, Waylon, I hadn't really thought about it that way. I feel like I'm in a whirlwind, my life has exploded on me, but I guess I do need to jump on this. I promise, I'll do it. By the way, what does 'obtuse' mean?"

His laughter roared in my ear. "I was wondering if you'd caught that one. Look it up, son, and when you find out what it means, try not to be that way from here on out. It's not a good thing. Trust me on this one. Seriously, son, I do wish you luck and I hope you get everything you've always wanted. Welcome to the big time. You're about to enter the land of the leeches where everyone sucks up to the smell of money. Take good care of yourself, pay close attention to what these pricks say to you and watch your ass." The phone clicked in my ear.

Following Waylon's advice, I bought my way out of my gig and headed back to Nashville that afternoon. On the way out of town, I stopped at a Barnes and Noble and bought a new dictionary.

I laughed out loud when I read the definition of obtuse. It was right on the money. Obtuse: slow to understand or perceive something, something that is not sharp.

THE NEXT TWO weeks were intense, meeting with one record company after another. All the deals were similar when it pertained to financial compensation, but Jimmy's offer from Mammoth Records stood far above the rest when it came to what really mattered. Mammoth offered me complete and total creative control of my projects. I would be in charge of the productions, not some bone head from the label watching over my shoulder, telling me what to do in the studio. I tried, but none of the other labels would budge when it came to creative control, so my choice became obvious.

On a gloomy, dark skied Thursday morning, exactly 5 weeks from the day I wrote *"What Am I Doing Wrong,"* I signed on the dotted line. Unfortunately, it was with Mammoth Records and Jimmy Proud, but as I signed that contract, I kept thinking about something my father used to tell me. It was an old saying he would quote from time to time: *Keep your friends close and your enemies closer.* It had taken thirty-eight years and I had to get in bed with the devil, but I'd finally made it to the big time.

Three weeks later, *What Am I Doing Wrong* hit number one on all the charts. You couldn't turn on the radio without hearing it. Suddenly, my face was everywhere you looked. I made the cover of all the trade magazines, as well as People, Time and I even made the cover of Newsweek. My album went gold the first month and platinum in two. It was one of the fastest selling albums in country music history.

In record time, Max Allen had become a household name and it was a strange veracity to deal with. As silly as it sounds, I had real trouble grasping the reality that this Max Allen guy, this big star in all the magazines and on the radio, was actually me. Everything had happened so fast, that deep down I didn't really believe it; however, the hard reality of it hit home the first time I ventured out of my house for a pack of cigarettes at the corner 7/11, I got mobbed.

For as long as I could remember I had dreamed about being a star, now suddenly I was a huge star, and honestly I hated it. When I would go out in public, I couldn't even go to the bathroom without someone wanting to shake my hand while I was busy at the urinal. If I went into a stall, some idiot would look over the top and ask me for an autograph. I actually made some guy's day by signing my name to a long piece of toilet paper I tore off the roll.

The invasion of my privacy was exasperating and frightening at the same time. Several times I found myself in the middle of a frenzied crowd on the brink of trampling me to death trying to touch me or snatch a piece of my shirt or hair. To protect me, the label hired three security guards to surround me and push back the mob of fans when I had to make public appearances. I honestly felt like a prisoner in my own home. It was a horrible existence. It changed my opinion and gave me a whole new respect for Elvis and the Beatles or anyone else who's had to live through this kind of sudden fame.

However, I must admit that it wasn't all bad. The feeling you get inside when twenty thousand people are applauding and screaming to your music is indescribable. It's why everyone in show business is in show business. No amount of money can equal that feeling and it almost makes all the bullshit worthwhile. Almost. The most surprising phenomenon I experienced from my instant fame was the astonishing rise in my sex appeal. Women, who two months earlier wouldn't have given me a second look, were now flashing me their tits and begging me to sleep with them. Every night I was surrounded by gorgeous women, fighting for my attention. They would literally crawl over each other trying to get me. I was always dumbfounded at the groupies. I'd heard about them all my life, but never really believed they actually existed, but trust me, they do.

The band and the roadies called them "Star Fuckers" and they loved them, because these groupies would do anything to get to me and that was my problem. I couldn't help but wonder how many blowjobs they'd given before my road manager would bring them into my dressing room to meet me. In the beginning, I thought it was a ridiculous perk and I didn't go along with it. However, I'm only human and the flesh is weak. Before long, I will admit to taking full advantage of the situation. Afterward I always felt a little sleazy and it often made me sad for the girls. Some were not only beautiful but also extremely intelligent; they didn't belong there. But I guess spending time with a famous person made them feel important somehow.

The next twelve months of my life was a complete blur. My life had changed so fast that before I realized what was going on, I was completely out of control. I had become a wild man living in a hazy fog, one concert after the next, lost in a world of sex, booze and country rock and roll. It should have been the best year of my life, a dream come true, but as it turned out it was the worst.

I was burning alive right before everyone's eyes; my manager, producer and everyone at the record label, but no one tried to extinguish the fire. In fact, they were the ones supplying the gasoline. The problem was that they couldn't see the fire because the huge stacks of money I was making blocked their view. I had forgotten my ambition, my goals and somehow had lost my soul along the way, but no one seemed to notice or care.

Life changing events always seem to happen to me in Arkansas. It's where my rocket ship took off and where it came crashing back down.

I was on tour opening for Hank Jr. and they tell me that the night before it happened, we'd performed at the Little Rock Amphitheater. Honestly, I don't remember being there except for a few flashes, but I'll never forget what happened after the concert.

The after show gathering was in my hotel suite as usual and we partied until daylight. I'm not sure what woke me the morning after, but suddenly I was wide awake and in desperate need of a bathroom. On my way to the head, I stumbled over ten or fifteen naked people lying in various positions on the floor around my bed. It was 8 a.m., I was still a little drunk and my head felt like it was the size of a basketball. After I'd finished my business in the bathroom, I did my best to make some coffee. It was a real challenge to my alcohol soaked brain cells figuring out where the coffee and water went, but eventually I got it started and plopped down on the couch holding my aching head.

I sat there an hour or so downing one cup after another and was on my second pot when the parade of half naked musicians and groupies began filing out of my bedroom. My normal routine was to sleep late and wake to an empty hotel suite, but this morning I was awake, surprisingly sober and got the opportunity to witness their humiliating exodus in all its glory. Twelve strange women and four of my musicians stumbled out.

To my knowledge, I'd never seen any of the women before in my life, but somehow they all seemed to know me. Most seemed embarrassed and made a bee-line to the door, but two of them showed no signs of humiliation and immediately snuggled up to me, still completely naked, on the couch. They were very young, very beautiful and apparently still very horny. My musicians had hurriedly beat it out the front door leaving me alone with the remaining two women. One man, two horny women may sound like heaven, but at the time, it seemed more like hell.

It took me a while, but I finally convinced the girls that the party was really over and pushed them half dressed out the door. It was just in time, because only seconds after I'd closed the door behind the last one, I lost my grip, rushed to the bathroom and with violent fervor, puked my guts out for fifteen minutes. I lost count of the times I threw up that day, but I'm sure I must have set some kind of record; every thirty minutes or so I found myself worshipping the porcelain god.

I'd never been that sick before and was grateful it wasn't happening on the cramped tour bus. Luckily, we were taking a rare break in our marathon non-stop schedule, leaving me with a couple of days off to do absolutely nothing but veg out on the king size bed, order room service and watch the game on the tube. That was the plan.

I ALMOST STEPPED ON HER. She was naked, curled in a fetal position on her side in the darkest corner of the bedroom. When I saw her lying there, my first reaction was anger. All I wanted was to be alone so I could catch up on my rest and I was in no mood to deal with a passed out, leftover groupie.

Standing over her, I yelled. "The party's over, darling! It's time for you to get dressed and go home." There was no response. "Hey! Wake up! It's time to go." I yelled louder, reaching down to shake her. When my fingers touched her skin, instinctively I jerked them back in revulsion. Her skin was cold as ice. Carefully, I lifted her arm to feel for a pulse, but there wasn't one. I found out later that her name was Victoria Lynard and unfortunately, for me, just two weeks shy of her 18th birthday.

From the moment my first record hit the airwaves I had been treated like some kind of god. Everyone I met bowed at the waist in some form or another and treated me special. I'm not saying that this is a good thing, but I will admit it's something that's easy to grow accustomed to, however, when the cops find a dead 17-year old girl in your hotel room, all that "special" treatment disappears fast. Before I knew what was happening, I was handcuffed and hauled off to jail. I went peacefully. I couldn't argue with them because honestly, in my fogged condition I wasn't sure if I'd been with the girl or not and had no idea what had happened to her. To the best of my recollection, I'd never laid eyes on Victoria until I found her lying there dead in my room. Disoriented, embarrassed and confused, I was photographed, finger printed and locked away in a six by nine cell.

The official autopsy report said that Victoria had died from a deadly mixture of cocaine and alcohol. It also showed that she'd had sex with multiple partners within hours of her death. I was charged with manslaughter, statutory rape, use of a controlled substance, and contributing to the delinquency of a minor. That night, my arrest was the lead story on all of the national news networks. Watching in horror from my cell, I saw my life disintegrate before my eyes. Within days, I'd fallen from grace landing into the pages of the tabloids magazines, labeled as a perverted, psychopathic criminal. I was sure my life was over, but it wasn't.

They had found a lot of alcohol, but no cocaine or any other illegal substance in my bloodstream. Because I was clean, so to speak, it put a big hole in the DA's "drugged out country/rock star" theory and made the prosecutors have to rethink what really went on in that room that night. I was addicted to fame, women and alcohol, but not drugs. I may have been an out of control egocentric wild man, but I wasn't a junkie. Due to this lack of evidence, reluctantly, they dropped all of the drug charges against me.

The other problem the prosecutors had was that the medical examiners couldn't connect me sexually to Victoria. She'd had several partners that night, but I wasn't one of them. My DNA didn't match up. I'll never understand that one. After all, she was naked and in my hotel room, but DNA doesn't lie and therefore, the statutory rape charges were dropped.

Things were looking better, but I still had the manslaughter and contributing to the delinquency of a minor charges to deal with. After two hearings and a very long trial, I was finally acquitted. A jury of my peers had found me innocent of having anything to do with Victoria's death since she had crashed my party and voluntarily taken the drugs, but unfortunately, I'd been tried and convicted by the court of public opinion. The press had crucified me, plastering my police mug shots on the cover of every scandal magazine on the rack, each rag sheet claiming my acquittal as another example of a guilty man getting off because of his wealth and fame. As far as America was concerned, I was guilty as hell and had killed Victoria with my own deadly hands.

Like rats deserting a sinking ship, so it went with my legion of fans and so called friends. Jimmy Proud was the first to call to let me know that, "although he'd fought for me, it was out of his hands. Due to all of the negative press, regretfully all my future projects had been shelved." What he was trying to say but just didn't have the balls was, that effectively I'd been dropped by the label. Although legally I was still under contract, the simple reality was that the label wasn't going to spend one more cent promoting me, or my records. No hit records, means no more concert dates as well.

Adieu, audios, goodbye, the end. It was hard to believe, but in less than two years, I'd completed the full circle: from the bottom to the top, then back to the bottom. I'd come crashing back to the bottom in flames this time and somehow it seemed much deeper than I'd remembered. I guess when you land on your face in disgrace you sink into the muck a little further.

To add insult to all of this injury, I was flat broke. I'd made millions, but only a fraction had made it back to me. After the label recouped their "promotion costs" and my agents and managers took out their cuts, there wasn't much left. What little I did have went to pay off my lawyers. The only thing I had remaining was a car, a few thousand dollars I'd hidden away, my clothes, some furniture and my boat.

I had lost everything, but for some reason I was not depressed about it. Of course, I was sad and a little embarrassed, but I was not depressed. Honestly, what I felt was relief. It was like I'd finally awakened from one hell of a nightmare, almost as if the last few years of my life had just been a dream or some wild fantasy. Intellectually, I knew it was real, but emotionally I had no feelings about it whatsoever, just a void. All I could think about was how lucky I was not to be in jail. It was a real wake up call. I'd been given a second chance to do something with my life. Apparently becoming a star wasn't my providence after all. I wasn't sure what my destiny was, but whatever it was, I knew I had to get it right this time.

I spent the next three weeks lying around my house in Nashville, hiding from the press doing nothing but eating and sleeping. Then in the middle of the night, I snuck out, drove to Texas and spent a few weeks visiting with my parents. As far as I could tell, the negative press had taken no toll on them. If it had, they showed no signs of it to me. All they showed me was love and compassion, never mentioning the groupies or the wild parties. We talked about everything else, but never that.

The only thing my father said that even came close was when he took me outside for a smoke. "You know, Max, everyone makes mistakes in their lives and that's OK, that's how you learn. Just remember that only a fool makes the same mistake twice."

That's my dad – a man of few, but usually profound words. I heard him loud and clear.

Still completely confused about what to do with the rest of my life, I packed a small bag of clothes, my guitar and a small sound system into my car and headed out to Florida. I hadn't seen my boat in a year, but she didn't disappoint me. She was glistening in the bright Florida sunshine, bobbing gently up and down with each small wave that slapped against her white hull.

I'd accidentally stumbled on her floating in a marina in Ft. Lauderdale. It was love at first sight and I knew I had to own her. She wasn't new, in fact, she was almost ten years old but she'd been pampered by her previous owner and looked pristine. At the time, I was on tour opening for Hank Jr. and buying a sailboat didn't make much sense considering my nonstop schedule, but I'd dreamed of owning my own sailboat my entire life and just couldn't resist. I paid cash for her and didn't tell a soul. I even registered her under my father's name.

For the next few months, I scrubbed, sanded and painted every surface on her. Next, I had her hauled out of the water and went to work on her bottom. One week later packed full of food, water and fuel, *Windsong* and I sailed across the Gulf Stream heading for wherever the wind might take us.

THE DISCOVERY

CHAPTER NINE

arla sat on the edge of her bed and picked at the food tray. She wasn't hungry, but the judge had gone out of his way to fix it, so she tried her best to eat. The coke tasted funny, but she was thirsty and finished it anyway.

Her mind was whirling in a million different directions. She couldn't get the image of the judge's menacing smile out of her mind. Why did he smile? It didn't make sense, but it wasn't just his smile that troubled her... it was the look in his eyes. It was evil, creepy. Just thinking about it sent chills through her body again. No, I'm just imagining things, she thought, the judge is a wonderful man. He probably smiled because... because... she thought for a moment, but couldn't think of an explanation. It doesn't matter, he's a wonderful man and that's that. She forced herself to think of something else.

Her thoughts shifted to the hospital. Why did she faint? What could have caused that? Was it the drugs? She knew that Morphine was a pain killer, Valium was a tranquilizer and Ecstasy was some kind of sexual enhancement drug, but she'd never even heard of Scopolamine. What in the world was Scopolamine and how did it get into her bloodstream? How did any of these drugs get into her blood?

A wave of nausea and disgust flowed through her body when she remembered the last thing she'd read on the chart. *Evidence of frequent aggressive sexual activity. Due to this evidence and my strong suspicions of date rape, the police have been contacted.* Date rape? Her nausea grew stronger. She convulsed and gagged at the horror of it all. She ran to the bathroom and threw up. She was vomiting and crying so violently she had to gasp for air between each wave. When she finally stopped, she pulled herself off the bathroom floor to the sink, rinsed out her mouth with water and toweled her face.

She stumbled back to her bed and laid down on her back. Her emotions swelled. "Oh, God, someone has drugged me... and raped me!" she yelled. Covering her face with a pillow, she released it all soaking the pillow with her tears. Finally, she regained some of her composure and wiped her wet face with her hands.

"Oh, God! Oh, my God." Using the napkin from the tray, she dried her face and wiped her eyes. Who would do something like this, and how?

The more she thought, the more the pieces of the puzzle fell into place. She *had* been losing track of time, blacking out, losing days sometimes. And, she had been having pain between her legs, but had thought it was something all girls went through. This was something no one should have to go through. Losing her train of thought, she tried to concentrate but couldn't remember what she was thinking about. She was getting sleepy, but fought it back. Oh, yeah, she remembered, the blackouts, the rape. It had to be someone at the college, she thought, but who?

She tried to think of the students she'd met. Maybe it was one of her professors. She tried, but couldn't recall their names; she was getting so tired. She could barely hold her eyes open. She tried to sit up in the bed, but she didn't have the strength, it was no use. Seconds before she drifted off, out of the corner of her eye she noticed a dark figure standing in her door. Slowly she turned her head and stared, trying to make out the shadowy figure. Gradually her eyes focused and instantly she understood everything. She tried to scream, but nothing came out. She couldn't move; she was drifting, her body paralyzed, barely conscious. He was standing over her now, smiling. When she locked eyes with him, a wave of terror rushed through her body. Staring into the judge's horrifying eyes, screaming inside her head, she floated away.

Doss, holding a syringe in his left hand, stood over her and waited. When she finally closed her eyes, he walked to the foot of the bed, skillfully spread her toes, inserted the needle and pushed the plunger.

Sitting on the edge of her bed, he hummed to himself as he waited patiently for the drugs to take effect. Between his legs, he could feel his erection throbbing. Soon, he thought, very soon.

CARLA OPENED her eyes and looked into absolute darkness. She lay there trying to order her thoughts, straining her eyes searching for any signs of light. Where was she? What time was it? She moved her right arm to the side of the bed and discovered her nightstand. After fumbling over the table a few seconds, she found the lamp and flicked it on. Locating her watch, she read the flashing digital numbers: 8:15. How can it still be dark at 8:15 in the morning? Moving in slow motion, she pushed her body up with her arms and swung her feet over the side of her bed. Staring at the floor, dizzy and a little queasy, she fumbled unsuccessfully with her slippers. Giving up on the shoes, she braced herself against the headboard and raised herself up to her feet. Instantly, a jolt of pain shot up her leg from her left foot, throbbing between her toes. With most of her weight supported by her right foot, she hopped to the window and jerked back the curtain.

The pool lights glowed brightly, illuminating Judge Doss' meticulously landscaped back yard. Over the fence line, she could see the greenish, golden glow of the halogen street lamps that lined the neighborhood. It wasn't 8:15 in the morning, she realized, it was 8:15 at night. She tried to recall when she'd gone to bed, but her mind was empty, a complete blank. Had she just wakened from an afternoon nap? Had she slept all day and into the night? She tried to think and concentrated hard, but she couldn't dredge up anything. She had no memory of even going to bed, let alone when.

Her stomach growled and she felt hunger pains. Again, she concentrated trying to remember when she'd eaten last. Sluggishly her brain cells began to fire and the image of a tray flashed into her head – a tray of food: fruit, turkey, crackers and... a coke. She could see it clearly now sitting on the bed beside her, but when did she eat from that tray? Was it today, this morning or was it yesterday? She had no idea. She couldn't recall anything and that worried her. A rush of panic flashed through her body. Oh God, another spell, another blackout. More lost time she could not explain. What was wrong with her? How could she not remember simple things like when she'd gone to bed or eaten last?

In the bright bathroom light, she inspected her sore foot and found a tiny scab between her toes. She assumed she'd stubbed her toe on something, but when? She examined it carefully. It was just a tiny puncture wound, but how it got there was a complete mystery. After she showered, she slipped on an old pair of sweat pants, an extra large T-shirt and hobbled down the stairs barefooted to the kitchen. She was famished and quickly dove into some leftover fried chicken she found in the fridge. After devouring two drumsticks and a thigh, she walked back to the fridge, located a diet coke and poured it over ice into a tall blue glass. When the sweet taste of the diet coke touched her tongue, her mind flashed to the tray of food she'd remembered earlier, specifically to the coke on the tray. The replay was vivid, complete with the sense of taste. The coke was... was bitter, she remembered, not sweet like this one. Her mind began to fill with more and more images. She remembered that the coke on the tray had tasted funny, but she'd been thirsty and had drank all of it anyway. She could see it clearly now. It was... it was last night. She'd just come home from the hospital and... her mind flooded with a million images playing in her head like a motion picture — she'd fainted at the hospital, there was a doctor. His image flashed in her head and she could see his face. Doctor White. The blood test, the pelvic exam... She could see the pages of her medical file. DATE RAPE!

What a horrible nightmare, she thought. It was a nightmare, wasn't it? She asked herself. It had to be just a dream, something she'd conjured up in her subconscious. Her mind was racing, vivid images flashing one after another. It couldn't be just a dream, the memories were too dramatic, too detailed, too exact. Did she really have a blood test? Does that explain the scab between her toes? Do they take blood from between your toes? She tried to push the pictures out of her head and force herself to think of something else, but the images were too strong. "It's true, oh God it's true," she whimpered, finally accepting the awful reality. Losing control of her limbs, she fell to the kitchen floor howling and shaking violently.

Terrified, she lay on the floor and wept uncontrollably for almost thirty minutes. Finally, her tears dried up and she stopped shaking, but her breakdown had taken every ounce of her energy. Stretching her body flat on the floor, she placed her face against one of the smooth white marble tiles. It was cool against her warm face, soothing and comforting her. She relaxed and let her mind drift, floating away from her anguish.

Images of her mother began to appear in her mind. She could see her clearly standing there in a bright yellow sundress, her long black hair pulled back into a ponytail with only a few long wispy strands framing her beautiful face.

She was standing over her. "Don't cry baby, let mommy kiss it away. It's just a little boo-boo. There, there let mommy kiss the pain away."

The memory was so lifelike Carla could feel her mother's lips touch her skin as she kissed her scratched knee. "See, it's all gone." And it was.

"Now, let mommy see your hands." Her mother took her hands and placed a kiss in each palm. "Those kisses are very special kisses. Save them up and use them if you ever get hurt and mommy's not around. To use them, all you have to do is think about me real hard, put your hands over your heart and the pain will disappear. Saved kisses are the best kisses of all, because they last for ever and ever and will always be there when you need them."

"Really Mommy?"

"It's true, honey. I have lots of saved kisses from my mommy and when I get hurt or don't feel so well, I think about her real hard, put my hands over my heart and I always feel better. Never forget about mommy's saved kisses. You can use them over and over again. They'll always be there for you."

Carla pulled herself up off the kitchen floor and looked at her hands. Thinking about her mother's beautiful face, she placed her hands over her heart. It did make her feel better, but she knew that all the saved kisses in the world couldn't take away the pain she harbored inside.

Although all of her pain was still there, the memory of her mother had sparked a new emotion, which began to grow deep inside her. It was irrational, but she couldn't hold it back. The feeling was anger and outrage. She was mad at her mother for dying and not being there when she needed her the most. She knew it made no sense, but couldn't hold back the rage that welled up inside her. It wasn't fair for her to be alone in the world – not now, not when she needed someone so terribly bad.

She didn't understand it, but the angrier she got the more it took away her fears and gave her strength. It helped her face the fact that she *was* alone in the world and the only one she could depend on for help was herself. A new understanding came over her and gave her resolve and purpose. She had to forget the fact that she was only thirteen years old. If she was going to survive in this world, she had to grow up. She couldn't be a little girl any longer. She'd always been told how smart she was, well… it was time to see how smart she really was. There was no one else, she had to take care of herself and to do that she would have to rely on her intelligence. At that moment, she made up her mind that she was going to find out who had done this to her and stop him from ever doing it to her again. She *would* survive this and go on with her life, somehow.

She searched the house. She wanted to talk to someone about what had happened to her, but the house was empty. It was 9:30 p.m. on a Saturday night and finding the house empty was puzzling. She wasn't surprised that Mrs. Doss wasn't there, she had such a busy schedule she was rarely home, but the judge was always there on weekends pouring over his cases in his study.

She walked into the judge's study and sat down in the leather chair behind the huge mahogany desk. It was in perfect order, covered with small perfectly stacked piles of court documents. She spun the chair to face the computer sitting on the credenza behind the desk. She hit the keyboard and the monitor came to life. The judge's computer was similar to the ones she used at college, so it didn't take her long to find what she was looking for. She hit the Internet Explorer icon and in the search area, she typed: Scopolamine. In seconds a list of web sites with the word Scopolamine in the title were displayed before her. One by one, she clicked the web addresses and hit the print button. After she'd explored and printed twenty or thirty of the sites, she logged off and shut down the computer. She waited until the screen was black, then gathered her printed pages and walked upstairs to her room.

On the edge of her bed, she scanned through the thirty or so pages. Most of the articles contained detailed descriptions of the chemical compound used in the make up of the drug. A few gave brief descriptions of its use, but most of them leaned toward listing the negative side effects. Finally, she found what she was looking for — a recent medical journal article. The author explained that Scopolamine was a popular drug used by anesthesiologists. When combined with Morphine, it was especially effective for colonoscopy procedures, because first, it put the patient into "twilight sleep" allowing the doctor to communicate with the patient during the procedure leaving the patient with amnesia of his discomfort afterward. Carla read the article several times digesting the information carefully. Each time she read the word "amnesia" her eyes would fill. Several times, she actually gagged, forcing back bile that had backed up into her throat.

"Keep it together," she told herself. "You can do this."

Now she knew how someone could have done this to her without her remembering. The blackouts, the lost days and the pain between her legs were no longer a mystery.

"Never again!" she vowed.

Her new knowledge filled her with frenetic energy. She was impatient to do something, but had no idea what that should be. She searched the house again. It was almost 11 p.m. and she was still alone.

She retrieved the card Dr. White had given her and dialed the number. "Could I speak to a Jane Griswald?"

"I'm sorry, but Dr. Griswald has left for the day. Could I take a message?"

"No, that's not necessary," she said disappointed.

"Dr. Griswald is on the schedule for tomorrow. You should try her then. She usually gets here by 7 a.m."

"Thank you, I'll call her in the morning. Ah... is Dr. White still on duty?"

"Yes, but unfortunately he's in surgery. I doubt you can reach him tonight. He'll be leaving as soon as he's out of surgery. His shift ends at 11:30. I can try to get a message to him if you'd like."

"That's OK, you don't have to do that. I'll try to contact him at his home later."

Carla hung up the phone and looked at her watch. It was 11:05. If she hurried, she might make it to the hospital by 11:30 and catch him in the parking lot before he left. It was a long shot, but she was desperate to talk to someone tonight. As fast as she could, she scribbled a note to the judge, taped it to the front door and ran down the street.

She was out of breath when the bright lights of the hospital came into view a few hundred yards away. When she reached the parking lot, the sliding glass emergency room doors parted and she saw Dr. White hurriedly walking out. She was about to yell for his attention when she stopped dead in her tracks. She was startled by someone flicking a cigarette out of the window of a parked car just two spaces away from where she stood. She recognized him immediately – it was Judge Doss, sitting in a dark green Ford.

Acting on instincts, she squatted down between the cars and watched Dr. White walk to his van and drive out of the lot. Judge Doss started the green Ford and slowly followed the doctor's van out of the lot with his lights off.

When she stood, her knees were shaking and her heart was pounding. She was petrified, but didn't understand her reactions. What was she afraid of? Why did she hide from the judge? She had no idea, but her instincts had taken over and forced her to hide. What was the judge doing there, in that strange car? Why did he follow the doctor? None of it made any sense. Exhausted and confused, she walked home.

It was after midnight when she made it back to the house. "Where have you been young lady?" Mrs. Doss was standing in the kitchen, her arms folded at her chest.

"Uh, I... Ah, went to see my father."

"At this hour you went to visit your father?"

"Yes, ma'am. I... I left a note."

"I got your note, but that is no excuse. Carla, it's not safe for you to be walking these streets at this hour. You know better than that."

"Yes, ma'am. I'm sorry, but I wanted to see my father again."

"I don't want to hear it now. I'll talk to the judge when he gets home and let him decide on your punishment. Go to your room, we'll talk about this tomorrow."

"Please don't tell the judge."

"Carla, I'm not going to discuss this with you. Go to your room. Now!"

Carla ran up the stairs and closed the door behind her. It was the first time Mrs. Doss had scolded her and it upset her, but what bothered her most was that soon the judge would discover she was at the hospital the same time he was there. Again, her instincts took over, her body stiffened, and a wave of fear came over her. She searched her mind trying to figure out why that frightened her so much, but she had no answer.

She tried to sleep, but each time she'd drift off, the nightmare would jerk her awake, her body covered in sweat, out of breath. She gave up on sleep. In the dark, she tried to recall the nightmare that kept jarring her awake, coming to her again and again. She couldn't remember at first, but eventually it came.

She's in bed and someone is standing over her... a dark, shadowy figure. She tries to scream, but can't make a sound; she's paralyzed. The figure is holding something in his left hand, but she doesn't know what it is. She can't see his face, but his movements seem familiar somehow. There's pain in her foot and the nightmare ends.

Replaying it repeatedly in her mind, she tried, but couldn't remember any more details, just the shadowy figure and the pain. It was horrible to think about, but she kept trying because she knew what it meant. She was dreaming about him; the horrible man who had drugged her and raped her and each time she replayed it in her mind, the anger inside her grew stronger. Someday, she vowed, he would pay for what he'd done to her.

At 3 a.m., she heard the front door slam; the judge was home. Her heartbeat quickened and beads of perspiration broke out on her forehead. Once again, she was terrified and once again, she had no idea why.

At 5:30 a.m., Carla watched the sun rise and paint her walls with golden light beams through her window. She hadn't slept all night; her terror wouldn't let her. At 6 a.m., she quietly dressed and slipped out the front door walking the twenty-six blocks to the hospital as fast as her feet would carry her.

She waited in the parking lot until 8 a.m. giving Dr. Griswald plenty of time to arrive. At 8:10, she walked through the main entrance doors and walked up to the reception desk.

"Excuse me. I'd like to see Dr. Griswald."

"Do you have an appointment?" the receptionist asked.

"Well, no... I was referred to her by Dr. White in the emergency room. He told me to come and see her if I needed to talk to..."

"Oh, that poor man," the receptionist interrupted wiping her eyes with a Kleenex. Her eyes were red and full of tears. "Did you know him well?"

"No, I just met him the other day, but he seemed very nice. He told me to talk to Dr. Griswald if I needed to talk to someone about my... ah... about what happened to me. You can call him if you'd like. I have his home number. I'm sure he'd..."

"Oh, honey, you don't know about Dr. White do you?"

"What about Dr. White?"

"He was killed last night. It was a hit and run. He died instantly," the receptionist broke down. "It's all in here," she said, pointing to the morning paper.

Carla read the headlines: LOCAL DOCTOR VICTIM OF HIT AND RUN. Trembling, she found an empty chair. The article stated that Dr. White had been hit and run over while walking from his van to his house, dying instantly from severe head trauma. The reporter stated that several witnesses had seen a dark green Ford speeding away moments after the doctor was struck. The police reported there had been several sightings of the green Ford heading south on I-45, but unfortunately, the car had not been located. They also stated they had no idea of motive and had no leads or suspects at this time.

Carla's body shuddered with the sudden epiphany. The revelation was inconceivable, but all the pieces fit. Rocking back and forth in the chair holding onto herself, she could see the face in her nightmare clearly now. It was Judge Doss' face and he was standing at the foot of her bed with a syringe in his left hand. Judge Doss was the man who had drugged her. Judge Doss was the man who had raped her and, it was Judge Doss who had killed Dr. White simply because he knew.

Overcome with fear and revulsion, Carla fought back her tears. She couldn't break down; she needed a clear head. By now, the judge had talked to his wife and knew she had been at the hospital last night. He would be searching for her, coming for her. She had to run, escape somehow, but escape to where? She had no money, no clothes, what could she do? Where could she go?

"Are you Carla Cecil?"

Carla looked up and saw a very tall, thin woman standing over her. "Yes, I'm Carla Cecil."

The woman reached out and shook Carla's hand. "I'm Dr. Jane Griswald. I understand you wanted to see me."

"Yes, I was a patient of Dr. White and he told me to contact you if I needed to talk to someone," Carla held up the newspaper. "I guess you know about this already."

Dr. Griswald's face dropped. "Yes I do. It is such a tragedy. I still can't believe it. He was a wonderful doctor and one of my best friends." Dr. Griswald could see that Carla was trembling. "Come with me, Carla, we can talk in my office."

Carla gathered the newspaper into her arms and followed the doctor down the corridor to her office. Inside the small office, she settled in a chair facing the doctor's desk. Dr. Griswald didn't go behind her desk; instead, she sat in the other chair beside Carla. "Before we begin, let's get this out of the way. Please call me Jane. I'm a psychologist and for me to do my job, you've got to feel comfortable with me. Removing all of the formalities between us is the first step in that direction. So, please call me Jane."

"Ok, Jane." Carla said shyly.

"That's much better. Now, tell me how can I help you? Why did Dr. White want you to talk to me? Start from the beginning and tell me everything."

Carla talked for the next hour, revealing to Dr. Griswald everything that had happened to her since her mother's death two years earlier. She ended her story with her suspicions about Judge Doss.

"Dr. Griswald... I mean, Jane, I promise I saw him last night in the parking lot. He was driving a green Ford. Dr. White was run over by a green Ford. I know it was him! He killed Dr. White because he knew what he was doing to me. I feel horrible. Dr. White is dead because of me! I don't know what to do. Please help me."

Dr. Griswald stood and walked behind her desk. She picked up the phone and dialed a number. "Hi Judy. This is Dr. Griswald. I need to see the file for a Carla Cecil. I believe she was a patient here within the last few days." Dr. Griswald settled into her chair and smiled at Carla as she waited.

"Did you say Carla Cecil?" the nurse asked on the other end of the phone.

"Yes, Carla Cecil," she answered.

"Well, she was a patient here, but there is a problem. We got a call this morning from a clerk from some state court judge ordering us to seal her file. I'm afraid I can't let you see it Doctor."

"Did this order come from a Judge Doss?"

"Hang on, let me look. Yes, it came from the office of state court Judge Bradford Doss."

"Judy, look. I've got Carla Cecil here with me in my office. She tells me that Dr. White wanted me to talk to her about her situation. Without that file, I don't know what her situation is. This is something that Dr. White obviously thought was important. I don't want to get anyone in trouble, but I don't suppose that file could fall into the copy machine before it got sealed. I promise you, it's for my eyes only. I'll shred it after I read it. You have my word."

Fifteen minutes later, Dr. Griswald's door opened and a woman dressed in green hospital scrubs walked in and dropped a stack of Xerox pages on the desk. "Anything for Dr. White." she said turning and walking back out of the room.

Dr. Griswald picked up the pages and began reading as Carla sat quietly. As a trained psychologist, Dr. Griswald had learned not to jump to conclusions. There was no doubt in her mind that Carla was not lying to her. Carla believed what she was saying to be the truth, but her story was so outlandish that before she even responded to her, she wanted to read the medical file to see what Dr. White had to say. Perhaps Carla's file would reveal facts from fiction and uncover any exaggerations conjured up by a thirteen year old mind.

She read and reread the file carefully, but found no exaggerations or fiction. Carla had told the truth, the poor girl had been drugged and raped repeatedly, but something else in the pages caught her eye.

"May I see that paper a minute," she asked Carla.

Carla handed her the paper. "What is it?"

"Oh, my God!" Dr. Griswald exclaimed. "Look at this."

Carla followed the doctor's finger pointing to a story printed just below Dr. White's article. It was a story about a police officer that had disappeared, vanishing without a trace. Carla read the article. "I don't understand," she said.

"Now read this." Dr. Griswald handed Carla a page from her file. It was in Dr. White's handwriting. He'd written the name of the police officer he'd contacted to report Carla's rape. The officer's name was John Colby, the same policeman who was now mysteriously missing.

JUDGE DOSS LIMPED, favoring his right side as he walked from his bedroom to the kitchen. His right knee was throbbing and both of his feet were sore and swollen almost to double size. The four plus mile trek from the old lake back to his car was a lot harder and had taken much longer than he'd calculated. He'd walked as fast as he could and it still took him over two hours to make it to his car. After driving another thirty miles north, it was well after 3 a.m. when he finally got to his front door.

He poured coffee into a large black mug and eased himself down at the kitchen table, resting his right leg on a chair across from him. The hot coffee helped push away his bleary haze. He hurt everywhere, but considering his gain, it was a small price to pay.

Things had gone down smoothly, without a single hitch. The doctor was first and it was quick and easy. Doss smiled, remembering how similar it was to hitting a deer on a highway. The doctor actually froze in his headlights. It was very quick – WHAM, bump, bump, so long doc.

Remembering the cop caused him to smile broadly. He had been the most fun of all. Doss laughed out loud when the image of the cop's surprised look flashed through his mind. It was a perfect move – one minute they were driving down the road, talking like two old friends and a second later the cop's eyes were on him, stunned at the sight of the needle sticking out of his neck. It was a perfect shot. A direct hit into his jugular. By the time he realized what was happening to him, the drugs were flowing through his brain paralyzing his body. He never moved, slumping in his seat, held upright by the seat belt. He now lay in the trunk of an old dark green Ford at the bottom of an old lake fifty miles southeast of Houston.

Doss eased himself out of the chair, poured himself another cup of coffee, then slowly walked to his study. On his desk was a hand written note from his wife with a smaller note attached. He picked it up and read the small note first:

Judge Doss,

It's 11:05 p.m. I know it's late, but I needed to go to my dad's hospital and no one was home to take me, so I walked there. Please don't be mad at me. I'll be back soon.

Carla

Confused, Doss read the letter from his wife:

Bradford:

I had to leave early this morning, but I'll be in my office most of the day if you need to talk to me about this. I thought you should know that I found this note taped to the front door last night when I arrived at 11:30. It was after midnight when Carla finally got home. I scolded her and sent her to her room.

I think I've made my position very clear on this matter. I've never wanted her here in our house and do not intend on assuming this kind of responsibility. Since you've insisted on her being here, I'm placing this problem back in your lap. You must talk to her and make her understand that this sort of thing is dangerous and not acceptable. Take care of this problem today. I do not want to find any more notes taped to our door.

Suzanne

Doss slammed the letter down on his desk, walked up the stairs and knocked on Carla's bedroom door.

"Wake up Carla. We have to talk." Getting no response, he knocked again. "Carla! Wake up! I want to talk to you!"

He opened the door and walked into her room. Her bed was made, but the room was empty. "Carla!" he yelled. "Where are you?"

He limped down the stairs and searched the house room to room, but couldn't find her. He looked at his watch. It was only 8:15. "Where the hell is she?" he yelled into the air. "Carla! Where are you? Carla!"

In his study, he reread the letter from his wife and the small note that Carla had taped to the door. Sitting in his leather chair staring at the letter and note in his hand, he concentrated trying to put things together. He glanced at his desk calendar –it was Sunday. Carla should be in her bed asleep. Where could she have gone? Why did she go to the hospital last night and why so late? He looked at the note again. If she left here at 11:05 walking, that would have put her there about 11:30. She couldn't have seen her father that late, visiting hours were over…

Suddenly an improbable scenario materialized in his mind. Could she have been at the hospital at the same time he was in the parking lot waiting for the doctor? He would have seen her unless… she saw him first. "That's absolutely ridiculous," he said out loud, "It's just too… too coincidental."

He wanted desperately to believe what he was saying, but his years on the bench had proven to him that nothing is too coincidental. Often simple coincidence was the final piece of the puzzle that allowed him to lock someone away.

A wave of fear came over him. It couldn't be true, not Carla. He loved her so much, more than anyone or anything he'd ever known. More than he could have ever imagined and he was sure she loved him too. She'd never hurt him, but if she was there and did see him…

"No! No!" he yelled, forcing himself to stop thinking about it. It was a very small possibility, nothing to panic about. He decided to wait for her to come home and simply talk to her. He didn't know where she had gone, but that didn't worry him. He assumed she'd walked to the college library to work on some assignment; she'd be home soon. When he talked to her, he would be able to tell instantly. Her body language would give her away. Or, perhaps her eyes, her beautiful blue eyes. He could see her face clearly, her blue eyes looking up at him as he thrust deep inside her. He no longer felt fearful. He could only think of one thing. With the erotic vision of Carla's naked body playing in his head, he slowly stroked his throbbing erection.

His orgasm was intense and shook his entire body. A calm came over him as he realized that he had nothing to worry about. Carla belonged to him and by now, she surely loved him as much as he loved her. They had shared so much together and he knew she loved every minute of it. Even if she had seen him, she would never turn him in. They were meant for each other. Any minute now she'd be walking in the door and everything would be as it should. He was the luckiest man in the world.

DR. GRISWALD

CHAPTER TEN

J ane Griswald's apartment was located on the 11th floor of an exclusive, high-rise building called the "Houston House." Although it was only blocks from the University area and Judge Doss' house, Carla felt safe there. She had awakened feeling fresh and rested, sleeping soundly through the night. Not once had she been jarred awake in a cold sweat.

After she dressed, she joined Jane for breakfast on the balcony. Overlooking the Houston skyline, Carla awed at the view and ate fresh strawberries, wheat toast with homemade peach preserves and drank freshly squeezed orange juice.

"I hope this is okay with you. I'm a vegetarian." Jane said.

" It's wonderful!" Carla said. "It's delicious."

"I hope you slept well, you're the first person to use that bed. Was it alright?"

"It was perfect, the first night I've slept in a long time. I guess it was because I felt so safe there. Dr. Griswald… I mean, Jane, how do I thank you for what you're doing?"

"Carla, there's nothing to thank me for. All I did was get you out of harm's way, but unfortunately, it's just a band-aid to your problem. We need to come up with a real solution to this."

"Why don't we just call the police and tell them about Judge Doss?" Carla asked.

"If we contact the police, I'm not sure what would happen to you. Judge Doss is obviously psychopathic and very dangerous. He has already killed two innocent people to cover his tracks. I don't think there is anything he wouldn't do to get his hands on you. If we call the police, I believe it's possible he could convince them that you're just an emotionally distraught teenager simply acting up. He *is* your legal guardian and a very powerful and respected person in this community. I don't think we can take that chance. All we have is your word against his and that's just not enough to keep you safe. We've got to come up with something else."

"But we have the copy of my medical file. We could show that to the police."

"Yes, but that's not any real proof, it's just circumstantial evidence. We need more before we go to the police. He's too connected and I'm not sure the police would take our side without absolute proof."

"How do we get more proof?"

"I have no idea. But until we figure that out, we need to get you to a safer place. Somewhere Doss wouldn't know about."

"I can't do that. I can't just leave. What about my father? I won't leave without my father, he's all I have left." Carla shouted.

Dr. Griswald had forgotten about Carla's father. He *was* all the girl had left and couldn't be left behind. She didn't want to frighten Carla, but considering the situation, he too was in grave danger. Something had to be done about him and quickly. "Tell me about your father," she said calmly. "What is his condition?"

Carla's expression dropped. "They tell me he's what you call non-responsive. He's physically awake, but doesn't talk or seem to notice his surroundings. He just stares out the window." Carla wiped away a tear. "He's been that way over six months."

Dr. Griswald stood and paced the balcony. Finally, she stopped and looked at Carla. "We have to get your father out of that hospital. Then we need to get you and him out of this city. And, Carla, we need to do it fast. Tonight."

Doss was livid. He'd waited patiently for Carla to come home all afternoon, but she never showed up. As night fell, his anger grew. When the clock struck 9 p.m., it became obvious to him that Carla wasn't coming home and his fury flared out of control. He rushed to his car and searched the streets around his neighborhood, but she was nowhere to be found. At 10 p.m., he went to her father's hospital room, but she wasn't there either. Where could she be? Had she actually seen him the night before driving the green Ford? Had she gone to the police? What did she know? No, he considered, if she'd gone to the police they'd have contacted him by now. Even if she had, they'd never believe her. After all, she was just a silly teenage girl and he was an important person in this town. He needed to think, sort this out.

Back home in his study, he read and reread Carla's note and the letter from his wife. He tried to convince himself that he had nothing to worry about... she'd never turn him in. She loved him. She was just confused and afraid, all alone out there hiding, but where? All he could think of doing was to go out and search for her again. He had to find his darling Carla and get her back home where she would be safe. There were a lot of bad people out there on the streets and he just couldn't survive if something happened to her.

Spinning in his chair, he noticed that the green light on his CPU was not lit. He touched the keyboard, but instead of the monitor screen coming to life as usual, nothing happened. Someone had shut down his computer. Pushing the start button, he watched the monitor flash and blink, finally coming to life. He'd always taken pride in his knowledge of the computer. He had not resisted this new technology like so many of his peers. Being able to access the law library and the files in his courtroom office from this small CPU had helped him enormously, allowing him to keep one step ahead of his huge caseload.

He searched the screen, but nothing seemed to be out of place. With a few tricks he had learned in his computer classes, he soon retrieved the most recent files that had been viewed on his computer.

Someone had researched the drug Scopolamine. He knew who it was. His suspicions had been correct; Dr. White must have told Carla what they had found in her blood. He was glad that he'd killed the bastard. But now he had another serious problem to deal with and although he hated the thought of it, he knew what he had to do.

THE PLAN WAS SIMPLE: Dr. Griswald would escort Carla into the hospital using her credentials to get past the security guards and the nurse's station. Carla's job was to locate a wheelchair and load her father into it. While Dr. Griswald distracted the nurses, Carla was to roll her father to the service elevator, take him down to the ground floor and out the side exit into the alley between the buildings. Dr. Griswald would simply leave the hospital, retrieve her car from the lot and pick Carla and her father up in the alley. After that was done, they planned to drive to Dallas and check into a hotel near the DFW airport. The next morning, Carla and her father would fly away.

"Once you get to Atlanta, my brother will pick you up and take you to our family farm," Dr. Griswald said. "You'll be safe there."

Carla sat quietly, almost in a trance gazing out the window at the Houston skyline.

"Carla, did you hear what I said? You'll be safe there I promise."

"Yes, I heard you," Carla whispered.

Dr. Griswald sat next to Carla and put her arm around her. "I promise, we can do this. Soon this will be over and you and your father will be safe."

"I don't know why I'm crying. I'm just so scared and I feel so bad that I've gotten you involved in all of this. You're taking such a risk. If the judge finds out you helped me... You're putting yourself in danger for me. Why are you doing this?"

Dr. Griswald wiped Carla's cheeks with a Kleenex, "Because I didn't help someone in my past and I promised myself that I'd never do that again."

"I don't understand."

"Carla, my father started molesting me when I was 11 years old. It continued until I went away to college. I never told anyone about it, not even my mother. I didn't tell, because he'd convinced me that I was the one in the wrong. Don't ask me how he did that, but I honestly felt that it was all my fault and I couldn't tell anyone about the horrible things I was doing. After I left, my father turned his interests to my younger sister, but it was different with her... she was very fragile and couldn't handle it. One night after one of my father's visits, she hung herself. The next day they found her diary and it all came out. My father died in prison and my mother has never been the same. My sister was only 15 years old when she killed herself. If I'd only said something, spoken up... I could have saved her. I've lived with that guilt for years. I realize now that my father had scared me into submission. I didn't do anything wrong, but it's taken me years to understand that and to get where I am today. However, if someone had been there for me who could have helped me understand sooner, maybe things would have been different. Do you understand? The reason I'm a psychologist today is so I can help people like you. It's why I have no choice here, I have to help you."

Dr. Griswald flashed her nametag to the security guards and they waved them through. She assumed it must have been break time, because the nurse's station was empty. Dr. Griswald waited at the station and Carla headed out in search of a wheelchair.

She located the wheelchairs right where she expected. She had her choice of three. She chose the lightest one and quickly rolled it out of the equipment room. Behind her, she heard footsteps and ducked into the nearest room, quietly closing the door behind her. Thank God, the room was empty. On the other side of the door, she heard the distinct sound of someone's heels clicking on the tile floor as they walked down the hall. She held her breath when the sound stopped on the other side of the door. After what seemed like an eternity, the clicking sounds resumed and she took a breath. She opened the door and

peered down the corridor. It was dark and empty. Pushing the wheelchair in front of her, she slowly made her way down the corridor to
the end. Then she turned right, passed three rooms and using her
backside to push open the door, she pulled the chair into her father's
room.

"I knew you would come. I've been waiting for you." Carla spun
around to see Judge Doss standing behind her father's bed. "Where
have you been? I've been worried about you." He took a step
toward her.

"Don't come near me! I'll scream!"

Doss tilted his head and stared at her, his face contorted, his
expression confused. "Why would you scream? It's me, darling,
Judge Doss."

"I know who you are, you monster! Don't come near me. I swear
I'll scream."

"Monster? You think I'm a monster? Carla darling, I love you. I'm
not a monster. I love you and you love me."

"Love you? I hate you! You're a horrible man! You killed Dr. White.
I saw you... in that car. I know you did it."

"Don't be silly. Now why on earth would I kill Dr. White?" Doss
said holding out his hands to her.

"Because he knew what you've been doing to me." Wiping away a
tear that had trickled down her face, Carla glared at Doss with hate
flying out of her eyes. "And I know what you've been doing to me too
and I promise you, someday you're going to pay for what you've
done!"

Doss stiffened, his arms still outstretched in front of him, frozen
like a statue of stone. Before her eyes, she witnessed his frightening
metamorphosis. His shoulders hunched, his eyes narrowed and his
nostrils flared. "You little slut! Don't you dare play high and mighty
with me. You know you loved it. I could tell. You didn't fool me. The
way you moaned when I was inside you. You loved it! Admit it! You
know you loved it!" Doss dropped his arms and began to rub his
crotch.

Clutching his erect penis bulging inside of his pants, Doss slowly tilted his head and smiled eerily. His smile triggered Carla's memory bank and suddenly the vision of him standing over her wearing that exact smile flashed in her head and a rush of fear overtook her body. She tried to scream, but couldn't open her mouth. She tried to run, but was frozen with terror.

Doss knew she had to die tonight, but when she walked in the door her beauty had overcome him and he had to have her one last time. "Now look what you've done to me. We need to do something about this. What do you say? Come over here and let me fuck you real hard. Right here on your father's bed. I'm sure he wouldn't mind." Doss walked around the bed and reached out his hand for hers. "Come my darling."

He knew she would come to him. Why wouldn't she, after all, she loved him. Just look at her standing there waiting for him to take her. She wanted it as much as he did. This time would be the best of all. This time there would be no drugs. This time she would take him inside her with all the passion and lust he knew she had for him.

With each step Doss made toward her, the screaming inside Carla's head became louder. Move! Run away! She screamed at herself. Run! Run Now! She tried but she couldn't move. Doss took another step toward her, her heart beat faster and her fear grew stronger paralyzing her further in its grasp.

He was beside her now, only a few feet away. She stared at his hands, his horrible hands reaching toward her. Then his hands touched her arm, gripping tightly and pain shot up her arm. "NO!" she screamed lifting the wheelchair off the ground with strength she didn't know she had. In one quick motion, she twirled her body around and smashed the wheel chair against him, knocking him to the ground. Standing over him full of rage, she lifted her right leg and kicked him in the crotch with all her might. He screamed and doubled over in pain. Still enraged, Carla kicked him again, smashing her boot against his forehead with a sickening thud.

She could hear the judge yelling for help as she flew down the corridor, out the emergency exit door and began hurling down the stairs two steps at a time. She had flown down the stairs past the fourth and third floor landings when she heard the door open below her and the sounds of someone running up the stairs toward her echoed through the stairwell. The judge's screams had alerted the nurses and they'd called security. Leaping over the second floor landing, she plunged to the ground floor ten feet below, streaking past the stunned security guard half way up the stairs. When she hit the ground, she pushed her way out the door and fell into the alley skinning her knees on the concrete.

Dr. Griswald screeched to a halt next to her. Pulling herself up off the pavement, Carla jumped into the car and they sped away seconds before the security guards pushed the exit door open and ran into the alley.

Sharp pains from Doss' groin shot throughout his body with each step. It was excruciating. He'd never felt pain like this before and he wondered if Carla had ruptured one of his testicles or both. With each jolt of pain, his love for her dissipated, replaced by growing detestation. Running his hand over his brow, he felt the knot on his forehead where she had kicked him. It was swelling, throbbing with each heartbeat. She had kicked him hard; it was a savage attack that could have killed him. How could she have done that to him after everything he'd done for her, after all he'd introduced her to, all the pleasure he'd given to her? She'd made a fool out of him in that hospital room, surprising him with her malicious assault, but the bitch would pay for it. He didn't know where she'd run to, but he would find her and make her pay for what she'd done.

When he reached his car in the parking lot, he opened the door and pulled himself behind the wheel, easing down onto the soft leather seat. The sitting position took some of the pressure off his groin and eased his pain. Resting there, he cleared his mind and began to evaluate his situation. Suddenly the solution became clear. It was so obvious he wondered why he hadn't thought of it sooner. He didn't have to search for Carla, he knew how to draw her out, how to make her come to him. He knew where she'd be at the exact time and the exact place. It would be so easy, so simple. He smiled. She'd have to come. She couldn't stay away. Yes, she'd be there.

JANE DIPPED the cotton ball into the alcohol and gently dabbed Carla's bloody knees. "I'm so sorry I wasn't there for you. I can't believe I let this happen. What was I thinking, letting you go in that room alone?"

Carla looked up and took Jane's hand in hers. "Please stop, this was not your fault. It was mine. I should have known he'd be waiting there for me. He knew I'd show up there eventually, all he had to do was wait. It was a stupid mistake."

"It was a mistake we both made. You are very lucky. He could've killed you."

"That wasn't what he had in mind," Carla said her body suddenly trembling, shaking out of control.

Dr. Griswald wrapped her arms around her. "It's OK. You're safe now. Calm down."

"I'm sorry, I can't stop shaking," Carla whispered. "It was just so awful."

"It must have been terrifying. What did he do to you?"

"It wasn't what he did to me, it was what he said. It was... so... so horrible. No one's ever talked to me like that before. The words he used were so filthy and disgusting."

Jane wrapped a blanket around her and hugged her tightly. "Carla, honey, listen to me. He can't hurt you anymore. You've got to put all of that out of your head. He's a sick man and I can only imagine what he said, but remembering his filthy words can only hurt you and make things worse. I know it's hard, but you've got to try to forget his words. His sick ramblings are not important. You're here with me and you're safe.

"What *is* important is for us to come up with a new plan to get your father out of that hospital. That's all that really matters now. We've got to come up with a new plan and soon."

EDWARD CECIL, Sr. was floating. He didn't know why he was floating he only knew that he was. He was hovering high above and could see them clearly. Little Eddie and Carla were lying on their stomachs on the rug in front of the fireplace. They were playing a board game, but he couldn't tell what it was, probably Battleship. Little Eddie loved to play Battleship. He could hear them giggling below him and from somewhere in the background he could just make out the tune his wife Judy was humming from the kitchen. It was an Elvis song, but he couldn't remember the name. She must be making dinner, he thought. She always hummed when she cooked dinner. She was a great cook. He could taste her famous mashed potatoes. Everything smelled so good. He wished he could float to the kitchen and see what she was making.

"I knew you would come. I've been waiting for you." Who was talking, he wondered. He didn't recognize the voice.

"Where have you been? I've been worried about you." There was that voice again. Where was it coming from?

Below him, he could see Carla and she was crying. Suddenly she screamed. *"Don't come near me! I'll scream! I'll run away!"* Who was she talking to? Why was she crying? What's wrong?

More talking from that strange voice, but he couldn't understand what he was saying. Carla answered, but it was just a mumble. What did she say? Who was Carla talking to? Where is little Eddie? He could no longer see him. Where is Judy? She's not humming anymore. Why can't Judy hear the strange voice?

"You little slut! Don't you dare play high and mighty with me. You know you loved it. I could tell. You didn't fool me. The way you moaned when I was inside you. You loved it! Admit it! You know you loved it!"

Oh God! Did he say that to Carla? Where was he? If he could just get his hands on who said that to her, he'd... he'd... Darkness. Everything is dark. He's not floating anymore. Where is he? Why can't he see anything? Quiet! Listen. Don't you hear it? Click, click, click. What is that sound? Footsteps? Yes, it's footsteps. Click, click, click. They're getting louder, closer, slower.

It's quiet now. No more footsteps. What was that? A shadow... there in the darkness. He could feel a presence around him, standing over him. Who's there? Ouch! Stop it! It hurts! Stop it! My foot!

"Goodbye Edward." Who said that? Was it him? The strange voice? Bastard! You bastard how could you say those filthy things to Carla? Who are you? Show yourself, you bastard! Click, click, click. He's walking away. Stop! Who are you? Come back here!

Floating again... So tired... Floating... Cold... very cold. A light. See it? It's blinding, so bright, but it's warm... so warm... Floating to the light... look at all the colors, so many

THE ISLANDS

CHAPTER ELEVEN

For my entire life, I was convinced that being a star was what I *had* to become, something I was born for and the true meaning of my life, but I was wrong. Somewhere along the way, I'd forgotten why I'd picked up a guitar at the age of five and could play it; why at the age of ten, I could sing. No doubt, it was a God given talent, but he didn't give it to me so I could become rich and famous, he gave it to me because it could give me freedom and happiness, if I let it. Being rich and famous had taken away my freedom and had forced me to become someone I was not. Instead of being happy, I was miserable and that had always confused me, but somehow sailing out there in the middle of the ocean, it became clear and I finally understood.

God gave me my talent to be free, not famous. Some people were meant to be famous, but I was not and for the first time in my life, I was actually OK with that. God gave me my talent not for fame, but to have the ability to earn my living anywhere I chose and to enjoy the freedom that comes along with that. My definition of freedom is simply having the spare time to do whatever I please – time to play, time to be creative, time to search for contentment. That kind of freedom is a privilege that most people don't enjoy in this hectic world of ours. Most people are chained to their mundane existences, living for the weekends and a two-week vacation. Because I was blessed with talent, I didn't have to live my life that way.

It had taken me almost 40 years to figure it out, but I finally realized that in my case talent, plus fame, equaled the loss of my freedom and soul. My inner peace came when I finally understood that I wasn't sailing away or running from anything. I was sailing *toward* something... my future, my happiness. I had no idea where I'd find it, but I knew that someday, somehow I would. In the meantime, I made up my mind to cherish my gift and enjoy my new life one day at a time.

ONE OF MY favorite movies is a flick starring Kurt Russell called "Captain Ron." If you're not a sailor, you may not appreciate it as much as I do, but if you *are* a sailor, you'll love it. One of the funniest parts in the movie is when Martin Short's character is questioning Captain Ron about his navigation abilities, suspecting that they are lost. Captain Ron just smiles at him and says, "Don't worry boss, if you get lost all you have to do is pull up to an island and ask somebody where you are."

That scene was playing in my head as I secured *Windsong's* anchor and unhooked my dingy. As I slowly rowed to shore, I couldn't help but laugh at myself, because the moment I got there, I was going to have to ask some stranger where the hell I was. I knew I was somewhere in the Bahamas, but I didn't have a clue what this particular island was. Like an idiot, I didn't have a chart with me. I'd sailed off into the Gulf Stream not really caring where I wound up, so having a chart of where I was going didn't seem very important to me at the time. Once I got out there and realized what it felt like to be completely lost in the middle of the ocean, my opinion changed quickly.

I had landed at Cornwall, a tiny island village located at the southern tip of the Abaco Islands. I later learned that I had been lucky as hell to have spotted Cornwall, because if I'd missed that island, my next stop would have been the east coast of Spain or Africa two or three months later, assuming I could have found it.

Following the coastline, I sailed north to Marsh Harbor and spent the next few months getting to know the wonderful people that lived there. Apparently, no one on that island had ever heard of the notorious Max Allen or let on if they did. In the beginning, the locals were a bit standoffish, cautious of the bearded, longhaired stranger who didn't say much in town, but would sit on the back of his boat, playing his guitar singing into the wee hours of the night. Eventually their curiosity got the best of them and my nightly concerts began to draw a good crowd.

One night, much to my surprise, the locals rewarded me with a round of applause after I finished singing a song. When I stood up in the cockpit and bowed politely they clapped even louder and cheered. I sang several more songs for my new fans, then waved at them and went below. The next morning I discovered my cockpit overflowing with fish and mounds of fresh fruit.

I'd planned on staying in Marsh Harbor for a week or two, but wound up staying almost nine months. I'd made some wonderful friends there. My weekly concerts had kept my icebox full of fish and my shelves full of fresh fruit, but hurricane season was approaching and it was time to move on. Reluctantly, I untied *Windsong* from the dock and sailed off for new adventures waving goodbye to the tearful faces of my new friends.

With the island disappearing off my stern, I tapped my new GPS and marked the pinpointed latitude and longitude on my chart. I had learned my lesson well and had purchased some new high tech navigation equipment for my long sail ahead. I was heading first to St. Thomas then on to the island of St. Martin in the West Indies. I'd always wanted to go there and now I had a reason to. I'd been offered a gig there.

AFTER ONE OF my weekly concerts in Marsh Harbor, the owner of a sleek 100-foot motor yacht had paid me a visit.

The tall and very large stranger handed me a six-pack of beer and without being asked, climbed into the cockpit of my boat. "I hope I'm not intruding, but I wanted to bring you this as a token of my appreciation for your music, I also wanted to meet you." Then he reached out and shook my hand squeezing my knuckles hard. "My name's Bill, Bill Heard."

"Nice to meet you, Bill," I said, "I'm glad you liked my music. It's the only thing I know how to do."

Opening two of the beers, I handed him one and settled across from him. "My name is Max Allen." I said quickly, waiting for the recognition to come over his face. It didn't take long.

"*The* Max Allen?" he said. "The country singer, Max Allen?"

"That's me."

"Well, I'll be damned. What the hell are you doing here? You on vacation?"

"Well, I guess you could say that I'm sort of on an extended vacation." I said. "And I don't plan on going home anytime soon."

"If I had all your money I'd probably do the same damn thing."

I laughed. "So you think I'm loaded, huh?"

"You're telling me you're not?" he said with a stunned look. "Don't tell me you pissed it all away?"

"Not that it's any of your damn business, but yep, I pissed it all away." I said smiling.

"All of it? On what?"

"Wine, women, song and lawyers."

Confused, Bill stared at me. After a moment, his eyes widened with understanding. "Oh, yeah, I remember now. You got your ass in some trouble with the law. What happened with all that? Are you on the lam?"

Normally, I wouldn't have opened up to a complete stranger, but there was something about Bill that drew me in. "No, I'm not on the lam and I don't really want to go into all of the gory details, just suffice it to say that I'm not in trouble with the law anymore, but it did leave me flat broke and brought my singing career to a screeching halt. After the trial, the press was relentless, following me everywhere, so I jumped into my boat and hauled ass. That's what I'm doing out here, trying to put all that crap behind me. I love it here. No one's ever heard of the famous Max Allen. You're the first person to recognize me."

"I think you're safe. To be honest, I *didn't* recognize you. Maybe it's all that hair, but I had no idea who the hell you were until you told me your name. Even then, I had to think about it for a second."

We finished off the six-pack and talked long into the night sharing stories and bad jokes like a couple of old friends.

"Max, I don't want to offend you, but I'd like to make you an offer." he said unexpectedly. I own a little joint in St. Martin called *Everyting's Cool*. It's right on the beach and we have a booming business selling everything from cheeseburgers in paradise, to rum punch to the tourists from the cruise ships. I was just wondering if you'd be interested in a gig. Now, I couldn't pay you what you're used to making, but it sounds like you could use a little cash flow. What do you think?"

"A gig huh? You have a stage?" I asked interested.

"I will by the time you get there. I'll build it myself – a big one. Look, you could anchor your boat right off shore and swim to work. Oh, yeah, I forgot the best part. We attract lots of babes there, very scantily clad babes. What do you say? We got a deal?"

"I don't know," I said, "let me think about it."

The next morning I met Bill and his wife for breakfast on his boat. We ate his wife's scrambled eggs and bacon and I agreed to play his joint under a few conditions. First, he couldn't advertise that Max Allen would be singing there. It would be me, but I'd be working under an alias. Second, my pay would be in the form of a little cash, food, booze and any repair/ maintenance costs that might come up on *Windsong* while I was there. He eagerly agreed to my terms and we shook on it. Just like that, I had a gig. The deal was, I would start June, 1st, 33 days from then. All I had to do was sail 1,280 miles to get there.

Fifteen days later, I dropped anchor in Charlotte A'malie harbor shaded from the sun by the tall beautiful green hills of St. Thomas.

After fifteen days and nights behind the wheel, sleep deprivation was taking its toll and I almost crashed into the dock before I got *Windsong* stopped. My mind and body were thrashed, so for the next 48 hours all I did was sleep, eat and marvel at the sights surrounding me in that harbor.

I finally felt rested enough to make it ashore and explored every inch of St. Thomas, dodging the horde of tourists, gorging myself in the great restaurants there and fearing for my life as I rode around the island in the out of control taxi cabs.

On my last day in St. Thomas, my waitress at a great little hamburger joint called "The Green House" recognized me and it got ugly. She almost dropped my cheeseburger when she realized who I was and by the time I'd finished my lunch, had retrieved her copy of my CD. She asked me to sign it and pose for a few pictures. She was sweet and I didn't mind signing her CD or posing for the pictures, but soon word got out that I was in the restaurant and a small crowd began to build.

"KILLER!" I heard someone yell. "PERVERT! MURDERER!" The chants became louder and louder as the crowd grew larger and larger. When someone began to chant, "OJ ALLEN," I dropped two twenty's on the table and made a hasty exit out of there before things got completely out of hand.

That night on my boat, I took out the clippers I had bought at the St. Thomas Walmart and fifteen minutes later, my long hair lay in a pile on the floor of *Windsong's* saloon. Next, I went to work on my beard. I hadn't seen my upper lip in 18 years or shaved my chin in 15. I needed a blood transfusion by the time I finished. I'd cut myself five times and had a hell of a time getting my shredded face to stop bleeding. Eventually it stopped and I got to take a good look at myself in the mirror. It was a dramatic transformation. I did not recognize the person staring back at me. I was looking at a stranger, not the face of the famous Max Allen. My new GI hairdo, combined with my clean-shaven face had transformed me. It was the perfect disguise.

That afternoon, I walked through the packed, tiny streets of St. Thomas testing my new anonymity and no one gave me a second look. My image change had worked perfectly, but its success was a double-edged sword that made me happy and sad at the same time.

When I was a kid, I used to daydream about what it would feel like to be famous. I must admit that when a fan recognizes you, a little rush of adrenaline shoots through you. It makes you feel special and if you're not careful, pumps your ego up to the size of the Grand Canyon. Although I'd lost the battle with my ego off and on during my brief 15 minutes of fame, I tried to keep in mind that fame didn't actually have anything to do with being special at all. Fame, in most cases, is the byproduct of simply being very, very lucky. And being lucky shouldn't give reason to expand your ego, but unfortunately, it does in most cases. It did in mine and because of it I lost control of reality and messed up my life.

Although I loved being recognized, my celebrity had changed from being famous to notorious and if I was ever going to find the happiness I was searching for, I had to become anonymous.

The next morning, after restocking *Windsong's* shelves with supplies, I pulled up her anchor and hoisted her sails. With the hills of St. Thomas fading behind me, I slowly tacked my way through the rest of the Virgin Islands. With five days left to get to my gig, a new unrecognizable face and my ego in full check, I watched the sky turn from gold, to pink, to purple as the sun set behind Virgin Gorda, the last island in the Virgin string. With a steady 15-knot breeze filling our sails, *Windsong* and I plowed our way across the open ocean on the final 90-mile leg of this long journey. With each gust of wind, *Windsong* lurched forward like a thoroughbred racehorse racing to the finish line. She seemed as impatient as I did to finally get to St. Martin and see what new adventures lay ahead.

BILLY DEAN

CHAPTER TWELVE

I 'd been sailing for almost 19 hours and beginning to question the accuracy of my new GPS, when off in the distance a hazy purple image of land appeared on the horizon. Like a David Copperfield illusion, the majestic emerald hills of St. Martin magically came into focus revealing more beauty with each passing mile.

"Land ho," I yelled. "*Windsong*, we did it!" Jumping out of the cockpit, I flattened my mainsail and cranked in on my jib sheet hoping to get a few more knots of speed, I couldn't wait to get there. Four very long impatient hours later, I dropped my anchor in Philipsburg harbor, just as the sun began to hit the water.

The next morning after a much needed sleep, I ate my breakfast in the cockpit, sitting behind the wheel in awe of the beauty of St. Martin. The turquoise water was crystal-clear and *Windsong* appeared to be floating on air. We were anchored in a gorgeous bay surrounded by lush green rolling mountains dotted with bright red rectangles – the roofs of the houses scattered throughout the hills. I had to keep reminding myself that it wasn't a painting, a postcard or a calendar. I was actually there. Behind me in the distance, I could just make out the shapes of the nearby islands of St. Barts, Saba and Anguilla. It had been a very long voyage, but well worth the effort. I was anchored in the heart of paradise and for the next hour, I just lay there in the cockpit sipping my coffee, listening to the waves slap against *Windsong's* hull, savoring the first day of my new life.

"Everyting's Cool" was located about a hundred yards from the beach, smack in the middle of all the action. It was easy to spot; the buildings that housed the kitchen, bar and bathrooms were painted bright neon yellow. On the sand covered wooden deck that jutted away from the yellow buildings, were numerous multicolored umbrellas shading small white plastic tables and chairs – every table was full. The joint was crawling with people, packed mostly with drunk, ghost-white or sunburned, overweight tourists dressed in baggy shorts, T-shirts and stupid looking hats. However, as promised there was also a very nice collection of tanned young babes almost wearing bikinis. Young firm butts barely covered by their thongs blurred my vision. Yep, I thought to myself, I'm definitely in paradise.

With a cold 'Carib' beer in my hand, I located an empty table and settled in for some serious people watching. My waitress brought me my cheeseburger and I dug in. It was huge, very sloppy and very tasty – perfect. I'd asked the bartender, but she had no idea where Bill Heard was, so I settled back in my chair and enjoyed the circus a little longer. He finally showed up around 2 p.m. and walked over to my table.

"What can I do for you?" He asked, not recognizing me.

I ran my hand over my bald head and looked up at him. "I see you've got a stage over there in the corner and was just wondering if you'd be interested in hiring a singer?"

Still not making the connection, he said. "To be honest with you, I've already hired a singer. Sorry about that."

"Yeah, I heard you were going to have some long haired asshole singing here. Some guy named Max Allen."

Bill froze in his tracks. "Where'd you hear that? Who told you that?" he said nervously.

"Hell, it's all over the island," I said.

Bill's face flushed and his eyes widened. "I don't know who told you that, but it's not true. Who ever told you that was full of shit and I promise..."

"Relax you dumb ass, it's me. I'm just fucking with you," I said with a smile.

"Excuse me?" Bill said, totally confused.

"It's me, you dumb shit. Max. I cut off my hair. I'm Max."

Bill stared at me for a long time, then pulled out a chair and plopped down. "Well, I'll be God Damned! Is it really you?"

"In the flesh," I said. "You like my new hairdo?"

Bill wiped his eyes with his hand and looked at me. "I've got to tell you Max, I would have never recognized you in a million years. Son, you are one ugly bald headed dude. Until your hair grows back, I think you should consider wearing a hat."

"Good to see you, too." I said, laughing.

He jumped up and gave me a bear hug lifting me off my feet. "When did you get in?"

"I dropped my hook last night," I said, pointing toward *Windsong* bobbing on her anchor in the bay.

After the tourists cleared out, Bill introduced me to the staff and showed me around the place. The stage he'd built was smaller than I'd expected, but adequate. It had plenty of power and with a bit of adjusting, would hold all of the equipment I'd had my father ship there.

The night before I opened, Bill invited me to his boat for dinner with his wife and we drank ourselves to a stupor, brainstorming to come up with my new stage name.

"What about Johnny Nelson? You get it? Part Johnny Cash and part Willie," he said

"That's just stupid," I interrupted. "No damn way am I going to call myself Johnny Nelson."

"Ok, ok. How about Rock Stone? Sounds like a movie star," his wife suggested.

"No offense, but I think you're drunker than we are."

"I think you're right," she giggled.

"Come on guys. I've got to come up with a name. I open tomorrow. Think, damn it!"

"We need margaritas. I do my best thinking when I'm drinking margaritas," Bill said.

"I'm not sure that's a good idea. I open tomorrow and I can barely function now. If we don't come up with a name soon, I'll be drunk tomorrow and really suck."

"Hey no problem mon. That's the way we do it here in the islands – the drunker the better. Come on, you wussy. Drink up," he said, setting a very large salted margarita in front of me.

We were on our second round when his wife spoke, slurring her words. "What was your brother's name?"

"His name was Dean," I slurred back, mocking her.

"Ok, smart ass. Dean it is," she said.

"Yeah, that's good," Bill added. "Dean something. Or something Dean."

"Something Dean. Actually that's not bad," I said.

"Hey, my real name is Billy." Bill yelled, hanging on to the table as he stood to make his point. "Why don't you call yourself, Billy Dean, now that's a great name for a country singer. Yeah. Billy fucking Dean."

"Ok, Billy fucking Dean it is," I said, lifting my glass, toasting my new name.

With the worst hangover I'd ever had in my life, I opened the next day and surprisingly had a blast. The people were great, singing along with me, especially when I sang Jimmy Buffett songs. "Wasting Away in Margaritaville" took on an entirely new meaning that day. Although I felt like hell, the crowd's response pumped me up and got me through it. When the day was finally over, Bill and his entire staff toasted me and declared that Billy Dean was an official hit, soon to be the biggest thing on the island. In celebration, Brenda, the head bartender, presented me with a straw panama hat. Everyone got a big laugh out of her present and all pleaded with me to wear the hat until my hair grew out a little. They said that I was scaring the customers.

With my new straw hat on top of my bald head, I settled in and found my niche singing six days a week to the tourists. Life was sweet; I was content knowing that I had taken the first step in my search for happiness.

WHEN THE CRUISE ships were in the harbor, I sang to the tourists, but when the big ships weren't there and the huge docks were empty, I was off. That was my schedule at Everyting's Cool. When I had the day off, I pulled up my anchor and explored St. Martin and the surrounding islands. *Windsong* and I sailed into every harbor deep enough to clear our keel and a few that were not. There's an old sailor's saying: if you haven't ever run aground then you've never been sailing. I took that to heart and found myself sitting high and dry often. Fortunately, I never hit a coral reef, but I did tear the hell out of a few sand bars. Eventually, I figured out where to steer to stay out of trouble and spent my days off anchored in some of the most beautiful places on this earth.

I was having fun and just like that old saying, the days, months and years just seemed to fly by. I was content and didn't pay much attention to time; it just didn't seem to matter much. I was happy living on island time in paradise and thoughts of my past or plans for my future weren't part of the equation. I had assumed the island attitude of *no problems mon, everyting's cool.*

One day I looked up and realized that I'd been in St. Martin for almost five years. The last time I'd paid attention, I was in my thirties. In the blink of an eye, I was 44 years old closing in on 45 fast. I'm not sure exactly why, but the sudden realization of my age began to bother me. I kept telling myself that I was being stupid, it was just a number. I preached to myself about how I had it made; I was living in paradise, had a lot of great friends and the perfect gig, but when I thought about how fast the last five years had flown by and how in another blink of an eye I'd be 50, none of that seemed to matter.

The sudden realization that I had become a middle-aged man scared the hell out of me and made me start to question my mortality and what I was doing with my life. It forced me to think about my future for the first time in years. For the next few months, I searched my soul and tried to come up with some kind of plan for my life. I even bought a few books about retirement planning and setting long-term life goals, but reading those books made me realize that I just didn't want the same things out of life that most people wanted. I had no desire to acquire a lot of money; I'd had money, lots of it, but it hadn't given me anything but grief.

Money or the lack of it wasn't my dilemma, nor was being famous or powerful or being a "somebody" important to me. My quandary, I finally realized was very basic. What was scaring me was the thought of growing old... alone. I had everything I wanted in my life except someone to share it all with.

In the last five years, I'd dated several women – a few local island women and several young French girls visiting St. Martin on holiday. There were loads of women from the cruise ships, but they were only there for a day and although they were fun and always promised to come back to the island to see me again, they never did. Honestly, getting laid was never the problem, but finding someone I wanted to talk to afterward, was.

THE FIRST TIME I laid eyes on her, she was drunk. I was in the middle of a nice ballad when she staggered into Everyting's Cool with five other equally drunk girlfriends. Along with the rest of her friends, she made a very impressive entrance. As luck would have it, the table directly in front of the stage was empty, so the six of them made a beeline toward it, only to trip and fall on their asses in a pile in the middle of the sandy dance floor. The crowd loved it and gave them an instant round of applause. After they untangled themselves, showing no signs of embarrassment, they all stood up, knocked the sand off, stretched out arm and arm into a make shift chorus line and bowed gracefully from the waist. This got them a roaring standing O.

I didn't start my next song until all six of them were successfully sitting upright in their chairs and that took a few minutes. When I finally started singing again and finished a song, the girls would whoop, whistle and yell at the top of their lungs which would incite a small riot from the rest of the crowd trying to keep up with their enthusiasm. It was the rowdiest audience I'd performed for since I'd opened for Hank Jr.

After my set, I stopped by their table to meet them. I shook all of their hands and they all told me their names, but I only remembered hers. It was Michelle, Michelle Parker. They were dancers performing on a cruise ship. Michelle told me that she had just signed on the ship for a six-month contract and would be in St. Martin every Tuesday. She told me this squeezing my hand and staring into my eyes. It was an awkward moment. I wasn't sure how to react to her obvious interest in me. It honestly shocked me a little because she was in her early twenties and the most beautiful thing I'd ever seen. The recent revelation of my age was fresh on my mind and a voice inside my head screamed loudly, *don't be stupid, she's drunk, you're old enough to be her father.* She was too young and way too beautiful for me, so I wrote off her flirting and interest to her obvious state of intoxication, slipped my hand out of hers as gently as I could, excused myself and walked away.

When I returned from my break, her drunken friends were gone but she was still there. For the next forty-five minutes, as I sang my set, she never took her eyes off of me, studying me so intently it made me nervous and caused me to break a sweat. I did my best to play to the rest of the crowd, but no matter how hard I tried, I always wound up singing each song to her. A couple of times I actually forgot the words when I found myself lost in her beautiful green eyes. I'd been stared at a thousand times before. I'd been winked at, flirted with and even flashed a few times. Being watched intently is all part of being on stage, but no one's gaze had ever had this affect on me.

Between songs, I reminded myself how old I was and tried to convince myself that what she was doing didn't mean anything; she was just drunk, too young, too pretty and way out of my league. Then I'd get lost in her eyes again. At the end of each song, I checked my watch. Time seemed to have stopped, it was the longest set of my life. I couldn't wait to finish it so I could talk to her again and see what the hell was going on. Finally, I'd worked my way down the list to the last tune, but in the middle of the song, she stood up, waved at me and walked out the door. My heart sank as I watched her leave.

The following Tuesday, it took me almost an hour to get ready for work. I primped on my hair longer than normal and shaved my face closer than I had in months. I dug through my locker and found some clothes I hadn't seen in years. I tried on several different shirts and pants before I finally gave up and put on what I usually wore to work – a worn out T-shirt and a pair of faded jeans. Then I loaded my guitar into the dingy and rowed to shore.

I was bent over snapping the lock to the chain that secured my dingy to the dock when I heard a voice. "Hello, Billy. Remember me?"

Looking under my arms straining to see behind me, I saw Michelle. "Hi," I said in shock.

"She told me you would be here. The girl behind the bar I mean, I forgot her name," she said nervously. "I thought I'd come and surprise you. I hope it's OK."

"It's a wonderful surprise," I said walking down the dock toward her. "I can't believe you're here. I never thought I'd see you again."

"Why would you think that? Didn't I tell you I'd be in St. Martin every Tuesday?"

"Yeah, you told me, but you were a little... ah... how do I say this politely... drunk as a skunk?"

She dropped her head in embarrassment. "I'm so sorry you saw me like that. I've never been that drunk before. I made a fool out of myself, didn't I?"

"On the contrary. You brought down the house and if I remember correctly, you guys got a standing ovation. It was quite a show."

"Oh God, I'm so embarrassed. I've thought about it all week. That's why I ran here as soon as I got off the ship this morning. I wanted to apologize to you and hopefully convince you that I'm not like that. I wouldn't want you to think that about me."

I felt my heart actually skip a beat when she reached out and took my hand in hers. "Don't think bad of me, Billy. It's important to me that you don't think badly of me. I've worried about this all week long," she said almost in a whisper, staring directly into my eyes.

The way she said "Billy" melted me. It felt like it was the first time I'd ever heard someone call me that before. Of course, it wasn't, but it was the first time hearing my new name had meant anything to me. "Michelle, don't be silly. It was your first time in St. Martin and you guys were just having fun. Honestly, I thought it was funny as hell. If you want to know the truth, I've been thinking about you all week too and was really hoping you'd come back today so we could talk again."

She flashed her beautiful smile at me and squeezed my hand tighter. "You've been thinking about me? All week? Seriously?"

Thinking about her was the understatement of the century. I hadn't been able to get her out of my head for a second. The feelings that had rushed through my heart when I'd first looked into her eyes had made me feel like some love struck high school kid. When I could sleep, I dreamed about her. It was crazy. I'd been battling with myself all week. She was a complete stranger. She was half my age, from a completely different generation, she probably wouldn't have anything in common with me and yet, I couldn't think of anything else but looking into those eyes again. And now, unbelievably, she had gone out of her way to find me. It didn't make a damn bit of sense and I had no earthly idea what she possibly saw in me, but there she was holding my hand, looking at me with those mesmerizing, heart stopping eyes.

I had practiced what I wanted to say to her a thousand times, but couldn't remember a single word. My mouth was dry as sand. "Michelle, last week when you were watching me sing... the way you were watching me... I got the feeling... uh... well, I thought that maybe... DAMN IT! I'm such an idiot!"

She laughed and moved close wrapping her arms around my waist. "It's ok, Billy, just relax. What are you trying to say?"

"I'm sorry, I'm not very good at this sort of thing and I'm a little nervous. Give me a second. OK... I think I'm ready. What I wanted to say to you is... is... Michelle you're *all* I've thought about – every minute, every second, of every day. When I first saw you and looked into your eyes, I got lost. I've been lost in there ever since."

Michelle dropped her arms from my waist, took a step back and looked up at me. I thought I'd said something wrong and was trying to remember what I'd actually said when she suddenly jumped forward into my arms and kissed me. "Oh, Billy," she whispered in my ear then she kissed me again and again and again. I didn't make it to work that day.

That afternoon we made a bed on *Windsong's* foredeck and snuggled together watching the white fluffy clouds pass by. "Look, there's an elephant," she said.

"Where?"

"Right there. See his trunk and the ears?"

"Yeah, sort of... I guess. Kind of a skinny elephant isn't it?"

She sighed. "It's not supposed to be exact. You have to use your imagination a little. You find one."

"Ok. Let me see... there's something. See it?" I said pointing to the sky. "The big round one. It's a snowball."

"You are hopeless," she said running her hands over my chest pulling gently on the hair.

"Hey watch it, that's attached."

"It's sexy," she said twirling the hair around her finger.

"Oh yeah? What's so sexy about it?"

"I don't know. There's just something about it." She rolled on top of me and rubbed her bare breasts against my chest. "I love the way it feels against my skin. It's just one more thing about you that drives me crazy."

Thirty minutes later, we slid off the deck and swam naked together to cool off our bodies and wash away the sweat that had coated us from our lovemaking in the sun. In the cockpit, I dried her muscular body with a towel and marveled at how incredibly beautiful she looked with no makeup and wet hair. With the bright sunshine highlighting her emerald green eyes, she blinked her long lashes and asked, "What are you thinking about?"

I laid down on the seat and resting my head in her lap, pulled her hands to my mouth and kissed her palms. "I'm thinking that I'm the luckiest guy in the world. And I'm wondering what on earth I've done to deserve you."

Running her hands through my wet hair she said, "You know, for someone who claims that he's not very good at this sort of thing, you're doing pretty good. Billy, that's the sweetest thing anyone has ever said to me."

I THOUGHT I was going to have to quit before Bill Heard finally agreed to give me Tuesdays off. Eventually, he gave in and for the next six months, every Tuesday morning I motored *Windsong* over to the cruise ship dock to pick up Michelle. Then we would spend the day together sailing, talking and making love. On the days her ship wasn't in St. Martin, she would call me, feeding quarters in a pay phone from some other island. We would talk until she ran out of change. For six months, I lived for Tuesdays. Each time her ship pulled into the harbor my heart would beat like a drum inside my chest. And every time I saw her, held her in my arms and looked into her eyes, I fell deeper in love.

After her cruise ship contract ended, Michelle went home to visit her parents for a few weeks, then as she'd promised, against her parents wishes, she flew to St. Martin to be with me. The plan was for her to take a few months off so we could do some sailing, then fly back to the States once a month or so to make a few auditions which would hopefully land her a spot in a new show. Fortunately, she'd saved some money working on the ship and could afford the time off. With her savings, combined with the little I had, we calculated that we'd have six to eight months before she'd have to start looking for work.

Over the next few months, we island hopped south all the way to Barbados and then back to St. Martin. As we sailed along, we talked about everything. She told me her life story from the day she'd been born. I did the same, except for one part. I couldn't bring myself to tell her about Max Allen, the country star. What we had between us was almost too good to be true, and that's what scared me and shook me awake late at night. Life had kicked me in the nuts more than once, leaving me cynical but wiser with the knowledge that real life comes with vicissitudes. What scared me was the knowledge that no matter how hard I tried to prevent it, this impossible dream we were living would undoubtedly change one day. I was afraid that telling her about Max would bring on that inevitable change sooner than later.

I'd finally found the happiness I had been so desperately searching for and fought with all my might to keep it. I cherished our life together so much I hid my past and wouldn't even discuss what was going to happen when the money ran out. She tried to bring it up occasionally, talking about dancing again, wanting to make some long-range plans, but I'd instantly change the subject. I could tell this was a frustration to her, but how could I explain the reality of the world to Michelle? She was so young and naïve, she had no idea how cruel people could be or how truly harsh the real world was. She was so innocent to life, she didn't realize that what we had was truly unique and could only exist in the fairy tale land of love we'd created out there on my boat in paradise. A place where it didn't bother anyone that she was only 21 years old and I was 46, a place where no one cared that I had no money or ambition to earn any. It was a place where the only thing that truly mattered was the love, romance and passion we felt for each other. We were living an impossible dream, but Michelle was too much in love, too happy and too innocent to realize it..

GUS WALTERS

CHAPTER THIRTEEN

The charity of the honorable Judge Bradford Doss was limitless. He took charge with the same competence and vigor he'd displayed during little Eddie's funeral. He insisted on handling every detail of the funeral, and of course, paid for everything. Everyone in Tyler couldn't stop talking about how wonderful he was. The rumor around town was that he even used his influence to prevent the Houston medical examiner from performing an autopsy on poor old Edward. After all, he was already dead; there was no reason for them to cut him up like that. Judge Doss even paid for the cremation, as well as the beautiful brass urn that held Edward Sr.'s ashes. He was truly a great man and everyone at the service made a point to shake his hand and tell him how they appreciated everything he had done for the Cecil family.

It *was* curious that Carla wasn't at the funeral. It appeared that even the judge was surprised. Throughout the service, the entire congregation kept expecting her to show up, but she never did. At the gravesite, the judge continually scanned the crowd, obviously searching for her. A few people noticed that his actions had been a little curious, but they didn't say anything about it. After all, it had been a very stressful day.

Carla's absence was especially troubling to John Jackson, the owner of The Jackson Box Factory. He was stunned she had not shown up for her father's funeral. He had planned on spending some time with her after the service. He needed to talk to her about something important.

The first time John Jackson saw Carla, she was only hours old. He was by her father's side the night the nurse told him that he had a daughter. He loved Carla and had always thought of her as his adopted granddaughter.

He'd watched her grow up before his eyes, but hadn't realized how much she'd grown until he observed her during little Eddie's funeral. He couldn't believe how she'd matured and how well she'd handled herself, taking care of her father during that terrible time. It was inspiring for him to see how well adjusted she seemed, despite the tragedies in her life. That's why it was impossible for him to understand her absence. Something was wrong, there had to be a reason.

Each day that passed with no sign of Carla, John Jackson's suspicions increased. After a week, he placed a call to Judge Doss' chambers. He was told that the judge was in session, but would return his call. He waited for two days before he gave up and called back. This time, he was told that the judge was "in a meeting" and couldn't be disturbed. He left his number again and waited for the return call. This went on for almost seven days. Finally, he reached the judge at his home.

"I'm sorry, Mr. Jackson, but Carla is unavailable at this time, in fact, she's not in the country. She was so distraught over the death of her father I felt it best for her to get away. I arranged for her to spend some time touring in Europe. I assure you when I do hear from her I'll tell her that you called and I'll give her your regards."

"You sent a thirteen year old girl to Europe? Alone?" Jackson asked.

"Mr. Jackson you've nothing to worry about, she's properly chaperoned. I'm sorry, sir, but I'm very busy and have to get back to my caseload. Thank you for calling."

The phone clicked in his ear before he could answer. "Pompous asshole!" he yelled, slamming down the phone.

"What in the world?" John's wife asked.

"Bastard says she's in Europe."

"Who's in Europe?"

"Carla. Judge Doss just told me that she's in Europe. Do you really think that girl would take off on a trip like that without at least visiting her father's grave first?"

"Doesn't sound like Carla to me," she answered.

"Damn right it doesn't!" he roared. "Something's wrong here. I want to know where in the hell Carla is. I don't know why, but that bastard is lying to me and I'm going to find out."

The next morning, John drove to Houston and located the judge's house. He knocked on the door, but no one answered. He waited in his driveway for almost an hour before he finally gave up and cranked his car. As he was backing out, a car pulled into the driveway of the house next door.

"Excuse me," he said to the woman in the car. "I'm trying to find Carla Cecil. I understand that she's living with Judge Doss next door. I rang the bell, but no one seems to be home."

"Oh, that poor sweet girl. She doesn't live with the Doss' any longer. She lost her father and the poor dear was so distraught, she quit college and moved back home. It was a shame. She had such a bright future. I believe the judge told me that she's living with her relatives in Tyler now."

"Judge Doss told you that she's in Tyler?"

"Yes, I'm sure he said Tyler. It was her hometown."

"Thank you very much. You've been a big help to me. Don't worry about telling the judge I was here. I'll call him at his office. Thanks again."

John backed out of the driveway, drove straight to the Houston police department and told the officer behind the desk his story.

"Please have a seat, sir. I need to talk to my captain about this." The policeman walked down the corridor to the captain's office.

"You're kidding," the captain said. "This guy is accusing Judge Doss? Are you sure it's Judge Bradford Doss?"

"That's what he said, sir. He claims the judge is lying to him about the whereabouts of a thirteen-year old girl. Supposedly, the judge is her guardian. He said the judge told him that the girl is in Europe, but one of his neighbors claimed the girl is in Tyler. This guy is convinced that something is wrong and wants us to check it out."

"Look, I'm not about to check out anything on a state court judge just because some nut case thinks there's something wrong, especially this state court judge. You don't fuck with Judge Doss. If he says the girl's in Europe, well that's good enough for me."

"What do I tell the guy?"

"Don't waste time on this. Give it to the rookie. What's his name? Walters. Tell him to be sympathetic with the guy, fill out a report, but not to do a damn thing with it. I'm sure the girl will show up and it'll blow over."

Officer Gus Walters guided John Jackson back to his small desk. "Have a seat sir. Now tell me again what you told the desk officer."

John repeated his story.

"When was the last time you actually saw the girl?" Gus asked.

"It was about six months ago, at her brother's funeral."

"She lost her brother six months ago and then her father only a few weeks ago?"

"Yes. She also lost her mother two years ago," John added.

"And she's only thirteen? Poor girl."

"That's why I'm so concerned officer... she's all alone. I'm the closest thing she has to a family left. I have to find her. Please help me find her."

Gus's instructions were to be sympathetic, fill out a report and do nothing, but that didn't make any sense to him. This man was no nut case. Jackson's concern was real and Gus couldn't just ignore everything he'd heard.

The next day, the Captain stormed into the room and slammed a file down on his desk. "Walters, what the hell is this?"

Gus looked at the file. "It's my report, sir... on the Judge Doss case."

"I told you to fill out a report, not to file it!"

"But, Captain this Jackson guy is for real."

"Shut up and listen, I'm trying to help you here. I realize that you're just a rookie and don't know your ass from a hole in the ground, but I assumed you had something up there between your ears. Do you have any idea who Judge Bradford Doss is? How powerful he is? What he could do to you if he got wind of this?"

"I've never heard of him," Gus answered.

"Obviously, because if you had, you would have never filed this report. Fortunately for you, I discovered it and removed it from the system. Just let this one go, son. You're fucking with fire. Take my word on this. Even if they're standing over a body with a gun in their hand, never screw with a judge, especially Doss. Do you hear me?"

"Yes, captain. I hear you loud and clear."

"Good. Now get rid of this. I don't ever want to see it again."

Gus took the file and tossed it into the trash, but the moment the captain cleared the room, he pulled it out of the can and stuffed it into his briefcase. Rookie or not, he hadn't joined the force to turn a blind eye to anyone. Officially, he couldn't do anything, but what he did in his spare time was his own business.

FOR AS LONG as Gus could remember, he'd wanted to be a cop. When he was a kid and all his friends fantasized about being astronauts or rock stars, he was dreaming about being Sherlock Holmes. His favorite books had always been stories about police detectives. He discovered Patricia Cornwell novels in high school and became fascinated with her books. He loved the way her lead character, Dr. Scarpetta, used forensic evidence to catch the bad guys. Although he had no interest in medicine, he was intrigued with forensic science and how it could be used in police work. There was never a question about his major in college and one week before he began his extensive training at the Houston Police Academy he graduated from the University of Texas with a Bachelor of Science in Criminology. At 22, he was considered the old guy at the police academy, with a majority of his fellow cadets in their late teens, joining the force shortly after graduating high school. In fact, he wasn't the oldest; two of his fellow cadets were his age and one was two years older joining after a four-year stint in the military, but Gus was the only one in his class with a college degree. So, naturally, he soon became known as "College Boy" and that moniker had stuck.

At first, he didn't mind the nickname, but when it became obvious that it wasn't being used in jest, but rather in the form of an insult, he started taking offense to it. He went to college with the assumption that having a degree would help him rise through the ranks, but because most of his superiors were not college educated, his degree seemed to be working against him and as ridiculous as it sounded, it appeared to be holding him back.

He kept trying to convince himself that it was just his imagination, but in the year he'd been on active duty he'd been taken off patrol and stuck behind a desk working shit cases while his fellow academy classmates were out on the street doing real police work. His captain was the only one who called him by his name, to everyone else in the squad he was "College Boy."

He opened up his briefcase and took out the Doss file. He spread the report on the table in his tiny efficiency apartment and read it carefully. He had the same sensation roll through his gut he'd felt during the initial interview with John Jackson; this man was telling the truth, he was no nut case. Jackson's only problem was whom he was accusing. If John Jackson had accused anyone but a state court judge, Gus was sure this case would have been assigned to a detective carrying a gold shield, not him.

All through his academy training, Gus had heard about the so-called "Blue Rule." The unspoken pact that simply meant, you never rat on a fellow officer… no matter what! The "Blue Rule" was never officially discussed, but every cadet heard about it on the sly. Gus had been informed and understood the rule, but it never set well with him. He'd put it in the back of his mind, hoping he'd never have to invoke it, but now it was staring him in the face.

He had a big decision to make–ignore his captain's advice and put his career on the line for a complete stranger, or invoke the "Blue Rule" and just let this one go. He wrestled with it for hours, then he began to wonder what his childhood hero Sherlock Holmes would have done if put in the same situation, and he had his answer.

His problem was how to conduct an investigation on a powerful and connected man like Judge Doss without being detected. Because it would have to be deep undercover, he couldn't use normal police procedures without tipping his hand. Every move he made had to be done with great caution and no one, especially his fellow officers, could know what he was up to. Before he did anything, he had to find out if the missing girl was actually missing or, as the judge claimed, safe and sound touring Europe with a chaperon. He had an idea how to find out, but didn't have the skills to pull it off, however, he knew someone who did.

His college roommate was one of the weirdest guys he'd ever met. His name was Clyde Parker and he was the biggest computer nerd on campus. He claimed to be a direct descendent of the infamous Bonnie Parker, of Bonnie and Clyde fame, but no one took him seriously. The running joke between them was that one day, Gus would be the detective that would bust him when the inevitable happened and his inherited criminal genes eventually surfaced.

"You start your crime spree yet?" Gus said the second Clyde answered.

"Walters! How the hell are you? he yelled. "You made detective first grade yet?"

"It's only a matter of time," said Gus, "but don't worry, I'll have it before you get up enough guts to rob your first bank."

"Well, you better hurry up, I'm getting tired of this nine to five crap and I'm pretty sure I've already met my Bonnie. In fact, I'm glad you called. I need your address to send you an invitation to my wedding. Can you believe it, I'm getting married."

"Hey, that's great," Gus said. "Congratulations, but I'm not sure I want to meet her. She's got to be weird as hell if she's marrying you."

"No way, that's the best part, she's actually an earthling. She's normal as hell, a fucking accountant and she's pretty too. Real pretty. I don't understand what she sees in me, but I love her, man. The wedding's next month, hope you can make it."

"You can count on it. I'll be there."

"So what's up?"

Gus thought for a moment, trying to come up with a simple explanation for his call, but couldn't, "Well, it's sort of a long story. Could I buy you lunch?"

Over hamburgers, Gus laid out the entire scenario to Clyde. "So that shit's true?" Clyde asked. "Cops clam up and cover each other's asses no matter what? That sucks man. Don't seem right."

"It's not right, that's why I've got to do this, state court judge or not."

"You better watch your ass. If this dude finds out you're checking up on him, you're gonna find yourself in a world of shit." Clyde took a bite out of his hamburger and studied Gus's face. "So, I guess that's why you called me. You need my help checking on this judge."

"Not on the judge, but I do need you to do some hacking for me."

"Hacking?"

"Yeah, hacking and don't tell me you don't know how to do that."

"Of course, I know how to do it, but that's illegal, man. If I go down, it ain't going to be for cracking open some mainframe."

"Clyde, think about your heritage. Aunt Bonnie and Uncle Clyde, they're probably looking down and laughing right now. Seriously, I really need your help."

Clyde smiled, "Bonnie was my cousin, not my aunt. Ok, ok, what am I looking for?"

"I need to know if someone's used a passport or acquired a visa in the last three weeks."

"Shit man! You want me to bust into the US Custom's system? I don't know... that would get me into some serious shit if I got caught."

"Come on, Clyde, you're too good to get caught and besides, you're not going in to place a virus or erase anything, you're just in there to look something up. I'm not even sure it's a crime."

"Trust me, it's a crime, but you're right about one thing."

"What's that?"

"I am too good to get caught," he said smiling broadly.

Two days later, Clyde called Gus with some interesting information– Carla Cecil did not have a passport and no visas had been issued to her. Without a passport or visa, she couldn't be touring Europe; the judge was lying. The question was... why would he lie and where was the girl?

On his day off, Gus drove to Tyler and met secretly with John Jackson. He brought John up to date telling him what he'd found out and explained in detail the reason his investigation had to be kept quiet.

"Tell me more about her father," Gus asked John. "How did he die?"

"No one really knows how he died. Judge Doss stopped the coroner from doing an autopsy and had his body cremated. At the time, no one thought anything about it, but now it seems a little suspicious, doesn't it?"

"Let's not jump to conclusions. Right now my concern is finding the girl, we'll worry about how her father died after we find her. Where did he die?"

"In his hospital bed, in Houston. I think it was called Ben Taub? It was something like that."

"I'm familiar with that place, it's a county hospital, in the medical center. I'll see what I can find out. Well, I guess that's all I need for now. I'll be calling you with any updates and please call me if Carla shows up."

Clyde had no trouble breaking into the hospital's computer to download Edward Cecil's medical file. "I got his file and something else I think you'll find interesting," he said to Gus on the phone.

"Something else?"

"Yeah, looks like Carla Cecil was admitted into the emergency room of that hospital a week before her father died."

"Why was she there?"

"Don't know, her file has been erased from the system. Says it's been sealed by court order. Interesting, huh?"

"Yeah, very interesting. I wonder what court sealed it."

"You'll love this. It says here, by order of state court Judge Bradford Doss. That fucker is dirty as hell."

"Clyde, this is getting to be a little muddy and dangerous. Are you sure what you've done can't be traced?"

"Don't worry about me, man, but from here on, you better step lightly my friend. I checked up on this Doss guy and he's got lots of juice… big time friends in high places. Watch your ass, Walters."

"I'll do my best. Clyde, when a file is sealed is it really erased or just moved to another section of the computer? Could there be a special area that's perhaps password protected where court sealed files would be kept or, would they actually erase the file?"

"That's a good question, man. I'm sure they've got a hard copy somewhere, but it would only make sense to have it backed up in the computer. I'll look a little deeper and see if I can find it. I'll get back to you."

Gus immediately placed a call to John Jackson to find out if Carla had some kind of medical problem that would explain why she was in the emergency room of her father's hospital the week before he died. As far as John knew, Carla was perfectly healthy and he had no idea why she'd have to be admitted to the hospital.

An hour later, Gus's phone rang. "Dude, I think you need to come over here and read this file. It's too gruesome to talk about on the phone."

Gus read the file twice and his stomach turned with disgust. And to think he almost invoked the "Blue Rule" and walked away from this one? He was glad he'd let his intuition guide him forward this time and made up his mind that from that moment on, as long as he was a cop, his conscience would be his "Blue Rule."

He needed to know more about what had happened to Carla and the only person he could think of would be the doctor who treated her. He flipped the pages and located the doctor's signature. He had his name, but how could he talk to him about one of his patients without exposing his investigation? He had no idea.

Maybe, he considered, it was time to expose his investigation to his captain. Armed with Carla's file and everything else, perhaps he had enough to go back to him and convince him to open up a real police investigation on Doss. The more he thought about it he realized that, unfortunately, all he had was just circumstantial, none of it could be used as evidence in court because he'd acquired it illegally. All he really had was his suspicion that something was very wrong. He knew that Doss was dirty, but in reality, he had nothing to show his captain.

He looked at the file again and it made his skin crawl. He had to find this girl, but he was running out of ideas and the trail was getting darker. His only hope was that talking to Dr. White would shine a light in her direction.

THE SEARCH

CHAPTER FOURTEEN

I t was a risky move, but Gus had no choice, he had to tell Doctor White everything and pray. His only chance was that he would be as concerned for Carla as Gus was, and hold his trust.

Gus flashed his badge to the nurse behind the desk, "I'd like to talk to Dr. White," he said trying to be nonchalant. "Is he on duty today?"

The nurse put down her pen and looked up slowly. "Officer, did you say, Dr. White?"

"Yes, Dr. Ronald White."

Her face grimaced and she took a deep breath. "I'm sorry, officer, but Dr. White passed away. He was killed by a hit and run driver a few weeks ago."

Gus was shocked, unsure how to respond. "Ah, OK, that explains it. I was following up on some paperwork he'd filed and now I understand why it was incomplete. Please forgive me, I didn't know."

That afternoon at the precinct, Gus pulled Dr. White's police file and discovered he'd been killed one day after he'd treated Carla in the emergency room. He went into the coffee room, pulled a bottle of water out of the fridge and sat down at a table. The room was packed and noisy with fifteen or twenty uniformed cops relaxing and drinking coffee. He knew most of them, but not well, so he just kept to himself and listened to their conversations.

"I'm telling you he just fucking vanished off the face of the earth," one cop said.

"Nobody just vanishes," another cop responded.

"Well, that's what happened," the first cop said. "One day Colby was on duty and the next day, poof he's nowhere to be found. They located his car downtown next to the courthouse. It was locked and nothing was missing."

"What about his house?"

"Clean as a whistle."

"Who are you guys talking about?" Gus finally asked.

The first cop turned toward him, "John Colby, a cop out of the twenty-first. He disappeared about three weeks ago."

The name sounded familiar to Gus, but he couldn't place him. "Was he a street cop?"

"No, he was a sergeant at the twenty-first, working the desk. I never met him, but I hear he was a good guy."

"He just vanished?" Gus asked.

"Looks that way. The detective working the case said they've got nothing. Not one damn lead, but the way I figure it the guy's been on the force twenty years and he's bound to have a few enemies. They'll probably find him locked in a trunk somewhere."

The name John Colby haunted Gus. He couldn't put it out of his mind. Where had he heard that name before? He racked his brain, but couldn't remember. After his shift, he drove to his apartment and sifted through the stack of papers covering his table. While he ate cold pizza and sipped a Heineken, he scanned the pages slowly searching for anything that might send up a red flag. He was at a dead end with the Doss case and needed something, anything, that might give a hint of what to do next. Frustrated, he called Clyde. "Sorry to bother you, but I'm stuck here. I'm looking at a brick wall and not sure where to go next. You have any ideas?"

"Sorry dude, chasing the bad guys is your specialty. I'm just a computer geek. But you can't give up, man, what about that little girl?"

"I'm not giving up, but at this point, I'm not holding out much hope."

"You're thinking that she's already dead?"

"She's been missing almost three weeks. Whoever was drugging her and raping her has... well..."

"That's cold, man. I don't want to think about that. You know me I'm the ultimate optimist. I figure she's hiding out somewhere, alive and well, waiting for you to show up and save her ass."

"I hope you're right, but even thinking positively, it's far fetched. Think about it Clyde, if she is alive where the hell is she? Where does a thirteen-year old girl hide for three weeks, alone with no money? I don't think a teenager could pull that off."

"Maybe a normal teenager couldn't, but Carla's not a normal teenager."

"What are you talking about?"

"Come on Gus, think about it. Nobody gets into Rice University at thirteen by just being bright. I pulled her high school transcript, she's got an IQ of 163. Trust me, this girl is brilliant and I'd bet she's very much alive. Don't give up on her."

"I never put that together. When Jackson was describing her to me, all I could see was my sister when she was thirteen and how alone and scared she'd be. I never added Carla's intelligence to the equation."

"Hey man, when you add an IQ of 163 to any equation, the whole scenario changes. She's out there, man, and you've got to find her before this Doss asshole does."

"Maybe you're right, but there's got to be something I've missed... another direction to take. By the way, does the name John Colby ring any bells for you?"

"Sure, he's in the file."

"What file?"

"Carla's medical file. He's the cop the doc called," Clyde said.

"What are you talking about?"

"It's somewhere near the end of Dr. White's report, where he talks about reporting his suspicions of date rape to the police. It says that he called and reported it to officer John Colby at the Houston Police Department."

Gus snatched up the file and scanned the pages. On the last page of the doctor's report, he read the name, Sergeant John Colby. "Oh, man!" Gus yelled, "I think we just hit the jackpot here."

Gus checked with the twenty-first and found out John Colby was reported missing one day after Dr. White reported Carla's rape to him. The very same day Dr. White was killed by a hit and run driver. Two people knew that Carla had been drugged and raped. The very next day, one wound up dead, and the other one disappeared. It was quite the coincidence and one thing he knew for sure, the first rule of being a good detective was there was no such thing as a coincidence.

"Clyde, where's Darrel these days?" Gus was asking about his other college roommate.

"That's weird, man."

"What's weird?"

"I just hung up talking to him. Just five seconds ago, talking to him about the wedding. That's weird man, you asking about him like that, kind of spooky don't you think?"

"Yeah, I guess it is, but I need to talk to him, where is he now?"

"He's big time, man. He's head of ER at Ft. Worth General. He's making a ton of money, but he's working his ass off for it. What do you need to talk to him for?"

"I need some medical advice."

Gus smiled when he heard the nurse refer to his old friend as "Dr. Wells." He felt pride for him that he'd actually made it through medical school and fulfilled his dream. Unfortunately, he was in surgery when he called, so Gus left a message with his nurse.

It was 1 a.m. when his phone rang, jarring him awake, "Hello," he growled.

"Wake up asshole," a voice boomed in his ear.

"Wells, is that you?"

"That's Dr. Wells to you."

"Well, excuse the shit out of me, doctor," Gus said laughing.

"How've you been, Gus? Clyde tells me that you're with HPD. Can you believe that Clyde has actually found a woman who can stand him?"

"Ain't that some shit? I can't wait to meet her and see what species she is or what planet she's from."

"My money's on Mars," Dr. Wells chortled. "So, what's up? I haven't heard from you in ages. You calling about Clyde's wedding?"

"No, I wanted to ask you something about a case I'm working on. I'm working undercover on this one, so you need to keep this conversation between us."

"Sure, no problem. What do you need to know?"

"Let's say that a thirteen year old girl is admitted to your hospital. She fainted and they brought her to you to check out. What would you do?"

"Well, first I'd check her vitals, then draw some blood and send it to the lab."

"Ok, so when the blood comes back from the lab and it says there's large amounts of Morphine, Valium, Ecstasy and Scopolamine in it... what would you do then?"

"Did you say Scopolamine?"

"Yes, Scopolamine, Ecstasy, Morphine and Valium."

"Why in the world..." Dr. Wells thought for a minute. "Well, because of the Ecstasy and Valium, I'd probably do a pelvic exam to see if the girl was sexually active. I'm not sure what I'd think about the Morphine and Scopolamine. You said that this girl is only 13."

"Yes, but remember these are just hypothetical questions."

"Yeah, sure they are. What's going on, Gus, why are you asking me this?"

"Come on, Darrel, you know I can't tell you. I just need to know the procedure that would be followed if this really happened."

"Alright, I understand, but I need to know a few more things. If I ran a pelvic exam on this hypothetical 13 year old girl, would I find that she's been sexually active?"

"You would find that her hymen was ruptured and there were

slight tears in the walls of her vagina and anus. What would you do next?"

"Do you know what Scopolamine is used for?"

"No, I've never heard of it before."

"I'm reading about it now. It used to be used during childbirth, but it was too dangerous. Damn! It says here it's been used by the CIA as a mind control drug. Some kind of truth serum. Sometimes it's used by anesthesiologists in minor surgical procedures... why in the world would it be in a thirteen year old girl's bloodstream?"

"I was hoping you could tell me that. What does it do to the body?" Gus asked.

"Says here when combined with Morphine, it puts the patient into a twilight sleep allowing communication during a medical procedure with a positive after-effect of amnesia."

"Amnesia?"

"That's what it says," Dr. Wells thought for a moment. "I guess it could be used in a date rape situation. Yeah, that fits. It's possible to have someone sexually turned on by the Ecstasy, but barely awake due to the Scopolamine and Morphine. When it was all over, she wouldn't remember what happened. Yeah, that could work... give her Valium to knock her out... then inject her with the other drugs. But that's a very dangerous combination. Man that's sick. Did someone actually do this... to a 13 year old? What a sick fuck!"

"Again, I'm not pulling you into this. Let's just keep it hypothetical. Ok, so that's what you've found, now what's next?"

"Let me think a moment. My next logical move would be to contact the girl's parents, get permission to do a rape kit on her and then get her to a rape specialist for psychological counseling as fast as I could."

"A rape specialist? Would that be someone on staff at the hospital?"

"That depends on the hospital, but most hospitals either have a psychologist on staff or on call."

"Would the psychologist be named in your report?"

"Of course. We see too many patients to remember the details, so it's standard procedure to write it into the report; all recommendations, even the names of the doctors we refer a patient to."

"So, if there's no mention of a psychologist in a report, then more than likely there wasn't one called?"

"Yeah, that'd be my guess, but no doctor with a brain would allow this girl to leave the hospital without at least talking to a psychologist. Something like this needs serious counseling. I wish you'd fill me in, Gus, maybe I could help this girl."

"Sorry old buddy I can't do that, this could be dangerous. But I promise who ever did this to this girl... is going down hard. I've got to go. Thanks for the information. I'll see you at the wedding."

Gus hung up and immediately began searching Carla's medical file for any mention of a psychologist or rape specialist, but there was none. Only Dr. White's hand written recommendation that Carla receive counseling, but no specific psychologist was named.

Gus asked Clyde to run a search on the hospital employment records and found that the hospital employed two licensed psychologists, but only one was on duty the week Carla was there. If Carla *had* talked to a psychologist, chances were that she'd talked to this one, but once again he was faced with a serious dilemma—how to talk to Dr. Jane Griswald without exposing his investigation?

According to the hospital employment records, Dr. Griswald lived at the Houston House, an upscale high-rise apartment building nestled among the downtown skyscrapers. Gus opted to approach the doctor at her home rather than her office, because it wasn't actually official police business. To get in to see her at the hospital without an appointment would take a flash of his badge and that would be a little too high profile. The fewer people that knew about his visit to the doc, the better.

He pulled into the Houston House visitor's parking lot, killed his engine but didn't get out. In his rear view mirror, he could see the doorman and the two security guards sitting behind the reception desk of the small lobby. His badge would get him past the doorman, but getting up to the fifth floor was the problem. Before the security guards would let him on the elevator, his name and badge number would be written in the log and the doctor would be contacted. She'd want an explanation for his visit and of course, he couldn't tell her, not there in the lobby with the guards listening. He had to find some other way in.

He noticed several cars pulling into the "owners only" entrance of the building's parking garage. From where he sat, it appeared there was no entrance security gate, or any kind of mechanical arm blocking the drive. He cranked his car, backed out of the visitor's lot and followed a black Jaguar into the garage. He was correct, there *was* no security to get in, however, once inside the garage, he discovered that to operate the elevator required a pass code he didn't have. Frustrated, he got back into his car and sat in the dark, trying to think of what to do next.

The elevator doors opened behind him and a teenage girl and a woman in her mid thirties walked out. Perhaps a mother and daughter he thought, studying the face of the young girl as she walked past. Suddenly recognition flashed in his mind. Jerking his briefcase open, he fumbled through the papers and located the picture John Jackson had given him. He studied the picture. There was no doubt about it, it was the same girl. Carla Cecil was alive.

He watched them get into a white Mercedes and followed them out of the garage. They turned left on Main and headed south toward the Medical Center. He allowed a few cars to get between them, but kept a close watch on the Mercedes. They stopped at a small out of the way Mexican restaurant. Two tables down, he drank his beer waiting for them to finish their meal.

"Excuse me, but aren't you Dr. Jane Griswald?" he said approaching their table.

They looked up in shock. "Uh, yes I am," she said nervously.

"What a coincidence, I was just on my way to see you," he said, showing her his HPD badge and ID. "My name is Gus Walters, I'm with the Houston Police Department. Would you mind if I sat down?"

"Actually, we were just leaving. Why don't you drop by my office tomorrow," she said as she stood.

"I'm sorry, Doctor, but I need to talk to you now. Please, this will only take a moment."

Dr. Griswald sat back down in the chair and looked at Carla who was frozen with fear.

Gus sat a chair at the table and looked at the young girl, "Carla, please don't be afraid. There's nothing to be frightened about."

Carla looked up at Gus with wide eyes then turned to Dr. Griswald. "I'm sorry, Officer Walters," Dr. Griswald said. "You must be mistaken, her name is not Carla."

"Dr. Griswald, please, let's not play this game. I know this is Carla Cecil. I've been searching for her for three days and to be honest with you, I thought she was dead until I saw her walk out of that elevator with you. I'm not here to arrest her or take her back to Judge Doss. Dr. Griswald, I've read her medical file and I know what's happened to her. I'm not here to cause her more suffering." Gus turned and looked again at Carla. "Please trust me, Carla. I'm only here to offer you something I know you desperately need... my help."

Gus followed them back to the Houston House and rode with them in the private elevator up to the fifth floor. Once inside Dr. Griswald's apartment, the three of them settled in the living room.

"I have a question, Officer Walters," Dr. Griswald said.

"Please, call me Gus."

"Ok, Gus... how did you track Carla to me? What made you think that she was with me?"

"Honestly, I didn't know. I only came here to talk to you. I had no idea Carla was here."

"May I ask a question?" Carla said shyly.

"Of course," Gus said.

"Why were you looking for me in the first place?" she asked.

"John Jackson told me about you."

"Mr. Jackson from Tyler?"

"Yes. He's very concerned about you, Carla. When you didn't come to your father's funeral, he suspected that something was wrong, so he called Judge Doss and asked about you, but he didn't believe what the judge told him, so he came to my precinct and filed a report."

"What did Judge Doss tell him?" Carla asked.

"Something about you being in Europe."

"Europe?"

"Yes, but he didn't believe that, so he drove down here to talk to him in person. Doss wasn't home, so he talked to his next-door neighbor who told him you'd moved back to Tyler. After he heard that, he knew that something was wrong, so he came to see me." In detail, Gus explained to Carla and Dr. Griswald what had transpired from there.

"So, other than you, no one knows about Judge Doss and what he has done?" Dr. Griswald said.

"That's correct," Gus answered.

"I'm sorry, but I don't understand. If you know all of this, why haven't you arrested him?"

"I wish it was that simple, Dr. Griswald, but I don't have any solid evidence. I can't arrest him just because I think he's guilty."

"He raped me and murdered my father!" Carla yelled, jumping to her feet, "And, he killed Dr. White just because he knew what he'd done to me. He's a monster, isn't that enough proof?"

"I'm sorry, Carla. I know what happened to you is horrible, but I don't have any real proof that Judge Doss was the one who raped you, or murdered your father. I wish I did, but there's just no solid evidence of that. I also believe he killed Dr. White, as well as Sergeant Colby, but I can't prove that either. All I have are my suspicions and some circumstantial evidence. That's not enough to arrest him, Carla. I wish it was, but it's not."

Carla sat on the couch, pulled her knees to her chest and rocked back and forth nervously. "If he finds me, he's going to kill me too," she murmured terrified.

"Carla, look at me," he said. "Doss is never going to touch you again. I promise, but we do have to get you out of Houston to a safer place."

"Do you think he could track her here?" Dr. Griswald asked.

"Judge Doss is extremely intelligent. If I found you, I have to assume that he could too. I think it's imperative to get Carla out of Houston as soon as possible. I'm also concerned about you, Doctor."

"Me? Why would you be concerned about me?"

"Obviously, Doss didn't trust Dr. White to keep Carla's rape a secret, that's why he killed him. In Dr. White's report, he recommended that Carla see a psychologist, that's why I came to you. You were the only psychologist on duty that night. We have to presume that since Doss had the file sealed, he knows what's in it. I'm concerned he may be thinking the same thing I did and will be coming after you next."

"What are you suggesting?" Dr. Griswald asked. "That I hide from Doss as well? I can't do that. It's taken me years to build my practice. I can't just pack up my life and run away."

"I understand, but if Doss is who we think he is, he'll stop at nothing to cover his tracks. I believe you are in danger, Doctor. Is your practice worth your life?"

"Officer Walters, my practice is my life," she said. "I can't just leave it. I'm not going to let this man destroy everything I've worked so hard to get. I'm sorry, but I'm not going anywhere."

"Ok, but I think you're making a mistake. At the very least, you need to alert security at the hospital and here at your apartment building. Tell them you've received a death threat and they'll keep a closer watch on you. Hopefully, I'll find something solid on Doss soon and this will be over."

"Ok, I'll contact security," the doctor said. "But what about Carla? Where will you take her?"

"I'd like to take her to Tyler to see John Jackson first. He needs to know that she's safe. He also told me he had something very important to talk to her about. I'm not sure what it is, but he made me promise that I'd bring her to him the second I found her. After that, I'm not sure, but she needs to go to a place totally unconnected. Somewhere Doss wouldn't think to look."

"My family has a farm in Georgia. What about that?" Dr. Griswald asked.

"Sorry, Doc, but it can't be connected to you either."

Gus loaded the few possessions Carla had in his car and headed to Tyler. Two and a half hours later, he rang John Jackson's doorbell. It was after midnight. When John opened the door and saw Carla standing under the porch light, he rushed to her and threw his arms around her. "Thank God you're alive," he said. "I've been worried sick about you."

At the dining room table, John's wife brought Carla hot chocolate with marshmallows and poured Gus and John steaming coffee. "John, I think I need to tell you there is a possibility that your house is being watched. You need to be very careful and keep Carla out of sight until I get back here tomorrow night. My shift ends at 8, I should be here by 11 at the latest."

"You think Judge Doss is out there somewhere watching my house?" John asked startled.

"No, not the judge, but it wouldn't surprise me if he'd had someone here in Tyler keeping an eye out for Carla. I don't know that for sure, but this would be a logical place for him to look. That's why we have to get her out of here as soon as we can. As long as she's here, she's in jeopardy and so are you and your wife. Doss is dangerous and Carla and everyone connected to her is a threat to him. I wouldn't put anything past the judge, so please be careful."

John pointed to an electronic panel mounted on his wall, "I have a good security system in this house and I'm pretty good with a gun, don't worry she'll be fine tonight, but I agree we need to get her out of Tyler. Do you have any ideas where to take her?"

Gus felt awkward talking about Carla as if she wasn't there, but she didn't appear to be paying attention, lost in thought quietly sipping her hot chocolate, staring out the window. "Not really, but it needs to be somewhere new, someplace she's never been before so Doss won't track her there. To keep her hidden, she's going to need a new identity and money to survive."

"Money is something she doesn't have to worry about," John said.

"I promise I'll pay you back every cent," said Carla, surprising both of them that she'd been listening.

John looked across the table at her, "You won't have to pay me back a cent. You don't need my money, Carla... you have your own. Your father's life was insured."

Carla lowered her cup to the table. "Insured?" she asked.

"Yes, he was insured. When he was my general manager, I took out a key man policy on him and it was still in place when he died. The money is yours."

"How much money?" she asked softly.

"Five hundred thousand dollars," John said. "That should take care of you for a long time."

ON HIS DRIVE back to Houston, Gus called Clyde and woke him out of a sound sleep. "Dude, do you know what time it is?" he growled.

"Somewhere around 3 a.m. I guess," Gus said.

"Don't you ever sleep? What do you want now?"

"I was just wondering if you had any friends on the net who could help set up a new identity for someone."

"You found our girl?"

"Yes and I need to make her invisible fast. Can you help me with that?" Gus asked.

"Now you're talking, man. Give me 24 hours and I'll have her hidden deeper than Elvis. You do know that he's still alive, don't you? I figure he's living it up on some exotic island, laughing at all of us."

"Clyde, you've always been delusional, but I love you anyway. Call me when you've got it set up."

It was almost 5 a.m., when Gus opened the door to his apartment and collapsed on his bed. Four hours later, he was sitting behind his desk at the precinct, working on his third cup of coffee when the call came in. Dr. Griswald had been found dead in her apartment. A rush of panic shot through his body. He grabbed his cell phone, ran out the front door and called John Jackson.

"Is Carla alright?" He asked the second John answered.

"Yes, she fine, she's here with me. Why? What's wrong?" he asked.

"John, listen to me carefully. You've got to move Carla right now, right this second. Jane Griswald was killed last night. It had to be Doss and if he forced her to talk before he killed her, he knows everything. We can't take any chances. Get her out of there, now. I'll call his clerk to see if he's holding court today, if he's not... he could be in Tyler now."

Gus placed a call to Judge Doss' clerk and was relieved to hear that he was in session and would be there all day. It still didn't answer the provocative question in his gut. Did Jane Griswald talk before she died? Could she have endured his horrible torture without talking? Did Doss know about him and where he'd taken Carla?

His cell phone rang. "We're out of the house, where do you want us to go?" John Jackson asked.

"Is your wife with you?" Gus asked.

"Yes, we're all here."

"Good. I want you to drive to Dallas, to the DFW airport and take the next available flight to Colorado Springs. When you get there, check into a hotel near the airport. Use a different name and pay with cash. I'll meet you there tomorrow."

"Colorado Springs? What's there?"

"I think I know a place where Carla will be safe."

Gus hung up and dialed the phone again. "Darrel, it's me, Gus."

"Hey buddy, what's up?" he said.

"I hate to do this, but I can't think of anything else. I'm sorry, Darrel, but I really need your help."

"With what? What's wrong, Gus?"

"Remember the hypothetical thirteen year old girl I told you about?"

"Yeah, in fact, that story has been haunting me ever since you told me about her. Is she in more trouble? Do you want me to see her?"

"No, it's nothing like that. I wish it were that simple. Remember our ski trip in college? When we went to Colorado?"

"Sure, but what's that got to do with anything?"

"On the way, we stopped and spent the night with your aunt, in a cabin in the mountains."

"Yes, in Woodland Park, it was my Aunt Martha's place."

"Does she still live there?" Gus asked.

"Of course. The only way she's coming down off that mountain is in a box. She's a lot older now, but still tough as hell. Why do you ask?"

"Darrel, I have to be honest with you. This girl is in *real* trouble. The guy who raped her is searching for her, and he'll kill her if he finds her. I need some place to hide her. Some place he wouldn't know about. Do you think your aunt would mind a thirteen year old genius living with her for a little while?"

"She'd love it. I know she's lonely up there by herself and would love the company. I think it's a great idea. Ah... did you say genius?"

"Yes. This girl has an IQ in the 160's, but she's in real peril. If I'm going to save her, I've got to move fast. If you're sure it's OK, I'd like to take her to your aunt's cabin tomorrow. Would you call her and set it up? Tell her not to worry about any extra expenses, the girl has money to take care of herself. We should be there around 3 p.m."

Back at his desk, Gus booked a flight to Colorado Springs leaving at 8 a.m. the next morning. When his shift ended, he drove to Judge Doss' house praying that he'd find his white Lexus sitting in the driveway. It was and his heartbeat returned to normal for the first time in hours. He parked across the street and fought to stay awake the rest of the night. A black Volvo pulled into the drive around 11 p.m., which Gus assumed belonged to Doss' wife. Nothing else happened after that. An hour later, the house went dark and remained that way all night. At 7 a.m., Gus cranked his car and drove to the airport.

The flight attendant woke him only moments before the plane touched down in Colorado Springs. It was 11 a.m. and he'd slept all the way. He rented a car and drove to the nearest breakfast joint he could find. He hadn't eaten in two days and was running on fumes. He'd just finished his pancakes when his cell phone rang.

"What do you think about the name, Leigh Ann Brooks?" Clyde boomed in his ear.

"I like it," Gus said. "It sounds sort of sophisticated. So, that's her new name?"

"That's what is says on her new birth certificate and social security card. By the way, do you think she can pass for sixteen?"

"Well, she looks young, but when you talk to her, she comes off much older. Yeah, I think she can pull off 16."

"I hope I get to meet her someday. She sounds cool."

"Let me get her settled in first and make sure she's safe, then we'll take a trip to Colorado. She wants to meet you. I've told her about everything you've done for her and she's very grateful. You'll like her, Clyde. And by the way, she *is* cool."

Before Gus drove up 'Ute Pass' to Woodland Park, he took Carla shopping. If she was going to live in the mountains, she'd need some warm clothes: sweaters, a warm coat, snow boots and a good pair of gloves. After the shopping trip, they drove up the snow packed mountain path to Woodland Park. It took him a while to locate the entrance to the property, but eventually he found it and slowly rolled down the quarter-mile long snow-covered drive leading up to the beautiful old cottage.

Aunt Martha opened the front door and stepped out on the porch as they pulled up. "Welcome," she said, waving.

Carla stepped out of the car, taking in the panoramic view surrounding her. "Oh, my," she said. "It's beautiful."

The cabin was nestled between six snow covered aspen trees, resting on a small rise overlooking a winding mountain stream. Behind the cabin, off in the distance, was a clear view of Pike's Peak towering majestically above them.

"Child, I've lived here thirty years and it still takes my breath away," Aunt Martha said. "I think it's some of God's best work. You must be freezing, come in. I have a good fire going and I've made you and Gus some homemade stew. I hope you're hungry."

Gus opened the trunk and began gathering up Carla's new clothes when she walked up and threw her arms around him. "Thank you, Officer Walters. For everything you've done."

He put down the clothes and hugged her back. "It's Gus, remember… and you are very welcome young lady."

While Carla put away her things and hung up her new clothes, Gus explained the situation to Aunt Martha. He didn't tell her everything, but enough for her to understand the need for Carla to be there. She seemed genuinely happy to have her and for the first time in days, Gus relaxed. Carla was safe, the stew was delicious and the fire was warm. In mid conversation with Aunt Martha, he drifted off, falling sound asleep on the couch.

The next morning he woke to the smell of frying bacon and fresh brewed coffee. It took him a moment to realize where he was, but after a few minutes, his brain cleared and he made his way to the kitchen. Carla was standing behind the stove poking bacon with a fork. "Good morning," she said, smiling.

Gus found the coffee and poured himself a cup. "Where's Aunt Martha?" he asked.

"She went into town for some fresh bread, she'll be back in a few minutes. I really like her. She's sweet."

"So, you think you'll be OK here."

"I love it here," she said. It's beautiful. I can't stop looking out the window."

"Yeah, it's quite a view," Gus said sipping his coffee.

Carla's smile disappeared. "Dad would have loved it here. He loved the snow," she said wiping her eyes.

"Carla, it's OK to cry. You've been holding it in, but you're safe now. Judge Doss can't find you here. This is the perfect place for you to rebuild your life, but before you can do that, you have to have closure to your old one. You need to grieve for your father, Carla... and, for Dr. Griswald. Just let it all out. It's important to get it out."

"I'm not ready for that yet. Maybe someday I will be, but not now," she said turning the bacon. She put down the fork and sat at the table across from Gus, "Someday, he'll pay for what he's done."

Gus saw genuine rage in her eyes and it concerned him. "Carla, I can't imagine what you've lived through in the last few weeks. I know you're full of hate and anger, but don't let that destroy you. If you do, then he's won. Don't let him win, Carla. Your best revenge would be to take back your life and do something good with it. I'll get Doss... I promise I will. Leave that to me, that's my job.

"You think you're all alone in the world, but that's not true, there are a lot of people who care about you. And remember, you can always count on me. I'll be checking on you every week and I'll always be there for you if you need me."

The next day, Gus flew back to Houston barely arriving in time to make his shift. From his desk, he called John Jackson and was relieved to hear that they were safe. That night he followed Judge Doss home from the courthouse, staked out his house until daybreak, but nothing seemed out of the ordinary. His wife arrived around 11 p.m. and the house went dark two hours later. The next morning he tailed the judge back to the courthouse, then went to work. Surviving on fast food, coffee and short catnaps in his car, Gus watched the judge's house for a week. Finally, after the eighth night, he drove home and slept in his own bed, satisfied that Judge Doss had not been successful.

He couldn't imagine the horror she must have endured, but it was obvious that Dr. Jane Griswald had not talked. She had resisted Doss' torture, protecting Carla to her death.

THE TRUTH

CHAPTER FIFTEEN

"I think that's my father," Michelle said suddenly, jumping up in the cockpit.

"Your father? Where?"

She pointed toward a small speedboat heading our way. "There in that boat," she shouted nervously. "Oh, God he's coming out here! What's he doing in St. Martin?" She was shaking, wrenching her hands.

I knew that eventually I'd have to meet her father, but I'd always assumed that I'd have the time to think about what I was going to say to him and I also assumed I would be wearing more than a pair of cut off jeans, however there was no time to do anything but run to *Windsong's* stern, catch the line he threw to me and attach it to the cleat.

Her father didn't take my helping hand and climbed into the cockpit unassisted. Looking me up and down, he locked eyes with me. "I'm here for Michelle. Where is she?"

Before I could answer, Michelle appeared in the companionway opening. "Daddy, what are you doing here?" She moved to his side and hugged him.

"Your mother and I came here to see where you've been living and to meet Mr. Dean. We'd like to take you to dinner tonight and talk to you about something that's come up. It's important and we wanted to talk to you about it face to face."

"Mom's here too?"

"Yes, we're staying at the Holland House. She's there waiting to see you now."

"Well, sure... uh... let me get dressed and I'll go back with you, Billy can meet us later for dinner."

Her father cleared his throat and shot me a hard look. "If it's OK with Mr. Dean, your mother and I would like to talk to you alone if possible."

Michelle flashed me a concerned look. "Michelle, it's no big deal," I said bravely. "Go get dressed and have a nice visit with your parents."

She wrinkled her brow. "Are you sure? I hate to leave you alone."

"I think Mr. Dean will be fine without you for one night," her father said firmly.

It only took Michelle a few minutes to throw on a dress and brush her hair, but it seemed like an eternity. I tried several times to make small talk with her father, but it soon became clear that he wasn't interested in shooting the shit with me; he was only there to collect his daughter. My heart ached as I watched them speed away to shore. I stood there watching the little boat disappear trying to shake the feeling of doom that had suddenly overtaken my body. Although she'd only been gone a few seconds, I missed her desperately and feared the worst.

She didn't come back to the boat that night. I assumed that her parents had convinced her to stay with them in their hotel room, but I was a little surprised and hurt that she hadn't called to let me know. I didn't even try to sleep. I couldn't bring myself to lie down in the bunk without her. I couldn't even stay below in the saloon – it was just too quiet and lonely down there. I made a bed on the forward deck and spent the night praying, worrying and staring at the stars.

My cell phone rang at 7 a.m. "Can you meet us for breakfast?" Michelle asked. Her voice seemed strained and different.

As I rowed to shore, I kept replaying the phone call from Michelle. There was definitely something in her voice. Something wrong.

When I walked into the restaurant, Michelle waved at me, but didn't get out of her chair to greet me as I had expected. Instead, she just motioned me to sit in the chair across from her. She smiled at me, but it was forced and she avoided making eye contact.

"So this must be your mother," I said, offering her my hand. "It's nice to meet you." She politely took my hand and shook it but didn't respond. The tension hung in the air like heavy smoke. "So how was dinner? Where did you guys eat last night?"

Michelle looked at me and finally made eye contact. "We ate here in the hotel." She lifted her water glass and took a sip. Her hands were trembling.

"Are you OK, Michelle? What's wrong? You're shaking."

"Billy, I have to ask you something. And I want you to tell me the truth. Promise me you'll tell me the truth?"

I glanced at her father then to her mother then back to Michelle. Her eyes were red and her cheeks were swollen. "Michelle, honey, of course I'll tell you the truth. What's this all about?"

She reached under her chair, came up with a copy of my CD and laid it on top of the table. "Is this you? Are you Max Allen?"

I stared at my bearded smiling face staring back at me from the CD cover. I didn't know what to say, so I just shook my head yes.

I'd never seen her cry before and it broke my heart. "So you're not Billy Dean? You're this Max Allen guy that was arrested for raping and killing a 17 year old girl?"

I jumped out of my chair knocking it over behind me. "I was not arrested for raping and killing a 17 year old girl! That's a fucking lie!" I yelled. The restaurant was suddenly silent and everyone was staring at me in shock.

"Sit down and stop yelling!" her father said under his breath. "You're making a scene."

Ignoring him, I spoke directly to Michelle. "I never touched that girl and I had nothing to do with her death. Yes, I was charged, but I was acquitted because I was innocent. Michelle, I could never do anything like that, you've got to know that about me. Please don't believe the things people have said about me. It's all lies. Think about it. You know me, Michelle. Do you honestly think I could have raped and killed anyone? Do you?"

"Why didn't you tell me about this before? I thought you loved me."

"Michelle, I do love you. More than anyone or anything I've ever loved before. I don't know why I didn't tell you. I guess I was afraid of something like this happening. I was afraid I'd lose you."

Michelle covered her face with her hands and cried. I wanted to go to her and hold her in my arms, but I didn't dare.

"I've heard enough. Come on Michelle. Let's go collect your things. We've got a plane to catch," her father said, standing up from the table reaching for her.

"You're leaving me. Like this? Now?" I said.

"Yes, Mr. Allen. She's leaving with us, now," her father said glaring at me.

Michelle didn't take her father's hand. Instead, she stood up from the table and looked me in the eyes. "No, Daddy. I'm not leaving today. Billy and I have a lot to talk about. Go home and I'll call you tomorrow and let you know my plans."

"Michelle, I insist you come with us now! I forbid you to stay!"

"I'm not your little girl anymore. I'm a grown woman and old enough to make my own decisions. I listened to you and mother last night. I think it's time I hear Billy's side of the story."

"But."

"Shut up, Jack. You've said quite enough," Michelle's mom said as she hugged Michelle goodbye and pushed Jack forward. When they had walked around to my side of the table her mother stopped directly in front of me. "It was nice to meet you too," she said holding out her hand. "By the way, what do we call you? Billy or Max?"

I took her hand and shook it. "Take your pick. I'll answer to both," I said smiling.

Her mother leaned in close and whispered in my ear, "Max, she loves you. Don't break her heart."

With my deck shoes in my left hand, I walked barefoot along the beach, waiting impatiently for Michelle to return from seeing her parents off at the airport. I had to continually fight with the little voice inside my head that kept bringing up the possibility that she wasn't coming back. I could hear her father's words in my head, and could picture him trying to convince her to board the plane with them. Although she'd looked me in the eyes and promised me that she'd be back, I honestly didn't know for sure until I saw her walking down the beach toward me.

When she got close, she slipped out of her shoes, reached for my hand and for almost an hour, we strolled along the shore together, not a word spoken between us.

We found an empty table at a tiny beach side bar, sat down in the shade of a huge umbrella and ordered two beers. Michelle drank almost half of hers before she finally spoke. "I'm going to miss calling you Billy," she said gazing out at the water.

"Why would you stop calling me Billy?"

She tilted her head and looked at me curiously. "Because your name is Max. Billy Dean doesn't really exist."

I turned away from her and stared at the ocean. I didn't know how to respond. She reached across the table and took my hand in hers. A single tear appeared in the corner of her eye and slowly ran down her cheek.

"Why didn't you tell me?" she asked.

"I've been asking myself that all morning. I guess it was because you fell in love with Billy, not Max, and I was afraid you'd feel different if you knew about Max."

"I fell in love with you! And I fell in love because you were sweet and gentle and I thought you were the most open and honest person I'd ever met. I told you everything about me, all of my darkest secrets, and I thought you'd done the same with me. I feel so... so, betrayed."

I'd been a fool. I should have told her, but now it was too late and I wasn't sure if the damage could be repaired. I pulled her out of her chair into my lap, held her in my arms and let her cry on my shoulder. "I'm so sorry," I said, wiping away her tears. "Do you have any idea how much I love you? Michelle, you are my life. I love you. Truly, truly love you and I know that I'm gonna love you until the day

I die. Don't let this destroy us. Don't stop loving me. Please forgive me."

Michelle lifted her head away from my shoulders and stared up at me. "You're crying? Oh Billy, don't cry. I forgive you. Don't cry baby, I could never stop loving you. Don't cry, baby."

I hadn't realized it, but I *was* crying and once I started, I couldn't seem to stop. I tried to speak, but my words were so slurred she couldn't understand me. Finally, I regained my composure and over the next several hours, I told Michelle every gory detail of my sordid past.

It was well past midnight when we rowed back to *Windsong*. Back on board, we watched what was left of the waning moon come up and snuggled together in the cockpit. With her head resting on my shoulder, I stroked her hair with my hand and gave her baby kisses on her forehead.

"Do you have a middle name?" She asked smiling up at me.

I laughed. "Actually, Max is my middle name. My first name is Dan."

"Dan Max Allen? No, no, no, no," she said laughing. "I could never get used to calling you Dan. Ok then, Max it is."

"I'm not so sure about that," I said. "I think I'd miss the way you say Billy. When you say it, it makes me kinda tingle all over. Tell you what. Why don't we leave it like it was before. Max was someone from some other life. He doesn't exist anymore. I like this life a lot better. Call me Billy."

"You sure?"

"Yes, I'd like that."

She leaned up, touched my face gently with her hand and kissed me for a long time. "B..i..l..ly," she said playfully. "Are you tingling yet?"

THE NEXT MORNING, being careful not to wake Michelle, I untangled myself from her arms and slid out of the bunk. In the galley, I turned on the propane, lit the fire under the coffee pot then climbed up the companionway ladder to the cockpit.

I was on my second cup when Michelle finally climbed up the ladder and snuggled in my lap.

"How long have you been up?" she asked.

"I've been awake for hours. I've only been up here thirty minutes or so."

"Poor baby, couldn't sleep? Why didn't you wake me?"

"You had a pretty rough day yesterday, so I thought I'd let you sleep in. Besides, I loved watching you sleep."

"You watched me sleep? Ewww! I must have looked awful."

I touched her face and kissed her. "You looked like an angel, a beautiful sleeping angel, and I couldn't take my eyes off you."

For almost an hour, we sat in the cockpit watching the boats buzz around the bay, sharing my coffee until it was gone. Then we went below to make breakfast. I cooked eggs, bacon and toast, but Michelle didn't eat much, she seemed preoccupied. A few times, she looked across the table at me as if she wanted to say something, but withdrew and looked away. Finally, she spoke. "Billy, we need to talk about something." She was biting her bottom lip.

I stared back at her, studying her now serious face. "Sure, honey. What is it?"

"I've been waiting for just the right time to bring this up. I wanted to tell you last night but…" She bit her bottom lip again.

"Just tell me, Michelle. What's wrong?"

"There's nothing wrong, it's something good, at least I think it is. Billy, I've had an offer… for a show in Myrtle Beach. In a theater there."

"There's a theater in Myrtle Beach?"

"Oh, yeah! There's a lot of theaters in Myrtle Beach, but this isn't just any theater, it's the biggest and best one there. Dancing in this show is something I've dreamed about my whole life. When I was a little girl, my parents took me there to see the shows. This theater was my inspiration to become a dancer. I can still remember how I felt watching the dancers spinning around on that stage. When I was ten or eleven, I made a promise to myself that one day I'd be up there on that stage and now I actually have the chance to do it. Billy honey, please understand, I have to do this. I can't pass this up."

She was on the verge of tears. "Why would you even think about passing it up? Did you think I was going to try to talk you out of it?"

Michelle dropped her eyes and shook her head. "Yeah, I thought you might."

"Michelle, we've talked about this before. We both knew that one day you'd get another show. I can't believe you thought I'd try to stop you from doing something you loved. Why would you think that?"

"Please don't be mad at me Billy. I didn't know how you'd react. We haven't talked about me dancing in a long time. It's just that in the past... when I tried to bring it up, you wouldn't talk about it. I just assumed..."

I put my finger over her lips. "Shhhhhhhh. Michelle, you don't have to explain." I cupped her face in my hands and kissed her lips. "When do you have to leave?"

"I'm supposed to be there Monday to start rehearsals."

"Monday? Day after tomorrow Monday?"

"Yes," she said, "But... I don't have to do this if..."

"Michelle, if this is important to you then it's important to me. You have to do this. I'm going to miss you, but you have to do this."

She looked up horrified. "Billy, no! I can't do this without you. I can't leave you. You have to come with me."

I pulled her into my arms. "Wait... slow down, you didn't let me finish."

"I'm sorry, but..."

"Michelle, hush... you're jumping to conclusions. What I was trying to say... I'm going to miss you until I finish the season here. I promise, the second it's over I'll be on my way to Myrtle Beach. You wouldn't want me to just walk out on Bill Heard and leave him without entertainment, would you?"

"No, I guess not, but how long will that be?"

"Three or four weeks at the most."

"You said, on your way? Are you going to sail there? How long would that take?" She asked.

"I'm not sure. It depends on the wind and the weather. If I'm lucky, about two weeks."

"You don't have to bring *Windsong*, I'll have an apartment," she said.

"I know, but I can't leave her here during hurricane season. It wouldn't be safe. And besides, I'm pretty sure your parents aren't expecting me to show up in South Carolina. It's going to be bad enough when I do, but if they think we're living together, well, that's going to go over like a whore in a church."

"But they know we're living together here on your boat. What difference is it going to make if we live together there?"

"Michelle, they just spent about two grand flying down here to bring you the news about this job and about me, I mean about Max. Trust me, they weren't planning on us staying together and if they think we're living together again, they'll make your life miserable. They hate me, Michelle. I just think it would be better to have *Windsong* there, so we can at least keep up the façade of me having my own place."

"Maybe you're right, but you *are* going to live there with me, right?"

"Of course, but for a while, let's not tell your parents. Let's give them some time to get to know me first. Who knows, maybe I'll win them over. It won't take me that long to sail there."

"Two weeks… if you're lucky." she said hugging me. "Add that to the four weeks before you can even leave… that's almost two months, Billy. What am I going to do for two months?"

"Well, dance in your new show and miss me a lot… I hope," I said kissing her cheek. "I don't like it either baby, but we'll get through this. I promise I'll call you everyday."

The next morning, we took a cab to the airport. In the back seat, I held Michelle in my arms and she cried all the way. I waited at the airport until her plane pulled away from the gate. I could see her waving goodbye through the small plane window; she was still crying. I didn't cry, but when I got back onboard *Windsong*, I dug through the cabinets until I found the Johnny Walker and proceeded to get very drunk.

∼

I CALLED Michelle every morning and sent her e-mails every night. The time just seemed to creep by, but eventually the season ended and my obligation to Bill Heard and Everyting's Cool was over. It took me most of the afternoon to get everything ready and the sun was already hitting the water when I pulled up the anchor and sailed out of Philipsburg harbor. *Windsong* was riding low, packed to the brim with supplies and fuel but had no problem cutting through the chop plowing our way back to Michelle.

Sixteen very long and sleepy days later, I pulled into the Myrtle Beach Yacht Club. Michelle was standing on the dock. When I saw her, I killed the engine, jumped over the rail and lifted her off her feet with my embrace. In between our kisses, we wiped each other's faces soaked from our tears.

"Hold me, Billy. Thank God, you're here. Promise we'll never be apart again." Michelle whispered as I squeezed her.

"I promise. Never again, baby, never again."

That night after her show, we returned to the boat and made love until daylight. Entangled in each other's arms, snuggled as close as humanly possible, we finally fell asleep and didn't wake until the afternoon. I had timed it perfectly, it was Monday, her day off, so that evening we had a romantic dinner and afterwards she drove me to Myrtle Beach to see her new townhouse.

I was stunned when I walked in. The furniture and floors were stacked high with unopened boxes. The only room that showed any signs of life was the bedroom. This room was also full of unopened boxes, but in the corner on the floor was a double sized mattress with a pillow and a wrinkled sheet in a pile on top of it.

"Haven't you been here almost two months?" I asked.

"Almost," she said.

"Why haven't you unpacked any boxes? It looks like you just moved in."

She threw her arms around my neck and kissed me. "I didn't want to unpack until you got here."

"Why not?"

She looked me in the eyes. "Because this is *our* new home. I didn't want to set it up without you."

I kissed her a long time, savoring the taste of her lips. "I love you," I said as I threw her over my shoulder and carried her out the front door.

"What are you doing?" she giggled.

"We need to make this official." I sat her down, then picked her back up and held her in my arms. "Here's to our new home," I proclaimed as I carried her across our new threshold.

WOODLAND PARK

CHAPTER SIXTEEN

I n 1954, John Wells bought twenty acres of land, nine miles west of a tiny Colorado mountain town called Woodland Park. On his property, he built a small Swiss styled cottage for his wife, Martha. On their tenth wedding anniversary, he took her for a drive in the mountains and surprised her with it. They lived there happily for 30 years. On May the second, 1984, John suffered a stroke and died two days later in a Colorado Springs hospital. After John died, Martha contemplated selling the place and moving into a retirement center in Denver, but changed her mind...

She was driving back from visiting her sister in Golden, Colorado when the snow began to fall. It snowed all the way to Woodland Park, but when she made the final turn and pulled onto her property, it finally stopped. At the gate, she trudged her way through the deep, fresh powder to her mailbox. On her way back to her car, she paused and looked around at the picturesque scene before her. Everything was white; the mountains, the trees, the bushes were all blanketed with snow. Suddenly the clouds parted and a single brilliant ray of sunlight shown down illuminating her cottage, like a huge spotlight from the heavens. The white snow on the roof glistened, reflecting a rainbow of colors like a prism across the landscape. At that moment, she realized that she'd never be happy living anywhere else.

For the first few years, she was lonely, but eventually she became content living alone. She kept herself busy knitting sweaters for her nephews and nieces and canning jams and vegetables, most of which she gave away to her church for the needy.

She had grown to love her simple life of solitude, passing each day of the last nine years doing things at her pace and on her schedule. When her nephew, Darrel, called asking if she'd mind taking in a 13 year-old girl she agreed, but she *was* apprehensive. She wondered how long the girl would have to stay there and dreaded how the teenager's presence would disrupt and change her simple daily routines. However, in less than a week, all of her apprehensions disappeared. Carla Cecil was not what she had expected.

Martha Wells was childless. She and her husband had tried for years and although she did get pregnant several times, she could never carry to term. After several miscarriages, they stopped trying, resolving themselves that obviously raising children was not in God's plan for them. Instead, they spoiled their nieces and nephews, covering their walls with their pictures and they always looked forward to their yearly visits. Her two sisters had delivered their children within weeks of each other, one sister with two boys and the other with two girls. Martha fell in love with each child at first sight. She spent as much time as she could with them and every year all four of them, in a group, would come and play in the snow with her and her husband for several weeks. They loved having them there each year, but as they grew older, it became more and more of a challenge. When they reached their teens, their yearly visits became almost more than they could handle. She remembered how quickly they had changed once they reached puberty, all four of them became sullen and moody and at times down right hateful. Fortunately, they grew out of it and all of the children had developed into happy and successful adults.

Living through the terrible teens with her nieces and nephews was the root of her apprehensions about Carla. However, Carla didn't seem to possess any of the negative traits she'd expected to see. She was a polite, quiet and gentle girl who went out of her way to be helpful. Carla's bedroom was neat as a pin and without being asked she took over most of the household cleaning chores. Martha's oak wooden floors hadn't shined this bright in years and the kitchen seemed to sparkle after one of Carla's thorough cleanings.

Carla spent most of her time reading or surfing the web, as she called it, on her new computer. Martha had no idea what that meant, but it seemed to be very interesting to Carla. The thing that impressed her most was how often Carla would stop what she was doing, just to see if there was anything she could do for her. Often she would surprise her by carrying in a tray with fresh brewed tea, cookies and a vase holding flowers she'd pick out of the garden. Carla had a sweet soul and it didn't take Martha long to fall in love with this wonderful young woman.

ALLOWING Carla full access to her father's insurance money without creating a paper trail had been a real challenge. Since the insurance policy was written as 'key man' coverage, the original beneficiary was John Jackson and the check was made out to him. That was good. However, getting that much money to Carla undetected was the problem. John couldn't just write her a check without alerting the IRS and possibly giving away her location. He had to get the money to her without any obvious link to him.

To accomplish this, he formed a new Colorado corporation, naming Carla, or rather Leigh Ann Brooks, as the President and CEO. Once the new corporation was formed, John Jackson purchased five hundred thousand dollars worth of stock and transferred the funds into the corporate checking account. With Carla in complete control of the new company, she could use the corporate funds any way she deemed necessary. The only taxes owed would be on any money she drew out as salary or profit the company earned from interest or dividends from its investments.

Six months later, John drove to Woodland Park to check Carla's books and make sure she was keeping the proper records. He was staggered to discover that Carla had spent almost all of the money, buying stocks in several small, unknown companies. He was horrified and wanted to scold her, but instead, he kept his misgivings to himself. After he reviewed her records, he told her that her books were in perfect order and insisted that she call him if things should turn bad with any of her investments and she needed more money. When he returned to Tyler, he called Gus and told him about Carla's foolish use of her father's insurance money. Gus was shocked she'd do something like that and was very concerned for her future welfare. They both blamed themselves for not realizing how stupid it had been to allow a thirteen-year old girl access to so much money.

Six months later, John returned to Woodland Park to check her books once again, fully expecting to find her checking accounts completely empty. He was astonished to discover that most of the small-unknown companies in which Carla had invested in so heavily, had grown rapidly, increasing the value of their stock ten fold. In less than a year, Carla had increased the net worth of her company to over a million dollars. John and Gus stopped worrying about her welfare and never questioned her stock purchases again.

Carla's uncanny ability to pick the right stocks wasn't luck; it was based on solid research using a debt to asset ratio formula she'd come up with in college. In utter amazement, John and Gus watched Carla build her company's assets to over ten million in less than six years. Twice a year, John drove to Woodland Park to check her books and each time he was impressed and overwhelmed at what he found.

As her company assets grew, so did Carla, changing from a shy, skinny teenager into a beautiful young woman. Although she'd spent her adolescence living like a recluse in a small mountain cottage, spending most of her time behind a computer, somehow Carla, AKA, Leigh Ann Brooks had developed into a woman with style, grace and confidence. She possessed a certain sophistication that impressed John Jackson every time he visited her. He attributed her remarkable transformation to Aunt Martha's guidance. Martha Wells was a classy lady and it had obviously rubbed off on Carla.

On her nineteenth birthday, Aunt Martha surprised Carla with a party. Secretly waiting in a restaurant in Colorado Springs was John Jackson and his wife, Dr. Darrel Wells, Clyde Parker, and newly appointed Detective First Grade, Gus Walters.

Through the years, they had all fallen in love with Carla, watching her grow up. For most of them, it had been years since they'd seen her in person and almost three years for Gus. However, they all had kept in touch with her through the Internet. Gus thought talking to her through a computer was cold and impersonal, so instead, he called her on his cell phone and had done this every week for six years.

It was a weekly ritual. Every Saturday after his shift, Gus would pick up a pizza and eat it in bed talking to Carla. When he called, she too would eat pizza in her bed and they would talk for hours. She would tell him about her new stock interests and he would tell her about his job. They both looked forward to their weekly talks and had become very close.

The day he got the promotion, all he could think about was how she would react to the news and he wasn't disappointed. She screamed in his ear, dropped the phone and danced around the room.

The weekly phone calls had begun as a fulfillment of his promise to stay in close touch and keep her informed of his progress investigating Judge Doss. Unfortunately, there had been little to report. Through the years, he had watched the judge's every move, but he seemed to be a model citizen. It was frustrating, but Gus knew that one day the judge would slip up, and when he did, he'd be there to take him down. The only positive thing was that it appeared he wasn't searching for Carla any longer.

It had been six years since they'd all helped her escape to Colorado. The whole gang was there and it was time for Aunt Martha to bring Carla in for her grand entrance, time for everyone to jump up and yell surprise, but when she walked through the door, they were speechless. Carla had changed dramatically and everyone except John Jackson, who had seen her recently, was in complete shock. They all assumed that she might look a little different, but no one expected to see such a vision of beauty walk through that door. Everything about her was different. She was much taller, having grown at least three inches since they had seen her and her face structure had changed from the round little girl face to a fashion model oval with pronounced high cheek bones set off by her beautiful blue eyes. Her waist length hair was pulled up with long blonde curls trailing down her back. She was wearing an ankle length knit dress that hugged the curves of her lean but shapely body, a body no one even knew she had until that moment. She looked like she belonged on the cover of a fashion magazine. The restaurant went silent and every head in the place turned to look at this beautiful creature that had just walked into the room.

Finally, Clyde yelled, "Surprise!" and everyone around the table in unison yelled, "Happy Birthday!"

Carla screamed at the top of her lungs and ran to the table hugging and kissing everyone there.

Their table buzzed with loud conversation. Carla was ecstatic, having the time of her life. Throughout the dinner, Gus couldn't keep his eyes off of her, trying to find the slightest trace of the scared teenager he'd saved so many years ago, but she wasn't there. A confident, positive happy woman had replaced the shy, petrified little girl he once knew. He was pleased she hadn't let the anger and rage she'd felt for Judge Doss destroy her life.

Several times, Carla caught him staring at her. When their eyes met, Gus would turn away shyly, but when he looked back, she would hold his gaze and smile at him coyly. Every time she did this, he could feel his heart flutter.

After the dishes had been cleared, they presented Carla with her birthday gifts. She may have looked like a sophisticated super model, but all that poise disappeared when she saw her presents. She tore into them like a little girl under a Christmas tree and everyone in the restaurant seemed charmed by her over the top exuberance.

Gus had searched for weeks for just the right present and had maxed out two of his credit cards to buy it. When she reached for his gift, his body stiffened. Suddenly, he was nervous, confident he'd made a terrible mistake, he was sure she wouldn't like it. It was an autographed first edition copy of "The Stockbrokers' Clerk" a Sherlock Holmes novel. As she peeled back the wrapping paper, he cussed himself for buying her such a dumb gift.

"Is this a first edition?" she exclaimed.

"Ah... yeah," he fumbled for words, "I thought maybe you'd..."

"Is this Sir Arthur Conan Doyle's signature?"

"Yes."

"I didn't know there was a Sherlock Holmes novel about a stockbroker. Where on earth did you ever find it? Oh, Gus, it's perfect! I can't believe you bought this for me, I'll cherish it forever!" She ran to his chair, threw her arms around his neck and kissed him on the lips.

Everyone at the table broke into a smile watching Gus blush, his face turning the color of his wine. He tried to act nonchalant, but he didn't fool anyone. He was beaming, obviously loving the kiss and elated that Carla had understood his gift and realized its true value. She knew that to Gus, it was a priceless treasure. That he cared enough to give it to her, was the biggest gift of all.

ON THE PLANE RIDE HOME, Clyde unhooked his seat belt, moved down the aisle and sat next to Gus, "So, when's the wedding?"

"What wedding?" Gus said.

"Your wedding."

Gus stared at Clyde curiously, "What the hell are you talking about?"

"Look, man. I only know three absolute truths. One, I'm going to die someday, two, while I'm alive, I'm going to have to pay taxes and three, Gus Walters would never, ever give away a first edition Sherlock Holmes book unless..."

"It was just a birthday present," Gus said. "Don't jump to any conclusions, she's just a kid."

"I'm not sure where *you* were tonight, but I was at a birthday party for the most beautiful *grown* woman I've ever seen. Hey, man, she is not a kid any more."

"Yeah, I guess so, but it's still hard for me to grasp that concept. Who would have ever dreamed that scared 13 year old girl would grow up to be Christy Brinkley?"

"That's your problem, man. All you can see is that little 13-year old girl you saved, but that was a long time ago. Gus, it's 1999, Carla is 19 years old and all grown up, and... she's in love with you, man. It's written all over her face every time she looks at you. You're her hero."

"Clyde, heroes don't hit on their heroines. They just save them and walk away. And besides, after what's she's been through with Doss and everything else... it wouldn't be right. She trusts me. I'm her friend and I could never do anything to destroy her trust or ruin that friendship."

"That's bull shit, man. The last I heard, loving someone was a good thing. How can loving her hurt your friendship or destroy her trust? Dude, it's obvious you've got it bad for our girl. Just fess up and tell her how you feel."

Clyde returned to his seat leaving Gus to contemplate his words. His mind flooded with thoughts of Carla. There was no question he had feelings for her, but was it love? Had his feelings of concern for her safety grown into love? And, if that was true, when did that happen? Is that why he'd spent every spare minute of his life for six years tracking the man who'd raped her? Is that why he'd never found anyone interesting enough to date? Would anyone ever be as interesting to him as Carla? Probably not, he conceded. Being honest with himself, he realized that Carla was actually the only woman he ever thought about. However, before this trip, when he thought of Carla, in his mind's eye he saw a scared little girl, now the vision of her walking into the restaurant played in his head and each time he saw it, he melted a little further.

He had to admit to himself that what he was feeling for Carla was more than just friendship or concern, but he wasn't sure he could ever tell her. So, he hid his true feelings and kept quiet. The only thing that changed between them was their weekly phone calls. The week following her birthday party, he began calling her in the middle of the week. Some weeks, he called her two or three times. His phone bill was getting out of hand, but he couldn't resist.

It had been two days since he'd heard her voice and he was thinking about calling her when his phone rang. "It's Aunt Martha," Carla's voice broke, "I think she's dying."

Gus caught the next plane and was by Carla's side when Martha died. She was 83 and her heart had simply stopped. At the funeral, Carla clung to him crying uncontrollably in his arms.

They buried Martha next to her husband on a small hill that over-looked the beautiful cottage they'd built and lived in for so many years. The following day they read Martha's will. No one was surprised that she had left all of her money and most of her posses-sions to her nieces and nephews, but we all were surprised to hear that she had left the 20 acres of land, and the cottage, to Carla. The only problem was that she'd left the land and cottage to Carla Cecil, not Leigh Ann Brooks. For the first time in six years, Carla Cecil's name would be on a public record and that worried Gus.

"Do you really think it matters?" Carla asked.

"I don't know, but if the judge is still searching for you, it would be an easy way for him to find you."

"It's been six years, Gus. Don't you think if he was still looking he would have found me by now?"

"No, he couldn't have tracked you here. Clyde made sure that your identity couldn't be traced. Carla Cecil simply disappeared and until now, there's been no trace of your name on any record, anywhere."

"What do we do?" she asked.

"I'm not sure, but the thought of you out here in the middle of nowhere, alone, doesn't feel right," Gus thought a moment. "To be safe, I think we need to find you someplace else to live."

"What about Manitou Springs?"

"Where is that?"

"Just down the pass, it's close to Colorado Springs. Aunt Martha and I used to go there for Sunday brunch and shopping trips. It's beautiful, very quaint. In fact, I'd been thinking about buying a small used bookstore that was for sale there."

"You've been thinking about buying a bookstore?" Gus asked with surprise.

"Yes. There is a back room big enough to set up an office. The market has been precarious, so I haven't been doing much trading lately, and I was thinking it would give me something to do, to occupy my time. Gus, I need to keep myself busy, especially now with Martha gone."

"I understand, but I'm not sure that's far enough away," Gus watched her face drop. "But maybe I'm wrong, let's go check it out."

They drove down the pass and walked hand in hand through the narrow streets of Manitou Springs. Although Gus didn't like that it was only 22 miles from Woodland Park, he loved the idea of Carla living in this happy little community. The people were friendly and he knew they would welcome her with open arms. It was time for her to have a real life and make new friends. Carla seemed thrilled with the possibility of living there, so Gus put aside his misgivings and gave in.

Walking through the surrounding neighborhood, they found a beautiful old two story ginger bread style house for sale only blocks from the bookstore. Carla fell in love with it at first sight. Carla was ecstatic when she discovered the bookstore was still for sale. She closed the deal with the owner on the spot, and then dragged Gus down the street to a real estate office and bought the old house. Gus called his captain and took a few vacation days due him, and spent the next four days helping Carla move into her new home and reorganizing the bookstore.

The only concession Carla made to Gus's concern for her safety was to allow him to install a state of the art security system in her house and bookstore. The system included advanced video surveillance equipment that covered every room of her house and every room of the bookstore. The cameras were miniature and virtually undetectable. The system was so sophisticated it allowed Carla to view each room of her house from her bookstore, as well as, view her bookstore from her house. From four different monitor locations in her house and two locations in the store, Carla could easily scan every square inch of her property. At the first sign of trouble, all she had to do was hit a panic button and the local police, as well as a private security force would be alerted. Hitting the panic button also activated six digital video recorders that stored the images from all of the cameras on a hard drive. It wasn't failsafe, but it was as close as Gus could get to it.

With Carla settled in her new home and after checking and rechecking the new security system, Gus reluctantly said goodbye and caught the next plane back to Houston.

CARLA UNDERSTOOD Gus's concerns for her safety, but honestly, she had grown weary of hiding from Judge Doss. She'd had nightmares about that horrible man for most of her life. Fulfilling her promise to Dr. Griswald, she had spent thousands of dollars in therapy because of him, although, she'd never used the judge's real name and the psychologist only knew her as Leigh Brooks, the terrifying story was the same. It had taken her years, but the therapy had helped dissipate the deep phobia she once had for Judge Doss. She no longer feared him and the nightmares had stopped.

Honestly, there was a part of her that wanted him to find her. Perhaps it was the years of her martial arts training she had worked so hard to perfect rather than the therapy that had given her confidence and taken away her fear, she wasn't sure. It didn't really matter, all she knew was that she wasn't afraid of him anymore. Instead of trembling at the thought of him, often she caught herself fantasizing about kicking him in the throat or ramming the cartilage from his nose into his brain with a quick chop from the palm of her hand. She knew it wasn't healthy to fantasize about killing someone and tried to put those thoughts out of her mind, but once a month or so, especially when she was alone, the fantasies returned.

She had bought the house and the store in her company name and had registered the utilities under the name of Leigh Ann Brooks, but as a test, she had her fax phone line installed in her home under the name of Carla Cecil. She knew it was a risk, but she was tired of wondering if he was still out there searching for her. Gus would have gone ballistic if he'd known, but it was time to find out the truth. If he was still looking, it wouldn't take him long to discover she had a phone in Manitou Springs. Come and get me you bastard, she thought to herself, I'm waiting for you and things will be different this time.

TESTICULAR CANCER WAS the diagnosis and his only hope for survival had been invasive surgery. In effect, they had castrated him taking away all of his sexual urges in the process. Now, five years later, the diagnosis was prostate cancer and he would have to endure another surgery followed by six months of intensive chemotherapy. He was only 64 years old and already technically a eunuch. Now, he was going to lose what was left of his manhood. Oh, how he hated her for doing this to him! She had started it all with the savage kick. Before she had attacked him, he was fine, perfectly healthy. But look at him now.

Every single night for six years, he'd searched for her, running traces for her name in every state. He searched property records, utility records and phone records. She was nineteen or twenty now, so he expanded his search to voting records and political party lists looking anywhere he might find her name.

When he viewed her old videotapes, he no longer felt sexually aroused, the doctors had taken all of that away. All he felt now was rage and hatred for the girl that had ruined his life. His pedophilia had filled a void in his life. It had excited him and made his life worth living, but she had taken that away from him. Now he was just a sexless shell of a man. But one day he would find her and she would pay, she couldn't stay hidden forever.

She was also the only person alive that could expose him, the only person who knew the truth about him and another reason he continued his search. Destroying his manhood was enough reason to kill her, but she possessed information that could take away his freedom and put him in jail. This would never happen to the honorable Judge Bradford Doss. One day he would find Carla Cecil and when he did, she would die in his hands.

THE GAME

CHAPTER SEVENTEEN

I t took us several days, but we finally made our way through most of the boxes and had our new apartment looking reasonably good.

"What's all this?" I said, opening one of the remaining cartons.

"Oh, cool," Michelle said. "They're my games!"

"Games?"

"Yeah, look!" She reached in and started pulling out board games — Monopoly, Clue, Parcheeze and Battleship. "Oooooh, check this out."

From the bottom of the container, she pulled out a small green rectangular box, set it on her lap and opened the lid. It was a Ouija board.

"Don't tell me you believe in that crap," I said scoffing.

"It's not crap, it's fun."

"Yeah, some fun."

"I'm serious, I had a blast with this thing in college." She unfolded the board and ran her hands over the surface. "And it really works, too."

"Come on, Michelle. You don't really believe that, do you?"

"Yes I do. Billy, I'm telling you this thing will freak you out. It's scary as hell. I've seen some really strange things on this."

"Oh, yeah I bet. In fact, you're scaring me a little now."

"Very funny. I'm not kidding, it's like it's alive. It used to scare the hell out of us when it would come back with a specific answer to our questions. I'm telling you, it knew things it couldn't possibly know."

"Michelle, you can buy these things at Walmart! Of course it knew the answers to your questions, you guys were pushing it around spelling them out."

"No, I'm serious," she insisted. "It just sort of takes off on its own. You can't control where it goes."

"Yeah… sure." I walked into the kitchen, opened the fridge and pulled out a bottle of wine. "It's all a bunch of bull shit," I mumbled to myself.

"I heard that," she yelled loud enough for me to hear through the walls.

"Hey witchy woman," I yelled back. "You want some wine?"

Michelle walked into the kitchen. "You are such a comedian tonight," she said. "You know, Max, I didn't realize how cynical you were."

I poured a glass of wine and handed it to her. "I'm not cynical, just a skeptic," I said sipping my wine. "I'm a realist. I know there's things that can't be explained in this world, but, Michelle please… a Ouija board? Come on, it's so obvious how it works."

"Oh, really," she said. "Ok then, Mr. Know-it-all, let's play it and when it totally freaks you out, then I want you to tell me how obvious it is."

"No way."

"What's wrong? Are you chicken?"

"No, I'm not chicken. It's just a waste of my time."

"Oh, yeah you're soooo busy. Come on you big chicken. Let's do it, just for a few minutes."

I took another sip of my wine and thought about it for a moment. "Ok," I said. "I'll do it, but with a few conditions."

"What conditions?" she asked.

"I'll play this stupid game if you wear a blindfold. And, if you turn the board upside down, so I can't make out the letters. If it works that way, maybe I'll believe it. We got a deal?"

"Deal," she said, unfolding the board on the coffee table. "You sit on that side and I'll sit here."

I tied a red scarf around her eyes making sure she couldn't see through it, and then guided her hands to the small plastic triangle in the middle of the board.

"Do you have your fingertips on the triangle?" she asked.

"Yes, but I'm scared," I joked

"Ha, ha, ha. OK, here goes. Let's do it."

Using a low husky tone I hadn't heard before, Michelle said, "Is anybody there?" It was difficult, but I managed not to laugh out loud. Nothing happened, so once again, she asked, "Is anyone there?"

I couldn't hold it back and started laughing, but stopped when the plastic triangle began to move under our fingertips. It circled the board two times then stopped over the word **YES**.

"You did that," I said.

"Did what?"

"You were pushing it."

"I was not! I swear!" she insisted. "Where did it stop, what did it say?"

"It stopped on yes."

"Cool, we've made contact with someone! Whom are we talking to?" she asked.

The triangle slid up to the letter *E*, then across the board and stopped on *C*.

"What did it spell?"

"E C," I said.

"Your name is EC?" she asked.

The board circled once and stopped over the word **YES**.

"What did it say?"

"Well, *you* said yes." I answered.

"Damn it, Max, I swear I'm not doing anything. I'm blindfolded remember, I can't see."

I jerked my hand up to her eyes, checking to see if she was cheating, but she didn't flinch. "Let me ask it something," I said.

"OK, go ahead."

"Ah… Mr. EC, ah… how old are you?"

The board moved to the number *1*, then to the number *4*.

"So, you are 14 years old?" I asked.

It moved back to the word, *YES*.

"When were you born? What year?"

1… 9… 8… 2

"What did he say?" Michelle asked.

"1982."

"Is that right?"

I calculated in my head for a moment. "Yes it is."

"What is your full name?"

E… D… W… A… R… D… C… E… C… I… L

I'd been calling out the letters as the board moved. "His name is Edward Cecil?" Michelle said. "Ask him if he's dead?"

"What kind of question is that?"

"Sometimes they're not dead," she said.

"What the hell are you talking about?"

"I don't know exactly, but once in college we contacted a spirit who said he was still alive. Maybe he was in a coma or something. Just ask if he's dead or not."

"Ok… Edward, are you still there?"

YES

"Are you dead?"

YES

"When did you die?"

1… 9… 9… 1

"How old were you when you died?"

9

"How did you die?"

C… A… R

"Were you hit by a car?"

NO

"Were you killed in a wreck?"

YES

I jerked my hands off of the triangle. The answers were coming too quickly and honestly, it was freaking me out a little. Either Michelle had memorized the board and was guiding the triangle from her memory, or she was somehow peaking through the blindfold or, and this was the part that was freaking me the most, she wasn't doing either one and something was actually happening. "Michelle, you swear you're not fucking with me? Because if you are, I'm telling you it's not funny. Tell me the truth, are you guiding this thing around?"

"Max, I told you this was spooky. I swear I can't see the board. I'm not doing anything."

I put my fingertips back on the triangle. "I'm sorry, Edward, but I'm a skeptic. It's hard for me to believe that I'm talking to a dead person. Can you tell me something that would help me believe?"

B... R... O

"I'm sorry, but I don't understand."

B... R... O... H... E... R... E

"I think BRO means brother," Michelle said.

"Are you trying to spell brother?"

YES

"Brother, here. Is that what you're saying?"

YES

"Whose brother?" I asked.

M... A... X

"Me?"

YES

"My brother? You're saying that my brother is there, with you?"

YES

"Billy," Michelle whispered. "I don't like this."

I continued, "If my brother is there, then tell me his middle name."

F... R... A... N... K... L... I... N

"Is that right?" Michelle asked.

"Yeah," I said as a chill slowly crept down my spine.

"What's our father's middle name?"

F... R... A... N... K... L... I... N

"Fuck!" I yelled, jerking my hands away.

Michelle pulled off her blindfold. "I think we need to stop, Billy. This is scaring me."

"I know, it's scaring the hell out of me too, but... how could he know their middle names?"

"Come on. You're the one that said that it's just a silly game."

"I know, I know, but, Michelle he spelled their middle name. I've never mentioned that to you before and I know I wasn't pushing the damn thing. Something's going on, we can't just stop now."

"Edward, are you still there?"

YES

"Is my brother still there with you?"

YES

"I don't mean to be difficult, but I need more proof to make me a believer. I want you to ask my brother to tell me something that only he and I know – something that happened only between the two of us. Something that no one else could possibly know."

Nothing happened for a few minutes and then the triangle began to glide across the board.

S... I... N... G... R... O... S... E... S

The letters didn't mean anything to me. "I'm sorry, but I don't understand."

S... I... N... G... R... O... S... E... S

I concentrated hard trying to comprehend what he was trying to communicate, but my mind was blank. Michelle looked at me across the board and shook her head no. She was as confused as I was. "Help me, Edward, tell my brother that I need something else to understand this."

After a few moments, the triangle began to move.

L... A... S... T... S... O... N... G

When I saw those letters, my heart jumped out of my chest. Suddenly, I felt weak and clammy, instantly breaking out into a sweat, and my hands started trembling.

"Billy, you're shaking. What's wrong?" Michelle took my hands in hers.

"My God, Michelle, this thing is real. I'm talking to Dean!"

"How can you be sure?"

I told her about the party I played two weeks before my brother was killed, and about *Run For The Roses*. "Michelle, no one else was around. It was the last song I ever sang for him. Until now, I'd never considered the significance, but obviously Dean has. *SING ROSES* was the *LAST SONG!*"

For several minutes, we just sat in silence, sipping our wine, looking at each other. When we finally went back to the Ouija board, we didn't have to ask the next question. The second our fingertips touched the triangle it began to spell.

B... E... L... I... E... V... E

Michelle didn't get it at first, but I understood. "Yes, Edward I believe you now."

H... E... L... P

"You need help?" I asked.

YES

"You want us to help you?"

YES

"How can we help?" Michelle asked.

C... A... R... L... A

"Carla?" Michelle said. "Who's Carla?"

S... I... S

"Carla is your sister?" I asked.

YES

"You want us to help Carla?" Michelle asked.

YES

"How can we help her?" I asked.

D... A... N... G... E... R

"Your sister is in danger?"

L... E... A... V... E

"Leave? You want us to tell her to leave?"

D... O... S... S... C... L... O... S... E

Michelle looked at me confused. "Edward," I said, "we are not understanding you. What does DOSSCLOSE mean?"

K... I... L... I...

"Kill? Killer? Are you saying DOSSCLOSE is a killer?"

D... 0... S... S

"Wait," Michelle yelled, "I think I've got it. Edward, are you saying that you want us to warn Carla because Doss is close to her and he is a killer?"

YES

"Who is Doss," I asked.

K... I... L... L... M... E

Michelle jerked her hands off the board. She was terrified. "Oh, my God, Billy, Doss is the guy that killed Edward and now he's coming after his sister. I don't want to do this anymore! This is scaring me, Please, Billy, let's stop."

It took some serious coaxing, but I finally talked Michelle back to the Ouija board. I glanced at my watch, it was 1 a.m. We'd been on the board three hours. Michelle was frightened and we were both exhausted, but we had to go on. Over the next two hours, with Edward spelling out fragmented words, we deduced the rest of his story. He told us that a man named Bradford Doss had kidnapped him, but the car he was driving had crashed. Edward was killed, but Doss survived. Now, this Doss character was after his sister, Carla. We didn't know why, just that he was. Edward was asking us to warn Carla that Doss knew where she lived and that she needed to run away.

"Where does she live? How do we find her?" I asked.

R... E... D... M... O... U... N... T... A... I... N

"Red mountain?" Michelle said. "She lives at Red Mountain?"

NO

"Help us Edward, we don't understand," I said.

G... O... D... G... A... R... D... E... N

Michelle sighed, "Come on Edward, give us more. What state does she live in?"

G... A... R... D... E... N... G... O... D

"Hold on," I said, "I have an idea. Where did we put that atlas?" I found it and flipped through it to the state of Colorado. "Yes, that has to be what he's talking about. Look," I said, pointing to the map.

Michelle followed my finger. "Garden of the Gods?"

"Yes, it has to be. It's close to Colorado Springs. I went there once. It's beautiful and the mountains are red. Red mountain. Garden God. He's talking about the Garden of the Gods, in Colorado. Are we right, Edward?"

YES

Michelle scanned the map again, "But this is a state park, do people live there?"

"Let me see that," I searched the map. "There's a place called Manitou Springs next to it. Maybe she lives there."

"Edward, does your sister live in Manitou Springs?"

YES

"Why didn't he just tell us that?" Michelle asked.

"He's just a kid, I don't think he knew how to spell it," I said. "Ok, Edward, we promise we'll try to contact Carla and warn her about Doss. You have our word."

G... O... D... B... L... E... S... S

"Is my brother still there with you?"

YES

"Could I talk to him?"

YES

"Are you sure that's a good idea?" Michelle asked.

I looked at her and shook my head. "I don't know, but I think I have to." I took a deep breath and said, "Dean, are you there?"

YES

My hands were shaking so much I couldn't keep them on the triangle. My heart was racing. "Is this really happening? Is this really him?" I said to Michelle.

"I don't know, Billy, but I think so."

"God! What do you say to your dead brother? I don't know what to ask him. This is so fucking weird."

"Ask him if he's happy," Michelle said.

I didn't have to ask. When I touched the triangle, it began to move.

L... O... V... E... U

My eyes filled and tears dripped down my face onto the board. "I love you too. Are you OK?"

B... E... E... N... B... E... T... T... E... R

We both laughed out loud.

Y... O... U

"I'm doing great. I'm in love with Michelle and I'm very happy. What do you think about her?"

B... A... B... E

We both laughed out loud again, "This is Dean alright. Yes, she's quite a babe."

H... E... L... P... E... C

"Yes, we're going to help Edward."

M... U... S... T... G... O

"No, don't go. Not yet."

L... O... V... E

"I love you too."

There was so much more I wanted to ask him, but the triangle stopped moving. I kept trying, but got no more answers... he was gone.

We went to bed, but neither one of us could sleep. Michelle finally dropped off around daybreak. She had me in a vice grip, her arms and legs wrapped around me squeezing tighter than normal.

Communicating with Edward and my late brother went against all logic and contradicted everything I'd ever believed. Lying there with Michelle in my arms, I kept asking myself the same questions. Did it really happen? Was that really Dean? It sure sounded like Dean and what's all this about Carla Cecil and this Doss character? Should I actually try to contact Carla?

I thought I understood how a Ouija board worked. I'd heard the wild stories before and had rationalized that the triangle was guided around the board maybe not consciously by the players, but subconsciously. And, because it was guided by their subconscious, the answers surprised and shocked them. My theory held water when it came to talking to my late brother. It could have been my subconscious guiding the triangle, but how could I explain Edward, Carla and this Bradford Doss character? Their names were uncommon. To the best of my recollection, I'd never heard of an Edward Cecil, Carla or Bradford Doss. Perhaps they were in Michelle's subconscious. There had to be a logical explanation. There had to be.

When Michelle finally woke, I took her out for breakfast. Purposely I didn't bring up the Ouija board until we'd finished eating. "Billy," she asked, sipping her coffee, "was it just a dream or did we actually talk to your brother last night?"

"If it was a dream, then we had the same one. I don't know what the hell that was."

"Do we actually try to contact Carla?"

"I'm not sure. Michelle, have you ever known anyone named Bradford or Doss or Cecil, maybe someone from your college days or your childhood?"

"I've known a few Carla's and I met a few guys named Ed or Edward, but no one named Bradford or Doss. There was a guy named Cecil in my high school, but I didn't know him very well. Why do you ask?"

"I'm just trying to figure this out. Maybe we were just fooling ourselves and only talking through our subconscious mind."

"I guess that could explain it, but remember, I was blindfolded in the beginning, when we first made contact with Edward... and... it seemed so real."

"Yeah, that's the problem. I'm not sure what to do, but I guess it couldn't hurt to see if there's a Carla Cecil living in Manitou Springs."

I called 411 and asked the operator for the number. Instantly, the phone clicked and a recorded voice gave me a number. "Oh, shit," I yelled. "I just got her number."

"Call it," Michelle said.

"You think?"

"We promised Edward. Dial the number."

The phone rang two times then clicked and I heard a fax signal in my ear. "It's a fax," I said.

"Try it again, maybe you misdialed."

I tried it again, but got the fax signal again. I called information back, but there was only one number listed for a Carla Cecil in Manitou Springs. We tried the number several times during the day, but only got the fax signal.

"Why don't we send a fax?" Michelle asked.

"How?"

"I can send faxes from my laptop."

Michelle pulled out her computer and I went to work. After I'd finished the letter, I looked at Michelle and she gave me the thumbs up. I smiled back at her, clicked send and waited for confirmation that the fax had been sent successfully. It only took a few minutes.

FAX
February 16, 1999

To: Carla Cecil, Manitou Springs, CO
From: Billy Dean & Michelle Parker, Myrtle Beach, SC

NOTE: *We are not sure you are the correct Carla Cecil. Please ignore this letter if this does not pertain to you; however, if you know an Edward Cecil, or know of someone named Bradford Doss please LEAVE YOUR HOUSE NOW. You are in grave danger!*

WE NEVER GOT a response to our fax. We waited a week before we tried to contact Carla Cecil again, but when we called, the phone had been disconnected.

"Do you think she got the message and moved away?" Michelle asked.

"I have no idea."

"Maybe we should try the Ouija board again?"

"No way," I said. "I don't ever want to do that again. We've done all we can do—we fulfilled our promised to Edward. Maybe Carla saw our fax and ran away. Maybe this is all a bunch of nonsense—just our subconscious playing tricks on us. Who knows? To be honest with you, I don't think I want to know. Let's just try to forget about it. But just in case it was real... maybe we should burn that damn Ouija board."

I was serious, but Michelle wouldn't let me burn it. Instead she hid it away somewhere deep in a closet. After that, we never talk about it again.

THE ESCAPE

CHAPTER EIGHTEEN

I t had been an unusually busy day at the bookstore. The new flyer had worked incredibly well, bringing in a steady stream of new customers to sample her gourmet coffee and the free Internet access. If this kept up, Carla realized, she'd need to hire some help. She barely had time to check the stock markets in between her customers.

Although she was exhausted, it was such a beautiful evening she decided to walk home and left her car parked behind the bookstore. She took her time window-shopping on the way. When she turned the corner, she could see her beautiful house waiting for her at the top of the hill. She'd only lived there a few months, but had fallen madly in love with this lovely old home. At the front door, she turned the key and walked inside, but the warning alarm didn't sound. "Damn!" she said. "I did it again." Setting the alarm before she left each morning was something she just couldn't get used to. At least once a week she'd forget to set it. She smiled thinking about Gus and what he would be telling her now if he knew she'd forgotten to set it again. "How can someone with an IQ of 163 forget to set her alarm?" he would say. "Why did I go to all the trouble hooking the damn thing up if you're not going to remember to set it?" She'd listen to him vent for a while then she'd start laughing. "It's not funny, Carla. It's serious." Then he would calm down and laugh with her.

She knew it was a dumb thing to do and promised herself not to forget next time. She gathered her mail on the floor under the slot and scanned through it as she walked up the stairs. She dumped the mail along with her keys and coat on the bed and headed to the bathroom. Something caught her attention out of the corner of her eye, but before she could react a white cloth covered her mouth and nose. The smell was sickening. A huge arm wrapped around her body and squeezed her hard. She tried to move away but suddenly she was woozy. She held her breath and tried to clear her head, but she was dizzy and off balance. Instinctively, she shifted her body to the right and jabbed backward as hard as she could with her left elbow. She caught Doss off guard, smashing her elbow into his rib cage. She heard him yell in her ear. He fell on the floor and gasped for air. Carla fell forward against the dresser and tried to steady herself on rubbery knees. The ether from the white rag had her disoriented.

In a dream like state, she watched Doss rise from the floor cursing at her and holding his side. She shook her head trying to get control, but before she could move Doss lunged at her, knocking her to the ground. Instantly he was on top of her, choking her with his fingers around her neck. She couldn't breathe and felt herself slipping away. She tried to pull his hands away from her throat but he was too strong, she couldn't break his grip. She was about to die, and it was all her fault. She had foolishly led him to her, wanting this battle, but he was too big and too strong. Had all her years of martial arts training been for nothing, she thought? NO, she screamed inside her head, gathering all of her rage, letting it fill her body with strength. In one quick motion, she went for his eyes. Doss screamed and fell backwards, covering his face with his hands. Blood dripped down his fingers. Free of his grip, Carla jumped to her feet and flew out of the bedroom running as fast as she could down the stairs. At the landing, she stopped, hit the panic button and ran out the front door.

She ran to the bookstore, but when she got there, she remembered she'd thrown her keys on the bed with the mail. In a panic, she broke the back door glass with a rock, and ran to the alarm keypad. She hesitated for a second, wondering if she should just let the alarm go off, but she was afraid the loud noise would draw Doss' attention, so she punched in the off code.

At her desk, she searched the video security monitors to see if Doss was still in her house. Her body shuddered when she saw his image on the screen. He was in the kitchen rummaging through her drawers. His face was bleeding where her fingernails had sliced the skin around his eyes. "Where are the police?" she screamed. She listened on the monitor for the alarm, but it wasn't sounding. "Oh, God! He must have disconnected it!" She checked the rest of the house in the monitors and saw the wrath of his destruction. He had trashed every room, smashing pictures and breaking her beautiful furniture into small pieces.

She watched him shatter her dishes and glasses on the kitchen floor. Then he stopped suddenly and turned toward the back kitchen cabinet. She turned up the volume on the monitor and listened carefully. The phone in the kitchen rang once, then the fax machine turned on and began to click and buzz. Someone was sending a fax to her home and this confused her, because she'd only connected the machine to that line three days earlier and hadn't had a chance to tell anyone. The fax began to print and Doss moved closer and stared down at the machine.

Having that specific line ring as she watched Doss move around inside her house was an eerie reminder of how foolish she had been to use her real name for that phone line. She had two other lines in the house, but that was the only line registered to Carla Cecil. She had no idea who could be sending her the fax, but in horror, she watched Doss pull the paper out of the tray, hold it up to his eyes and read it. He crumpled the fax in his hand and slammed his fists down on the counter yelling obscenities at the top of his lungs. She had no idea why, but the fax had infuriated him, sending him into a violent frenzy. He lifted the fax machine and smashed it on the floor.

He moved to the dining room and pushed over her antique hutch, shattering her crystal and china into pieces. He walked to the table, lifted a chair and smashed it against the wall. At the edge of the table, he shoved a stack of colored paper that was sitting there onto the floor. She picked up the phone and dialed 911, but put down the receiver when she saw Doss suddenly stop and pick up one of the sheets from the floor. Carla panicked when she realized what was in his hand. It was the new flyer for her bookstore.

In the security monitor, Carla could see his bloody face clearly. He was staring at the flyer and smiling. She froze as chills raced through her body. Suddenly, she was 13 years old again and Doss was standing over her smiling with that same horrible smile. In the security monitor, she watched him step over the stack of flyers on the floor and walk out the front door. He knew where she was and he was coming for her.

Terrified, she jerked open the desk drawer and frantically searched until she found her spare car keys. Pulling open the bottom drawer, she grabbed a red canvas bank bag full of petty cash, then scooped up her laptop computer off the top of her desk and ran out the back door to her car. Driving as fast as she could, she flew down the mountain pass to the freeway entrance, turned right and floored the accelerator heading south.

GUS HAD BEEN TRYING to reach Carla all night and was trying not to jump to conclusions, but when she didn't answer at the bookstore at 9 a.m., he knew something was wrong. Carla was never late opening the store. In the few months she'd owned it, she'd built a booming business selling fresh gourmet coffee, bagels and homemade muffins to the locals. He tried her cell, but it didn't ring, instantly switching to her voice mail.

He lifted the receiver to his desk phone and started to dial, but dropped it back into the cradle, having second thoughts about calling the Manitou Springs Police Department. What if he was just overreacting? What if Carla had met someone and had just taken a few days off to go skiing? After all, she was a beautiful woman, no longer hidden away in that mountain cabin. She was out in the open, in full view of anyone who might pass by her store. It only made sense that she'd meet someone someday. What kind of fool would she think he was, if he called the police and they tracked her down out on a date? She'd never talk to him again. What right did he have to monitor her personal life?

Two hours later, he called her house again, but there was still no answer. He dialed the bookstore expecting the same results, but on the second ring, a man answered. "May I speak to Car..." he caught himself, "Ah... may I speak to Leigh Brooks."

"May I ask who's calling?" the man asked.

"This is Gus Walters. Is she there?"

"Mr. Walters, may I ask your relationship with Miss Brooks?"

Gus was surprised by the question. "Well, I can't see how that's any of your business, but I'm a close friend of hers. May I speak to her, please?"

"Mr. Walters, this is Officer Phillips with the Manitou Springs Police Department. I asked the question because we're trying to find some way to contact her family. I was hoping that perhaps you were a family member or a relative."

"Oh my God!" Gus yelled. "What's happened?"

"I'm sorry, Mr. Walters, but since you're not a relative, I don't have the authority to give out any details."

"Officer Phillips, I'm also a policeman. I'm a detective with the Houston Police Department. You can call and check that out. I understand your situation, but you need to know that Leigh doesn't have any family. I'm the closest thing she has to that. I'm one of her best friends and I know she'd want you to tell me what's going on. Please, tell me... is she alright?"

"Well, I guess since you're a police officer...." Officer Phillips paused.

"Please, cop to cop, tell me what's happened. I'm going nuts here. Is she all right or not?" Gus pleaded.

"Well, we don't know what's happened to Miss Brooks, she's nowhere to be found, but someone broke into her bookstore last night and tore the place all to hell."

"What about her house? Have you checked there?"

"We sent an officer over there, but no one answered the bell. That's why we were trying to locate a relative. We need permission to go inside to look around."

"I'm giving you permission to do that now. I'll take full responsibility. Please call me here at my office once you're inside."

Gus hung up then immediately dialed the number for Judge Doss' clerk. He was mortified when the clerk told him that the judge had gone out of town due to a family emergency. Carla's beautiful face flashed in his mind and trepidation overtook him. He knew the judge had found her.

His desk phone rang. "Detective Walters, we're in the house and it's in worse shape than the bookstore. Someone has really ripped this place up."

"Did you find Carla?"

"Excuse me?"

"I'm sorry, I meant Leigh. Did you find Leigh?"

"No sir, there's no signs of her here, but we have found what looks like blood droplets. It's not much, doesn't look like anyone was mortally wounded, but it's definitely blood. Most of it's upstairs in the bedroom, then a few spots here and there scattered through the rest of the house. The bedroom also shows signs of a struggle. Looks like who ever did this, must have attacked her there first. Officer Walters, is there anything you can help us with here? Did Miss Brooks have someone after her?"

Gus thought for a moment considering if he should tell him about Doss. Deciding against it, he said, "No, not that I know of. Is her car there?"

"No sir, there's no sign of that either."

"What about forensics? Do you guys have good people there?"

"To be honest, not really. We have a small force here and normally it's a sleepy little town, we don't have much call for a forensics expert around here."

"Don't touch anything else. I'll make a few calls and see if I can get someone down there from the Denver CSI unit. What you've described to me doesn't sound like a clean crime scene. I have a feeling that whoever did this left a lot of trace evidence behind."

Gus spent almost an hour arguing on the phone, trying to get someone from the Denver CSI unit to sweep Carla's house, but because Manitou Springs was an incorporated independent city, they couldn't touch it without a formal request from the Manitou Springs Police Chief. To do this, the Chief would have to admit that his force wasn't equipped to do the job and Gus was confident that wasn't going to happen. Gus got the same response from the Colorado Springs unit. Frustrated, he called the Chief of Police for Manitou Springs anyway, and as he expected, he rejected the need to bring in outside help. The Chief assured him his force could handle the investigation and he was confident that the blood samples had been collected correctly. He promised Gus that every inch of Leigh's house and bookstore would be dusted for prints and he would forward the results to him in Houston. It wasn't what Gus wanted, but it would have to do.

Instinctively, Gus ran to his car and started driving toward the airport. All he could think to do was to get to Colorado and start searching for Carla. On a whim, he pulled out his cell phone and punched in Carla's cell number. It didn't instantly go to her voice mail as he expected, instead it rang in his ear. His heart beat faster with each ring. On the fourth ring, she answered.

"Carla! Thank God!" he yelled. "Are you all right?" He could hear her crying. "Carla! Answer me. Are you OK?"

"He found me," she cried into the phone.

"I know. Where are you? Talk to me!"

"I don't know where I am," she whimpered.

"I hear noises," Gus said. "Are you driving?"

"Yes."

"Is Doss with you?"

"No, I got away," she began to wail in his ear. "It was horrible."

"Carla, listen to me. You've got to get control of yourself. What road are you driving on? Look for a sign."

"I think I'm in Texas," she said.

"Where in Texas? Tell me what the signs say around you."

"There are no signs. Wait, I see one. It says Interstate 28."

"Ok, great. Now tell me what direction you're driving. East or west?"

"I guess I'm going south. The sun is on my left."

Gus pulled over to the shoulder and grabbed his road atlas from the car pocket. "I'm looking at a map and Interstate 28 runs through Amarillo to Lubbock. Do you see any other signs?"

"Hold on, I think I see one coming up. Yes, it says Canyon 14."

"Ok, I see where you are. Now listen to me. Are you listening?"

"Yes," she said softly.

"Do you have any cash with you?"

"Yes, a little. I have my petty cash sack."

"Great. Now listen carefully. When you get to Canyon, I want you to find a motel and rent a room. Pay for it in cash, but don't use your name, come up with some fictitious name. Do not use Leigh Brooks or Carla Cecil. Do you understand?"

"Yes," she sounded like she was in a daze.

"Carla, are you paying attention? Did you hear what I just said?"

"Yes."

"Repeat it back to me." She repeated it.

"I want you to call me on this number the second you get into the motel room. Do you understand?"

"Yes, I understand."

"Good. Now I want you to do one last thing for me. Promise me that when you get into the room you will not leave until I get there. I'll be there soon. Remember don't leave the room and don't answer the door for anyone."

"Ok, I promise," she said, sounding like a little girl on the other end of the phone. She was in a slight state of shock, but at least she was alive.

It took him almost four hours to fly to Amarillo, rent a car and drive to Canyon. He called her room as he was driving into the motel parking lot. When Carla saw Gus pull up in front of her room, she opened the door and ran to him. He picked her up in his arms, carried her back in the room and locked the door behind them. She tried to talk, but he stopped her. He ordered pizza and forced her to eat something. Then he held her in his arms until she fell asleep.

The next morning when she woke up, she seemed better. He watched her at breakfast and she appeared to be in control, with no signs of shock. Her hands weren't shaking and her voice was steady and calm. When they finished eating, he let her tell him what had happened.

"I know it was stupid," she said, "but I was just so tired of running from him, as if *I* was the criminal. You don't know how horrible it is to always be looking over your shoulder..." She lifted her head and looked him in the eyes. "He's never going to stop, is he?"

"No, I don't think he will, but maybe we can stop him. He really screwed up this time."

"What are you talking about?"

"He left his blood in your house and we should have him on video. You did hit the panic button didn't you?"

Carla lifted her eyes. "Yes, but it didn't work. I think he must have disconnected it somehow. The alarm didn't go off and the police never showed up."

"Don't worry about it," he said reaching for her hands. "We still have his blood and prints in the house," Gus lifted her index finger and gently scraped under her nail, "And this."

"What's that?"

"I'm betting it's Doss' skin. We can get his DNA from this and place him at the scene."

Carla looked down at the scraping. "What good is that going to do, it's still his word against mine."

"Yeah, but he won't be able to deny that he was in your house.

That's at least breaking and entering. It's not murder or rape, but it might be the first crack in his foundation."

"Gus, that's not enough... not for the honorable Judge Bradford Doss and you know it. He's too powerful and has too many friends. They'll never lock him up for that. He'll find a way out. I wouldn't doubt he'd accuse me of assaulting him. No, this is not enough. Gus, he's killed three people that we know of and there's no telling what else he's done. There's got to be more, something that will put him away forever."

"Carla, I've been trying to catch him for six years."

"I know, but there has to be something we can do. I can't hide for the rest of my life."

Because Doss had discovered Carla's new identity and had the connections to trace her car, they left it in the motel parking lot in Canyon, then drove Gus's rental back to Amarillo and caught the next flight to Austin, where Clyde now lived. To protect her money, she had to move fast and to do that she needed Clyde's computer system. Working out of Clyde's home office, Gus watched in awe at the speed she moved her money in and out of several private offshore accounts. Occasionally, she would look up at him and smile, and then return her full attention back to the computer screen.

In less than six hours, she had liquidated all of her stock holdings and had transferred the money in and out of five different coded offshore accounts leaving behind no possibility of an identity trace with each transfer. She explained to him later that she'd set up the five offshore accounts years before for just this possibility. She was brilliant, and the more he watched, the more hopelessly in love he fell.

"What did you say?" She asked glancing up from the computer.

"I said I love you." She didn't respond, just returned her gaze to the computer and continued typing.

"Well?" he said frowning at her.

"Gus, I'm sorry, but I can't talk right now."

He was shocked at her response. Dejected, he rose out of his chair and walked out of the room. He was sitting on the back deck when he heard her behind him.

"That wasn't fair," she said.

"What wasn't fair?"

"Hmmm, let me see... I'm running for my life, in the middle of transferring millions of dollars and you tell me something like that... maybe that wasn't fair."

"I'm sorry, I was out of line, just forget I said it."

"Oh, no, you're not getting off that easy." She sat down next to him and took his hand. "Gus, I've dreamed of hearing you say those words my whole life. But right now.... with everything that's happening..."

"Carla, you don't have to explain. My timing was all wrong... I'm sorry."

"Don't be sorry," she leaned over and kissed him. "Give me a little time and then tell me that again."

CLYDE INSISTED that Carla stay at his house until he could come up with another untraceable identity for her. It *was* a safe place for her to hide, so Gus left her in his care and caught the next flight back to Houston. When he walked into the precinct, his captain immediately confronted him.

"Where the fuck have you been?" He was yelling in his face, their noses almost touching.

Gus stepped back, "Ah... helping out a friend," he said.

"Leigh Brooks? Was that your friend in need?"

Gus froze. "How do you know that name?"

"In my office, Walters! Now!" Gus followed him in and closed the door behind them. "I just got off the phone with a very angry judge and he wants your head on a platter."

"Judge Doss?" Gus asked.

"Judge Doss? No, not him, some fucking hick-town judge in Colorado. He presides over some place called Manitou Springs. He tells me that you've been sticking your nose into one of his cases. Is that true?"

"I guess I did sort of push my way in a little," Gus said.

"A little! According to this judge, you insulted the hell out of his chief of police. Did you really call the Denver and Colorado Springs CSI units trying to get them involved with this case? And, did you really ask the fucking *chief of police* of this town if he knew how to dust for fingerprints?"

Gus smiled. "Yeah, I guess I did."

"It's not funny, Walters, wipe that fucking grin off your face. Now... you want to tell me what the hell's going on?"

It was time and Gus knew it. To hell with his career, to hell with the consequences, it was time to talk and expose this murdering, child-molesting bastard. "Captain, I don't really know where to start."

"Why don't you start by telling me why you thought I was talking about Judge Bradford Doss."

Gus took a seat and gathered his thoughts. He reached into his briefcase and pulled out Carla's medical file. "Here, read this. I'll fill you in on the rest when you're done." After he finished reading the file, Gus told his Captain every detail of his case against Doss.

Stone faced, his Captain listened silently, occasionally scribbling notes on the legal pad in front of him. "I left Carla with a friend of mine. She's safe, but still pretty shook up." Gus sat back in his chair and waited for a response.

Still expressionless, his captain stared at him tapping his pen on the desk. "Gus, that's one hell of a story. You know, I've been married now almost thirty-five years. In fact, I have an anniversary coming up next month. I don't suppose you know who the best man at my wedding was."

Gus had no idea where he was going. "No sir, I don't."

"John Colby. We went through the academy together and wound up partners working the streets together. He was a damn good cop and good friend."

"I'm sorry, sir. I had no idea you two were close."

"We weren't just close, Gus, I loved him like a brother. I've fought to keep his case open for almost six years now. And, for the six years we've been looking for him, not one thing, not one shred of evidence has turned up. Now you tell me that you suspect that a state court judge killed him. And this prominent, respected, very powerful state court judge murdered him simply because John just happened to answer a call from a doctor and found out some information he shouldn't have. That's what you want me to believe?"

"I know it sounds far fetched, but it's the truth."

"Detective Walters, it's my job as your captain to tell you that everything you just told me is crap, purely speculation on your part. Not one ounce of solid evidence, just a lot of circumstantial B.S. that would never hold up in court. Ok, so he trashed her house and her business, got in a fight with her and she scratched him. What's that? Nothing! Sounds like a domestic squabble to me. Your girl's right, Doss would turn it around on her, maybe claim she was his mistress who threatened to tell his wife. So, he confronted her, she attacked him and scratched him, which sent him into a rage. All you really have is a possible B&E, but he'd claim she let him in. That leaves a misdemeanor vandalism charge. He'd walk in ten minutes."

Gus was frustrated, he knew he was right, "Yes, but..."

"Wait, let me finish," he said holding up his hand. "That's my official response. Now let me tell you my unofficial opinion. Walters, I've watched you for six years. You're a good detective. You're smart, thorough and don't make mistakes. What I'm about to say to you can't ever leave this office. Are we clear on this?"

"Of course," Gus said.

"Officially I'm telling you to drop your investigation on Judge Bradford Doss. You have zero evidence, absolutely nothing that implicates this man of any crime. So, if you fuck up and this blows up in your face, remember... I warned you. You're on your own, I can't back you up without a hell of a lot more. However, off the record, if this motherfucker had anything to do with John Colby's disappearance... well, Gus, take this sorry sack of shit down hard."

Gus smiled, grabbed his briefcase and stood. "I'm not going to fuck up," he said.

The captain wrote something on the back of a card and handed it to Gus. "My private number. Keep me in the loop and let me know if there's something you need."

Walking back to his desk, Gus felt the weight he'd been carrying on his shoulders disappear, although, nothing had really changed. Doss was still out there and Carla was still in danger, but he now had a powerful ally inside the force. He didn't know how or when, but with the captain in his corner, he knew something was about to break; he could feel it in his bones. Doss was going down.

THE WRONG GUY

CHAPTER NINETEEN

For the next few months, we lived at Michelle's apartment during the week and on *Windsong* in the yacht club on the weekends. Myrtle Beach is not a great sailing area, but we made do with a few trips south to Charleston and a couple of trips to the outer banks of North Carolina. More often, we spent our weekends sailing donuts off the Myrtle Beach coastline.

It was almost impossible to believe, but it had been three years since Michelle had stumbled into Everyting's Cool. We were living proof of the old saying that time flies when you're having fun, because we were. Things were so good between us, we used to kid about our relationship being a real life fairy tale. The only time things weren't perfect, was when her parents would show up.

On their visits, I would hide away on *Windsong* in the marina. Michelle would sneak phone calls to me when she could get away from her mother during one of their many shopping trips. I wouldn't hear from her again until her parents finally went to bed. She would call me from her bedroom whispering like a thief in the night trying her best not to let them hear her talking to me on the phone. I hated the deception and missed her desperately.

My presence wasn't a secret, her parents knew we were seeing each other, but didn't know that we were living together. Her father had made no effort to hide his wretched disapproval of me, so rather than create a family war, we did our best to deceive them. Honestly, I think they knew, but never admitted it to us.

To keep up the ruse, I wasn't allowed to answer our home phone. A few times when I'd forget, I'd hear her father cussing in my ear, slamming down his receiver. The man hated my guts. When I accidentally answered her mother's calls, she would at least say hello, then ask politely to have Michelle call her back.

Over the months, I had gotten to know her brothers and fallen in love with her nieces and nephews. Her brother, Jake, was a great guy and I liked him a lot. He was an attorney with a thriving practice in Williamsburg, Virginia. Every month or so, he would come for a visit and the three of us would have a blast together and close down all the bars in town. He loved to party. Jake was my only ally inside Michelle's family and the only one I thought truly understood what we had between us.

We'd been living together for almost a year when one night our doorbell rang. "Jake, what a surprise," I said. "Come in. You just missed Michelle."

"I know," he said with a serious expression, "I've been waiting across the street. I wanted to talk to you alone."

"Sure, come on in."

"No thanks, I'd rather not."

He was acting strange, almost as if he was angry with me but I had no idea why. "Ok, suit yourself. What's up?"

"Billy, I think you know that I really like you. You're a nice guy and I know that you love Michelle and would do anything in your power to make her happy. That's what I want to talk to you about, making her happy."

I wasn't sure where he was going, but I was getting a bad feeling in my gut. "Jake, this is silly, come in and let's talk about this inside."

"No, Billy, I don't want to do that. It would just make this that much harder. I don't have much time anyway, I've got court in the morning and have to drive back to Virginia as soon as I leave here."

I sighed and shook my shoulders. "Ok, so, what's on your mind?"

"When I was here last weekend, after you'd gone to bed, Michelle and I stayed up and talked. It was the first time I'd had a chance to be alone with her in a while. Billy, you've got to know that Michelle loves you madly. She'd do anything for you, and I mean anything. She wants to marry you for God's sake. Hell, that's all she could talk about. I know you guys have been together for a while, but honestly, it shocked me when she started talking about marrying you. I don't mean to offend you, but I've always thought this was just a fling between you two and eventually, you guys would break up and Michelle would move on with her life. After our talk the other night, I realize that's not what's in Michelle's head and I haven't been able to sleep since. I know you love Michelle and want what's best for her, but you've got to know that marrying *you* isn't it. You're the wrong guy. I know this may be hard for you to hear, but someone has to face the facts and say it out loud. Simply, you're too old for her. If you stay together, you'll be stealing her youth and taking away any chance she may have for a future. Michelle can't see it because she's head over heels in love with you and too young to understand it, but I know you understand. Don't do this to her. Please don't screw up her life... she deserves more than you'll ever be able to give her and I think you know what I'm talking about. All I'm asking you to do is to think about all the things she's going to miss out on if you stay together—like children... You know how much she loves children. Do you really want kids at your age?

"I think you know how Dad feels about you, as well as the rest of the family. They'll never accept you, Billy. If you guys got married, Dad would disown Michelle and the rest of the family would turn their backs on her. I know that sounds harsh, but I know my family and that's the way it would go down. And if that happened, where would Michelle be in twenty years? What if you die? She'd still be young, a widow, alone with nothing and no family to fall back on. There are a million other reasons why you're the wrong guy Billy... the list is a long one. I love my little sister and don't want to see her miss out on anything in her life. Do you? Do you really want her to miss out on her life?"

I'd heard every word he'd said, but I couldn't respond. He had blindsided me with thoughts I had considered early on in our relationship, but had buried somewhere deep in my heart. I had nothing to say in my defense, so I just stood there like a stone.

After several minutes of awkward silence, Jake finally spoke again. "I hate doing this, but I had to tell you how I felt. I hope you don't tell Michelle I was here, she'd be furious and probably never speak to me again. I'll leave it up to you.

"Billy, I like you. Honestly, I do, but I don't like what you're doing to my sister. Michelle worships you, but you are a negative influence in her life. If you love her, truly, truly love her, then prove it and let her go. You know she'll never leave you, so you have to be the strong one. You are the only one that can save her and I'm begging you to do it. You have to convince her somehow that you're the wrong guy."

His swollen eyes were red and his lip was quivering. "I have got to go. I've said all I can say. It's all up to you now. I can only pray that you love Michelle enough to let her have the life that she deserves." He wiped his eyes with his sleeve, turned around and walked away leaving me shell-shocked standing in the doorway.

That night I held Michelle tighter than normal, savoring the feel of her warm skin against my body. Wide-awake, I watched her sleep in my arms with Jake's words echoing through my head, wondering if he was right. Could my love for her really ruin her life? I fought with that question all night long, not wanting it to be true, but unfortunately, the answer was yes.

That night my feelings for Michelle changed from undying love, to guilt, and from that day on, every time she looked into my eyes and told me how much she loved me, the guilt inside me grew like a cancer, destroying any possibility of our relationship surviving.

Every night when Michelle would leave for her show, I would walk along the beach, praying, asking God to help me find a solution, some other way out. Some way to keep Michelle and yet give her a rich full life, but the answer never came.

There was only one thing to do, but how do you leave someone you love with all your heart? How do you just walk away from true love? How do you tell someone who's in love with you to stop loving you? How could I leave Michelle without destroying her in the process? How could I survive the pain of losing her? I had no idea, but she deserved more and somehow I had to do it.

The change had been subtle, but eventually Michelle noticed that something was wrong.

"Billy, are you mad at me? Have I done something wrong?"

"Of course not."

"Do you still love me?"

"Are you serious?"

"Yes, I'm serious. You haven't told me that in a long, long time."

"I'm sorry, baby, of course I love you, I've just had a lot on my mind lately. I guess I've been a little preoccupied.

"Yeah, I've noticed. Do you realize we haven't made love in over a month?"

"Has it been that long?" I knew exactly how long it had been, but every time I touched her, I felt like I was doing something wrong.

"I know I've lost some weight and probably don't look as good as I used to, but..."

"Oh, no honey. That's not it at all. You're beautiful. It's not you, it's me."

"Then what's wrong?"

She had caught me off guard and I hadn't yet found the words to tell her what was going on, but the opportunity was there and she deserved to know what was in my heart. "Michelle, I don't know exactly how to say this, but... maybe it's time for us to move on with our lives."

"WHAT?" she gasped, dropping the glass she was holding. When it hit the tile floor, it shattered and sharp pieces of glass scattered all over the floor. Dropping to her knees, she started picking up the sharp fragments, cutting her fingers in the process. "What do you mean, move on with our lives?" she said not reacting from the blood streaming from her fingers.

"Michelle, my God, you're bleeding!" I pulled her to the sink, ran water over her bloody fingers, then wrapped them with gauze. While I was bandaging her fingers, she stared at me with a look of horror in her eyes. "Don't you love me anymore?" she whimpered, with tears streaming down her face.

Those words ripped out my heart. "Oh, Michelle, that's not it at all. I love you with all my heart, but honey, that's the problem... I'm the wrong guy. You deserve more."

She pulled away from me and ran into the living room, falling face down on the couch. She was crying so hard she began to hyperventilate, gasping for air between her wails. She tried to speak, but nothing came out except the sounds of her gasps. I ran to the couch, pulled her into my arms and made her breathe into a paper bag. Finally, she stopped hyperventilating, but her entire body was shaking violently and she was as white as a ghost. "Please don't leave me, Billy. Please... please don't leave me."

"I'm not going anywhere, baby," I said pulling her close. "Calm down, everything's going to be alright." I'd caved in. I couldn't hurt her anymore. Not then, not that suddenly. Instead, I kissed her forehead and rocked her in my arms until she stopped shaking. Her hysterics had zapped her energy and soon she was out, sound asleep in my arms.

Her reaction had left me numb, and honestly a little scared. I never expected Michelle to have a complete emotional and physical breakdown. I felt horrible for what I'd done to her and had no idea what to do next.

She slept for almost three hours. When she woke, she immediately walked upstairs, took a shower and began getting ready for her show. I stayed downstairs sitting alone in the dark. I didn't hear her come down the stairs.

"If you were the wrong guy, I couldn't possibly love you this much," she said wrapping her arms around me from behind.

"Are you sure about that?" I asked.

"God is not that cruel. He'd never let that happen. Billy, we are meant to be together and you know it."

"Let's talk about this after your show. But before you go, I want to say something. Michelle, you've got to know by now that nothing is more important to me... than you. Whatever happens between us will never change the way I feel about you. My love for you is infinite and absolutely nothing can make that love go away."

When she got home from her show that night, I could tell that she didn't want to talk. She was exhausted and could barely keep her eyes open. She curled up on the couch and I massaged her feet. Before I knew it, she was out. I carried her upstairs, tucked her in, returned to the couch and laid awake under a blanket, alone in the dark. At 3 a.m., I saw her standing on the stairs, rubbing her eyes.

"What are you doing down here?" she said in her little girl voice.

"I couldn't sleep and I didn't want to wake you."

Still half asleep, she stumbled to the couch, pulled back the blanket and laid down next to me. "I don't know what's going on, Billy," she said, "but I know you love me. Whatever is wrong, we can work it out, but right now I need you to hold me." So I did. And for the first time in weeks, it felt right.

For the next few days, Michelle did her best to act like nothing had happened. I didn't have it in me to break her heart again, so I let things go on status quo. The days passed and Michelle seemed happy and content; it was as if I'd never said anything. Finally, on her day off, we went sailing and she brought it up.

"I guess we have some things to talk about," she said.

"Yeah, I guess we do." I said, studying her face for signs of tears or emotion, but she seemed calm and in control.

"I know this is serious, Billy. I've been watching you and I know something is not right between us. You've pulled away from me and I don't know why."

"Michelle, if we talk about this, you've got to promise me that you won't go to pieces on me. You scared the hell out of me the other night."

"Don't worry, I've been thinking about this all week. I've tried to prepare myself for the worst. Just tell me what's wrong."

I took down the sails and let *Windsong* drift with the current. I sat down beside her in the cockpit and held her hands in mine. "Michelle... I love you so much it's almost impossible for me to say the words, because deep down in my heart, I *don't* want to talk about this. It's the last thing on this earth I want, but because I love you so much... I have to."

"Billy, I don't get it. If you love me and I know that you do, and I love you and you know that I do, what could be so terribly wrong?"

"That is the problem, Michelle. We do love each other and it's a real and true love, but honey... I'm the wrong guy for you to be in love with. I'm too old and could never give you what you deserve to have in your life. You'd miss out on so much with me."

"Is that it? That's the horrible problem? You think that you're too old for me? Billy I don't care how old you are. I've never cared about that."

"Michelle, you're only 23 years old. If we got married, you'd be a widow at 40. I just can't do that to you."

"Don't you think I've thought of that before? My God, I thought you knew how I felt about this. Billy, I'd rather have one minute with you than fifty years with someone else. I want to have your children and spend my life with you. I don't care how many years that may be, I just want to spend every one we may have together."

"I know you believe that with all your heart now, but Michelle, it's just not that simple. I'm not sure I want children at my age. Think about it honey, if we started right now, more than likely I'd be 50 before that could happen. I'd be 68 when the kid graduated high school. And what about your parents? You know they'll never accept me. Neither would the rest of your family. Do you really want to live the rest of your life without your family?"

She wiped her eyes and stared down at the ground. "I don't care what my family thinks, this is my life. And I know you'd be a wonderful father. Billy, I can't change how I feel. I'm in love with you. I don't want anybody else. I only want you."

I held her in my arms and wiped her eyes with my hand. "I'd give anything in the world if I could turn back the clock and be young again, but I can't. I've searched for you my whole life and now that I've found you, the last thing I want is to give you up."

"Then don't do it, Billy. Please, don't leave me."

I was the one who lost control that time. I tried to speak but nothing would come out, so I just held her in my arms and cried.

OVER THE NEXT FEW WEEKS, Michelle and I shed a lot of tears trying to come up with a different ending to our fairy tale love story. She fought me every inch of the way, but eventually accepted the unfathomable truth. There *was* no other solution; we had to end it. Although Michelle was willing, I couldn't allow her to sacrifice her life for me. Sadly, we resolved ourselves to accept our reality and started making plans for the difficult road that lay ahead. I packed my things and moved back to *Windsong* at the yacht club. We still spent most of our time together, but it was at least a step toward the inevitable.

The only intelligent thing I'd done during my hit record days was to keep the publishing rights to my music. The annual BMI royalty checks had been my lifesaver, sustaining me financially through the years. The money always appeared in my mailbox in March and I was expecting it to show up any day. I wasn't sure I could actually do it and I hadn't told Michelle, but my plan was to sail away the moment the check arrived. I'd have no more excuses to stay.

Although we both knew that our relationship was over, nothing had really changed between us. She was either with me on *Windsong* or I was at her place every night. We rarely had sex, but we slept in each other's arms every night. We knew it wasn't healthy, but we just couldn't seem to stop. When I would try to leave, she'd beg me to stay and I always gave in.

One weekend Michelle's mother came for a visit and as usual, I was banished to spend the weekend alone. They did their usual shopping routine, but on Saturday night, her mother convinced Michelle to go out to a nightclub with her. Michelle didn't really want to go, but her mother insisted. The next morning, she called me when her mother was in the shower.

"So how was it? Did you have fun?" I asked.

"Yeah. I had fun," her response was forced and seemed strange.

"What's wrong? Are you OK?"

"I need to tell you something."

My heart began to race and my hands shook. I knew what it was before she said it. "So what happened? Did you meet someone?"

"Well... actually I did."

Blood rushed through my body and suddenly I felt light headed. I couldn't answer.

"Please don't be mad, Billy. Isn't that what you wanted me to do?"

It was exactly what I'd been telling her to do. I had no right to be mad, but I was. I was furious, enraged and jealous. I didn't say a word and hung up in her ear. My phone rang three more times, but I didn't answer. I was acting irrational, but I couldn't control myself. I started throwing things all over the saloon. I broke dishes on the floor and smashed her pictures against the walls. I was out of my mind.

Michelle called me all weekend, but I never answered or returned her calls. I was afraid of what I'd say. Honestly, I was too drunk to talk. She finally stopped calling and a week passed before I saw her again.

My royalty check had arrived and *Windsong* was loaded with food and water. I was at the fuel dock when I saw Michelle walking down the ramp toward me.

"Going somewhere?" she asked.

"Yeah, thought I'd head down to Key West. Maybe find a gig there."

"You were just going to leave. Just like that, without telling me?"

"No. I was going to call you first."

"YOU WERE GOING TO CALL ME?" she yelled. "HOW COULD YOU JUST CALL ME, THEN SAIL AWAY?" she covered her face and cried in her hands.

I didn't know what to say, so I just stood there like an idiot watching her.

"Didn't you want to see me again?" her voice was trembling. "How could you just leave me like that?"

"How's what's his name?" I said coldly.

She dropped her hands and looked at me confused. Her face was streaked with mascara. "Who?"

"The new guy. My replacement. You know who I'm talking about."

Her eyes flared with anger, "His name is Thomas. He's a nice guy and he's not your replacement. He's just a friend."

"Well, I hope you and Mr. T will have a wonderful life together." I said as I hung up the diesel hose and stepped on to *Windsong's* deck. "I'll be sure to include a big hello for him in my postcards."

"Billy, why are you acting this way? How can you be so mean to me? I'm only doing what you wanted me to do. I haven't done anything wrong."

She was right. She hadn't done anything wrong. She was only doing what I'd begged her to do for months, but I couldn't handle the reality of it. "I'm sorry, Michelle, I know you're only doing what I told you to do, but I can't deal with it. I have to get out of here. I know I promised you that I'd be here for you and we'd love each other through all of this, but I was wrong. I'm not that strong. I guess I'm just a coward after all."

Michelle stepped onto the deck and stood next to me. "You're not a coward, Billy. You just love me too much. You know I never wanted to hurt you. Nothing's happened between Thomas and me. He's a nice guy, just someone I can talk to. We've only been out a few times, for coffee. I promise that's all there is to it. You're the only one in my heart, Billy. I love you, not Thomas."

She rode with me back to the slip and helped me secure Windsong to the dock. "I'm sorry I'm acting so stupid, but I just can't stand the thought of you being with another man, even if it's only talking, over coffee. It's killing me, Michelle."

"I know honey, and I'm so sorry I've hurt you. I hadn't planned on this happening. He was at the club, asked me to dance and things just sort of progressed from there. So, when he asked me out for coffee, I accepted. That's all there is to it."

"You danced with him? You let him hold you?"

"Please don't do this to yourself, Billy. You know that didn't mean anything to me. He's just a friend. I promise that's all he is."

"I'm sorry for being such a jealous fool. But I can't stand this, Michelle. I have to leave. I can't stay around here and watch you date. That would kill me."

"But I don't want you to go."

"I know you don't, but I have to."

Michelle stared out over the marina for a long time, wiping her tears away with her hand. "Billy, if you leave, promise me that you'll never lose touch with me. I want you to promise me that you'll always be in my life, in some way... forever and ever. Promise me, Billy. Swear to it."

"Michelle, I'll never stop loving you and I promise that I'll be in your life as long as you want me there. You own a piece of my heart and you'll be in there for as long as I live."

"Even if I get married to someone else?"

"Nothing you ever do is going to change the way I feel about you. As far as being in your life after you're married, well, that's sort of up to your new husband, but I promise if you ever need me, I'll be there for you."

My heart shattered, realizing how well I'd done my job. It had taken months, but Michelle was actually dating and considering the possibility of marriage to someone else. What had I done? Hearing her say those words ripped through my body like a knife and drained the life out of me. The thought of Michelle being with someone else was unfathomable, eating me up inside. As much as I didn't want to, it was obvious that the time had come for me to sail away from the woman I loved and try my best to get on with what was left of my miserable life.

She pulled my arms around her and snuggled in my lap. "When were you planning on leaving?"

"Tonight." I said, kissing her on the forehead.

"No, not yet!" she burst into tears. "I'm not ready yet, please don't leave me now. Oh Billy, not tonight."

"Please don't do this, Michelle. God only knows how much I don't want to leave you, but can't you see how this is killing me?"

"I know, Billy and I understand, but please don't leave tonight. I'm begging you. Stay one more night... with me. I need you to hold me and make love to me one last time."

The next morning I backed *Windsong* out of the slip and left my beloved Michelle bawling on the dock behind me. When I hit open water, I headed south, hugging the South Carolina coastline on my way to Key West.

MICHELLE

CHAPTER TWENTY

The bailiff stood before the courtroom. "All rise, the honorable Judge Bradford Doss is now..." he stopped in mid sentence, caught off guard by the sight of the judge. Doss walked past the bailiff, climbed the two steps to his podium and sat down in his chair. His appearance had drawn every eye in the courtroom.

Doss glared down at the bailiff. "You can close your mouth now." The room vibrated with laughter. "I'm only going to say this once people, so listen carefully. I had a slight automobile accident and received some minor cuts around my eyes. It's nothing serious, but I will have to wear these bandages for several days. That's the whole story and I don't want to hear another word about it. For any reporters who may be in this room, this is not the result of cosmetic surgery. I'm warning you, I better not read anything in the morning papers about my new eye job. If I do, there will be serious repercussions. Now, Mr. Bailiff please finish your speech so we can get on with this and start the day."

From the back of the courtroom, Gus's boss, Captain Ralf Williams shook his head and smiled. "Automobile accident my ass," he said to himself. "She almost gouged out your fucking eyes, didn't she, you bastard?"

At 6 p.m., Judge Doss opened the front door of his house and rushed to his bedroom. The cuts around his eyes were driving him crazy, itching and throbbing with pain at the same time. Staring at his reflection in his bathroom mirror, he slowly peeled back the bandages and inspected the cuts; they were red and inflamed. He covered them with antibiotic cream, reapplied a new bandage and swallowed four Tylenol extra strength tablets.

In his study, he settled behind his desk, hit the space bar on his keyboard and waited for the screen to come to life. He typed Carla Cecil/Colorado in the search area and hit the return button. The program he'd written would search all of the public records in the state. He'd try Leigh Ann Brooks next, but didn't expect to find anything new from either search; Carla was too smart for that, by now she was far away with a new identity.

Unconsciously he rubbed his eyes and wrenched in pain. The Tylenol had worked and for a second he'd forgotten about his injuries. The pain triggered the image of Carla's hands rushing toward his face and he flinched at the vision. Suddenly, he was out of breath, his heart pounding in his chest. Leaning back in his chair, he relaxed his body, taking in slow deep breaths. After a few minutes, his heart rate slowed and his breathing returned to normal. It was the drugs again, he thought. He'd put off the prostate surgery as long as he could; it was scheduled to take place in two days. Supposedly, he'd be back on his feet in a few months and as good as new in six, but without testicles and a prostate, how good could that actually be?

The drugs supposedly helped prepare his body for the operation, hopefully slowing the growth of the cancer, but he hated taking them, they sapped his strength. That's what had happened in Colorado. If he'd had his strength, Carla would be dead. She was in his hands, but he just couldn't hold her down. She'd moved like a cat and surprised him by slashing at his eyes. He'd underestimated her two times now, the first time in her father's hospital room, but he would not make that mistake again, next time he'd have a weapon in his hand.

The computer beeped and flashed her Manitou Springs phone number and address on the screen, but it had found nothing new. He sat up and typed *Leigh Ann Brooks/Colorado* and started another search. He opened his desk drawer, pulled out a crumpled piece of paper and smoothed it against his desk with his hand. Holding the page up to the light, he read the fax again and smiled.

"Carla my darling, you're safe for a few months, but as soon as I'm back on my feet, I'll be taking a trip to South Carolina. Perhaps with a bit of persuasion, Billy and Michelle will help me find you."

IT HAD TAKEN Max almost three weeks to sail to Key West. He wasn't in any particular hurry to get there, so he'd stopped a few times along the way. He'd spent almost three days in Ft. Lauderdale, working on his engine and checking out the local nightspots. Along the way, he'd called Michelle a few times, but he was always so messed up afterwards, he'd swear he'd never call her again. But after a few days would pass, he'd give in and dial her number.

Hearing her voice was like picking at a scab on his heart, making it bleed all over again. She always cried and begged him to stay on the phone, but it was too hard to talk to her for very long. He never cried while she was on the line, but more than once, he'd embarrassed himself hanging up, then losing control in public.

When he arrived in Key West, he tied *Windsong's* bowline to a public mooring in the harbor, caught the water taxi to downtown Key West and called Michelle to let her know that he made it. After he hung up, he proceeded to get very drunk, and stayed that way for almost two weeks.

Eventually, he sobered up enough to find a gig, singing three nights a week at Captain Tony's, a place Earnest Hemingway immortalized in one of his books. Legend has it, Hemingway was a regular there and a serious drinking buddy of Captain Tony. It was a dump, but a famous dump and Max liked playing there. The tips were good and nobody seemed to care about his constant state of inebriation.

He hadn't talked to Michelle in over a month when he finally gave in and called. "Are you drunk?" she asked irritated.

"Am I awake?" he joked.

"That's not funny, Billy. I'm worried about you."

"Nothing to worry about here. So, what's up with you and Mr. T these days?"

Michelle took her time answering. "He's fine."

"So, when's the wedding?"

"Billy, I'm not going to talk to you about Thomas. It's none of your business."

"Well, excuse the fuck out of me!" he yelled slamming down the phone.

The next morning he realized what he'd done and tried to call her back to apologize, but she didn't answer. He tried several more times during the day, but she never answered her phone. That night at Captain Tony's he couldn't stop thinking about Michelle. He shouldn't have called her drunk. On his break, he tried her again from a pay phone, but she still didn't answer.

When he walked back inside the bar, a waitress yelled at him. "Billy, somebody wants you on the phone."

He wondered who could be calling him there. Cautiously he lifted the phone to his ear. "Hello?"

"Billy, can I come see you?"

It was Michelle and his heart skipped a beat when he heard her voice. "Michelle? How did you find me here?"

"I called your father. Billy, I need to see you. I'll come down there. We need to talk about something."

"I don't think that's a good idea, Michelle. What good could possibly come of that? I don't think I could handle seeing you."

"But, I've got something to tell you. It's important, Billy."

"Why can't you tell me now?"

"Not over the phone. Not this."

Max knew what it was. Obviously, things had progressed between Michelle and Mr. T. He'd asked her to marry him or at least move in with him. His stomach was in a knot and he was trying to control his anger... she'd moved awfully fast. It had only been two months since he'd left. "I'm sorry, Michelle, but I don't want to see you. Maybe we should just let this go and put some time between us."

"But, Billy, I need to tell you someth..."

"Michelle, whatever it is can't be that important," he interrupted. " I'm sorry, but I don't want to hear about it. Don't you understand? It's over between us. It's time you go on and live your life and let me live mine. I love you, but we both know that nothing you've got to say is going to change a damn thing! I'm sorry, but I have to go. I'm late for my set."

He could hear Michelle crying, but she didn't say a word. "Michelle, I promise I'll call you someday. Maybe in a few months, I don't know exactly when, but someday. I promise."

"I love you, Billy," she whispered then hung up.

He couldn't do the next set, so he faked sick and took the water taxi back to *Windsong*. He felt numb and a little sorry for himself, but he didn't get drunk, he'd lost his taste for alcohol. Sitting alone in the cockpit and painfully sober, he stared up at the moon and tried not to think about Michelle and what he'd just done.

IT HAD BEEN ALMOST three months since he'd talked to Michelle, but he still struggled with the urge to call her almost everyday. He missed her immensely, but wasn't strong enough to hear about her new life with Mr. T., so he fought off the urges.

One night after one of his sets, a stranger walked up and handed him a card. "You ever considered working on a cruise ship?" the man asked.

Max read the card. "You're head of entertainment for Golden Cruise Line?"

"Yes I am and I'd like to offer you a job. I think you'd do great on our ships."

Two weeks later, Max signed a six-month contract with Golden

Cruise Lines, found a good boat yard to look after *Windsong* and caught a flight to San Juan, Puerto Rico. He didn't call Michelle.

Because he needed a passport to board the ship, he had to use his real name, but no one except a few musicians on board recognized him. The lounge he sang in was next to the casino and the passengers seemed to like his music. He was surprised at how small his cabin was, but it was efficient and soon he settled into ship life. Every night after he finished singing, he would go to the back of the ship and watch the huge prop wash streaming behind. It was soothing and therapeutic. He would sit there for hours watching the foamy water streaming away, talking to himself, healing his wounds.

Time on the ship was marked by the number of cruises rather than days and some cruises were seven days long and some were ten, so before he knew it, he'd lost complete track of time and four months had slipped away. Often, he had to look at a calendar to figure out what day of the week it was. It had been almost nine months since he'd seen Michelle and seven since he'd talked to her on the phone. Enough time had passed and he felt he was ready to see her again or at least talk to her. The hours he'd spent on the back of the ship watching the ocean had helped. The agonizing pain in his heart had finally gone away and he could actually think about Michelle without getting emotional. The old saying was true—time had healed his wounds. He knew the scars would always be there, but he wasn't bleeding for her any longer.

He called her number from San Juan, but her phone had been disconnected. He went to an Internet café and tried to send her an e-mail, but her e-mail address was invalid. As a last resort, he bought a post card and mailed it to her. Two weeks later, he got it back stamped *return to sender, address unknown.* His only hope was to call her parents, but when he did, her mother refused to give him her new address or phone number.

Six weeks later, he signed off the ship and flew back to Key West. It had been nine months since he'd heard Michelle's voice. He considered the possibility that she'd gotten married during that time, but that didn't matter to him. He wanted her to be happy. He'd prayed for her happiness every night for the past six months and sincerely hoped she had found it. He wasn't trying to find her to get her back or to mess up her life, he just needed to hear her voice again, to know that she was all right and to tell her that he was fine with everything.

Max could come up with only one possibility. There was only one person who might understand his need to talk to Michelle. Holding his breath, he dialed Jake's number.

"Jake Parker," he said, answering on the first ring.

"Jake, this is Billy Dean. How is Michelle?"

"Billy! Where in the hell have you been?" Jake yelled into the phone. "I've been searching for you for months!"

"I've been working on a cruise ship for the last six months," he said. "Why have you been looking for me? Has something happened to Michelle? Is she all right?"

"Calm down, Billy. She's fine, well sort of."

"What do you mean, sort of? Is she sick? What's wrong with her?"

Jake hesitated, sighing deeply. "Billy, Michelle's gone through hell since you left. We have a lot to talk about. Are you on a pay phone?"

"No, I'm on a cell phone. Keep talking. What the hell's wrong with Michelle?"

"Billy, she's just real messed up and it's all my fault."

"Your fault?" Max asked. "How'd you mess her up?"

"Well, I guess the simple explanation is… I broke you guys up."

"How did she find out it was you? I swear, Jake, I never told her."

"I know you didn't and she doesn't know it was me. Thank God she doesn't, I'm not sure what she'd do if she found that out."

"Jake, you're talking in circles. Why is she so fucked up?" Max said.

"I honestly thought that she'd get over you, meet someone else and move on with her life, but that didn't happen. When you left, she just lost it. She quit her job and wouldn't come out of her apartment. She stopped eating and got down to almost 80 pounds. The only time she would eat anything was when I forced her to. She was in real trouble, Billy. She almost died."

"Is she still that way?" Max asked.

"No, she's eating now and gained back a little weight. There's nothing wrong with her physically, but she's still in trouble."

"What do you mean?" Max asked confused.

"Billy, I've got to tell you something that's going to shock you and I'm not sure how you're going to take it."

"Jake, for god's sake, just tell me."

"I honestly believe that Michelle wanted to die. She stopped eating because she didn't want to live her life without you, but something happened that gave her a reason to live."

"And what was that?" Max asked.

"Billy, there's no easy way for me to tell you this... She started eating again because she found out she was pregnant."

"She's pregnant?" Max said shocked. "Who's the father?"

"She's not pregnant anymore, she had the baby two months ago. It was a girl. Her name is Jessie. As far as the father is concerned, well, she's not sure."

Anger raced through Max's body. "What do you mean she's not sure? How many guys was she fucking?"

"Please, Billy, don't do this. You don't have any idea what your leaving did to her. She wasn't herself and did some very stupid things because of it."

Max took a deep breath and tried to think of something to say, but he was so stunned, his brain couldn't formulate a sentence.

"One night she went out with one of her friends and met a guy in a bar. She didn't even know his name. You know that doesn't sound like Michelle. Yes, she screwed up but it wasn't her fault. She was out of her head, Billy. She's never loved anyone else but you."

"I don't know what to say." Max finally said. "This is a lot to take in."

"Billy, I don't know how you feel about her right now, but I know that you loved her once. I fucked all that up and I'm so sorry. I just wanted her to be happy, but I was an idiot, because she *was* happy and I just couldn't see it. I had no right to do what I did. Please, Billy, you've got to help me fix this. I don't know if you guys can patch things up, I sure hope so, but even if you can't, at least go to her and help her to get on with her life. She's living out in the country, just north of Myrtle Beach. It's just her... and Jessie... out there all alone. I'm begging you, Billy... go to her, help her, she needs you."

Max considered what he'd said and thought about Michelle and her baby. "What about your parents? They'll go nuts if we get back together. I tried to contact her a few months ago, but her mother treated me like I was a stalker or something."

"Don't worry about mom or dad or anyone else in the family, I'll handle them. Just go to her. Please."

THE OLD HOUSE sat in the middle of a twenty-acre plot surrounded by dense woods. Michelle's nearest neighbor was almost a mile away and that was the biggest problem her parents had with the place. They didn't think it was safe for her to be alone out there, especially so soon after her delivery, but there was a hospital only a few miles away if she needed it and after what she'd just gone through, being alone was exactly what she wanted. She liked the idea of not having close neighbors, it was a nice change from living in an apartment with too many nosy neighbors asking questions that were none of their business like, "Are you married?" or, "Who's the father?"

It did take her awhile to get used to the quiet. She actually missed the sounds of the traffic passing beneath her window at night, but that went away the day Jessie was born and she first heard the sounds she made while sleeping. Ever since then, she'd cherished the quiet, peaceful solitude of living alone with her daughter in the country.

Michelle had just laid Jessie down for her afternoon nap when her doorbell rang. She assumed it was her father who, much too often, dropped by unexpectedly. Or, it could be her brother, Jake. She hadn't seen him in a while and that would be a nice surprise.

Standing on her front steps, the honorable Judge Bradford Doss pushed the doorbell for the second time.

MY BILLY

CHAPTER TWENTY-ONE

The Delta commuter jet had been delayed in Atlanta and was almost thirty minutes behind schedule when it finally touched down at the Myrtle Beach International Airport. Max checked his watch in frustration. He grabbed his overhead carry-on and pushed his way through the crowd to the baggage area. While he waited for his luggage, he walked to the Avis counter and filled out the paperwork for his rental car. Fifteen minutes later, he loaded his bags into the trunk and sped out of the parking lot.

He couldn't wait to see Michelle again, although he had no idea what he was going to say when she opened the door. From the moment he boarded the plane in Key West, he'd been trying to come up with something. He'd battled with his emotions the entire way; one minute he was angry at Michelle for making such a stupid mistake and then the next moment, he wondered how it was going to feel to hold little Jessie in his arms. Jessie... He thought about her name. His grandfather's name was Jessie. Is that who she's named after? Probably not, he thought. He wasn't sure he'd ever told Michelle his grandfather's name. His mind was bouncing around like a rubber ball, jumping from one thought to another. He was a nervous wreck. He needed to calm down, but the excitement of looking into Michelle's eyes again and holding her in his arms was building inside him like a furnace. Before he realized it, he was doing 90 miles an hour, flying down the freeway. He let off the accelerator and carefully watched his speed, driving 60 until he saw the sign for Hwy 9.

He took the exit and pulled to the side of the road to check the directions. It was only a few more miles to the turn off that would take him down the road to Michelle's house. It was mid afternoon and the sky was growing angry. He hoped that he could find her house before it started to rain. Jake had told him that once he made the final turn he'd be able to see Michelle's house sitting alone in the field. His heart was in his throat when he made the turn and saw the house setting a few hundred yards off the road, about a mile away.

As he drew close, he saw Michelle's silver Saturn sitting under the carport. Parked a few feet behind it, was a large black SUV and he wondered who it belonged to. When he reached her driveway, he couldn't stop. What if that was her father's SUV, he thought. He wasn't prepared for that kind of confrontation, so he drove past the house a few miles and pulled to the side of the road. He waited there a few minutes then turned around and headed back. He didn't care if it was her father, he'd deal with it. Michelle needed him and nothing was going to stop him from seeing her again.

As he topped the hill, the black SUV was backing out of her drive. Max slowed and watched it speed down the road toward him. As it drew close, he held his hand up to hide his face, glancing at the driver through his fingers. It wasn't her father. It was an older man he'd never seen before, with gray hair and strange piercing eyes.

Turning into Michelle's driveway, he noticed her front door was standing open. He walked slowly to her front steps and knocked on the doorframe. After a few seconds, he yelled through the open doorway, "Michelle? Are you here?"

In the distance, he could hear a baby crying. He yelled again, "Michelle, it's Billy! Hello?"

"Bil...ly," he heard Michelle's voice, but it was just a whisper.

"Michelle?" Where are you?" He took a step into the doorway.

"Help me, Billy," Michelle's voice was faint. He could barely hear her.

He took another step further into the house and saw her lying at the bottom of the stairs. She was covered in blood. He rushed to her, falling to his knees beside her. "Oh my God, Michelle! What's happened?"

"Pull it out... it hurts," She moved her hands and Max saw the bloody handle of a butcher knife sticking out of her chest.

"Oh my God, Michelle!" he wailed, "Oh, baby who did this? Instinctively, he grabbed the knife and began to pull. Michelle screamed. "I can't do it, I'm sorry baby but I can't do it."

"Help me," she whispered.

Max ran to the phone and called 911, "Please help," he cried, "she's dying! Please hurry!"

"Who's dying sir?" the 911 operator asked.

"Michelle! She's been stabbed! For God's sakes hurry!"

"Sir I need you to tell me your location. What's the address sir?"

"I don't know the address. It's out in the country. Off of Highway 9... Barnet Road I think. Yes, Barnet Road that's it... Please help her. Please!"

"We have a unit on the way sir. Is she breathing?"

"I think so. I have to go to her now. Please hurry, please, please."

Max ran back to Michelle and pulled her into his arms, brushing her hair away from her face. "Hold on, baby. You're going to be OK. They're coming. I'm here now, you're going to be fine. Open your eyes, Michelle. Please baby, open your eyes for me!"

Michelle's eyes flickered and opened. "B...i...l...l...y," she whispered.

"I'm right here, baby. You're going to be fine."

"My Bil...ly?"

"Yes, it's me, your Billy and I'll never leave you again."

"I... lo...ve... you." He could barely hear her. "Al... ways... lo... ved... Bil...ly," her eyes closed.

"NO!" he yelled. "Wake up, Michelle! Open your eyes. Please, honey, hold on just a little longer."

"Sing… ro…ses." She coughed blood.

"Please God!" he begged. "Don't let her die. Pleeeeease God! Not now… please." Max pulled her close and kissed her face. "Don't die, baby, please don't die!"

Michelle opened her eyes, "Don't… cry… Bil…ly."

"Oh, baby, I'm sorry. I'm just so scared. Please don't go away. Hold on, please don't die!"

She lifted her hand and touched his face. "Doss," she whispered. "Sing… ro…ses."

"Doss? From the Ouija board? He did this?"

"Yesss," she wheezed. She lifted her eyelids slowly and searched for his eyes, "Jes… sie."

"I know about Jessie. Please don't worry, you know I'll love her too." Michelle's lips curled faintly, then she slowly exhaled. Max felt her breath on his cheek as her head fell gently against his chest. Her hand dropped and her body went limp in his arms. Her eyes were open, but they were empty gazing up at him. Max knew she was gone.

"NOOOOOOOOO! GOD, NOOOOOOOOOOOOOO!" he wailed over her body. "PLEEEEEASE! OH, GOD NO! NOT NOW! PLEASE GOD PLEASE!"

Suddenly, everything was still and quiet, the only sound was his breathing. Max stared into Michelle's vacant eyes for a long time, then pulled her close and caressed her in his arms. In the distance, he could hear a siren gradually growing louder. Gently, he lifted her head and brushed the hair from her face. With his finger, he closed her eyelids, then gently pressed his lips to hers and kissed her goodbye.

When the EMS team arrived, they found Max lying on the floor holding Michelle in his arms drenched in her blood. They pulled him out of the way, laid Michelle on her back and checked for a heartbeat. They tried to resuscitate her for twenty minutes, injecting her heart with adrenalin and shocking her chest with quick jolts of electricity, but she'd lost too much blood. The medical examiner pronounced her dead at 5:05 pm. After taking several photographs of her, they loaded her onto a gurney, covered her face with a blanket and rolled her away.

Standing silently, only a few feet away, Max had watched it all. He hadn't noticed the policeman standing behind him until he spoke. "Can you tell me what happened here?"

Max turned and tried to focus on his face, "I didn't tell her I loved her. It… happened so fast. I forgot to say it."

"What's your name, sir?" the officer asked.

Max looked past him through the open door watching Michelle's body being loaded into the ambulance.

"Your name, sir. I need to know your name. Do you have any identification on you?"

Like a zombie, Max lifted his hands and stared at Michelle's blood dripping from his fingers. "What have I done?" he whispered as he fell to his knees.

∿

THREE DAYS LATER, Michelle's parents took her body back to Virginia and laid her to rest. After the funeral, her entire family gathered at her parents' home to talk and grieve together. They passed around pictures of her, watched old videos of her ballet recitals and relived their memories of her. It was a tearful family reunion.

Eventually the mood in the room evolved from remorse for Michelle's tragic death to anger and hatred for the man who had murdered her.

"I want to be there when they give him the gas," Frank Parker said.

Jake looked at his father, "Come on, Dad, you don't need to be thinking like that. We don't really know what happened to Michelle."

Frank jumped to his feet, "The hell we don't!" he yelled. "That murdering bastard tracked her down and killed her!" Overcome with emotion, he broke down, "He stabbed my baby girl to death and I want to see him die!"

Jake stood and put his arm around his father. "Dad, I know you never liked him, but just because they arrested him doesn't mean he's guilty. You're hurting, Dad, and you're lashing out, but just think for a second," he said, "Billy loved Michelle. Why would he kill her? It doesn't make sense."

Frank jerked away from Jake, pushing his arm off his shoulder. "Why are you taking up for that son-of-a-bitch?"

Jake glanced around the room. Everyone was staring at him startled, all wondering the same thing. He sat down in a chair and dropped his head. "I've been waiting for the right time to tell you this. Billy didn't track Michelle down, I sent him there," he said staring at the floor.

"You sent him there!" his mother said. "What are you saying?"

"Mom, she was miserable!" he yelled. "And we all knew why, but none of us would dare admit it. I couldn't stand seeing her that way, so sad and lonely. So, I begged Billy to go to her and that's why he was there. He wasn't there to kill her, he was there to save her."

His mother's face was flushed and her eyes were full of tears. "But he was the only one there… his finger prints were everywhere… the knife and all the blood…"

"I know what it looks like," Jake said, "but there had to be someone else."

"He confessed, Jake. Have you forgotten that?" asked his father.

"Dad, I talked to the DA down there and even he's not convinced it was a confession. All Billy said was, 'what have I done?' That's not a confession."

"Sure as hell sounds like one to me," his brother said.

Jake stood and faced his brother. "I know you're devastated by Michelle's death, so am I, but can't you at least admit that none of this makes any sense. Don't you want to know the truth? Maybe Billy did kill Michelle, I don't know, but I can't just stand by and accept what the police are telling me." Jake walked to the bassinet in the corner, picked up Jessie and cradled her in his arms. "I don't care what any of you think. This little girl deserves to know what happened to her mother and I'm going to find out the truth… for her sake *and* for Michelle."

THE INTERVIEW ROOM was smaller than Jake had envisioned. He took a seat at the table in the center of the room and waited. Five minutes later the door opened and he watched the guards lead Max through the door. He was dressed in a bright orange jump suit. His hands were secured behind him with handcuffs that were connected to ankle chains that clanked loudly as he shuffled into the room.

"Are those really necessary?" Jake asked pointing to the shackles.

"Standard procedure," the guard barked.

"Take them off," Jake said.

The two guards looked at each other, "I'm not sure that's a good idea, sir, he's a murderer..."

"*Accused* murderer," Jake interrupted firmly. "Please take off his shackles and leave us alone."

The guards reluctantly unlocked the shackles and shoved Max down into the chair. "We'll be outside," he said, giving Max a hard look. "Just yell if you need us."

Max avoided Jake's eyes and stared down at the table. "I'm so sorry," he said softly.

"Billy, tell me what happened?"

Max lifted his head and stared at Jake. "Don't call me that. She called me Billy. I can't stand to hear that name."

"Ok, then, Max, tell me what happened."

"Don't you read the papers?" Max said turning away. "I tracked her down and, in a jealous rage, stabbed your sister to death."

"Yeah, I've read all of that and I've seen the police report, but that's not what happened and we both know it. Come on, Max, tell me what the fuck really happened in that house!"

Max looked in his eyes, "No one is going to believe what happened. Jake, I appreciate you coming here, but you're wasting your time. Go back to Virginia and get on with your life. I'm a dead man."

Jake wrinkled his brow and shook his head. "You're talking in circles, buddy, not making sense. Why wouldn't anyone believe what happened?"

"Because what happened is not possible."

"Max, you've lost me. What are you talking about? How can it not be possible, Michelle's dead and someone killed her and I know it wasn't you. Who did it, Max. I think you know."

"That's the whole problem, Jake. I do know who killed Michelle, but no one's going to believe *how* I know."

"Try me," Jake said. "I'll believe it."

Max ran his hands through his hair and leaned back in his chair. "You ever play with a Ouija board, Jake?"

"Yeah, sure. Why?" Jake asked confused.

"Do you believe they work? Did you actually believe you were talking to someone on the other side?"

Jake thought a moment before he answered. "Well, honestly it was weird, but no, I didn't actually believe I was talking to someone on the other side."

Max sighed and stared back at Jake. "I rest my case counselor."

That evening, Jake ate his dinner alone in his hotel room going over his notes. He'd angered Max at the jail making him retell the Ouija board story repeatedly, grilling him like he was a hostile witness on the stand. He had used all of his skills and every trick in the book trying to trip him up, but Max never faltered. He had no doubt that Max was telling him the truth about the Ouija board. Jake didn't know whether it really happened or not, but he was convinced Max believed that it did. Max was sure this Doss character had somehow discovered the facsimile they had sent to a Carla Cecil and because of that fax, he'd killed Michelle. That's why Max had said, "what have I done" to the cop. It wasn't a confession… it was his regret at sending the fax.

Jake closed his note pad and rubbed his eyes. Max was innocent and he knew it… but a Ouija board? How could he convince a jury with no plausible defense? He was out of ideas and unless he thought of something soon, Max *was* a dead man.

THE FAX

CHAPTER TWENTY-TWO

C aptain Williams reread the e-mail for the third time, and then hit the print button. When it finished printing, he took out the paper and read it again. It was just too much of a coincidence to ignore.

Holding the e-mail in his hand, Captain Williams dialed Gus's number. "We need to talk."

"I'll be right there," Gus said.

"No, not here. Meet me at O'Malley's in thirty minutes."

O'Malley's was a local watering spot and usually was packed with off duty HPD cops, but it was only 2 p.m. and the place was empty. Gus found a booth and ordered a coke while he waited. The captain arrived a few minutes later and sat down across from him. When the waiter took his order and walked away, he reached into his pocket and took out a piece of paper.

"Ever so often," Captain Williams began, "I get funny e-mails from other cops I've met around the country at conventions or seminars I've attended. We send each other police jokes, stupid criminal stories, crap like that. There's a top ten list for the most outlandish alibis. Some of the stories are damn funny, but I didn't find this one funny." He shoved the paper across the table.

Gus read it. "This was in an e-mail? Where did it come from?"

"I don't know, it was a referral, a group mailing. I'm not sure where it originated. I thought maybe your computer guy could track it down. What do you think?"

"I think it's bizarre," Gus stared at the page. "Some guy says he sent a fax to a Carla Cecil and claims that a man named Doss killed his girlfriend because of it. And, a Ouija board told him to send the fax? I don't know what to think, but he sure has the names right. It's weird, but we've got to at least check it out."

Two days later, Gus called Captain Williams on his private phone. "The e-mail came from Myrtle Beach, South Carolina. A guy named Max Allen has been arrested there for murdering his girlfriend. Apparently, he told the Ouija board story to his attorney."

"Did you say Max Allen? The country star?"

"I don't know, I hadn't considered that. I'll let you know when I get there."

MAX HOBBLED THROUGH THE DOOR, took a seat behind the glass and lifted the phone off its cradle. "Who are you?"

"My name is Detective Gus Walters. I'm a homicide detective with the Houston Police Department."

"Sorry detective, looks like you've wasted a trip, I haven't been in Houston in years."

Gus smiled. "So, are you *the* Max Allen?"

Max shook his head. "I used to be. You come all this way for an autograph?"

"No, I'm here because of a rumor, something you supposedly told your lawyer about Carla Cecil and Bradford Doss. Do you know those names?"

Max was stunned. "A rumor?" he said staring at Gus. "You heard a rumor in Houston about something I said to my lawyer... here in Myrtle Beach? That's one hell of a rumor."

"Yes, it is, but you didn't answer me, do you know those names?" Gus asked again.

"What difference does it make? Why do you need to know?"

"Max, I'm sorry, but I can't tell you why I need to know this. All I *can* say... is that it's important."

Max shifted in his chair and thought for a second. How could a Houston cop know about this? "I know this is probably a stupid question to ask a cop, but do you think I need to talk to my attorney before I answer you? Could this incriminate me in some way?"

"Look, Max, you don't know me from Adam and I understand your hesitation to talk to a cop considering your current circumstances, but I promise you I'm not here to trick you. I'm here because someone I love is in danger and I'm trying my best to protect her. That's it."

Max looked Gus in the eyes. "Doss is the danger, right?"

"That's right. Max, how do you know Bradford Doss?"

"I don't know him, but I know he killed Michelle."

"How do you know that?" Gus asked.

Max wiped his eyes and looked away. "She told me, before she died."

TAKING Max's case had driven a wedge between Jake and his family. His father hadn't talked to him in weeks and his mother just cried when he called. It had also created havoc within his law firm. His partners were threatening to kick him out of the firm. No one understood why he was defending the man who was accused of killing his own sister.

He was gambling his life and his career on an impossible case; the evidence against Max was overwhelming... the fingerprints, the blood and then there was his statement to the policeman, "What have I done?" It wasn't a confession, but how could he make a jury understand what Max was talking about? Tell them the Ouija board story? They'd laugh him out of the courtroom. Max's only chance was to plea temporary insanity, but Jake knew he'd never go for it. Even to save himself, he'd never admit to killing Michelle.

Jake jumped at the knock on his hotel door. When he opened it, Gus flashed him his badge and introduced himself.

"What can I do for you detective?"

"May I come in?" Gus asked. "I've got some information I'd like to share with you I think you'll find interesting."

Jake waved him inside and Gus took a seat by the window. "I just left your client, Max Allen and he told me his Ouija board story. To say the least... it's hard to believe."

"Detective Walters, I don't mean to be presumptuous, but aren't you a bit out of your jurisdiction? May I ask your interest in my client?"

"My interest in Max has to do with two people, Carla Cecil and Bradford Doss. I came here because, apparently, someone was listening in on your conversation when Max told you about the Ouija board. That story wound up on the Internet. That's how I discovered it."

"Fucking cops!" Jake yelled. "Sorry, no offense, but that was supposed to be a private meeting between my client and me! You say it's on the Internet?"

"No offense taken, I understand. And yes, my captain got it in an e-mail. It was a group mailing; his screen name was included with 23 other addresses. I think I need to tell you that Bradford Doss is a Texas state court judge and if he gets wind of this, you've got trouble."

"Detective, there's got to be more than one Bradford Doss in the world. What makes you think Max was talking about this particular judge?"

Gus leaned back in the chair and crossed his legs. "There are two reasons, but I'm not comfortable revealing much of this to you. In fact, my investigation has been undercover up to this point and I don't have to tell you how much power a state court judge wields and..."

"Detective Walters," Jake interrupted, holding up his hand. "Do you have a dollar bill on you?"

"Yes, I think so. Why?"

"Give it to me." Gus pulled a bill out of his wallet and handed it to Jake. "I'm accepting this dollar as my fee for legal advice. I am now your attorney. From this point on, everything you tell me is privileged and cannot be repeated even to a state court judge. Now let's stop beating around the bush. Tell me what you've got on this judge and how it connects to Max."

Gus smiled. "Pretty slick. Ok, if you're my attorney, can we bypass the formalities? Call me Gus."

"Deal. Call me Jake. Now tell me the two reasons you think Max is talking about *this* Bradford Doss."

"Well, the obvious one is the mention of Carla Cecil, but the real hook is where Max claims he sent the fax–Manitou Springs, Colorado."

"And why is that so important?"

"Carla Cecil has been hiding from Judge Doss for seven years. The only mistake she made during that time was to register a phone line in her name. It was in her house in Manitou Springs and the only line connected to a fax machine. Two weeks ago, Bradford Doss tracked her down by that number and attacked her in her house. She was lucky to have gotten away. Max sent a fax to a Carla Cecil in Manitou Springs warning her about a Bradford Doss. How could it be anyone else?"

"I see your point," Jake wrote a note on his yellow pad. "You said that Carla was hiding from Doss. Why was she hiding?"

"Because seven years ago, he drugged and raped her repeatedly. I know he did it, but I can't prove it. Jake, she was only thirteen years old. He also killed her father, the doctors and a policeman who knew about it."

Jake stopped writing and looked at Gus. "And now Michelle," he said softly. "Do you really think he came all this way to kill my sister because of this fax?"

"I'm sorry, Jake, I hadn't put that together. I didn't realize that Michelle Parker was your sister."

"Don't worry about it. It wouldn't be a natural assumption, me representing her accused killer, but yes, she was my baby sister. All the more reason I need to know everything you've got on Doss. He may be the only hope Max has of avoiding the death penalty."

For the next few hours, Gus filled Jake in on his case against Doss. When he finished, they drove to a quiet restaurant and ordered dinner.

Gus took a bite of his steak then put down his fork. "Jake, you know Max well and I assume he's your friend, so I don't really know how to put this, but is he, well, a nut case?"

Jake laughed. "If you're asking if he can't make a move without checking his horoscope first or holds regular séances, the answer is no. However, this Ouija thing, well, he's convinced it really happened."

"You don't think he could have just concocted the whole thing to cover up some other connection he may have to Carla or Doss."

Jake sipped his beer and shook his head. "I've asked myself that same question, but think about it, Max is charged with a premeditated capital murder. He's facing the death penalty. If he had any other reasonable explanation don't you think he'd tell me? As ridiculous as it sounds, Gus, I think he's telling the truth."

Gus chewed his food and considered the facts. "Ok, let's just go with the Ouija story. So, they find out about Doss on the board and send a fax to Carla. How did they send it? Did Michelle have a fax machine at her house? Did they send it from Kinko's?"

"I don't think Michelle had a fax machine and I've never asked Max that question. Why is that important?"

"I don't know about you, but if we could find evidence of that fax, this whole Ouija board story would be a little easier to stomach and it's a real connection between Michelle and Doss. If he sent the fax like he says, there should be some record of it somewhere. If he didn't, then there's something he's not telling us. If I could track it down, would it help you with his case?"

"At this point, Max doesn't have a case. I don't see how it could help, but maybe it could lead to something else."

"There's one more thing that bothers me about the fax." Gus said.

"What's that?"

"Assuming he sent it and Doss discovered it somehow, why didn't he go after Max? Why just Michelle?"

Jake shook his head. "I can see why you're carrying that gold shield, Detective Walters. I guess I'm just too close to all of this... I've never considered that before. I think we need to visit my client and ask him a few more questions."

BEFORE THEY MET WITH MAX, Jake gave a detailed explanation of the penalty for illegal eavesdropping to the watch commander and insisted on a different interview room. While he talked to Max, Gus checked the adjoining rooms to make sure no one was listening in.

"We used her laptop," Max said.

"Did you erase it after you sent it?" Jake asked.

"Why this sudden interest in the fax? What's up, Jake?"

"It may not be anything, but I need to know more about this fax. Did you erase it or not?"

"No, but Jake, we sent it over a year ago, Michelle could have erased it."

"Max, I need to ask you another question and I don't want you to take it the wrong way. I just need to know what you think."

"Ok, what?"

"If the fax was from both of you, why didn't Doss come after you?"

Max's eyes widened with agonizing comprehension. "God, Jake. I have no idea, but I wish he had. Maybe I'd have killed the fucker or he'd have killed me... maybe Michelle would still be alive."

The next morning, Jake contacted the DA to gain access to Michelle's house and he and Gus drove there to search for her laptop. Although Jake had been to his sister's house many times, as well as being there at the scene, the day Michelle had died, it seemed very different this time. His pulse began to race the second he walked in the door. He felt light headed and his forehead beaded up with perspiration. When he spotted Michelle's bloodstains on the carpet, he broke down.

"Jake, I can handle this by myself, it's what I do. Why don't you take a walk around the place. It looks like Michelle had planted some flowers in the back, I bet they could use a little water."

Gus searched every room of Michelle's house, but there wasn't a laptop or computer set up anywhere. He assumed she'd either stored it away somewhere or worse, gotten rid of it. He finally found it in her bedroom closet, but when he lifted the laptop out of the box, he froze. Lying under the computer was a Ouija board.

They drove back to Jake's hotel room and Gus plugged in the laptop, but it wouldn't boot up. He tried everything, but could not get it to turn on, so he gave up and called Clyde in Austin. "It's an IBM, but it looks like an old one," Gus told Clyde.

"Is it making any noise?" Clyde asked.

"Yes, I think the hard drive is spinning, but for some reason it's not booting up. Clyde, I know this is a lot to ask, but could you come up here and see what you can do? I'm not sure what's in here, but it could be important."

"What about Carla? Want me to bring her too?" Clyde asked.

"I'd feel better if she was with you, so yeah, bring her along. Maybe she'll see something we're overlooking."

Gus and Jake met them at the Myrtle Beach Airport that night and drove back to the hotel. As Clyde worked on the laptop, Jake filled them in on Max's case and told them the Ouija board story.

"I never received a fax," Carla said. "I'd just hooked it up a few days before Doss…" she stopped in mid sentence.

Gus looked over at her. "Carla, are you Ok, honey? You look strange."

Her eyes were open wide. "There was a fax," she said remembering. "Doss was in the kitchen when it came. I watched him read it and then he went crazy. It had to be Max's fax. It had to be!"

"Got it," Clyde said, holding up the laptop.

"The fax," Gus and Jake said in unison.

"Not the fax. The laptop. I got it to work. Give me a second, if it's in here I'll find it."

Carla was still staring forward trying to remember every detail of that night. "He crumpled it in his hand, then put it in his pocket. I can see him doing it. Doss has that fax. What did it say?"

Jake flipped through his notes. "Max just said it was sent to you in Manitou Springs and it was some kind of warning about Doss. That's all I know."

"Would you like me to read it to you?" Clyde said, turning the laptop screen toward them. "Or should we let Carla read it, after all, it's addressed to her." Clyde handed Carla the laptop and she began reading out loud.

"To Carla Cecil, Manitou Springs, Colorado. From Billy Dean and Michelle Parker, Myrtle Beach, South Carolina"

"Wait!" Jake yelled. "It says, Billy Dean?"

Carla looked at the screen. "Yes, Billy Dean and Michelle Parker. Who's Billy Dean?"

"Gus, that's why Doss didn't go after Max. He was looking for Billy."

"Who the hell's Billy?" Gus asked.

"It was Max's stage name. Doss was searching for Billy Dean, not Max Allen, but couldn't find him, because Billy Dean doesn't exist. What else does it say?"

Carla read from the screen again. "We are not sure you are the correct Carla Cecil. Please ignore this letter if this does not pertain to you; however, if you know of an Edward Cecil..." she paused looking up at Gus in shock. "My God, Gus he's talking about my father. How could he have known about my father?"

Gus shook his head. "I don't know, honey. Keep going."

"If you know of an Edward Cecil or know of someone named Bradford Doss please leave your house now. You are in grave danger!" Carla stared at the screen with tears rolling down her cheeks.

"Does it say when it was sent?" Gus asked. "Is there a date and time of the transaction?"

"Let me look," Clyde took the laptop from her hands and scrolled the screen. "Yes," he said. "It was sent February 16th, 2001 at 8:15 p.m."

"Shit!" Gus shouted, "That was the night Doss attacked Carla in her house. What time was it when you saw him read the fax in your kitchen?"

Carla looked at Gus, but didn't answer. Instead, she turned toward Jake. "Did Max tell you who they were communicating with on the Ouija board? Did this spirit give them a name?"

Jake sighed. "Honestly Carla, I was having a real problem with the Ouija board story and didn't take many notes. I'm not sure whom they were supposedly talking to."

"Would it be possible to meet with Max? I've got to know more about this."

"I'm not sure that's a good idea, Carla," Gus said. "I don't like the idea of you being that exposed. Doss is still out there and we don't know how much he knows about all of this. I'm not sure it's safe."

"Nothing is going to happen to me inside a jail," Carla said. "I have to talk to Max, to see if he talked to my father. I have to know."

"Carla, are you a believer in Ouija boards?" Jake asked.

She smiled. "Let's just say, I'm not arrogant enough to deny the possibility and, hopefully, intelligent enough to accept that there are many things beyond my comprehension in this world. I don't know if I believe in Ouija boards or not, but when total strangers learn something about my dead father from one, I can't just ignore it. That's enough for me and it gives me a reason to at least try to believe..."

Jake returned her smile. "Touché," he said. "I guess I have been a bit closed minded about this. I'll set up a meeting with Max in the morning."

PROOF

CHAPTER TWENTY-THREE

efore the meeting took place, Gus called his captain in
Houston to run a check on Doss. Impatiently, he waited by
the phone until Captain Williams called him back a few
minutes later to report that Doss was in session in his courtroom and
was expected to be there all day.

As a further precaution for Carla's safety and the need for absolute
privacy, Jake arranged to have the meeting take place at a local law
firm, rather than the Myrtle Beach Jail. To pull this off, he'd shown the
Internet e-mail to the presiding judge over Max's upcoming trial and
that was all it took. The judge was furious with the breach of
lawyer/client privacy and immediately sent down an order to have
Max escorted to the law firm's office.

Max was led into the room shackled and dressed in a neon orange
jumpsuit. With scowls on their faces, the two Myrtle Beach police
officers removed the shackles from Max's hands and ankles and left
the room. Max rubbed his wrists and took a seat at the table. He
looked thin and tired. He had dark circles under his eyes and seemed
distant.

"How are you doing?" Jake asked.

"Oh, I'm doing great. Never better," he said with weary sarcasm.

Jake glanced around the room and could read the concern for Max on Carla's face. "Max, I'd like you to meet Carla Cecil."

He raised his head and looked across the table at her. He'd noticed her immediately when he'd entered the room and wondered who she was. She was incredibly beautiful. "Is this some kind of sick fucking joke?" he said shocking everyone in the room with his language.

"Max, I know you must be going through hell in there, but everyone you see in this room is here because they want to help you," Jake said. "I'd appreciate it if you'd try to be civil and watch your mouth. This is no joke. This *is* Carla Cecil, the person you sent the fax to. She wanted to meet you and ask you some questions."

Max looked at Carla. "I offer you my apologies Miss Cecil, please excuse my language, but I hope you're not expecting me to say it's nice to meet you, because it's not. In fact, I wish to God I'd never heard of you."

"Ok, that's it, this meeting's over," Gus said jumping to his feet. "I'm not going to sit here and let you talk to her that way. You don't have any idea what she's gone through…"

"It's OK, Gus. Calm down," Carla said. "Max, I know you're hurting and I'm not surprised you feel this way. I feel horrible about Michelle's death, but it wasn't my fault and you know that. For whatever reason, our lives have crossed paths and I think it's imperative that we talk. Don't you?"

"She's right, Max." Jake said. "It's not her fault. I'm hurting over Michelle too, buddy, but I've got to be honest with you Max, you don't have a defense at this point. We've got nothing to help you get out of this. Maybe if you guys talk, something will surface that we've overlooked."

Max shook his head in agreement. "Ok, what do you want to know?"

Carla smiled. "Max, I'd like to talk about the night you and Michelle used this Ouija board," she said setting it on the table.

Max recoiled at the sight of the board. "Where did you get that?"

"Gus found it packed in a box with Michelle's laptop."

"In the same box? She packed her laptop in with her games?"

"It wasn't in a box of games, it was just the computer and this Ouija board." Gus said. "I swear I wasn't looking for it, I was searching for Michelle's laptop and it was packed underneath the computer."

"Max, is this the same Ouija board?"

Max looked at it and shook his head, fighting back his emotions. "I tried to get her to burn it, but she wouldn't do it. I thought she'd packed it away with the rest of her games. It doesn't make any sense that she'd put it with her computer," Max wiped his eyes. "She was always a little anal retentive about that sort of thing. Everything in its place..."

"I'm that way too," Carla said. "I think most women are and that's why I found this so interesting."

Max nodded his head in agreement. "It *is* a little strange. It's not like her."

"Was Michelle psychic or did she have premonitions?" Carla asked.

"No, I don't think so. She never talked about anything like that."

"Can we talk about the Ouija board night?" Carla asked.

"Sure."

"Who did you talk to that night?"

"At first to Edward then we talked to my brother, Dean."

"You actually talked to my father?" Carla asked excited.

"Your father? No, I was talking to your brother, Eddie."

"Eddie? You were talking to little Eddie?" Carla began to cry.

"Yes. He told me about Doss; how he'd kidnapped him and about the wreck."

Carla's entire body began to shake. She was gasping for air. "Oh, God no," she cried, covering her face with her hands. "Not little Eddie too."

"What did I say?" Max pleaded, looking over at Gus.

"She thought the Edward Cecil in your fax was her father. Doss killed him too," Gus said.

"Oh, God," Max turned toward Jake and stared for a long time. "Who is this guy, Jake? And, how the hell do we get him?"

"Max," he heard Carla's voice behind him.

When he turned around, she was standing next to him holding the

Ouija board in her hands. "Max, Bradford Doss has killed five people that we know of, including my father, my brother and now Michelle. When I was thirteen, he drugged and raped me. I've been running from him my whole life and I don't want to do that anymore. We have to stop him, Max. I believe Michelle had a premonition and packed this in a place she knew we'd look. This thing brought us together... maybe it can save us too."

CARLA OPENED the Ouija board and placed it between them on a small table. "What's next?" she asked.

Max guided her fingertips to the triangle and placed his on the other side. "Just barely touch it."

Her hands were trembling. "Ok," she said. "Now what?"

"Ask if anyone is there."

Carla cleared her throat. "Is anyone there?"

They waited a few moments but nothing happened. "Try again," Max said.

She cleared her throat again. "Is anybody there?" She gasped as the triangle began to move under their fingertips. It circled the board one time then stopped on **YES**.

"Is this Edward Cecil?" Max asked.

It moved across the board and stopped on **NO**.

"Is this Dean?" he asked.

NO

"Whom are we talking to?" Carla asked.

It moved to **M** then to **P**

Max took a breath, "Oh, God," he gasped, "Is this Michelle?"

YES

Max jerked his hands away. "I can't do this," he turned and looked at Jake. He had tears in his eyes. "Jake, it's Michelle."

"I know Max," he said calmly. "You can do it."

"Max," Carla said. "She needs to talk to you. I think she's been waiting for you to find the Ouija board."

Max took several deep breaths and placed his fingers back on the triangle. It began to move immediately.

J... E... S... S... I... E

"She fine, honey," Max said.

Y... O... U

"I'm good, too."

N O

"Ok, you're right. I'm not so good. I'm in jail. They think I... I... killed..." Max's tears were dripping on the board.

D... O... S... S

"Yes, we know it was Doss, but we can't prove it."

YES

"You know how to prove it?"

YES

"How?" Carla asked.

S... C... R... A... T... C... H

"I don't understand, honey," Max said.

Gus jumped to his feet. "Wait!" he yelled. "Ask her if she scratched Doss."

"Michelle, did you scratch Doss?" Max asked.

YES

"Jake was there any mention of fingernail scraping in her autopsy report?" Gus asked.

Jake thought for a moment. "No, I don't think there was."

"Are you sure? It's standard forensic procedure, they must have, and there should have been some DNA testing on anything they found."

Jake checked his file again. "There's nothing here about fingernail scrapings and no mention of any DNA tests."

"Jake, it's forensics 101," Gus said. "They wouldn't have overlooked something as important as that. Max you were there. Did the medical examiner bag her hands? Did he put plastic bags over her hands?"

Max thought for moment. "Yes. I remember wondering why he did that."

"Great," Gus said. "If they bagged her hands, I guarantee they took fingernail scrapings and if she scratched Doss, his skin was under there. Jake, I think we need to talk to the DA and find out what happened to those reports."

"Michelle, may I ask you something?" Carla said.

YES

"Is my father or brother there with you?"

NO

The disappointment read in her face. "Do you know anything about them?"

YES

"What do you know?"

T... O... G... E... T... H... E... R

"My father and my brother are together?"

J... U... D... Y

Tears rolled down her face. "They're together with my mother?"

YES

"Are they happy?"

H... A... P... P... Y

Carla was crying and smiling at the same time.

"Michelle," Max said. "Are you happy?"

M... I... S... S...U

Max couldn't hold it back any longer. He pulled his hands off the triangle and sobbed deeply. When he regained control, he put his hands back. "Michelle, I miss you too. I will always love you."

J... E... S... S... I... E

"I love her too," he said.

NO

"You don't want me to love her?" he asked confused

M... O... R... E

"You want me to love her more?"

NO

"I'm sorry, honey, but I don't understand."

J... A... K... E

"You want to talk to Jake?"

YES

Jake took Max's seat and carefully placed his fingers on the triangle. "I'm here, Michelle." His body stiffened when the triangle began to move.

M... A... X... J... E... S... S

"I'm sorry sis," he said, "but I don't understand what you're trying to say."

M... A... X... J... E... S... S... I... E

"You want Jessie to be with Max?"

YES

"You want him to raise her?"

YES

"That might be hard, Michelle. Mom and Dad are talking about adopting her."

NO

"Maybe I can talk them out of it."

YES

"I promise I'll do my best," he said.

M... A... X... J... E... S... S

"I understand," he said and paused a moment. "I love you, Michelle."

L... O... V... E

Jake lost it and moved away from the board. Max set back down, touched the triangle and again it began to move.

D... E... A... N... H... A... P... P... Y

"He's happy?"

YES

"I love you, Michelle," he said crying again.

N... O... C... R... Y

"You know me, honey, I'm just a big baby."

N... O... C... R... Y

"Ok, I promise. I won't cry anymore."

G... U... S

"You want to talk to Gus?"

NO

"I don't understand," he said.

C... O... L... B... Y

Gus was back on his feet. "Does she know where John Colby is?"

O... L... D... W... A... T... E... R

"Old water? John Colby is somewhere called old water?"

YES

"Ok, I think he understands."

M... U... S... T... G... O

"No! Not yet," Max yelled.

L... O... V... E... B... I... L... L... Y

A sharp pain shot through his chest remembering the sound of her voice when she called him Billy. "I love you too, Michelle. Please don't go yet."

The triangle stopped moving. Everyone in the room was crying and no one said a word for almost ten minutes. Finally, Gus spoke. "What do you think she was trying to tell me about John Colby. I've never heard of any place called 'old water'."

Max wiped his face with the sleeve of his orange jumpsuit and tried to pull himself together enough to talk. "Ah... well, it may not actually be called 'old water'. Edward never actually spelled Manitou Springs. He called it red mountains. I figured out he was talking about the Garden of the Gods which is next to Manitou Springs."

"So, 'old water' could be a description of something rather than a name?" Gus asked.

"Yeah, I guess it could be."

"Max," Jake spoke up. "I owe you an apology. Not just for scoffing at your Ouija story, but for not having enough criminal law experience to have noticed something as basic as a missing autopsy report. I thought I was helping you by taking your case, but my inexperience may have ruined everything."

"Jake, don't beat yourself up. I know criminal law is not your specialty, but if it wasn't for you, I'd be stuck with some snot nosed kid straight out of law school working in the public defender's office. I'll take my chances with you any day."

"Speaking of that," Gus said, "I'd like to get Carla safely back to the hotel under Clyde's watch and then we need to talk to the DA about that missing report. I'd be willing to bet he's conveniently misplaced it because the DNA didn't match Max's."

"Why would he do something like that? He knows he can't suppress evidence," Jake said.

"I work closely with the Houston assistant DAs and I have a good handle on how they think. Let's look at it from this guy's point of view. He's a small town DA with big aspirations for his career. Max is famous and this trial will more than likely be the highest profile case of his career. He thinks he has a slam dunk, but when the DNA under Michelle's fingernails comes back and doesn't match Max's DNA, well that sort of muddied up the water a bit. He has a strong case in every other area, so he conveniently misplaces that report. Trust me, he knows that you're a good lawyer, but he also knows that your specialty is not criminal law, so he is gambling that you wouldn't know to ask about the missing report. And if you never asked for it, then he hasn't really suppressed anything has he?"

It took a direct order from the Myrtle Beach judge before the DA's offices, without explanation, located the complete autopsy report and the missing DNA results. As Gus and Jake had expected, the scrapings found under Michelle's fingernails were human skin and it did not match Max's DNA.

Armed with this new evidence, Jake secured a two-week postponement, flew back to Virginia and convinced the five partners in his law firm that Max was innocent. When he returned to Myrtle Beach, a paralegal, two legal secretaries and the firm's best criminal attorney accompanied him.

They rented eight more rooms in Jake's hotel and went to work preparing Max's defense. With Clyde's expertise and Carla's money, they soon had everything they needed, including a state-of-the-art computer system.

"Do we have a match on the DNA?" William Patterson, the criminal attorney asked.

"We ran it through the system," Gus said, "but it didn't match anything in the data base, but that was expected. We know whose DNA it will match, but there's a serious problem with that match."

"And what would that be?" William asked.

"This guy is a Texas state court judge," Jake answered. "Unless it's absolutely necessary, I don't want to involve him with this case at this time."

"A frigging state court judge?" William said. "Wow! The last thing we need is to wake that dragon. However, if it comes down to it, we may have to draw our swords and swing in his direction."

"I understand," Jake said, "but if our defense is to prove reasonable doubt, why would we have to identify the DNA? If we can show proof that the skin of a stranger was found under Michelle's fingernails, wouldn't that convince a jury?"

William shook his head. "The problem is that a jury doesn't really get DNA. It's just a bunch of symbols printed on a blow up card, but if you can show them a face that the DNA matches, then they understand and can accept a reasonable doubt argument."

"Here's the situation, counselor," Gus said. "This isn't the only murder we think he's done. Although, I don't have any solid evidence to prove it, I know this guy is serial with at least 5 murders under his belt. He's also a pedophile rapist. He's bad news, but he's also a powerful judge with an impeccable reputation. Without solid evidence, no judge is going to subpoena his DNA. Until now, he's been brilliant covering his tracks. If he finds out that he's suspected in this murder, and we've got his DNA, I'm afraid he'll just simply disappear into thin air. He's got the financial resources to do that, but that can't happen. Remember, we're talking Texas here. When I take him down, he'll get the needle and that's what he deserves."

William paced the room. "Ok, if we can't expose the real killer, then we have to prove that the DNA found under her nails came from an absolute stranger who had no business being in that house. We'll need DNA samples from anyone who may have come in contact with Michelle; every member of her family, any of her friends, workmen, anyone, even her child," he glanced at his watch. "And people, we've got twelve days to do it."

"Is that possible?" Carla asked. "I thought it took several weeks to get DNA results."

William grinned. "Miss Cecil, I hope you were serious when you offered your financial help with this case, because I'm about to call your bluff. Get out your checkbook young lady, because you're about to donate a substantial research grant to a very lucky DNA lab."

THE TRIAL

CHAPTER TWENTY-FOUR

Doss traced the scratch running down the side of his cheek with his index finger and smiled. It was the first time he'd killed with a knife and he had to admit he enjoyed the feel of her blood on his hands. Although he was wearing gloves, he still felt the warmth under the thin latex on his skin. It was a shame he'd discovered this now... he was sure it would have been an erotic experience for him before his surgeries. His body couldn't respond to physical eroticism any longer, but the memory of Michelle's blood on his skin was strangely stimulating nonetheless. Perhaps he'd discovered something new to hold his interest... it was exhilarating... the blood, the look in her eyes when he stabbed her... it was almost sexual. Although it was a criminal act, that didn't matter to him any longer, the bitch had turned him into a murderer, he'd crossed over the line... and he couldn't wait to do it again.

EVERY NIGHT for the past four weeks, Doss had gone online and searched the Sun News' web site, the largest newspaper in Myrtle Beach for any mention of his name in connection to Michelle's murder trial. She *had* scratched him and he'd left his DNA at the scene, but so far, there had been no mention of it. Of course, he knew why; either they hadn't discovered it, and it wouldn't be the first time important evidence like this was overlooked, or the local DA buried it. Explaining how someone else's skin was found under the victim's fingernails would be a bit difficult. Either way, he was confident they'd never match it to him. The only possible connection to him was the fax locked away in his desk drawer, and Billy Dean.

Billy Dean *was* a serious concern because he was such a mystery. He'd searched for him for over a year, but he didn't seem to exist and that bothered him. As long as Billy Dean didn't show up and expose the fax, he would once again escape disaster. The jury would find Max Allen guilty, the file would be closed and it would be over. Poor dumb bastard, he thought smiling.

When he ran his nightly search, he only got one hit on Michelle's trial. It was a lengthy article about Max Allen's past music career. Doss had no idea that Max Allen had once been a famous country music star. He laughed out loud when he read about his past arrest. Although Max Allen had been acquitted, his former charges would weigh heavy on his current jury's mind, and unfortunately for Max, help seal his fate.

He decided to run a search for Max Allen on the net and was astonished with the number of hits. One by one, he clicked on the sites and read the information. They were all simple homemade web sites with posted letters, most supporting Max Allen in his current situation. Some were hate letters convinced of his guilt, hoping he got the chair.

The last site he checked was slightly different. These posted letters were all about the last time anyone had seen Max perform. One writer claimed to have seen Max singing in a small club in the Caribbean. He insisted it was him, although, he was performing under the name of Billy Dean. It took him a second to comprehend what he'd read. Slowly, he read the letter again. He couldn't believe it, after all this time he'd finally figured it out. This letter solved the mystery of Billy Dean and now he understood why his vigorous search had produced nothing. Billy Dean did not exist; he was only a pseudonym for Max Allen... a stage name.

Doss leaned back in his chair thinking about all the wasted time he'd spent searching for a ghost, but that really didn't matter now, he'd finally found him, however, he was locked up behind bars protected by armed police officers, but somehow he had to get to him. Max Allen, aka Billy Dean, was the only person alive who could connect him to Michelle Parker.

He'd been careless. He hadn't followed his plan of kidnapping Michelle and taking her into the woods; instead, when she scratched him, he lost control. The image of Carla slashing at his eyes flashed in his head and he flew into a rage, grabbed a knife off the kitchen counter and shoved it into her chest as far as it would go. When it was over and his rage subsided, he realized it wasn't Carla he'd stabbed. It was Michelle. It wasn't really his fault. He hadn't planned on killing her. All he wanted was to make her talk, to tell him where Carla was hiding. He had the drugs with him that would force her to tell him the truth. Nothing would have happened to her if she'd just told him what he wanted to know and come along with him like he said, but she was being difficult, fighting him. Then the bitch scratched him. Losing his temper was a stupid mistake, because by killing her and running away, he'd broken two of his cardinal rules–he'd left his DNA at the scene and had a connection that could lead back to him. He had to get to Max Allen to sever this connection. He knew it was going to be a challenge, but he loved a good challenge. Also, the thoughts of having warm blood on his hands again excited him.

He rolled his chair away from his desk and began pacing the room, considering the possibilities. Something just didn't fit. If Billy Dean was Max Allen, why hadn't he told them about the fax? Why hadn't he already connected him to Michelle? There must be a reason.

Doss stopped pacing. Suddenly everything was clear. He had nothing to fear from Max Allen. He should have realized it earlier. It was so obvious; the fax was sent to Carla. Max Allen wouldn't know that he was the one who'd received the fax and therefore, wouldn't have a reason to suspect that it was he who had killed Michelle. He

knew about them, but they didn't know about him. That's why Max
hadn't told the police about the fax and made the connection. He
broke into a smile. He had nothing to worry about. Max was no threat
to him after all. Even if they found his skin under Michelle's nails, all
they'd have is DNA from a stranger that they'd never match.

He walked into his bathroom and turned on the shower. The water
felt wonderful and revived him. His mind wandered. He began to
think about Carla. Where could she be hiding? What name was she
using these days? He wondered if she was doing the same thing he
was doing. Was she taking a shower someplace at that very moment?
How did she spend her days? Did she know that Michelle Parker was
dead? If she did, was she keeping track of the trial? Suddenly, he realized that he'd overlooked something. He'd been worried all this time
about the fax connecting him to Michelle and had forgotten about the
real connection. The fax was sent to Carla's house. It made perfect
sense... the fax was written in some kind of code... of course she
knew Michelle was dead. She was one of Carla's friends... close
enough for her to know her home fax number. A tingling sensation
flowed through his body. He looked at his hand and imagined the
warm water as Carla's blood dripping from his fingers. He knew
where to find her and this time he would not fail. He thought of
something that made him laugh. He repeated his thought out loud,
"Carla, with a knife, in the courtroom."

THE DA's opening statement was brief. "Ladies and gentlemen of the
jury, my name is Arthur Wilcox. I am the District Attorney for Horry
County and I'm here today to present to you a very simple case. Here
are the facts. Michelle Parker was murdered, stabbed to death in her
home. When the police arrived, they found the defendant literally
covered in her blood. The defendant was her ex-lover. His fingerprints were on the handle of a nine-inch butcher knife that was
sticking out of her chest. At the scene, the defendant said to a police
officer, and I quote, 'what have I done?'

"It's simple, ladies and gentlemen, very simple. My job here is to validate this overwhelming evidence to you. I promise you, ladies and gentlemen, I can and I will. And after I've done that and you've seen this mountain of evidence, I'm confident you will be convinced beyond any reasonable doubt that the defendant is guilty of murder in the first degree. Thank you."

Jake waited for the DA to take his seat, then walked assertively to the jury stand. "Ladies and gentlemen, over the next few days you're going to hear a very, very sad story about a beautiful young woman who was stabbed in the chest with a nine inch butcher knife and left to bleed to death," Jake paused for dramatic effect, looked up and lifted his hands to the ceiling. "Just up the stairs while this was happening, her two month old child was crying for her mother.

"You just heard the prosecution tell you how simple this case was and that my client, Max Allen, did this. During this trial, they're going to show you the murder weapon and tell you that the only finger-prints on this knife were his. They're going to show photographs of Mr. Allen covered from head to toe with Michelle Parker's blood, photos of his bloody fingerprints on her phone and pictures of his bloody footprints on her carpet. I would not doubt that they show you huge blowups of Michelle lying dead on the floor with the knife sticking out of her chest. Ladies and gentlemen, I've seen these pictures and I'll be honest with you; they are gruesome and difficult to look at. I sincerely wish that you didn't have to see them, but unfortunately, you do.

"Before I go any further, I think I should tell you that they are Max's fingerprints on the knife and on her phone and they are his footprints on her carpet. Max *was* there in the house the day Michelle was murdered. We do not deny those facts.

"Now let's talk about the things the state is not going to tell you. The part that's not so simple. I'm sure they're not going to tell you that Max Allen was desperately in love with Michelle. So much in love with her, he sacrificed his own happiness for her. No, they're not going to tell you that, but you need to know this, so you'll understand how he felt when he walked in and saw her lying there. He ran to her and tried to pull out the knife. That's why his fingerprints were on the handle! I don't know how you'd react, but I think I would have done the same thing. Not so simple anymore is it?

"Why would his bloody fingerprints be on her phone, you may ask? Now that's a good question. If you believe the prosecution's story that Max went there that day and killed Michelle in a jealous rage, then I ask you... why would he call 911, crying for them to save her, leaving his fingerprints on the phone in the process? Again, not so simple.

"There's also one other very important fact in this case that I doubt the state will dwell on and honestly, I don't blame them, because it blows a big hole in their *simple* case. Ladies and gentlemen, the medical examiner found skin under Michelle's fingernails. Fighting for her life, she reached out and scratched her assailant, taking some of his skin with her. The interesting thing is that the skin doesn't belong to Max Allen. In fact, no one knows whose skin it is. What does that tell you? It tells me that there was a stranger in that house that day. It was this stranger who killed Michelle, not the man whose arms she died in. I'm sure the DA wasn't planning on telling you this either, so I will... Michelle died in Max Allen's arms. That's why he was covered in her blood!

"Simple? I think not," Jake turned, took a few steps toward the defense table then stopped and turn to face the jury. "I apologize ladies and gentlemen, I forgot to introduce myself. My name is Jake Parker. Michelle was my sister."

The jury gasped. "Objection," boomed the DA. "Irrelevant!"

"Sustained!" yelled the judge. "Mr. Parker you know better than that!"

"I'm sorry your honor, but the death of my sister is not irrelevant to me."

"Your honor!" screamed the DA.

"Mr. Parker, I'm not going to warn you again. One more word in that direction and I'll hold you in contempt."

"I'm finished, your honor."

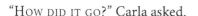

"How did it go?" Carla asked.

Jake plopped down in the chair and sighed. "We got a late start and only got in our opening statements, but to answer your question, I have no idea how it went."

"It went fine," William said, "And Jake was brilliant."

Jake shook his head and stared out the window. "Were you watching the jury during Wilcox's opening?" Jake asked.

"Yes I was," William said. "He's good, but he didn't even broach the subject of the skin found under Michelle's fingernails and I think that was a mistake. The jury seemed stunned when you brought it up. I still say your opening was strong."

"Carla, what's the latest on the DNA results?" Jake asked.

"I talked to the lab this afternoon and the news isn't so good. They need at least four more days to finish them all," she said.

"I'm not sure we've got four more days," Jake said. "Unless the DA has something up his sleeve that we don't know about, I believe he'll rest his case day after tomorrow. I'm not sure we've got enough to stretch until Friday. Call them back and tell them they've got to trim a day off. It's imperative that Martinez is ready to take the stand late Thursday."

"You're calling Martinez?" Gus asked.

"Yes, he's head of the lab. We're calling him as our DNA expert," William said. "But unless they've cleared every person on that list, we can't prove with absolute certainty the mysterious DNA belongs to a stranger. And without those results, our reasonable doubt argument is out the window."

"How was Max today?" Carla asked. "How is he handling the trial?"

Jake and William looked at each other, deciding who should answer. "Not well," William finally said. "He was very despondent."

"Morose is the best word I can think of to describe his disposition," Jake said. "I'm hoping he'll do better tomorrow. It's a negative read to the jury."

Gus's cell phone rang. It was his boss, Captain Williams, in Houston. "Gus, thought you'd like to know Doss cleared his docket yesterday for the next two weeks and we can't find him. I talked to his clerk and he claims the judge is having another surgery. I didn't want to press him too much, but he did tell me that it was a surprise to everyone. It sounds fishy to me. He's on the move, be careful."

"I will," Gus said. "Let me know if you locate him." Gus closed his phone and looked at Carla and Clyde. "Doss is out of place."

"Do you think he's coming here?" Carla asked.

"We don't know, but it's possible," Gus said. "Maybe you guys need to head back to Austin."

"No," Carla said firmly. "I'm not leaving until Max's trial is over."

"Carla, it may not be safe for you here and…"

"Gus, I'm not leaving and that's final!"

"Ok, ok, but you've got to promise you won't leave the room," Gus said. "Look at me, Carla, I'm very serious about this. Promise me you will not leave this room."

"I promise," she said reluctantly. "But Doss or no Doss, I'm going to be in the courtroom when they read the final verdict."

TWO FLOORS DOWN, the honorable Judge Bradford Doss fondled the switchblade, gazing out his hotel window admiring the Myrtle Beach skyline.

The knife felt good in his hand. He couldn't seem to stop opening and closing it. In the closed position, it looked innocent, measuring a little over five inches long, but with a push of a button, a razor sharp stainless steel blade flipped out and the knife took on an ominous appearance.

He walked to the bed and forced himself to lay the knife down next to the small snubbed nose 38. He opened his leather case and removed a few files. He placed the switchblade and the gun at the bottom of the case and carefully lowered the files back, resting them on top of the weapons. Next, he opened a plastic sack and took out a bottle of spirit gum, a fake beard, moustache and a hairpiece. It took him almost two hours of trial and error to apply them properly, but when he finished, he couldn't believe his eyes.

The next morning, without his leather case, he walked through the metal detector at the courthouse and smiled at the two uniformed guards as he walked by. He then turned around and introduced himself. "Excuse me, gentlemen," he said showing them his identification, "I'm a visiting judge here to observe the Max Allen trial. Could you please direct me to that courtroom?"

The guards read his identification and were impressed. "Of course, sir. Follow me, I'll take you there," the young guard said. "Would you like to meet the presiding judge for the case? I'm sure he'd like to meet you."

"No thank you. In fact, I'd appreciate it if you wouldn't mention my presence to the judge. It might make him a bit nervous and I wouldn't want that. I'm here as an official observer for the appellate court. This is a very high profile case and I'm here to make sure everything is handled properly."

"You can count on me, sir, and I'll tell Harry to keep his mouth shut too. He's the other guard. You can trust us. Mum's the word," the young guard said smiling.

"What was your name again, son? I'd like to have it for my report. I'll be sure to mention your cooperation to my colleagues." The guard gave him his name and Doss wrote it down. "Something like this can't hurt your career, son" Doss said smiling.

The guard was doing his best not to grin, maintaining his professional demeanor in front of this very important judge. "The Max Allen trial will be held in this courtroom, sir. It's scheduled to begin at 9 am. It's a little early, but you can go on in if you'd like."

"Thank you, son," he said shaking the guard's hand. "I assure you I won't forget all your help." The guard broke into a wide grin and walked away. *What a moron* Doss thought to himself as he took a seat at the back of the courtroom.

The room began to fill and Doss scanned every face carefully, but Carla wasn't there. The only person he recognized was Detective Gus Walters. He'd testified in his court several times and he wondered what he was doing here. What possible connection could a Houston robbery homicide detective have to this case? He watched him carefully and was surprised with his familiarity with the defense attorneys. He had no idea what it could be, but it was obvious that Detective Walters was involved in this case.

Detective Walters had scanned the courtroom several times, observing the crowd, and twice made eye contact with Doss, but showed no signs of recognition. His disguise was working well. The only person who gave him a second look was the defendant, Max Allen. Their eyes had locked and Max had held his gaze a little too long for comfort, so Doss had looked away. Several times during the day's proceedings, Max had turned in his seat and stared back at him with an inquisitive look in his eyes. To Doss' knowledge, he'd never seen Max before and didn't understand his interest. Although it made him uncomfortable, he was sure Max had never seen him before and there was no possible way he could recognize him, so he wrote it off as simple curiosity.

MAX WAS sure he'd never seen the bearded man before, but he was strangely drawn to him. There was something about his eyes. He'd racked his brain all day trying to place his face, but nothing came to his mind. Every time he looked at the stranger, an odd feeling flushed through his body. It must be someone from his past life, he thought, perhaps someone from Nashville.

DNA

CHAPTER TWENTY-FIVE

In the afternoon of the second full day of the trial, the prosecution rested. The judge adjourned the court for the day, with serious instructions to the jury not to discuss the case with anyone. The judge also expounded, in almost bias detail, for them not to formulate an opinion until they'd heard the upcoming defense portion of the trial. Jake and William took this as a positive sign from the judge that the prosecution's case had not been convincing. Perhaps because of this, the judge would allow them more latitude in presenting their side.

From the back of the courtroom, Judge Doss fumed in his seat. He couldn't believe what he'd just heard. Had this judge been asleep for the last two days? How could he not be convinced by now? In fifteen minutes, he'd destroyed two days of a brilliantly presented case against Max Allen. He was astounded at the judge's obvious predisposition. However, whether the jury acquitted or convicted Max Allen made little difference to him; either way it would not change his plans.

There had been no sign of Carla in the courtroom, but he was not discouraged; he knew she was somewhere close, he could feel it. And, if she was close, it was a certainty she was keeping track of the trial.

Eventually, her curiosity would get the best of her and she would show up. Maybe not during the actual trial, but he was convinced she'd be there for the final verdict.

When the verdict was read, guilty or not guilty, Doss knew the courtroom would erupt in utter chaos. He'd experienced it many times before in his own courtroom. It always happened with high profile cases – the reporters would rush out of the room colliding with the rest of the courtroom observers standing in the aisles blocking their way. There was always a huge traffic jam after a high profile verdict was read. During the bedlam, it should be easy for him to move behind Carla, bury the knife in her back just below her shoulder blades and slip away. If he placed the knife in the correct position, it would penetrate her heart and lung at the same time... before she hit the floor, he'd be lost in the crowd; just one more person rushing out of the room. Of course, if something went wrong, as a last resort, the gun would be taped to his ankle. One way or the other, he was not going to fail this time.

"Do you swear to tell the whole truth and nothing but the truth, so help you God?"

"I do," Dr. Alexander Martinez lowered his hand and took his seat in the witness stand.

"Dr. Martinez, you are the president and CEO of Carolina Forensics?" Jake asked.

"Yes, that's correct."

"What kind of doctor are you?"

"I have a PHD in genetic microbiology from Cornell University. I also have a medical degree from Duke University, however, I do not practice general medicine, my specialty is DNA research."

"You've published several books about your DNA research?"

"Yes, I've published two books and written several articles."

Jake looked up at the judge. "Your honor, may we assume Dr.

Martinez's credentials speak for themselves and classify him as an expert witness?"

"Any objections to this, Mr. Wilcox?" the judge asked.

Wilcox stood, "No, your honor, the state accepts Dr. Martinez as an expert in the field of DNA research."

"Very well, proceed Mr. Parker."

Jake walked to the defense table and retrieved a file. "May I approach the witness?" Jake asked the judge.

"Yes, counselor."

Jake walked to the witness stand. "Would you please identify this report as being the same report prepared by your company, Carolina Forensics and then explain to the jury what it contains?"

Dr. Martinez looked at the report. "Yes, that's my signature," he said then turned to face the jury. "This is a report of DNA test results my company prepared for the defense."

"How many different DNA samples, or people, did your company test?" Jake asked.

"49," he said.

"And where did you find these 49 people to test?"

"From the victim's parents. They compiled a list of people they believed may have had recent contact with their daughter."

"The people on this list likely came in contact with Michelle over what period of time?"

"Over the past several months," he said.

"Let me get this straight, Doctor. Michelle's parents compiled a list of every single person they could possibly think of that had come in contact with their daughter over the past few months and you took DNA samples from each one of them? Is that correct?"

"Yes, that's correct."

"What did you do with these 49 DNA samples?"

"We compared them with the DNA sample found under Michelle's fingernails."

"And what were the results of these comparisons?"

"There were no matches."

"Of all of these people, including her immediate family, her close friends, casual acquaintances and even her own daughter... no one matched the DNA from the skin found under Michelle's nails?"

"That's correct," Dr. Martinez said.

"In your expert opinion, doctor, what assumptions do you make of these findings?" Jake asked.

"Obviously, the skin found under her nails came from someone not on this list."

"A stranger then?"

"Yes, that's my opinion."

"Thank you, Dr. Martinez. I have no further questions for this witness, your honor." Jake walked to the defense table and sat down.

"Your witness, Mr. Wilcox?" the judge said.

" I only have a few questions," Wilcox said walking toward the podium.

"Dr. Martinez, do you honestly believe that you tested every single person that Michelle Parker knew? How do you know you didn't miss someone?"

"I don't. We only tested people from the list supplied by her parents."

"Do you have any friends your parents don't know about?"

"Of course," he said.

"So it *is* possible that this mysterious DNA came from one of Michelle's friends that her parents didn't know about. Someone she may have accidentally scratched. Could that be possible?"

"Objection, your honor!" Jake said. "He's leading the witness to make a conclusion he can't possibly make.

"Sustained," the judge said. "Counselor, your job is to ask the questions, not to testify."

"I was only asking if it was possible," Wilcox barked.

"You heard me, Mr. Wilcox. Now move on, or sit down!"

Wilcox stood silent for a moment, trying to regain his composure. "Are these tests 100 percent accurate, doctor?"

"No, to this date there isn't a procedure that is considered accurate to that degree, however, our standard of accuracy is widely accepted as verifiable evidence in a court of law."

"Were there any close matches? Perhaps one or two that gave you reason for a second look?" Wilcox asked.

Martinez shook his head. "No. Other than the DNA similarities between Michelle and her family members and of course, the intrinsic match between the mother and father of the child, there were no other DNA strings close. This is not just my opinion, Mr. Wilcox, it's the opinion of the nineteen other scientists that worked on this project. Not one of the 49 people we tested matched with the finger-nail DNA."

"Only a few more questions, doctor. What is the normal length of time it takes to get back a DNA test?"

"There is no real standard, it depends on how backed up the lab is, but usually the turn around time is between two and four weeks."

"How long did it take your lab to do these tests?"

"Ten days," he said.

"You did 49 DNA tests in ten days. Wow! Quite a rush job, doctor. Was this testing expensive?"

"Yes, DNA testing is very detailed and requires a lot of sophisti-cated equipment and long personnel hours from the scientist doing the work."

"Interesting," Wilcox said pausing. "Dr. Martinez, everyone in this courtroom that's watched the news is aware that Mr. Allen lost his fortune due to his previous murder charge. Who paid for…"

"Objection," Jake shouted.

The judge jumped to his feet and slammed down his gavel. "CHAMBERS, NOW!" he yelled.

Sitting in the last row of the courtroom, Doss laughed. It was a good question. Who was paying for Max's defense? *Carla*, he said to himself. Thank you Mr. DA, I hadn't thought of that. Now I know I'm right… she is very close.

It *was* a brilliant move by the DA, he thought. There was no legal way for him to introduce Max's past run in with the law; it was irrelevant to this case and not admissible evidence, but by blurting it out in the form of a question, he'd gotten it in anyway. Of course, he was risking a contempt charge and a possible mistrial, but more than likely, his only real punishment would be getting his ass chewed out by the judge, which was going on at that moment in his chambers. The brilliant part was that he wouldn't have to say another word about it. The judge would take care of that. All he really wanted was to remind the jury that Max Allen had been charged with murder before. It didn't matter that he had been acquitted; all he wanted was for the jury to remember the image of Max's mug shots plastered all over the television and newspapers. Because he'd introduced something that the jury shouldn't have heard, the judge would be forced to strike it from the record and instruct the jury to forget what he'd said, but of course, they wouldn't be able to. It's like telling someone not to think about an elephant, soon that's all they can think about. "Pretty slick, counselor," he mumbled to himself.

Fifteen minutes later, the judge and the attorneys returned to the courtroom. Just as Doss had predicted, the judge ordered the DA's last question to be stricken from the record and then spent a few minutes instructing the jury to forget what Mr. Wilcox had said.

"Mr. Wilcox, do you have any further questions for this witness?" the judge asked.

"No, your honor. I have no further questions for Dr. Martinez," Wilcox said frowning.

Jake stood and nodded approvingly to Dr. Martinez as he stepped down from the witness stand and walked by him. "The defense would like to call Mrs. Betty Parker as our next and final witness, your honor."

Jake's mother's hands were shaking as she settled in the witness chair. "Your honor, may I approach this witness?"

"Yes, you may, but Mr. Parker, don't you think it would be more appropriate if Mr. Williams questioned this witness?"

"I appreciate your concern, your honor, but I think everyone is aware that Mrs. Parker is the mother of the victim as well as my mother. If it's acceptable, I prefer to handle this witness myself."

Jake walked to the witness stand and stood a few feet from his mother. "Mrs. Parker, may I call you Mom?" The courtroom erupted with laughter.

His mother smiled and relaxed a little. "Jake, you look terrible, are you eating right?" Again, the courtroom vibrated with laughter.

"Mr. Parker," the judge said glaring down at him.

"I'm sorry your honor. Mom, you can't ask the questions, that's my job. I promise this will only take a few minutes. Don't be nervous. I need to ask you a few questions about Michelle."

"Ok," she said.

"When Michelle was a little girl, was she messy and dirty, always needing a bath?"

"No, just the opposite. Don't you remember, we couldn't keep her out of the bathtub?"

"Yes, I remember, but I think it's important that the jury hears from you, her mother, what kind of child she was. As she grew up, did her personal hygiene habits change through the years? Was she always clean and well kept?"

She looked at the jury. "I guess he's trying to get me to tell you that Michelle was sort of a clean nut."

The jury laughed. "Your honor!" boomed the DA.

"Mrs. Parker," the judge said. "Please don't expound, just answer the questions and address your answers to your son, not the jury."

"I'm sorry," she said, embarrassed.

Jake smiled at his mom. "In your opinion was Michelle concerned with her personal appearance, especially when it pertained to her cleanliness?"

"Oh, yes. She was very persnickety about being clean. I've seen her take a shower before she exercised." The jury laughed again.

"I only have one more question for you and I want you to think carefully about it before you answer. Knowing Michelle's obsession for cleanliness, do you think it would be possible for her to get something under her fingernails and leave it there, perhaps for hours or days?"

"Objection!" Wilcox yelled. "Calls for an assumption by the witness."

"Overruled! I'll allow that. Mrs. Parker, of all people, should have enough knowledge about her daughter's personal hygiene to make a qualified assumption."

"Go ahead, mom," Jake said. "What do you think?"

"I think she would have cleaned them immediately. She'd never touch her baby with dirty fingernails. I know that for sure."

Jake walked to the defense table. "Your witness," he said to the DA.

"No questions your honor," Wilcox said, deflated.

In that case," Jake said. "The defense rests."

THE LARGEST OF the five hotel rooms occupied by Jake and his staff had a full sized dining table. It was there that Carla, Gus, William and Clyde heard Jake's closing argument for the first time. It was the most important element of the trial. The rest of Max's life depended on these critical words, so Jake woke everyone up and made them listen. It had taken him five hours to draft it, but took only 17 minutes to deliver. When he finished, he walked to the bar, poured himself a scotch and sat down on the couch. It was 1:35 am.

"Well," he said, "comments?"

"I think it's good, Jake," William said.

"It's strong," said Gus.

"You convinced me," Clyde added.

Jake looked at Carla. "You're awfully quiet. Didn't you like it?" She seemed preoccupied, lost in thought. "Carla, what'd you think?"

"Jake, would you repeat the quote from Dr. Martinez?" She had a peculiar look in her eyes.

Jake took a swallow of his scotch and walked back to the table to refer to his notes. "Ah… OK, here it is. 'Other than the DNA similarities between Michelle and her family members and of course, the intrinsic match between the mother and father of the child, there were no other DNA strings close.'" Jake put down the pad. "Don't you think I should use that part? It's an exact quote."

Carla looked at him curiously. "Jake, aren't you listening to what you just said? 'The intrinsic match between the mother and father of the child.' Don't you understand what that means?"

Jake shook his head no, then suddenly lifted his eyebrows. "The father of the child!" he shouted.

"Yes," Carla said. "The father of the child."

Clyde and Gus looked at each other, both totally confused. "What the hell does that mean?" Gus asked.

"It means that someone on that list is Jessie's father," Jake said.

"And that's a good thing right?" Clyde asked.

Jake smiled. "Yes, Clyde, that's a very good thing." Jake motioned to Carla. "Call Dr. Martinez first thing in the morning to make sure."

"I will," she said, "first thing."

The next morning Carla was up early and placed the first call to Dr. Martinez at 7:30, but no one answered at the lab.

At 8:15, Jake knocked on her door. "Call me on my cell if you hear from Dr. Martinez before 9 a.m.," he said. "I'll have to turn it off after that."

"I've already tried a few times," she said, "but no one's there. How long do you think the closing statements will take?"

I assume we'll get started around 10," Jake said. "The prosecution goes first. I can't imagine his closing taking more than thirty minutes, maybe an hour at the most. We know mine only takes 17 minutes. The jury should get the case by noon."

"Do you think we'll hear today?" Carla asked.

"I hope not. The longer they're out tells us that they are at least considering reasonable doubt."

"Jake, I want to be there for the verdict."

"Yeah, Gus told me. I think Max would appreciate that. If they do come back today, we'll all go back together."

"Ok. I'll see you back here around noon. Good luck, Jake," Carla said giving him a hug. Then she whispered, "Jake... if Max is convicted... what happens to Doss?"

"Let's not think about that right now. First, let's get Max out of jail, then we'll go after Doss."

JUDGE DOSS HAD BECOME a familiar face to the guards running the metal detector at the front door of the courthouse. Each morning of the trial, he'd brought them fresh coffee and banana nut muffins from the Atlanta Bread Company.

Knowing that there was a possibility the jury could come back early, this morning he had the Atlanta Bread Company sack sticking out the top of his open leather case. The guards smiled and waved when they saw him approach. He held up his case and walked around the metal detector. The guards dug into the sack.

"What's in the case?" the young guard asked.

"It's case files. I thought I'd try to get in a little work while the jury is deliberating," Doss answered smiling.

"Do you think there's a chance they'll come back today?" the older guard asked.

"There is always that possibility. You can never tell with a jury," Doss picked up his case and walked past them down the corridor.

"Thanks again for the coffee and the muffins," the young guard yelled.

"It was my pleasure," Doss said smiling as he turned the corner.

IT WAS ALMOST 1 p.m. and Carla hadn't heard anything. She was getting anxious when her phone rang. "Jake," she exclaimed. "I've been so worried, how did it go?"

"I thought it had gone well, but we were just notified," she could hear the concern in his voice. "The jury's coming back. They were only out 45 minutes."

"Oh, no, Jake."

"Yeah, I'm afraid it's not good news. Have you heard from Dr. Martinez?"

"No not yet. I've been expecting a call from him all morning."

"Well, I guess that doesn't make much difference now. Carla, we've only got about 20 minutes, I'll try to run Gus down. As soon as I find him, I'll send him after you."

"I don't think there's enough time for that. I don't want to miss the verdict. Tell Gus I'll bring Clyde with me. We'll grab a cab and meet you there."

"He's not going to like it, but you're probably right, if you're going to make the verdict, you need to leave now. I'll have Gus save some seats for you down front. Be careful, Carla. I'll see you in a few minutes."

Carla hung up the phone, ran to the bathroom and quickly brushed her hair and packed her purse. She was just about to walk out the door when the phone rang. "Dr. Martinez," she said recognizing his voice, "I'm so glad you called."

IT WAS STANDING room only inside the courtroom, only minutes away from the return of the jury and Gus was out of his mind with worry; Carla and Clyde had not arrived. "I'm going to see if I can find them," he whispered to Jake and William. "I'll be right back."

"Carla and Clyde stepped out of the elevator only seconds after Gus had entered the other car on his way down to the lobby. When they opened the door of the courtroom, Jake saw them and motioned them to come forward and take the seats Gus had saved. Standing in the back of the courtroom, Doss' heart raced, watching her walk down and take the aisle seat. Inside his pocket, he clutched the switchblade.

"All rise," the bailiff announced as the jury began entering the room.

Once the jury had taken their seats, the judge rapped his gavel. "This court is now in session," he said. "Ladies and gentlemen of the jury, have you reached a verdict?"

The foreman stood, "Yes, your honor we have," he handed the bailiff a piece of paper.

The bailiff took the paper over to the bench and handed it to the judge. The judge read it. "Mr. Foreman, has the jury reached this verdict by unanimous decision?"

"Yes your honor," he said.

"Will the defendant please rise?"

William and Jake stood with Max in the middle. "Mr. Foreman, you may read the verdict. What say you?"

"The state of South Carolina versus Dan Max Allen on the charge of capital murder in the first degree... we find the defendant..." he paused and looked across the room at Max, "not guilty!"

The room exploded. The noise level of shrieks and screams was deafening. Max's supporters jumped to their feet and broke into applause, while the reporters rushed through the aisles trying to force their way out the doors. It was complete pandemonium.

Carla was on her feet crying and yelling at the top of her lungs. Max had closed his eyes and dropped back into his seat. Jake and William were staring at each other motionless, in a state of shock.

"Max! Max!" Carla yelled, trying to make her way forward through the crowd. "Max, I have something to tell you!"

Doss had slipped down the aisle and was only a few yards behind Carla when Max recognized Carla's voice and looked around searching the crowd for her. It took him a minute to locate her. She was yelling, waving her arms in the air.

Max smiled and waved back. A few yards behind her, he noticed the same bearded man he'd seen a few days earlier moving quickly down the aisle. He was smiling and had a sinister look in his eyes. Suddenly he remembered the black SUV pulling out of Michelle's drive and passing him. It was the same man... with those horrible eyes... It was Doss... then Max saw the knife.

Everything was happening fast. His memory of Doss and the sight of him rushing down the aisle with a knife was shocking and took him a moment to react. "DOSS!" he heard himself yell. "BEHIND YOU! HE HAS A KNIFE!"

Carla turned and saw him coming for her. She instantly recognized the smile and screamed. Doss pushed past the last two people and lunged at Carla. Out of nowhere, Clyde jumped in between them and the knife buried deep in his side.

Carla wrapped her arms around Clyde trying to hold him up. "It's Doss!" she shouted.

Judge Doss jerked the knife out of Clyde's side and slashed at Carla, missing her by inches.

Max jumped over the rail and leaped over two benches landing on top of Doss, knocking him to the floor, wrestling him for the knife. Max cracked his forehead against Doss' nose, stunning him long enough to reach up and grab his hair. Gripping his head in both of his hands, Max smashed Doss' head down hard against the tile floor repeatedly until he lost consciousness and dropped the knife beside him.

Max reached for the switchblade and straddled Doss' torso, pressing the blade against his neck. With his left hand, he grabbed the phony beard and ripped it off. "Carla, is this Doss?"

"Yes, that's him," she said crying.

"Wake up you bastard," Max yelled shaking him.

Doss opened his eyes, glaring up at him. "Before I gut you like a deer," Max growled, "I want you to tell me why you killed Michelle. What did she do to you?"

Doss spat blood out of his mouth. "I didn't kill anyone," he said. "Guards, arrest this man! He's assaulted me! I'm a state court judge! Arrest this man!" he yelled. The guards looked at each other unsure of what to do.

"One more word and I'll cut your fucking tongue out!" Max pressed the blade harder against his neck. "You have one last chance, judge. Tell me why you killed Michelle, before I cut your throat!" Doss could feel the sting of the knife slicing into his neck and he knew the blade was only inches from his jugular.

The guards pulled their guns. "Drop the knife, sir," one yelled.

"Please listen to them. Don't do it, Max," Carla yelled. "He's not worth it!"

"You better listen to her, Max," Doss said. "You've just been acquitted of one murder, you don't want to go back to jail do you?"

Max smashed his fist down against Doss' face. "Shut the fuck up! Do you really think I care about that? You killed the only reason I had to live. Now I'm going to kill you, and I'm going to do it slow, so I can watch your sorry ass bleed to death just like Michelle did. Say goodbye judge."

"NO, MAX!" Carla screamed. "You *do* have a reason to live! Jessie is your child! Don't do this! Think about her!"

Max froze. "What?"

"It's true, Max. Dr. Martinez discovered it with the DNA tests. Jessie is your daughter. She needs you, Max. Let him go. He'll get what's coming to him."

Max turned to Carla. "You're serious? Jessie is my child?"

"I swear," she said. "The lab confirmed the DNA today. Jessie is your daughter and she's going to need a father. Don't kill him, Max."

From the back of the courtroom, Gus had watched it all go down. He had tried, but there had been too many people in his way to get there in time to help Carla, but then he stopped in his tracks when he saw Max flying over the benches, landing on Doss. He listened silently as Carla pleaded with Max not to kill Doss. He was relieved when he saw him toss the knife toward the guards, stand up and walk toward Carla, but he was alarmed when Doss began to move behind him. Before Gus could pull his weapon, Doss reached to his ankle, came up with a gun and fired, dropping Max instantly to the ground. Then he turned and pointed the gun at Carla.

PSALMS 52

CHAPTER TWENTY-SIX

I t had taken seven years, but Carla was finally going to die. She was in his sights. Doss hesitated when memories of her naked squirming beneath him filled his head, then the kick that ruptured him and took away his manhood flashed through his mind and rage blazed inside him. "Die bitch," he yelled squeezing on the trigger.

He heard the shot, it was a deafening explosion, and then felt something hot in his back. In slow motion, his chest exploded outward. He watched his suit rip away and saw chunks of his flesh flying through the air. Suddenly, he was lying on his side on the floor. How did he get there, he wondered? He tried to move, but couldn't. Everyone was screaming and staring down at him with horror in their eyes. He tried to speak, but couldn't move his mouth.

Clearly, he could see Carla standing over him, but how could she be alive? What was she doing? He watched her bend down and spit in his face. Bitch! He yelled, but no sound came out. I'll kill you! I swear I'll kill you! He yelled, but only inside his head, he could make no sounds. He was cold, freezing and his vision began to tunnel and blur. He fought it, but the darkness overtook him.

W‍HEN HE OPENED HIS EYES, he was groggy and disoriented. He had no idea where he was. All he could see were white rectangular tiles in the ceiling above him. He tried to turn his head to look around, but couldn't seem to move his neck. He tried lifting his arms, then his legs, but that didn't work either. With all his might, he tried to turn his head, but nothing worked.

He heard a voice, and Carla's face suddenly appeared above him. "Oh great, you're awake," she said.

He tried to speak, but couldn't move his mouth. "If you can hear me Judge Doss, blink your eyes," she said.

He blinked.

"That's good. Now blink twice if you know who I am."

He blinked two times.

"Do you understand what I'm saying? Blink twice if you do."

He blinked twice.

"That's very good, Judge Doss. I have a lot to tell you. Do you feel up to a conversation?"

He blinked twice.

Carla moved out of his line of sight. "Wait just a second, I'm going to turn your bed so you can see us better." His bed was strapped to a platform connected to a large wheel. Carla pushed the control and the wheel began to rotate, turning his bed into a forty-five degree angle.

The movement made him dizzy, but in a few seconds, his vision cleared and he saw Carla standing at the foot of his bed surrounded by several people. "Judge Doss, you've been unconscious for almost three weeks, but don't worry, you weren't in a coma, the doctors kept you that way on purpose. It was to help your body heal.

"All of these people have been waiting for you to regain consciousness. We have a lot to talk to you about. We drew straws to see who got to go first and I won!" Carla flashed him a smile.

"I get to tell you the best news. Judge Doss, you are a quadriplegic. Detective Walters' bullet severed your spinal cord and your condition is irreversible. The noise you hear is a respirator. It's keeping you alive until the state of South Carolina executes you. Oh, I'm sorry, I'm getting ahead of myself. I'd like to introduce you to someone. Since you were at Max's trial every day, I'm sure you'll remember Mr. Wilcox.

Wilcox stepped forward. "Bradford Doss, I am the District Attorney for Horry County in the state of South Carolina. I'm here to inform you that you are under arrest for the murder of Michelle Parker and the attempted murder of Max Allen and Clyde Barker." He read him his rights and stepped back.

Gus stepped forward. "Bradford Doss, I am a homicide detective for the Houston, Texas police department. I'm here to inform you that you are also charged with the murder of Edward Cecil Sr., the murder of Edward Cecil Jr., the murder of Dr. Ronald White, the murder of Dr. Jane Griswald, the murder of Sergeant John Colby and the rape of Carla Cecil."

"You see, Judge," Carla said smiling, "we found traces of Michelle's blood in your rental car and also in your house. Oh, did I forget to mention that we went to your house? Yes, we did, and while we were looking around, we found the fax that Max and Michelle had sent to me. We also found your little playroom above your office and it was just full of videotapes.

She glowered down at him. "I was only thirteen years old, you sick son of a bitch!" She wiped her eyes and took a breath. "We also opened your safe and found all of your souvenirs. How many more were there, Judge Doss? How many innocent children have you raped? How many have you killed?"

Carla picked up the control for his bed and held it in her hand. "They tell me you'll probably get the death penalty for what you've done, but I sincerely hope it's years before they stick that needle in your arm. I want you to suffer. You deserve to live like this for a very, very long time."

Carla pushed the button and as the bed began to slowly roll backwards, she stepped close to Doss, only inches from his face and whispered,

"You were ingenious in plotting your evil tricks. Oh, how you love wickedness, far more than good. And, lying more than truth! You love to slander and you love to say anything that will do harm. O man with the lying tongue. But God will strike you down and pull you from your home, and drag you away from the land of the living... Psalms 52."

WHEN HIS BED came to rest, Doss stared up into Carla's eyes, but the sinister gaze she'd feared for some many years was not there. All she could see... was fear.

EPILOGUE

J ake explained to me that when someone is convicted of capital murder in the first degree, and receives the death penalty, an automatic and lengthy appeals process follows. It has taken almost six years for this procedure to run its course for Bradford Doss.

A month before his first trial, Doss' wife filed for divorce and stripped him of most of his financial assets. After the trial, as a convicted felon, he lost his law license and was removed from the bench. His medical condition deteriorated through the years and his quadriplegia did not improve. Blinking his eyelids continued to be his only form of communication.

Over the years, Judge Doss has received few visitors. His only human contact has been his doctors, the hospital attendants who change his excrement bags and bathe him every other day, and his attorney, assigned to handle his appeals. Other than that, for almost six years, the Honorable Judge Bradford Doss has laid in his bed, frozen in place, staring at the ceiling… alone. Perhaps I should, but I must admit, I do not feel sorry for him.

He received the death penalty for murdering Michelle and although it was a moot point, for the sake of closure for the families, he was also convicted for the rapes and murders of eleven other children. He was never prosecuted for the murders of the two doctors, but *was* convicted for the murder of Sergeant John Colby.

Colby's remains were discovered in the trunk of a green Ford sedan pulled from the bottom of an old lake, 80 miles southwest of Houston. As it turned out, this particular lake was proclaimed as one of the oldest bodies of water known in the state of Texas. Once again, the Ouija board had foretold the truth, "old water."

I can only imagine how slow time has passed for Judge Doss, but for the rest of us, the years have flown by and brought with them lots of change to our lives.

Although Clyde had to postpone his wedding for two months to heal from his knife wound, he finally walked down the aisle with his new bride. We were all at the wedding and I stood next to him during the ceremony... his best man. The newlyweds didn't waste any time—in five years they produced three children.

Carla put her money to good use and in the process, discovered her true calling. She established the *Edward Cecil Foundation for Sexually Abused Children* and built a beautiful three story children's dormitory in Woodland Park on the twenty acres of land Aunt Martha left her. The facility staffs five full time psychologists, specializing in sexual abuse of children. Each year her foundation offers security, food, shelter and psychological counseling to hundreds of abused children. In five years, Carla's foundation has grown to extraordinary heights and she has received countless humanitarian awards worldwide.

Gus is still a cop, but can't get used to being called *Captain* Walters. He finally got the timing right and eventually hooked up with Carla, but it took him almost four years to get up enough nerve to ask her to marry him. Together they have restored a beautiful old home in southwest Houston and Carla is currently expecting their first child.

One strange quirk of fate—Jake Parker received an appointment from the Governor of Virginia and is now a presiding State Court Judge. Life is funny.

Judge Doss' bullet had hit me in the back, just below my shoulder blade, shattering three of my ribs and puncturing my right lung in the process of passing through my body. I honestly can't remember getting shot and I guess that's a good thing. I'm a fast healer and was out of the hospital in less than two weeks; however, while I was there, I received over ten thousand cards and letters from my fans. My acquittal and consequent courtroom battle with Judge Doss made all of the headlines and apparently rekindled my celebrity. Suddenly, my old music flooded the airwaves and offers for record deals and concert appearances rolled in. I even had one call from my old buddy Jimmy Proud at Mammoth Records. It did feel good when I told him to go fuck himself.

Instead of falling into the same old trap of dealing with the record industry parasites, I called upon my friends. With Carla's brilliant business advice, Clyde's computer savvy and Jake's legal ease, I set up my own record company and launched *Max Allen dot com*. So far, we've sold over three million copies of my CD's online. Although I guess you could say I'm rich now, I live on an allowance, Carla is in charge of the rest of my money. The first thing she did was set up Jessie's college trust fund.

Yes, I do have custody of Jessie. When I'm on tour, she stays with her grandparents in Virginia. The rest of the time, she's with me sailing on our new boat, *Windsong II*.

JESSIE and I were cruising through the Windward Islands when my satellite phone rang. It was my father. He told me that one of my idols, Waylon Jones, had died. Apparently, his long running battle with diabetes had finally gotten the best of him. Waylon and I weren't actually close friends, but because of the sage advice he'd given me early on in my career, I wanted to at least send flowers and offer my condolences to his widow. I set a course for Antigua, the nearest island and trimmed the sails.

Just as the sun began to set, we pulled into the historic bay at Nelson's boat yard, motored toward the marina and got the shock of our lives. Standing on the dock was Carla, Jake, Gus and Clyde. We were twenty yards from the dock when little Jessie spotted her uncle Jake. She screamed with delight, dove over the side and swam like a dolphin to the pier. He plucked her out of the water and swung her around in the air as she giggled and laughed.

I threw my bowline to Gus. "What the hell are you guys doing here?" I yelled, grinning. "How'd you know how to find us?"

"I talked to your father," Carla said. "He told me you were on your way here."

"What a terrific surprise! What's the occasion?"

"We've got some news, Max, and we all wanted to be with you when you heard it," Carla said.

I secured *Windsong II* to the dock and invited them onboard. Everyone settled under the shade of the bimini in the cockpit and little Jessie, playing hostess, brought everyone cokes and cookies.

"I can't believe how she's grown," Carla said.

"I know. It's unbelievable. I can't keep her in clothes. She's quite the little hostess, isn't she?" I said, gazing at my beautiful child. "She is the image of her mother."

"If she's anything like her mother, I bet you're always out of water from her showers," Jake said laughing.

I laughed. "You've got that right. I had to install an extra water maker just for her."

After Jessie served everyone their drinks, she crawled into her uncle Jake's lap and started in with her usual million questions, completely dominating his attention.

"So, what's the big news?" I asked. "It must be something important to bring you guys all the way down here."

"Jessie," Jake said. "Why don't you show me around the new boat? I'd love to see your cabin." Excited, she jumped up and pulled him toward the saloon. He winked at us as they disappeared, closing the door behind them.

Once they were gone, Carla faced me. "Doss is dead."

"What?" I said shocked. "I thought his execution wasn't scheduled for another two weeks."

"Somehow, a couple of his fellow inmates slipped the hospital security and saved the state of South Carolina the trouble," said Gus.

"What happened, what did they do to him?"

"It's gruesome and no doubt the guards were in on it," Clyde added, "but it couldn't have happened to a nicer guy."

"They found him yesterday, Gus said. "Someone had cut off his penis and shoved it in his mouth. They also unplugged his respirator. He suffocated with his own dick in his mouth."

"Oh, man! Eeeeww!" The thought had me squirming in my seat.

"Honestly, I'm surprised this didn't happened sooner," Gus said. "Pedophiles don't live long in prison, at least not with their dicks still attached."

"The last thing I ever said to him, was a passage from the Bible,'" Carla said. "I probably shouldn't still feel this way, but I hope he's burning right now."

I took her hands in mine. "Carla, no one could blame you for the way you feel and trust me, he *is* burning. He got exactly what he deserved."

"Can you imagine what was going through his mind… not being able to move… watching somebody cut his dick off?" Clyde grimaced.

I squeezed Carla's hand and looked her in the eyes. "Carla, God always wins in the end and his pay back is *hell*… literally. Doss has just begun to pay for what he's done."

Everyone had cleared their schedules and had a few days to spend with us sailing, so after I wired flowers for Waylon's funeral, we hoisted the sails and set a course for St. Barts.

On the first night out, we all stayed up late talking, but eventually one by one, everyone retired and went below, leaving Jessie, who had fallen asleep in my lap, and me alone in the cockpit. It was almost a full moon, so I pulled back the bimini top and with our daughter asleep in my lap, I stared up at the sky thinking about Michelle. I wondered if she was looking down at us at that very moment. I hoped she was, and I prayed that she knew how much I loved this tiny blessing she'd left with me here on earth.

"A penny for your thoughts," Carla said from the doorway.

"Hi," I said. "I figured you'd be asleep by now."

"I guess it takes a while to get used to the motion. Mind if I join you two?"

"Of course not, have a seat."

Carla was carrying a small green box in her hand and laid it on the seat next to her as she sat down. "There was another reason I wanted to come to see you, Max."

I looked at her curiously. "Oh yeah? And what was that?"

She took the box and laid it between us. "I wanted to bring you this."

I picked up the Ouija board and held it in my hands. "I wondered what had happened to this."

"After we used it that day, I packed it up and took it with me. I guess it should have gone back to Michelle's house but no one ever asked about it, so I just hung on to it."

"You've had it all these years?"

"Yes. I thought you might want to use it again someday. Now that Doss is dead and this is finally over, I thought... Max, would you like to try it again?"

"I don't know, Carla. There's a part of me that wants to, but there's also a part of me that's afraid to do it again. I'd give anything to talk to Michelle, but something inside me tells me it's the wrong thing to do."

"Don't you want to let Michelle know that Jessie is with you and that you two are OK? Maybe let her know that Doss is dead?"

"I don't think there's anything I could tell her that she doesn't already know. Sure, I'd love to talk with her... see if she's happy, but the problem is I think she may also know the future and that's what scares me. Carla, I'm 57 years old. I don't know if I'll still be around to see our daughter graduate from college or to walk her down the aisle someday or to see my grandchildren... what if I ask Michelle and the answer is no? How would I deal with that?"

I brushed the hair away from Jessie's sleeping face. "So many things have happened in my life, but this beautiful child is the greatest experience of all. Every day Jessie surprises me with something, and when she does, it makes me realize how much I love being surprised. I believe life is supposed to be a mystery, full of unanswered questions. That's what keeps it interesting and worth living.

"What I really want is to hold Michelle in my arms again, to dance with her just one last time… But that's never going to happen, at least not in this life. But if I'm going to survive without her, I have to believe in my heart that she knows I've got Jessie and that we're fine. I want to believe that Michelle's gone on to a better place and is waiting for me there.

"No, I don't want to use the Ouija board again. I don't need it to tell me my future… I know what that is. I've finally figured out the real meaning of my life and it's given me the happiness I've been searching for all these years. Raising Jessie is my true destiny. I hope I'll be around as long as she needs me, but ultimately what happens is simply meant to be. And … I don't want to know what that is. I just want to cherish every single day I have with her. There are some things we're not supposed to know."

Gently, I moved Jessie from my lap, placing her head on a cushion and stood in the cockpit. I picked up the Ouija board and threw it as far as I could off the stern. Carla laid her head on my shoulder and we watched it float away in the trailing wake of *Windsong II*.

∽

The End

AUTHOR'S NOTE

Although this is a work of fiction, it was based on a true story. In fact, the first Ouija board story is true; it actually happened to me. What happened afterwards came from somewhere deep in my imagination. As unbelievable as it may sound, I really did talk to someone that night. Perhaps it was just my subconscious mind moving the triangle around and I was only talking to myself, I honestly don't know... but to tell you the truth, I'm still a little freaked and I haven't used a Ouija board since.

An interesting footnote: That night on the Ouija board, Edward asked me and my friend to help his sibling, *Carl* (I changed it to *Carla* in the book). He asked us to warn *Carl* about someone named *Bradford Doss.* To convince us the Ouija board was real, the board actually spelled *Sing Roses* (the part about the last song I sang for my late brother is absolutely true). It also spelled my brother and father's middle name, which is actually **Dean.**

Four years later, the friend who was using the Ouija board with me that night, married a man named... *Bradley*... who had a seven-year old daughter named... *Carley.*

One more thing... her new husband's middle name is... *Dean.*
Coincidence?

THANK YOU

Thanks for reading my book. This was my first novel and took me almost a year to write. **But there is more to this story...**

The Sequel to Sing Roses For Me

SERPENTINE ROSES

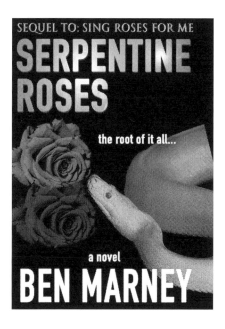

At 16, Ford Alexander and his autistic, but brilliant friend, Adrian Montgomery, write a revolutionary computer software program. With Carla Cecil Walters' investment and advice...they make billions.

Being one of the richest men on earth, autistic, sexually oppressed and easily influenced, becomes a dangerous and deadly combination when Adrian meets the wrong woman. Now, Forde, Adrian, Carla, Max...and everyone else they love...are running for their lives.

While you're on Amazon, check out my second novel, **Children Of The Band.**

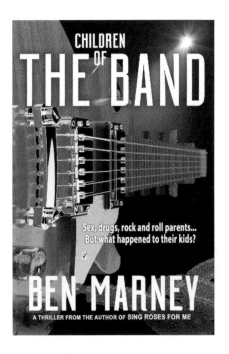

I spent my 20's singing and playing guitar in a touring rock band. Back in the 1970's, in every town and city in the United States, there was at least one bar that featured live entertainment. There were literally thousands of bands like mine, traveling the US performing in those bars. This was also the era the term "sex drugs and rock and roll" was invented. Unfortunately, traveling in many of those bands were their children, from infants to teenagers. I've often wondered and it's haunted me for years...what happened to those kids?

One more thing... Writing is a lonely job, so meeting and getting to know my readers is a thrill and one of the best perks of being an author. I invite you to join my **Private Readers' Group** and in return, I'll give you a free copy of *Lyrics Of My Life*. This is a collection of autobiographical short stories about my amazing life so far. I really would like to meet you! Get your FREE book and join my readers' group here: www.benmarneybooks.com

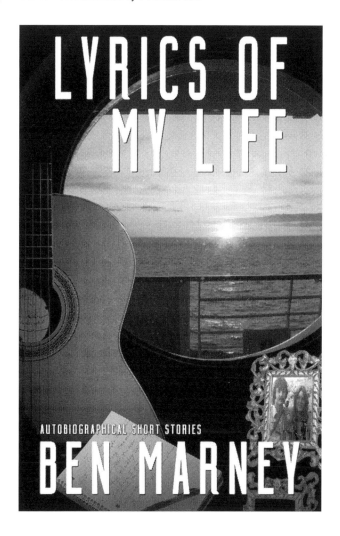